# Infinite
# LOVE

## BOOK ONE

# The Pursuit

# Infinite LOVE

## BOOK ONE
### The Pursuit

## Jeanine Mayers

This is a work of fiction. All of the characters, organizations, and events portrayed in this novel are either products of the author's imagination or are used fictitiously.

ISBN-13: 978-0-9854889-2-5
Library of Congress Control Number:  2014910029

First Edition: June 2013
10 9 8 7 6 5 4 3 2 1

Interior Design: Candace K. Cottrell
Cover Design:  Charlton Palmer (cptheartist.com)

JeanineWorldwide@yahoo.com
www.JeanineWorldwide.com

# Acknowledgements

First I would like to thank God for giving me the strength to write this novel. With him all things are possible. I would like to give thanks to my mom and dad, Mr. and Mrs. Mayers. I was blessed to have such wonderful parents who encouraged and pushed me to always reach my full potential. To my sister Angela Mayers-Williams: I love you, girl. You are my hero. Thanks to my brother, Michael Mayers. I would like to thank my hubby and stepson (Joe & Ryan Maldonado) for their continued support.

I would like to thank my friends for saying "Jay you can do this—don't stop—won't stop. I would like to thank my co-workers and focus group for taking the time out to read and provide genuine and honest feedback. Euclid Smith, Christina Reyes, my Connies (Brown and Scarborough-Burkes), Clara Barnes-Wright, Lelith Sharp-King, Stephanie Price, Dina Smalls, Kelli Sullivan-Forbes, and Donald Middleton, and last but never least, my left hand, Patrice George-Seth—thanks for standing by my side thick or thin.

To authors K'wan, Geoffrey McClanahan, and Rap Legend Dana Dane: I truly thank you all for your constant advice and brotherly love. I would like to thank my editor Candace for being so patient with me. I couldn't have asked for a more professional and personable person.

To all of those incarcerated in federal or state jails all over the United States, keep your head up!

This book is dedicated to the loving memory of my uncle Louis Emerson Ford and brother from another mother, Baby Chris Lighty. You may be gone, but you will never be forgotten. I know you are looking down on me smiling and saying "I'm proud of you. You did it!"

*Baby,*

*My God, how I wish you were here! I have a longing for you mere words cannot describe. This is me and how I feel after another dismal attempt at sexual gratification without you. My orgasms are reminiscent of unicorns or the Lochness Monster. They're fun to talk about, but no one has seen them or felt their magic. (Sigh) I mean, it's not bad with him, but it's not toe-curling, back-arching, or passionate beyond this world. It's good, but it's not great, and I know what great feels like . . . You! (Smile)*

*Is it crazy how I get more enjoyment out of our "phone dates" than I do his sex? How can your voice soothe me the way it does, more than his touch? I need you, Sin! You never left me aching for more, although you would leave me aching. (Smile) You always left me content mentally, physically, and spiritually.*

*I'd give anything to have you here or to hear your voice right now. One quick call from you would do the trick. You, me, the phone, and my "vibey." What an incredible team! (Ha Ha)*

*It's a shame that no matter how strongly I need and want you, it's 11:30 PM, and you won't be able to call. You're locked in that dreadful cell. Even if you weren't, it would be difficult for me to explain to Marcus why he was awakened out of his sleep by my moaning and crying out your name into the phone. (LOL)*

*I'm going to just run me a hot bubble bath and think of you. My thoughts of you and my fingers will have to do until you can "cum" and properly take care of this "Kitty Cat." (Smile) Listen to my horny ass! I'll write again this week, but know I'm thinking of you until then.*

*Loving and missing you always,*
*xoxo–Misty–xoxo*

# CHAPTER 1

## *Living without Sin*

I sat staring at the letter, wishing I had the good sense not to mail it. In my heart, I knew what I was doing was wrong, but this was the only way for me to have a piece of my dream—Garrett a.k.a. "Sin" Butler. He was the recipient of the letter and the man I was secretly in love with. The fact that he was sentenced to 60 years in a federal penitentiary did not dispatch or stifle the deep connection or intense emotions we share. If that and our extensive history didn't, then I honestly didn't know if there was anything that could. I knew the odds of us ever being together again in a sexual way were slim to none. I had a better chance of hitting the Mega Millions lottery. However, what I feel for him is so much deeper than a physical attraction. He is my infinite love.

The sexual frustration I described in my letter was merely a by-product of the true issue I faced. I was seriously involved and living with a man, yet I couldn't fathom living my life without Sin. We were divinely intertwined, and despite attempts to separate, we always found ourselves running to the other's call. We finally stopped fighting the inevitable. We had resigned ourselves to doing a tentative dance of secretly supplying each other with the mental, emotional, and spiritual nourishment we craved.

As I sat at my desk, thoughts of how he used to please me bounced around in my mind. I could clearly see the images of his strong, muscular body covering mine, lighting a fire within my belly that trickled like hot lava down into that sweet spot between my legs. I smiled and swept up the legal pad, envelope, and pen, then placed them into a folder. I stuffed everything in my briefcase then locked it, turned off the lights in my home office, and closed the door.

I felt a sense of hesitancy as I peered up the steps leading to the master bedroom where my man, Marcus Preston, awaited me. We had been seeing each other for the last three years, but the relationship lost its momentum in year one, and had been on a downward spiral ever since. Stepping into the bedroom, I inwardly sighed with relief as I found him asleep. A part of me felt guilty for loving two men—two good men, but it was complicated.

Marcus is the epitome of what society views as a worthy mate: college graduate, earning well over six figures, good credit, and living in a beautiful home. He's stable, consistent, and has structure. After the ordeal I went through with Sin, predictable and unadventurous were characteristics I wanted in a man. Yet with all his great qualities came drawbacks and Marcus's bullshit outweighed the good. It wasn't until after I moved in with him that I learned he had weird views on a woman's role in a relationship.

When Marcus and I first met I was residing in a brownstone on 134th Street & St. Nicholas, which I jointly owned with my best friend Charmaine. Although I dated him exclusively, prior to agreeing to move in with him, I really didn't spend a significant amount of quality time with him. After a year of random dates he asked me to move in with him. I was cool with the idea since we seemed to be on the same page and working toward the same goal. He had all the qualities I thought I needed in a man.

Everything was flowing up until I moved in with him. It was then that his true colors were revealed and I gradually discovered Marcus was happiest when I didn't have an opinion. As long as I agreed to agree, everything was all good with him. He wanted me to be subservient. He wanted a beautiful, smart woman on his arm that he could brag to his college buddies and business partners about—a showpiece. He wanted a woman he could marry then stick in a house alone and keep her barefoot and pregnant.

In addition to his primordial way of thinking he wasn't the easiest person to be around for any length of time. Living with someone is totally different than visiting. Marcus didn't relate to anything urban or the plight of the inner city people. I found him to be a snob—a typical privileged, want-to-be-white, suburban, upwardly mobile black man; a classic know-it-all. Over the months I saw it was a waste of time trying to tell or teach him anything. Why bother when he already presumed he had all the answers? I learned he was also negative, biased and judgmental. Who wants to be constantly critiqued or have someone's opinion jammed down their throat? Not me, that's for sure!

Most women would take Marcus and his bullshit over a convict any day, and under normal circumstances, I would too. However, if Sin's imprisonment was taken out of the equation he would be the embodiment of what all women would consider an almost perfect man. He's an attractive, dominant, masculine figure who's both book and street smart. He's a savvy businessman, a masterful lover, and a proven leader. He's firm, strong, and challenging yet fair, humorous, passionate, and attentive. He's tall, bald, and confident. To sum it up he's simply swagger-licious, and any woman would be proud to be on his arm.

Sin swept me off my feet in an instant and became the elevation in my flight, the air that fills my lungs, and the force that pumps my blood; my personal nirvana. My love for him was instinctive, pure, and without pretext. The love I have for Marcus was coincidental, learned, and then adopted. Yes, I love two men at the same time, but for very different reasons. I love them separately, but internally fight with the issues I have with both; which is what keeps me enthralled in this love triangle.

Don't try to understand this crazy thing I got going on, because I don't understand it myself.

My issues with Sin have very little to do with personality conflicts. We get along perfectly. At one time Sin's word was law, and if he told me to jump out of a window I would without asking a question because I knew he would have someone beneath to catch me. I know he still loves me, but his severing ties and then reconnecting once he was locked up left me apprehensive about his intentions. When the feds came looking for him years before he vanished like a ghost. He disconnected from everything and everyone. He took Robert DeNiro's character's line from the movie Heat—"Allow nothing to be in your life you can't walk out on in thirty seconds flat if you spot the heat around the corner"—literally. He went on the run and eventually disconnected himself from me as well.

I went through two years of depression before I pulled it together. He was eventually caught, tried, and convicted for the sale and distribution of heroin. He was given a 60-year sentence. I would never admit it to anyone back then, but there was this feeling of emptiness within me that wouldn't go away. I missed him so much that my heart ached. The pain was unbearable. I wanted to just crawl up somewhere and die. I felt like someone sliced half of my body off and threw it away. In time I started dating, but the truth was I never stopped loving or longing for him.

One day, out of the blue sky, I received a letter from him at my office. The return address was from Otisville Penitentiary. It had been years since Sin and I had spoken or seen each other, and the thought of holding a letter from him in my hands made my body weak. I sat down, read it, and never looked back. We gradually began corresponding. Old wounds had healed, and a renewed friendship blossomed. It was during the months of exchanging letters and calls that we began to supply each other with something most couples seek, but few achieve—unconditional love.

A friendly exchange of letters set off a raging, out-of-control blaze, and before knowing it we were talking love. Sin had me feeling things I hadn't felt in a long time as well as analyzing my current relationship. I was ready to leave Marcus and eager to see to what extent Sin and I could develop our relationship. We were talking several times a day and making plans to see each other. Everything was going great as Sin drew me in. I was happier than a star cloud-hopping in the sky.

I was so busy on cloud nine I didn't see the eye of the storm preparing to touch down. One afternoon while on the phone Sin decided to divulge something he had been purposely keeping from me. In fear I would no longer love him he intentionally waited until he felt I had fallen back in love with him before he told me. He confessed to fathering a child. All the changes I went through due to him leaving, only to find out he had gotten along just fine without me. I was pissed to say the least and crushed. I couldn't understand. Did he not miss me as I missed him? Did he not hear my soul crying out for him?

I was so hurt and, unbeknownst to him, it was Marcus's presence that made the crushing blow of Sin having a daughter tolerable. Marcus served as the safety net that prevented my fall. I became emotionally dependent on him to keep me afloat while I steadied myself for the all-consuming weight of loving Sin. I was no longer sure if I wanted to proceed with Sin, and I had already lost interest in Marcus. I didn't know what I wanted to do. Instead of making a decision, I chose to stay involved with both for my own selfish reasons.

For the years we were apart I wanted to forget Sin, but he was permanently etched in my heart and a part of my soul. His return made me hopeful only to find out he had a child with someone else. The one thing I always wanted. I never got the chance to tell him, but while he was on the run I had a miscarriage. Losing our child was my lowest point. I cut Sin off.

He did a whole lot of explaining and apologizing and the hurt and resentment waned. I, however, still internally wrestled with the issue. His departure damaged me, and then his having a child scorned me. It made me skeptical, envious, and angry. It made me realize how much I wanted my own child, and how his long stint shelved that for us. I found myself torn between what I wanted to do, what I was doing, and what I needed to do.

I made my way over to the edge of the whirlpool bathtub. I turned the valves, poured in some bubble bath and threw in a few bath beads. The hot water was exactly what my drained body needed. I began to relax. Within minutes of sitting back and letting the water jets do their job, my mind drifted back to my late teens and early twenties. Those were the years that shaped my mind, my outlook on life, and ultimately altered the course of my future. The carefree days—the days that made me the woman I am today. I thought back to that hot summer day in the early 90's when I first met Sin. . .

## (JUNE 16TH)

The day started off beautiful. I was going through a rough time with my then boyfriend, Black. I needed to get out and have some fun. I decided it was time to find a new man, and Harlem, USA was the perfect place to start. My crew and I had decided to start the afternoon at the Rucker basketball tournaments then work our way down 8thAvenue to 125th Street's Apollo Theater. These were places you could meet and greet the hot boys and girls from all over the city and surrounding states. My girls and I knew—or had heard of—just about anybody who was somebody, and if you let us tell it, if we didn't know you, then you weren't worth knowing!

The crew consisted of Charmaine, Toya, Jasmine, Nickelle, and me—Misty. We were all born and raised in the Bronx, attended the same high school, and loved each other like sisters; however, that's where the similarity ended. As much as we were alike, we were different. Jasmine and I grew up in the same apartment complex. Charmaine lived down the street in another apartment building, while Toya and Nickelle lived a few blocks away in private houses.

Nickelle was of Cuban, African-American, and Puerto Rican descent. She wore her hair in variety of styles, but at that particular time it was in a short, crimped DC style. She stood about 5'5", weighed 145 pounds, had fair skin, and was a bit naïve, but comical. Toya was a brown-complexioned, chubby, timid sister with big breasts and low self-esteem. She was extremely shy. Charmaine was the firecracker of the crew. She was the most daring and could outwit the best of the hustlers. She wore her long, black hair in a perfect Dubie, stood 5'7", and was stacked in all the right places. Last, but not least, was Jasmine. She towered over all us at 5'9". She played tennis all four years of high school and had a well-toned body. She was headstrong and appeared standoffish. She had an attractive face, but rarely wore any makeup or fitted clothes. She was like a tomboy.

I was the shrimp standing at a mere 5'2". I had a pretty face, fit a perfect size four, and had enough curves to turn heads. I had a mean shape. I was born to mixed parents, so I was blessed with the best of both worlds. My flawless skin had an olive tone like my half Puerto Rican, half African-American father, and appeared tanned all year round. My hair was dyed the color of honey, and it blended perfectly with my green eyes, which I got from my half white, half black mother. Some people mistook me for Spanish, but I proudly let them know I was indeed a beautiful African-American sister.

When we pulled up on 155th and 8thAvenue I got lucky. Someone was pulling out, and I got a parking space. The streets were abuzz with people. The Rucker basketball games were legendary, and all the hottest street ballers came out to show their talents. We looked around, and after accepting the fact that we weren't going to make it into the packed park, we opted to sit on a nearby car and take in the scene. We could hear the commentator over the speakers shouting out the score, describing a hot move someone made, or snapping on someone in the crowd. Nickelle, Toya, Jasmine, and I always pretty much stayed in one spot together while Charmaine wandered off and picked up stragglers. I spotted her coming up the block.

She was walking up 8thAvenue with a group. I instantly recognized three of the people, but the fourth was a guy I didn't recognize. There were two girls we'd met the week before, who were just as gold digging as Charmaine, and Lavon, the self-proclaimed party promoter. He was a ladies' man, whose sole purpose in life was to be the man. Sometimes I hated to run into him because he was always sticking a flyer in your face. There was a rap concert at Madison Square Garden the next day, and he was promoting an after-party.

"Ladies, ladies, what it look like? I got these flyers for the hottest party of the century!"

He passed each one of us a flyer. I looked it over.

"My man and I are promoting this party, and I tell you it's going to be off the chain!"

Each event he promoted was going to be the party of the century in his opinion, and every once in a while it would actually turn out to be hot.

"Hook us up with some comp tickets, and we'll roll through," I said.

"Oh, come on, Misty, the last two parties I gave you a pass for you didn't even show up."

"That's because the last two parties you only gave her one ticket, knowing it would be five of us going," Jasmine argued.

"Well how am I supposed to make money if I go around giving away tickets?"

"By making sure you give them to some fly girls. Duh? The guys will pay and buy drinks if your party has pretty women. I thought you had this," I teased. "Do I need to school you?"

Lavon's man, who I had never seen before, joined the conversation. "Yo, man she's right. Give the honeys five passes."

Lavon went to protest, but his anonymous associate shut him down quick.

"Look, it's not that heavy. The more pretty women show up, the more bread we gonna make, so give them the tickets."

Lavon could have died of embarrassment, but he played it off by saying, "It's your dollar, Sin."

The word "dollar" drew the attention of the two gold diggers. It was like a neon sign went off in their heads flashing "money, money, money." Charmaine was chilling because Terror, her latest flame, was in town and somewhere on 8th Avenue.

Lavon finally properly introduced us to his friend. "Oh ladies, this is my man Sin."

You couldn't tell much about him by the way he was dressed. He wore a pair of yellow linen shorts, a yellow-and-black party promotional tee shirt, and black sandals. However, if you judged his potential wealth solely on his jewelry, he was eating well. He wore a single two-carat diamond in his ear, and his wrist held a Presidential Rolex watch with diamonds around the bezel and band.

"Is that a real Roley?" one of the females asked with skepticism. "There are a lot of brothers out here fronting, and I don't have time for no wannabe hot boy."

Sin laughed. "It sounds like you're way out of my league. I guess you know a Timex when you see one."

She was instantly turned off with him and went back to watching the unofficial car show on 8th Avenue. He smirked then shook his head and chuckled under his breath. We stood there for a long time just shooting the breeze with them. Lavon was trying to impress us with his exaggerated stories of who he knew, all the while trying to convince one of us to give him some play. As if.

Sin, however, was much more enigmatic and mysterious. The whole time I silently watched him and attempted to size him up. He wasn't talkative like Lavon, and when he spoke he was articulate and his conversation had substance. He wasn't boastful or flirty, but reserved and laid back. A fascination for him was germinating within me.

He stood about 6'1", wore his hair short to his scalp, and had a medium muscular build, thick eyebrows, and the longest eyelashes I'd ever seen. He had full lips and skin the color of dark caramel. He was extremely handsome, and there was something definitely sexy about his smile.

Jasmine was standing next to me. She leaned over and whispered, "He's really cute."

"Yeah, I think so too!"

"Well I'm going to get those digits," she boasted.

I smirked. "Who told you that? Because I plan on getting that number!"

"Then let the best woman win."

"I'm up for the challenge, Jaz."

I knew the odds of him picking her over me were slim to none. She was a nice looking girl, but she couldn't capture and hold the attention of a man of his caliber. She just didn't stand out enough for a hot boy. She couldn't match their wit. I sat back and watched as she, as well as Charmaine's friend took every opportunity to gain his interest, but he brushed them off. I said to myself, *This guy is either married or his woman is close by, because there aren't too many brothers at the park who would pass up on an opportunity to get at either one of the girls.*

I broke the ice between us and asked, "Is Sin your birth name or a nickname?"

He went into explaining how he had gotten the nickname from his grandmother when he was a baby. She said eyelashes so long had to be a sin. We all began teasing him.

"Nigga, please, you got that nickname because you're one sinister-ass motherfucker," Lavon joked.

Sin didn't find the joke funny and shot Lavon a shut-the-fuck-up look and Lavon quickly checked himself. The whole time we stood around talking, Sin didn't make it obvious that he was interested in anyone in particular, but I did catch him sneaking peeks at me every now and again.

We actually got into a debate about the Chicago Bulls and New York Knicks. He later made mention that he was impressed with my knowledge of sports. I too was impressed after I tried to stump him by asking him a few questions about politics and history, and he answered every one. It's not every day you find a young African-American male in the hood who is educated, well versed, up on the world's current events, manicured, street smart, fine, got paper, and thorough. He was a polished thug!

Sin leaned his back up against the car and shuffled the stack of party promotion cards back and forth in his hands. I watched him as he eyed each one of us. His stare remained on me a little longer. He scanned me from head to toe, and when he realized I was watching him, he smirked. I walked off to the hot dog stand to get a grape soda. Seconds later he followed.

"Misty, that's a pretty name."

"Thanks. I caught you checking us out. So what's your synopsis of me?"

He laughed. "You don't hold any punches, do you?"

"Nope, and not much gets past me either." I laughed.

"If you must know, I was thinking—shorty is a cutie; pretty face, personality, real nice shape, long hair, manicured toes, and those eyes, they're beautiful!"

I smiled then replied sarcastically, "You must have been looking really hard to notice all of that, huh? Didn't your mother teach you it's impolite to stare?"

He smiled. "Yeah, but it's hard to turn away from those eyes."

I smirked and paid for my soda. "So what else did you observe?"

He laughed. "I noted there's something different about you. You appear to be more than a money-grubber like your friends. It's been a minute since a female peaked my interest, and I see a certain refinement in you I like."

I blushed as we walked back to the group. The sun had set and it had gotten dark. People dispersed from the park, and most were now looking to head down to 125th Street. The police were directing people off the Avenue. It was time for us to part ways. We said our goodbyes and were about to walk off.

"So will I see you at my party?" Technically, Sin could have been talking to any one of us, but his eyes were on me.

"Is that a personal or public invitation?" I asked.

"It can be whatever you want, Bright Eyes."

I looked him up and down. "I'd have to think hard on that one. I know how you party promoters are. You invite ten different females to the club, and then spend the night trying to avoid them."

"For one, this function is all about that cheddar for me. I can get with any female I want, anytime I want."

I grinned as I thought, Isn't he cocky?

"And for the record, I don't have those kinds of problems. Take my pager number down and hit me when you get outside the club."

"How are you going to know it's me? There's going to be a ton of people trying to reach you."

"Put in code 155 behind your phone number. I'll know it's you, and I'll call you right back."

"Sounds good, but don't have me standing around a pay phone waiting for you to call me back. That's not cool, Sin."

He grinned. "Don't worry, I got you. I'll call you right back."

I smirked. "I hope so. You may only get one chance."

"I'm a man of my word. If I say I'll call, then I'll call."

"Okay, we shall see, Mr. Sin. Why did you give me code 155 anyway? Am I the 155th chick you gave your number to?"

"Nah, it's nothing like that. I did meet you on 155th Street, right?"

I took the number from him. "What time is it?" He lifted his wrist and I read 7:12. I smirked because I knew he had lied earlier. "That's a beautiful timepiece."

Charmaine's friend spun around then chuckled because she thought he was a buster rocking a fake watch. I knew better because that bad boy on his wrist didn't tick. The joke was on her.

I later asked him why he'd lied to her and he responded, "Why entertain ignorance? Her question showed she had no class, and she wouldn't have known the difference anyway." He said chicks like her get strung along by broke-ass niggas every day.

I remember walking away from our first meeting thinking, *This is going to be an interesting summer!*

# CHAPTER 2

## *Black out.*

My boyfriend before meeting Sin was Harvey Johnson, better known as "Black" due to his dark chocolate complexion. He was my high school sweetheart, and a grade ahead of me. He was on the varsity football team and I was a cheerleader. Black stood 5'11", and was burly like a bear. He had bowlegs, broad shoulders, perfect teeth, and a bright smile. He was a nice looking guy with natural black curls. What stood out about him was his birthmark. It was a white, dime-sized spot to the side of his right eyebrow, but nearer to his temple. What I liked most about him was his sense of humor. We would meet up after practice and walk home together every day. He would tell me funny stories and make me laugh.

We were friends by the time we started dating. My father didn't want me to have a boyfriend, so initially we tiptoed around. He was my buddy, and our favorite places were the movies, skating, or carnivals. Once we got permission to date he would come over to my house, hang out, listen to music, or watch television. His mother was a home attendant and worked long hours, so most afternoons she wasn't home. Six months into hanging out, one thing led to another and one afternoon at his house I gave him my virginity. I really thought he was going to be my husband one day. How naïve was I?

In high school he wasn't the guy all the girls swooned over. He was liked, but he didn't get much play because he didn't have any money. He was cute, but cute and broke didn't cut it with the hot girls. He worked part-time at a print shop, but the pay was pennies. He barely made enough to treat me to a slice of pizza. Most times I paid when we went out. I had a part-time job, and an older brother and father who always gave me money. I didn't have an issue looking out for Black because he was fun to be around.

My senior year I started to notice a drastic change in him. His dreams of playing in the NFL changed to a pipe dream on Crack Row. Shortly after he started attending college in Texas, someone put him on to hustling drugs. He began missing classes, and his grades fell below the required GPA. His athletic scholarship was yanked, and he was thrown off the football team. Instead of getting a free education, he blew the opportunity. In a matter of weeks I watched him transform. He upgraded his wardrobe, purchased several flashy pieces of jewelry, and bought a used Jeep. He also started giving me lots of money. His time was replaced by material things—clothes, jewelry, and a car.

Once Black started seeing some real cash, things changed between us. I grew to enjoy the money and presents, but the lifestyle and his new attitude stunk. It was nice having a boyfriend who could now take me places and purchase me things, but his being gone all the time and messing around was not going to make it.

After a while I became bored with being bought. I guess the large sums of money and presents he gave couldn't erase the lies, unreturned phone calls, infidelity, and abuse. He became a real asshole. It got to a point where I couldn't stand the sight of him.

I no longer saw in him the person I once fell for. I didn't want to be bothered, and he knew it. To clear his conscience of his constant lies and cheating, he gave more and more money. When he realized the money wouldn't stifle my complaints, he took to quieting and controlling me through violence. It began with him threatening me, graduated to yelling, and then pointing his finger in my face. It intensified to him grabbing my arm, and ultimately ended with him pushing or smacking me. I wasn't raised to have a man hitting on me. I wasn't sure how, but I had to leave him.

At first he was sending for me to visit him in Texas twice a month, and that abruptly stopped. He started giving me excuses why he didn't want me down there. He said his crew had beef, he was constantly moving, and it wasn't safe for me to be there.

There were little signs of his cheating in the beginning. He started taking a long time to return my calls if he did at all. He had every reason in the book from his battery dying to he left his pager somewhere. I noted when his pager went off at home he wouldn't return the calls, and if he did he whispered. I found phone numbers and once a pair of panties in his bed. He claimed he let his friend and his girl use his room, but I knew it was a lie because we had to sneak in his house before he was able to afford a hotel. I was nobody's fool.

One time, he came home unexpectedly, determined to make up with me. At that point, if something didn't change, I was done. He sexed me all morning, took me shopping, and assured me things would get better between us. He said he missed me and he was going to start sending for me again. I wanted to believe him. I was happy he was trying. Later that same evening we were at the movies when his pager went off. He walked off to use the pay phone, while I remained at the concession stand.

I noticed a female roll up on him. I could see he was trying to ignore her. I wondered what it was all about. I got our items then strolled over to him. When he saw me approaching, he picked up the receiver and pretended to be making a call. She refused to budge. He turned his back on her then started punching in numbers. She was pissed. When I stood next to him she yelled, "Who the fuck is this bitch, Black?"

She obviously didn't know who I was. I said nothing. I waited for him to respond.

"Don't fucking play yourself, Tamika! That's my girl!"

"No motherfucker, don't play yourself! You told me you broke up with the person you were dating months ago! You never said anything about having a girl! Up until I told you I was pregnant, I thought I was your girl!"

I was totally surprised. I had to make sure I heard her correctly. "You're pregnant from him?"

"Yes, I am!"

"How long have you been dating, and how many months are you?"

"I've been dealing with him off and on for like six months, and I'm three months pregnant."

"If this bitch is even pregnant, that shit ain't mine," Black blurted out.

She started yelling. "I know who my baby's father is! This is your baby! I was fucking you and only you for like three months straight. Sometimes we used condoms, but most of the time you hit this raw so don't act like it's impossible."

I stood with my hand on my hip in disbelief.

He looked over to me with pleading eyes. "Misty, I don't know what she's talking about. This bitch is crazy!" He grabbed my arm. "Come on. Let's go!"

"You're not going to call me crazy and walk away from me! I wasn't crazy when you were sending money through Western Union every time you wanted me to fly down to Texas to see you, motherfucker! You had me down there with you for two months straight, and now you don't know me?"

I pushed him in his chest.

"I know you're not about to believe this ho over me! I wasn't fucking with her, Misty. She was bringing work down there for us. That's all."

I shook my head in disgust. "You're pathetic. Who do you think you're dealing with, Black? Her bringing work down to Texas is like me bringing cocaine to Columbia."

Tamika spun her head around like Reagan from *The Exorcist* then pointed in his face with her long, fire-engine-red nails. "Bringing you work? I wasn't bringing shit down there, but me! You a lowdown motherfucker, Black! How you gonna act like you ain't mess with me? If you didn't fuck with me, how would I know you got a birthmark on your left butt cheek to match that one on the side of your face?"

My mouth flew open. "That's it! Fuck you! I don't need you, Black, and I don't need this shit! She can have you! It's over!" I went to stomp off, but he grabbed my arm.

The shouting caused people to stare at us.

"You stinking-ass bitch! You trying to break me and my girl up? Get the fuck out of here with this bullshit before I slap the shit out of you!" He mushed her in the face hard, sending her stumbling backwards into the payphone, causing the receiver to fall.

She came right back at him and started pushing him. People were looking at us like we were insane. I walked off in total embarrassment. I exited the theater in tears. He chased after me with her in pursuit. I flagged down a cab, but before I could get all the way in he snatched me out by my arm. He pulled then pushed me into his car before shoving Tamika to the ground.

He took me back to his house, tried to apologize then basically threatened me. He put a gun to my head and told me I wasn't going anywhere, and if I tried he'd kill me.

My reply was, "You can make me stay by force, but don't act surprised when you find out I've been messing with someone else." He thought I was just talking out of anger, but I really had other plans. He left that night, and the very next day I met Sin.

The following day I went to the concert then headed home to change for Lavon and Sin's official after-party. I decided to wear a red suit with red 3½-inch heels. We all looked cute, but my red suit and red car took me to the next level. The club was packed, and the line was around the corner. Thank God we knew the bouncers and had no problem walking right in. As soon as we entered the club I spotted Sin, Miguel, and Lavon talking by the bar. Sin was sipping on something clear and looking clean in his cream-colored linen suit and Fedora hat. There was a pay phone on the wall by the door.

"Wait up a minute," I told my girls. "I want to page Sin and see if he calls me right back."

Charmaine pointed toward the bar. "But he's right over there."

"I know, but I want to see if he's really a man of his word." I pulled out his number, pushed the coins in the slot, and then typed in his digits. At the tone I entered the pay phone number followed by 155. I hung up then put my back to the phone.

"I'm not about to stand by this pay phone all night, Misty!" Jasmine stated.

She was still salty I pulled Sin, but she would just have to get over it.

"Chill. Do you really think I'm going to stand here past a minute? He's either going to get the beep and call me right back, or he's going to look at his pager and ignore it."

After a minute or so I noticed him reach into his pocket. He pulled out the pager and fumbled with it before pressing the button. We all watched as a smile spread across his face.

"Is that the reaction you were looking for?" Charmaine asked.

Feeling myself, I replied, "Yup!"

We watched as he excused himself and walked toward the back of the club. Shortly after he disappeared, the pay phone started ringing. "Hello."

"Did someone page somebody from this number?"

"Why give a person a code and then act like you don't know who it is when you call them back?"

He laughed. "Okay, may I please speak with Misty? Is that better, Bright Eyes?"

"Yes, much better."

"Are you outside?"

"No, but did anyone tell you how extremely debonair you look tonight?"

"How you know how I look?"

"Because, I got my eye on you."

He laughed. "Where you at?"

"I'm in the front by the door. I'll meet you over by Lavon and Miguel."

Sin strode up twirling a red straw around in his mouth. He examined me as he approached. My skirt was tight and short—sexy, not slutty. The matching jacket was cropped so he got a full view of my flat stomach, small waist, and high ass. He said hello to both Charmaine and Jasmine then gave me a special greeting. He was looking down at me real sexy like.

"Hi there, Bright Eyes! I love the red."

"Thank you and I like your hat! It was the perfect touch."

"You're looking like a fresh strawberry!" Miguel teased.

I playfully modeled for Miguel, hoping Sin was paying close attention. He leaned his back up against the bar and played with the straw in his mouth as I twirled around. I stood next to him, and signaled for the bartender.

Like a ventriloquist, Sin mumbled under his breath while still swirling the straw. "I wonder if that strawberry is as sweet as it looks?"

After ordering my drink and without turning to look up at him, I whispered back, "Oh, but it is, especially with a sprinkle of sugar, a dollop of whipped cream, or a drizzle of champagne."

He turned around, placed his drink on the bar, and then slightly pressed his side into mine. His body was so close he gave me goose bumps.

I could feel the heat from his breath on my neck as he lowered his head, brought his lips directly to my ear, and softly whispered, "Whenever you're ready to let me taste it, I'll be happy to let you know which I prefer it with."

INFINITE LOVE: THE PURSUIT

I turned my head and looked up at him surprised. He winked then walked off.

Later that evening, the party was in full swing, and we were on the dance floor. I put a little extra in it when I saw Sin watching.

He made his way over to me, stood between me and some guy I was dancing with, and then said, "Chocolate."

I was confused. We had not spoken since the bar. "What about chocolate?"

"I decided I want to taste your strawberry with melted chocolate."

At that moment, I knew if I continued this dangerous game we were going to eventually fuck. Jasmine was standing next to me, and huffed under her breath.

"What perfume is that you're wearing?" Sin asked me.

The guy I was dancing with sucked his teeth and walked off.

"It's Calyx by Prescriptives."

"It smells really nice on you." He moved in closer. "Do you mind?"

I looked at him strangely.

He smirked. "I just want to get a better whiff."

I tilted my head slightly to the left and back. He leaned in, gently pushed my hair to the side, and then slowly sniffed up my neck. The tip of his nose grazed my skin as he sniffed from my collarbone to the back of my ear. He made chills run down my spine. He lit a match under my skirt, and I instantly became aroused. My breathing became heavy as he pulled away.

"Yeah, you smell delicious!"

I couldn't let him see me lose my cool although I felt flushed. I bit down on my bottom lip, released it, looked into his eyes then said, "I'm glad you like."

"Would you like a drink?"

I nodded and we all walked over to the bar. "I'll take a Sex on the Beach."

He got the attention of the bartender and signaled for her to come over. "What would you ladies like?"

Charmaine ordered the same while Jasmine tried to get cute and order a bottle of champagne. I took offense.

"Stop playing yourself, Jaz, and order a mixed drink. You don't even like champagne like that!"

She rolled her eyes at me then ordered a Blue Hawaiian with an attitude.

He placed our order. We stood there sipping, talking, and watching the crowd.

We were about halfway through our drinks when Jasmine snapped, "Are we going to stand here all night? I want to walk around!"

I cut my eyes at her, but before I could respond Sin said, "Go ahead and have fun. I'm getting ready to get up out of here anyway."

"You're leaving so soon?" I was honestly disappointed.

"Yeah, I have to bounce out of town real quick."

"But I thought this was your party?"

"It is, but real business calls."

Not wanting to seem pressed to spend time with him, I left it at that. "I understand, and thanks for the drink."

Jasmine grabbed Charmaine's hand, who then grabbed mine, and before he could ask me for my number they started pulling me back into the crowd. I waved bye.

"I'll see you again, shorty."

I mouthed back, "I hope so."

# CHAPTER 3

## *Marcus the Carcass*

The sound of Marcus stirring about awakened me out of my daze and brought me back to my current milieu.

He opened the bathroom door. "You've been in here for thirty minutes already. You're going to look like a prune when you get out of that tub. Are you okay?"

"I'm fine; just unwinding. I'll be out shortly."

He shook his head and walked back into the bedroom. The memories I housed in my mind of those early years were held dear to my heart. Back then I lived to travel, party, and shop like there was no tomorrow. Today my business and my sanity was what I was trying to maintain. I stepped out of the tub, reached for the lotion, and began oiling my skin. I could hear the sound of the television playing in the adjoining bedroom. I figured he was up and wanted to make love. Sometimes I fretted giving him some of my Kitty Cat. Having sex with him was like taking an express train that missed your stop.

Don't get me wrong; he was a decent lover, but because he was not fully in tune with my body it was a constant challenge for me to reach my sexual pinnacle. I often felt like it was every man for himself in our bed. You either worked and got yours off, or you went to bed frustrated. It was a continual contest of who could cum first. An experienced lover knows how to build an orgasm and bring it to fruition. A selfish lover hurries to extinguish their own fire, unaware or unconcerned with the frustrated feelings of their cheated partner.

Marcus had it all; a great job, nice physique, and a nice sized penis, but couldn't work it. The life I had with him was comfortable. We lived in a four-bedroom house in Fort Lee, New Jersey, collectively owned three cars—a Porsche, a Mercedes, and an X5 BMW—and had plenty of money at our disposal. We were living the American dream, but something was wrong with this picture. He lacked finesse and panache. He just wasn't the type to walk into a room and draw the crowd's attention. He lacked creativity and courage. If you asked him a question, the answer would always be analytical. He would surely select the longer, but safer route, and never dare to explore the quicker, but riskier course.

Often people want to know why good girls fall for bad boys. The answer is simple—confidence! There's something about a man who reeks of confidence that turns a woman on like an aphrodisiac. If she believes in that man, then she will trust him to lead her, and will follow him to the ends of the earth. This can be dangerous because she can end up with a dud; a rocket that dies midair.

Marcus was a beast in the boardroom, but lacked that same energy and flair in the bedroom. His specialty was executing contracts, not pussycats. He reached his apex each time he closed a big deal. He'd spend months on conference calls, in board meetings, and revising proposals to win a deal. I only wished he put 10% of that energy into satisfying me in the bed. Maybe if I had never experienced complete sexual fulfillment I wouldn't have such had a high standard to measure him by.

Sex with Sin was another story. It was out of this world; passionate, uninhibited, new, and spontaneous every time. Like a sculptor he molded my body to conform to his, and with each of his strokes our bodies became harmonious like the sounds of a sonata being played by a symphony.

There's a scene in the movie *Species II* that reminded me of the sexual frustration I encountered each time I hungered for Sin's loving. In the movie there are these two characters, female and male, half human and half alien who are deliberately kept apart by a glass partition so that they could not procreate.

The glass didn't stop their sexual desires. Each time they were within close proximity of each other, their hormones would go crazy, and a desperate animalistic yearning overcame them. Their chemistry was electric, and you could empathize with the sexual hunger they felt for one another.

The one thing that was always consistent with Sin was great sex! He knew how to satisfy me yet leave me yearning for more. Whether we were making love, getting a quickie, like or lust, the sex was always incredible.

I heaved a sigh and took a final look at myself in the mirror, put on my robe, and walked into the bedroom. I was prepared to be touched, teased, and then left frustrated once again. Twenty minutes after entering the bedroom it was over. Just as I expected—what should have been an all-night sex-a-thon ended up taking all of seven minutes from start to finish.

The next morning when I rose I saw that Marcus had already left for his business trip. I took the day off and planned to take care of a few errands. Growing up I always wanted to be an entrepreneur, and am fortunate to now have the option of working from home, going in the field, or reporting to my office. I am the broker of my own real estate company. I got into the housing market early enough where I was able to reap the benefits.

There were times when I wondered if real estate was still the right move. The market had dried up terribly, and people were not buying like they used to. I was lucky Marcus paid all the bills. He pretty much took care of the entire household, which allowed me to spend and save my money at my discretion. Although I protested, this was the arrangement he wanted when he first asked me to move in. I took advantage and stashed like a squirrel.

I stretched, popped in a Pilates DVD, and got my morning started. Breakfast was the normal turkey bacon, egg whites, whole-wheat toast, orange juice, and a cup of decaffeinated Chamomile tea. Just as I sat down to catch CNN, my cell phone rang.

"Hello. Miss Bishop speaking."

"Misty! Misty! You're not going to believe this!" Nickelle was hyped.

"What is it?" With her you could never be sure what she had going on. I could only imagine the story she was about to tell me.

After a dramatic pause she finally yelled, "I was approved by the bank! I got the loan! I'm going to be opening that new salon!"

We both screamed, "Yeaaaahhhhhh!"

"Oh my God! Congratulations! This is great, Nick! My little sister is blowing up! Little boss lady gonna have two hair salons now."

"I couldn't have gotten this far without your help."

"I might have given you some pointers, but it was you who applied the knowledge, sacrificed, and remained disciplined. I'm extremely proud of you, Nick."

Nickelle had wanted to open up another hair salon for some time, but didn't pursue it because she didn't think a bank would approve her. Due to past indiscretions, her credit score was low. She needed to do some major repairs before any lender would take her seriously. Everyone was feeling the strain of the economy and was being more frugal with their dollars. I personally felt the effects and had to make some difficult choices in the last three years. I had to downsize my office space and lay off five people. We all took it hard, but there was nothing I could do.

I was fortunate to have Sin advising me, and he saved me a lot of potential losses. He warned me about the impending crisis long before it actually hit. He recommended I unload a chunk of my holdings right before the market went bust. I was able to sell off some properties my company owned and was highly invested in.

For seven years straight I had seen a steady increase in all my properties' values, so I thought he was losing his mind when he told me to unload a majority of his and my assets. He said all he had to do while in jail was work-out, read, manage his interests, and work on getting the hell out of there. He said he was in there all day and didn't have the same distractions most people had. He said he had the advantage of looking at situations with a clear mind and from all angles. He asked if I trusted him. I did, and he was right! I sold and managed to dodge a major loss. He saved us both a whole lot of money.

"So what's the next move, Nick?"

"First, I want to go out and celebrate with my girls. Dinner and maybe listen to a little music tonight, and then I'll worry about a location starting next week."

"Have you spoken to anyone else yet?"

"No, you're the first person I told."

"I'm flattered."

"The budget and savings plan you created for me really helped. I was able to pay off all my debt and increase my credit score by almost 170 points. Those two things and the advice along the way made all the difference. I wanted to make sure I called you early before 'Mr. Know It All' made any plans."

She didn't like Marcus, and only tolerated him. "He went to Detroit on business this morning. He won't be back until Tuesday night sometime, so you have me all to yourself."

"Good, because Trey will be with his great aunt the whole weekend. How's everything with you? How's business?"

"Business is good. Matter of fact, as long as I stay in the black, it's great!"

"How's my big brother doing?"

At one time Sin spent so much time at the brownstone it was like the five of us lived together. "He's fine; trying to stay busy. It's me who's going crazy missing him. I wish my baby could get out of there already."

"Between you two and that team of lawyers you got, you'll find a way."

"Someone better!"

"So what's up with you and that other one?"

"Who Marcus? Girl, please don't get me started. Things aren't going anywhere. It's the same shit, but on a different day. The only reason I think it's lasted this long is because he's gone most of the time. I don't want to hurt him, but I can't do this anymore either. I need to move out and on with my life."

"I told you he's bipolar. They just haven't diagnosed his ass yet. Nice guy, but not for you. I do understand why you stayed this long though. He takes good care of you and—"

"Wait a second, Nick. I didn't stay this long because of money. I don't need Marcus, or any man for that matter, to take care of me. One thing Sin did before leaving was made sure I had the means to take care of myself. When most guys had their girls laying up he was paying for me to take real estate classes, accounting courses, and small business seminars. He used to say his woman had to be more than just another pretty face. He said his lady had to be intellectual, street savvy, and able to handle a nine at the drop of a dime."

Nickelle and I giggled. "Putting all kidding aside, Nick, I knew I could never be completely dependent on a man—not after Black. Sin might have given me the startup cash, but I did the right thing with it. I didn't jack it off. I was smart and knew what I wanted. I put in those long hours making my company a success. It's been me, all by myself, all this time, maintaining my lifestyle, and for many years yours too. Not Marcus, Sin, Pop, or anybody else. I made wise investments and I save. I never splurged like Charmaine or squandered like you.

"Now I won't try to take anything away from Marcus. He is a great provider, and if it was all about the money, without thinking twice, I would stay, but it's not. I stayed in a relationship years ago for money, and I swore I would never do that again. My issues are bigger than that. For one, physically there's no chemistry, and two, our personalities clash. He has many good qualities, but there's so much he lacks."

Nickelle laughed. "And I guess with Sin in the picture all of Marcus's flaws are in living color!"

"That's not true, Nick, and Sin is far from perfect."

"Maybe, but he's the closest thing to perfect for you! What are you going to do? Leave Marcus to start a new relationship and face the same issue?"

"And what issue might that be?"

"Sin! He's your biggest obstacle. I've watched you over the years get involved with men then cut them off for inconsequential reasons. No man will ever compare or match up to him, Misty, nor will you ever find a man who'll be okay with you still being in love with him—at least not one deserving of you. That, in a nutshell, is your issue."

"So what do you suggest I do? I've tried to move on before, but I found myself missing him so much I literally got sick. You were there! It's like I'm an addict, and the interventions don't help."

"Then figure out a way for you two to be together. I light my candles and pray for you two all the time. I want you to be happy and not cursed with the burdens that come with loving him. You can't play with people's feelings, and that includes your own. You always tell me to either take a shit or get off the pot. Make a decision, because one way or the other, one will be made for you."

I remained silent and thought. She had made valid points, but I didn't need to hear it from her. I already knew it. In a perfect world I would have who I wanted and not be faced with eventually having to make a decision. I couldn't conceive having to make that kind of choice, but she was correct. Ultimately, I would have to decide.

"I hear what you're saying, and I'm going to really think about that." My tone wasn't convincing.

"Yeah, whatever. We both know, Misty, when it comes to Sin you're going to do what your heart says. You're going to ride with him, and that's cool. I'm rooting for him anyway. Tell Marcus I said good riddance! And I'll make sure to let your next man know big brother is still the regulator of that Kitty Cat, and to not get too comfortable."

I chuckled. "Ooh, be quiet. Why don't you go tell all of this to your procrastinating-ass big brother the next time you speak to him? He's the one who needs to stop dragging his tail and figure out a way before somebody beats him to punch."

"I will, as soon as he calls Trey this afternoon."

"And after you do that, go look for a boyfriend. It's about time you had a man. How long has it been?" We laughed. "Let me get off this phone. I've got a few things I need to take care of. Call me back later when you set everything up."

"I'll text you later with the specifics."

*Click.*

I hit the remote and turned up the volume on CNN. This was the first time in American history an African-American held the Presidency of the United States. Senator Barack Obama made history. I also loved the fact that he had a normal life prior to running. He has an attractive, educated African-American wife and two beautiful little girls. I was hopeful he would make a change, and I was willing to vote him in ten times to see it happen. Most Americans believed he related to the common man's plight and would lead our country further into greatness. I hated to be selfish, but I was hoping he would give relief to those families unfairly affected by the federal sentencing structure.

# CHAPTER 4

## The Crew

I couldn't help but reflect on Nickelle's good news. To think of the woman she has become made me very proud. I felt like I had a hand in that. Who would have ever known way back then how our lives would have turned out?

We were all young and happy-go-lucky when we first met. We started really running around back in high school. She was three years younger than the rest of us, and I took her under my wing. Everyone believed she was my little sister. I was shocked when she first told me she was pregnant by her first love, Treyvon. She was infatuated with him, so I wasn't surprised when she said she was going to keep the baby.

I didn't turn my back on her even when Treyvon and her family did. Her Cuban mother was a religious fanatic who followed the beliefs and practices of Santeria to the 150th power. She spent all her time outside the home praying. Her stepfather was an abusive drunk who I later found out molested her. They put her out as soon as she started showing. Her mother said she brought shame to the family. I couldn't understand how her mother could just put her out on the street, pregnant.

She was stuck on Treyvon. He was all that mattered until he flipped on her in her fifth month. He decided he wasn't ready to be a father. Everything came to a grinding halt when he said he didn't want to deal with the responsibilities and took off. It was over between them.

He moved to Connecticut with his grandfather before the baby was even born. His mother bought things and watched Lil Trey every now and again, but there was no interaction from her son. Nick was on her own and too young to do anything for herself. I spoke with my father, and he said it would be fine for them to move in with us. My brother was living in California, and his old room was empty.

The following year when Charmaine and I got our own place, Nickelle and Lil Trey moved in with us. I was financially responsible for her until she was old enough to get a real job. I was always looking out for them because being a mother was something she was not prepared for. She had him six months after her sixteenth birthday, and Trey's father didn't try to reappear until he was ten. Could you imagine being a mother and yet not be old enough to get into a club? I stayed on her to get her GED and I financed her through cosmetology school, and thank God it paid off. Now that little heifer was trying to give me advice!

In high school my life revolved around Black and my girls. Charmaine and I met when we were nine at a local dance school and had been friends ever since. She was the wild child of the crew. She lived for a party and loved to be the center of attention. She was a very attractive girl with her sun kissed skin, chinky eyes, and long black hair. She was what most men would consider a dime, and had the ability to pull just about any guy she wanted.

Wanting to keep one was another story. She didn't want to be locked down in a relationship. She didn't want to have to answer to anyone. Her single mother was a flight attendant who was never at home. This provided her with the freedom to come and go as she pleased. Nine out of ten times she was in the wrong places and doing the wrong things, but she managed to never get played or disrespected. She wasn't a slut and was selective about who she slept with. Money didn't guarantee anything from her, especially some ass. She was more of a free spirit who chose to play according to her own rules.

Toya and I met our freshman year in high school. We had the same gym and English classes. Our aerobics teacher assigned partners and we happened to be paired up. She was timid. At first I thought she was a nerd, but as the days passed I found her to be hilarious. She had a great sense of humor and a sweet disposition, and we quickly became friends. She had a southern hospitality about her, and was the type to take the high road and turn the other cheek.

Her home life was the complete opposite of Nick's or Charmaine's. Ms. Jones owned a flower shop and worked nine to five. She wasn't having any slip-ups when it came to her only child. Toya's adolescent and pre-teen years were spent solely with her mother or grandmother. She was a homebody who spent her free time reading, cooking, or watching television. They had a hard time letting go when she became a teenager. It wasn't until she started hanging with us that her mother loosened up on the reins a little.

I can picture Ms. Jones now standing in her living room asking us twenty-one questions. "Where are you ladies going, how are you getting there, how are you getting home, and what time should I expect her back?" This was a pain, but we had to go through the routine every time if we wanted her to go. Little did Ms. Jones know, we ad-libbed most of the information we provided her.

Jasmine was always the most responsible out of the clique. I used to tease her and gave her the nickname, The Funburster. We lived in the same building but didn't speak. She was actually Toya's friend first and was introduced to us by her. Jasmine focused on pleasing her parents and lived her life according to what they wanted. Her mother was a nurse and her father worked for the post office. Their dream was for her to go to college and go into the field of medicine.

Her personality was the complete opposite of Charmaine's. Although they liked each other, they just couldn't see eye to eye. They had different views on men, relationships, dressing, and music. They could be like night and day. If one said red then the other said blue.

Jasmine would say, "Your lifestyle is going to get you in trouble one of these days. You live too much on the edge."

Then Charmaine would reply, "When you get a life then you can tell me how to live mine. You're too square."

Jaz was a prude. Even Nickelle, the baby of the crew, lost her virginity before her, but we see where that got her hot-ass—pregnant at fifteen. Charmaine was a little too carefree for Jaz's taste. Cha could meet someone she was attracted to at a club and leave with them that night. I think Jaz was a little jealous because those guys were sweating, chasing, and trying to lock Charmaine down while she tried hard, but couldn't keep a boyfriend. We tried to tell her if she let up on the attitude they might stick around a little longer, but she was adamant she was not going to change.

I would have liked to see Charmaine with a steady boyfriend, but she didn't want one. In tenth grade her basketball player boyfriend, Carl, hurt her. She found out he was sleeping with a girl from another high school. He begged for her forgiveness and got her an engagement ring, but the damage was done. Within a month it was over. She complained about the many guys who tried to push up on her while she was with him. There were guys with cars who had something to offer that she turned down for him. She felt like a fool and swore off having a boyfriend.

Charmaine believed all men were dogs, and if you couldn't give her something, you weren't worth dealing with. There were a select few she slept with while the rest were for dinner, shopping, movies, or anything else she wanted. She got what she wanted or you could get lost. I knew she was smart and could take care of herself. It was just in her personality to be in the mix. She loved that hustler mentality, and the fast money turned her on.

I was a lot more reserved than Charmaine, and I preferred having a boyfriend. I gave my virginity to Black and never considered sleeping with anyone while we were together—that is, until I met Sin. Before the passing of my mother, all I witnessed in my home was a woman loving her man, catering to him, and supporting him. I was a lot like her; the nurturing, care-giving, affectionate type. I witnessed a man and woman in love, enjoying life, and working as a team to keep it together, and I wanted what I saw. I wanted a man to love me like my father loved my mother.

Now that I think about it, the situation I was in with Black back then would have been perfect for Charmaine. As far as she was concerned, a person like Black was good for two things: sex and money, and the less he was around, the more opportunity for her to get around. She wouldn't have cared if he was out sexing someone else, as long as he brought that money home to her.

I received the latest news on Barack Obama, terrorism, and the economy then got dressed, and prepared to shake a leg. On my to-do list was to stop at the post office to drop off a letter for Sin and mail a package to the law firm I found to work on his appeal. I threw on a pair of jeans, a sweater, my Ugg boots, and a black mink jacket then headed out into the cold. I despised living in New York City during the winter months. It was just too damn cold! If I had my way, I would live in New York four months, and float around between Atlanta, Miami, and LA the rest of the year.

I started my truck, selected Life Jennings's "Must Be Nice" on the iPod, and then cranked the stereo system as loud as it could go. I loved the song! Sin put me up on it and told me the words reminded him of me. If my stereo wasn't hooked up to my iPod then it was tuned into one of my favorite radio stations: Hot 97, Power 105.1 or 107.5 WBLS. Traffic was moving pretty smoothly, and I was able to handle my business in record time. I stopped at Nickelle's salon to get my hair and nails done then headed to the liquor store and supermarket. I also made it to the post office in time and while there checked my P.O. Box.

The box had a bunch of junk mail, and disappointment set in. It had been two weeks since I'd heard or received a letter from Sin. I was now starting to worry and wonder if he was all right. Exiting the post office, the wind felt like it could have blown me away. I made a mad dash for my jeep. My cell phone started ringing, but I was not about to stop and start digging through my pocketbook. After I hit the alarm, I jumped in, pulled off my glove, and was able to retrieve the phone before the call went to voice mail.

I hit the talk button. "Hello?"

"You have a prepaid call and will not be charged for this call. This call is from Garrett Butler, an inmate at a federal penitentiary. Hang up to decline the call or to accept dial five now."

My face lit up, my heart skipped a beat, and those damn butterflies started fluttering around in my stomach. I pressed 5 and waited to hear his voice.

"What's good, Baby Girl? Can you talk?"

"Yes, Daddy, I can talk! How are you doing?"

"I'm good, boo!"

"I was starting to get worried about you. No letter, no calls, is everything okay? You know if I don't hear from you I get concerned. What's been going on over there?"

"They shut the joint down. There were a couple of fights and a stabbing, but nothing for you to worry about." Sin always minimized the violence so it wouldn't bother me. He made it seem as if the things going on around him didn't affect him. "I sent you an email right before they shut it down."

"I got it, but that was a while ago." I was thankful for www.corrlinks. com. Through that website, federal inmates could communicate by way of email with friends and loved ones. We took advantage of any way he could reach out from within there.

"You know every junkie needs their fix, and you're my drug, Daddy. You got me spoiled, and I look forward to hearing your voice or reading your letters. I know you love when I send you kisses in the mail or when you open my envelope and that sweet scent of my perfume fills your room. I mailed you something today."

"I sent you a letter a few days ago too. You didn't get it yet?"

"No, and I just left the post office. I'll check again tomorrow. Nickelle called and said she got the loan. She's going to be opening up that new salon we were talking about."

"Nice! Tell her I said congratulations!"

"Actually, you can tell her yourself. She said you're supposed to call Trey today."

"Oh yeah, I almost forgot. I'll hit him in a few. So what are you getting into?"

"Tonight we're all going out to celebrate."

"That sounds like fun! And don't be out there getting too drunk."

"I'm going to be with my girls."

"I know, but I also know how you can get when you got a couple of drinks in you."

"You remembering how I use to throw this thing on you after a function and a few drinks, huh?"

"Like it was yesterday. I put a lot of hard work into sculpting that cat, so you better treat it like the prized possession it is."

"You know this is your kitty! It's stamped with your name inside and out! Only one getting some of this is Marcus, and you should be thanking him."

He got serious. "Thanking him for what!"

"For maintaining it! As big as your dick is if it wasn't for him you wouldn't be able to get in it. You don't want to come home and find cobwebs in my coochie."

"You swear you got all the game, Misty."

I chuckled. "I learned from the best, Sin. Seriously, you should know I'm not out looking for sex. It would take a superhero, swooping down from a tall building and rescuing me, for me to forget how sweet my Sin-namon stick is. I wish I could have some of that right now. If only the feds would allow conjugal visits."

"If the feds allowed conjugal visits, I would have married you yesterday!"

"Is that the only way you would marry me? If you can get sex out the deal?"

"You know better than that. If I had my way I would have married you a long time ago. I told you here is not the place. You deserve better than a jailhouse wedding. We already discussed this, and I feel getting married could ruin what we have. It would complicate things and add unnecessary pressures." He noticed I got quiet and tried to make a joke. "But best believe if they opened these doors to conjugal visits all of that shit would go out the window and we would be the first on line for the I do's! We wouldn't have any complications if I could hit you off with some of this dick every now and again. Keep that butt in line."

"It's okay. You're a gambling man. I just hope no one calls your bluff and steals your pot of gold."

"Stop talking craziness. Nobody is going to steal you away. Only a fool would try to take something that is already possessed by me. I got your mind and soul, and I'm working my way back to that body. The day I walk out this hellhole I am going to make you my wife. Being married in here could destroy our relationship. I've seen too many couples take that leap of faith without being fully aware of the sacrifices they would have to make in order to maintain such a high level of commitment."

"Any woman I call my wife could never be out there with another man, Misty, in any way. Are you ready to retire that kitty for me? Now that's something to think about, ain't it? I don't want you to give up your life for me. My relationship with you is the closest thing I have to perfection . . . to freedom. I would rather have our love forever than take the risk of getting married and helplessly watching it fall apart behind the walls of a prison. What if it became too much for you? I could lose you again, this time maybe forever. I can't take that chance. You know I love you, right?"

"Yeah, I know. If I didn't, we wouldn't be having this conversation."

"Do you know that I love you like crazy?"

"That's exactly what it is—crazy."

"Baby Girl, all I'm doing is giving you an out if you want it."

"No, all you're doing is giving the next man a way in. Nick and I were just talking about this exact same thing earlier."

"What she say?"

"When you call Trey, speak with her and ask her about her views on this topic. Hopefully she'll be as opinionated with you as she was with me."

"Do you know what I want to do right now?"

"What?"

"I want to apologize and then have make up sex!"

I chuckled. "You are so silly. Can you ever be serious?"

"I am dead serious." He was laughing as the phone hung up.

### ***SIN***

I walked away from the phone with a smile, shaking my head. The banter between me and Misty always lifted my spirits.

My man, Blaze, was leaning up against the wall waiting for me to finish my call. When he saw me hang up he walked over. "Let's go hit the yard." As we walked out the unit Blaze noted my smile and teased. "I see baby got you open, man."

"Open is freshmen in high school, son. Honey got me conscious."

"Conscious? Get the fuck out of here! What? Now you see the light?" Blaze joked.

"What happens when a person of little means come into great wealth?"

"You mean like hitting the lottery? If that's what you mean they get to tricking!"

"No I mean like a self made individual, like you going through the trenches to get that money?"

"I would appreciate that shit because I worked for it! The pressures of needing it would be gone, and my life would be better. I'd be hella smart about the way I'd spend it because I'd know what it took to get it. I'd be trying to find ways to flip that bread and make more money, more money, more money!"

"Exactly, and that would happen because of your awareness to the possibilities you didn't see before."

We stopped and I bought two sodas from an inmate selling them for stamps—the currency in federal jail—then passed him one.

"So what are you saying?" Blaze asked opening the soda.

"I'm saying when wealth is gained by hard work a person finds themselves weighing the options and considering different avenues to grow that wealth. There's a certain understanding you get when you know you possess something that makes things possible; things that you otherwise wouldn't have the presence of mind to consider."

"Okay, so what does that have to do with that goofy smile I saw on your face?" Blaze took his fingers and stretched his mouth out like the Joker.

I laughed, "I found that wealth in Misty. After all the shit it took for us to get to this place, I feel emotionally richer and due to her love for me, I now see possibilities I never imagined. My girl got conscious, son."

"My girl had me conscious too, Sin. Every time she gave me head she blew my mind."

As he laughed I shook my head.

# CHAPTER 5

## Pool Party

Within a month of meeting on 155th Street and 8th Avenue then flirting at his party, Sin and I hooked up again—It was June 21st to be exact. This was the day a match was placed to a trail of gunpowder. It started out a scorcher, and when the sun finally set the temperature dropped down to a comfortable 92 degrees. It was a perfect summer evening for a pool party. I was lying across my bed watching television when Miguel paged me. He typed in his code and added 411-911 behind it. I called him right back.

"I got your page, what's up?"

"I meant to call you yesterday, but I got distracted. I'm hosting a pool party out in New Jersey tonight, and I want you to roll through."

"I don't have any plans. I'll come."

"Perfect, because somebody has been pressing me to make sure you come!"

"Who's pressing you?"

"I don't know if it's luck or skills, but you got 'The Man' checking for you. Yo, what did you do to him?" He laughed.

"Did to whom?"

"Sin! He called me from out of town last night and again today wanting to know if I invited you to the party. He's on his way back to NY and wants to see you! He got an attitude when I told him I didn't get a chance to speak to you. He then demanded I get on my job and make it happen. I had to remind him I'm his man, and not his employee."

"He requested my presence?"

"Yeah, and he asked for your pager number too! I wanted to make sure it was okay before I gave it to him."

Since he brought his name up, I felt comfortable asking a few questions. On the low I was intrigued and wanted to see him as well. "Where do you know him from?"

"From out in Washington, DC."

"So what's up with him?"

"He's my peoples. He's a good dude!"

"So what makes him *The Man?*"

"You really don't know who he is, huh?"

"No, not at all, but I think he's really cute and smart!"

"All I'm gonna say is, he's all about that paper and well respected. I don't have to tell you how to play your cards because you're a smart girl, but he's definitely a good look for you."

I rubbed my chin. "Interesting. So he wants to get up with me?"

"Hard body too! When I spoke to him earlier he said he would definitely be here and asked specifically for you. You should feel honored. That nigga don't be checking for chicks—they check and chase after him."

"Good thing I'm not just some chick. I'm a lady and he's gonna need sneakers when he gets to chasing after this ass. He may not be used to it, but he's gonna have to work for this one, and let him know it ain't up for sale either!"

Miguel burst out in laughter as I schemed. Black was in Texas, and the party was in New Jersey. The likelihood of someone seeing me with Sin was slim.

"Tell him I'll be there, and he can get my number himself."

Miguel joked about the way the two of us were digging each other at the club. He said he knew if given the chance something was going to develop between Sin and me. Miguel was cool with Black, but said Sin was his man. His allegiance was to him, but at the same time he didn't want to see them bump heads. It would get ugly. Sin was not a man to be played with. Yet Black was no punk and would bust his gun. Miguel said Sin had the capability to squash an opponent like a grape, but preferred peace. There were stories about Black and how grimy he could be. Yet, he was no match and not equipped to go to war with Sin.

"Just watch your back, Misty. I don't want your man questioning me or you."

"Don't worry about my soon-to-be-ex man. Black's already got one foot out the door, and the second close behind. He might be replaced sooner than expected if your man is all that you say he is. Is he all that?"

"Hell yeah, I wouldn't do you like that."

"So he's worthy?"

"For sure!"

"Okay, I'm gonna trust you, Miguel. You already know I got one clown on my hands I'm trying to get rid of and I don't need another one."

He cracked up. "Nah shorty, my man is far from a clown. He's an official nigga. He is the real deal."

"Does he have a girl?"

"Now, that I don't know. You're gonna have to find that out on your own."

"Yeah, I bet. Okay, I'll see you there."

He gave me all the information before we disconnected the call. As soon as I hung up I called Charmaine to find out if she was down to go to the party.

She picked up the phone on the first ring. "Speak to me!"

"Is that the way you answer your phone?"

She giggled. "Hey, sis, what's cracking? I thought you were this guy from Brooklyn trying to holler at me. We're supposed to go out tonight."

"Well, Miguel just called and invited us to a pool party out in New Jersey. You wanna go?"

"Dilemmas, dilemmas," she teased. "I wouldn't mind getting up with Miguel's fine Puerto Rican ass! I haven't seen him since the after-party."

"The party starts at nine o'clock. Are you down to go or what, because I'm definitely going!"

"Yeah, I'm down, but why you so eager to go? I normally have to beg you to go out."

"Because Sin sent me a personal invitation, that's why."

"Get out of here. That's what's up, but you better be careful. I told you what I heard about him. He ain't no regular nigga. He's a hot boy, and you don't want to get caught out there by Black. Fuck it. It's your call. Hold on. Let me see if Jaz wants to go. She's in the bathroom washing dye out her hair."

Charmaine had done some investigating and found out Sin was indeed The Man. He was getting major paper out of town and had a multitude of females trying to pull him. No one had been seriously linked to him as of yet, but word was he was a player. The few females rumored to have fucked him were club bangers— met at the club and banged out directly afterward. One girl said he was hung like a horse. The fellas didn't know much about him except he kept it low and was very selective about the people he dealt with. I had plans to give Sin a run for his money.

After what seemed like five minutes she finally came back to the phone.

"Okay, we're both down!"

"I'll be over there at ten, so be ready. I'm not waiting for anyone tonight."

I hung up and was excited. I had to look just right. I headed to my closet to find the perfect outfit. After an hour I found a cute cream-colored short wrap dress. Underneath I wore a white bikini I had purchased from Nordstrom. I took a long shower, oiled my body down, sprayed on some perfume, and swept my hair up in a clamp. I was pleased when I looked at my reflection in the mirror. I already had a nice tan from sunning at Orchard Beach.

Nickelle was walking around my father's apartment with her bottom lip poked out. She wanted to go, but didn't have a babysitter, and it was my rule that she could not ask my father. I had watched Trey two weekends in a row, and I wasn't having it tonight. I picked the girls up, and by 11:45 we were pulling up in front of the New Jersey mansion. The house was huge, and there were all kinds of cars parked outside.

"I wonder whose house this is," Charmaine asked.

"I don't know, but they must be rich," Jasmine replied.

We made our way through the front entrance of the massive house, and it was packed with people. We could hear music and laughter coming from the backyard. The DJ had the place rocking. I searched the room, but Sin was nowhere to be found. We made our way outside into the backyard.

Miguel waved us over. "I'm glad you made it," he slurred. I could tell he had started drinking early. He looked over at Charmaine. "Damn! You look good enough to eat!"

She grinned. "If you act right, I might just let you savor the flavor, later."

He pretended to bite down on his knuckles, and we all giggled. They had a thing for each other, and every now and again she would hang out with him, but she refused to let him be her man.

Miguel pointed. "Come on, the bar is over there!" He grabbed Charmaine's hand and directed us to the upstairs patio.

I asked as if I didn't care, "So where's mister man at?"

"Oh, he just left, but he should be right back. He went to the liquor store."

Jasmine and I walked over to the bar. There were some New Jersey cats standing nearby trying to look cool. One reached out for her hand.

"Excuse me, miss, but I just had to introduce myself."

When I turned around, there stood all six feet four inches of him, Mitchell "Sweet Feet" Seth, recently drafted outfielder. He had the deepest dimples, and a neck as thick as my thigh. Jasmine didn't care who he was and was genuinely attracted to the hulk of a guy. He remained holding his hand out as she stood frozen in awe.

I decided to break the ice and stuck out my hand. "Hi, Mitch! My name is Misty, and this is my friend Jasmine."

"How did you know my name?"

"I watch the news," I laughed. "Nah, just kidding. My dad is into baseball."

"Cool! It's nice to meet you."

Jasmine was still standing there looking stupid. I nudged her and she finally said hello.

"Thanks for coming out to my party."

"Oh, this is your house. My friend Miguel and Sin invited us."

"Those are my boys. So you're Misty, the girl with the prettiest eyes?"

One of Mitch's friends tried to join the conversation, but he shooed him away. "Nah, duke, that one's already taken. She's here with my man Sin." I looked at him strangely and he smiled. "He was talking about you earlier."

I blushed. "Really? And what did he have to say?"

He smirked. "Nothing much except you was coming. He should be back in a couple of minutes. Please make yourself at home."

Mitch turned his attention back to Jasmine. I was glad she met someone. Now I wouldn't have to worry about her having an attitude with me all night. I made my way back down to the pool and found a seat. The sky was so dark and clear you could count the stars. At 12:35 the night air was still hot, and instead of sitting alone I decided to take a quick dip. There were a few people in the pool.

As I was about to unwrap my dress, I noticed out of my peripheral vision Sin standing on the upstairs patio talking to Miguel and Charmaine. I saw Miguel point in my direction, and as soon as he turned to look at me I untied my dress and let it fall to the floor. I repositioned my bathing suit bottom, stretched, and dove into the water. When I reached the other end of the pool he was leaning on the banister with both hands dangling over the railing watching me.

I made sure to lift myself out of the water very slowly. I picked up my towel then patted my face dry. The moonlight was glistening off my oiled skin, and I looked positively edible. Knowing he was looking, I waited a few seconds before I turned around and acknowledged him with a wave. I smiled then slid back into the water. He smiled and waved back. He acted as if he was listening to Miguel, but I could see he was really studying me.

Charmaine approached the two them, had a brief conversation, then disappeared into the dark house. She decided to stand behind the curtain and listen in on their conversation. She wanted to see what he had to say. Once she heard enough she ran downstairs to the pool and filled me in before Sin came down.

"Sis, let me tell you what I just heard! Sin and Miguel were upstairs talking and I got an earful. Let me recap the convo for you. It went like this . . ."

*"Miguel, you got those digits for me?"*

*"Nah, she said you can get it yourself. You my man, so I'm gonna keep it real with you. She got a man so be easy with her."*

I was upset that Miguel ratted me out, but didn't comment.

*"And? That's never stopped me before."*

*"Yeah, but her man's stupid when it comes to her."*

*"He won't have to worry. I don't know if I'm trying to keep her yet anyway.*

How about I borrow her for a minute and drop her off when I'm done? He can have her back when I'm finished."

"Nah, man, she ain't one of these chickenhead broads. I've known her for a long time, and she's a good girl. She got caught up with the wrong dude, but she's official."

"Who's her man again?"

"This kid named Black from uptown. He used to play football. He getting that first bit of shine, got a little team running with him, so his head's on swole."

"I heard his name before. He be out in Texas, right?"

"Yeah. I know you ain't tripping, but I felt you should know. She's definitely worth having, though. Like I told her, I think the two of you would be a good look."

"I don't know about all of that, but she's definitely someone I could see me chilling with, maybe hit that real quick."

"Are you listening to me, dawg? She ain't the kind a girl you just hit. She's the kind of girl you wife! A lot have tried, but she ain't given up shit! She's a good girl. If I didn't meet that crazy-ass Charmaine first, I would be pushing up on her myself. All I ask is that you be discreet no matter what you do. She's been with him for a while. She told me she's ready to leave him, but I don't want to see her fucked up in the process. Don't get her caught up, because he will literally kill her if he finds out. He be acting out and embarrassing her and shit. He tried to grab her up one time we were around and we were gonna pound his ass out."

"Get the fuck out of here! She's too pretty to be having a nigga hitting on her. That shit's for chumps. I wish that nigga would try that shit while she with me!"

"Yo, she be pulling official niggas, duke, and trust they be coming at her hard, but I've never seen her stray. She really likes you, man. I can tell! That's why I'm telling you to be discreet. She doesn't need him getting wind of you and taking it out on her."

"*Don't worry, I got her. I won't let anything happen to her, and I'll play it fair.*"

"*Oh, yeah, she wanted to know what was up with you.*"

"*And what you tell her?*"

"*I told her we knew each other from D.C., but she doesn't have the slightest idea what you got going on.*" He laughed then teased, "*But she thinks you're soooo cute and smart! But trust she'll eventually figure out you're that nigga with Charmaine on the case. Now that one is another story. She's a handful.*"

"*Hopefully by the time that happens I'll know where Misty's head is at.*"

We watched as they gave each other a pound. He then motioned with his hand that he would be down shortly.

Charmaine rose from the edge of the pool. "You take it slow with Sin until I can find out what's up with him."

"I will. I only plan on testing the waters for now."

She walked off and I admired Sin as he made his way through the crowd. He was a nice looking brother, and his fresh bald head was sexy as all outdoors. About ten different women tried to stop him on his way down to me. I wanted to yell, "Back off bitches, that one's gonna to be mine!"

He gave me a bright smile then kneeled down to the edge of the pool. "What's good, Bright Eyes?"

"Everything! Enjoying the weather and this warm water. It's so relaxing."

"You're wearing the shit out of that bathing suit."

I flirted with my eyes. "Thank you."

"You want a drink? We got everything. I just went and got more champagne."

"That sounds nice."

"Let me go get us some." He walked over to the bar and came back with two champagne flutes, a cup full of strawberries, and a bottle of

Moët. I made a mental note not to drink too much as he sat the items down on the table. He picked up my towel. I got out and he stretched it open for me. I stepped into it, and he dried me off. I wrapped my dress back around my body and followed him to the back of the yard, where we sat on a double chaise. He popped the cork and poured us both a glass.

"Did you have a good time at my party?"

"Yeah, it was nice. I didn't stay long, though. I left shortly after you did."

"Why you leave so early? You got a curfew or something?"

"Nah, Nickelle wanted to go to your party, so I went home to watch Trey."

"Who's Nickelle and Trey?"

"Oh, she's like my little sister, and Trey is her son. I wasn't stressing it. I got to see who I wanted."

He smiled. "Is that so?"

I blushed. "Yeah, that's so."

We continued talking and wound up drinking two bottles of Moët. His conversation was actually stimulating. He told me how he was in the process of opening up a new business and of his desire to invest in real estate and the stock market. Finally, a man with a plan! All Black ever wanted to invest in was a fresh pair of sneakers. I shared with him some of my career goals, and he was very supportive. He was suave, charming, and sure of himself.

"I know you must have a bunch of women trying to get with you."

He grinned then sucked his teeth. "Nah, I don't know what you're talking about."

"Come on, you don't have to lie to me. You can be honest."

"How about we play a game?"

"What kind of game?"

"The game of Absolute Honesty. If we're going to be around each other, then I'm gonna need to know everything there is to know about you."

"I've never heard of this Absolute Honesty game?"

He smiled. "You wouldn't have because I made it up! It will lead to us discovering things about each other and ourselves that we don't even know. Do you want to play?"

"How do you play?"

"It's simple. We take turns asking each other any question you want, but you have to give an honest answer. If you lie, you have to take a shot."

I was already a little tipsy, but I was willing to try. "Okay, I'm down!"

He got up, went to the bar, and returned with a bottle of Absolut and a plastic cup. He opened it and poured a hefty shot. "You ready?"

"Yeah, I'm ready—but wait, how will you know if I lie?"

"I won't; only you will. That's why the game is called Absolute Honesty. Only you will know if you're telling the truth. You can't lie to yourself. I'll tell you the purpose of the game when we're done. I'll let you go first."

I sat and thought. "Okay, what type of man are you? Body, face, brains?"

"I'm greedy! I want my woman to have it all; a nice ass, some tits—not necessarily big—a small waist, pretty feet, smart, with a beautiful face. I guess if I had to pick one attribute to seal the deal I would have to say I'm a heart man. The woman I choose will have a heart of gold like my grandmother. Now it's my turn! What could I get you to do for ten stacks?"

"Ten thousand dollars? That's a lot of money! You can put me to work."

He smirked. "And what kind of work would you be willing to put in?"

"Any kind! I'm not too proud to earn an honest dollar as long as it doesn't entail me doing anything sexual or demeaning."

He laughed. I knew he was trying to see where my head was at, and I was nobody's whore.

"If you had a choice right now to be anywhere in the world, where would it be?"

"It would right here with you, Bright Eyes!"

"Yeah, right! Take a drink."

He stared into my eyes. "That's the honest to God truth. Didn't Miguel tell you I wanted to see you?"

"Yeah, he did."

"Then you know I'm being honest. I made some moves just to be here with you tonight." I blushed. "So tell me, Misty, how many people have you had sex with? Men and women."

"Sex with a woman?"

"Yes, with a woman. What's wrong with that? Two women can have sex. Have you ever considered it?"

"No, never! I'm not into women. Have you ever considered being with a man?"

"Don't play yourself!"

"Well then don't play yourself. Now back to your question. You did mean intercourse, right?" I could feel my face turning red.

He grinned. "I can see I'm going to have to be specific when asking you a question. Yes, how many men have you had intercourse with?"

"Just one."

He picked up the cup. "Take a shot! This is called Absolute Honesty."

I got serious. "I am being honest! I've only been with one guy in my life. He's the only person I've ever slept with."

He stared into my eyes and searched for the truth. "What about getting your pussy eaten?"

I giggled and became a little embarrassed. "Two other people."

"Is that Absolute Honesty?"

"Yes, that was Absolute Honesty." I dropped my eyes and waited for him to tease me.

"If you're being honest, why you lower your eyes?"

"Because Charmaine sometimes cracks jokes about how inexperienced

I am."

"Well, I personally don't see anything wrong with it." He grinned. "I'm a great teacher. Whenever you're ready, I'll be happy to give you personal lessons and private instructions free of charge."

I giggled. "I'll keep that in mind, nasty boy. My turn . . . umm . . . okay, I got one!" It had been a while since I had my Kitty Cat properly eaten, and the way he licked his lips made me think he could do it well. "Do you eat Kitty Cats?" I giggled. "I meant do you do oral sex?" His looking down between my legs caused me to pull them together.

He chuckled. "So that's what you call it." He smiled. "That's cute. Yeah, I have, but I'm very choosy about who gets that from me." He looked down between my thighs again. "But you look like your kitty would be very pleasing to my palate. I can't wait to taste it, and that is Absolute Honesty. Do you suck dick?"

My eyes opened wide, and I took a deep gulp. I was hesitant, but told the truth. "I've done it a few times, but I haven't in a long time."

"And why is that? You don't like doing it?"

"No, that's not it. I guess I'm choosy like you. I believe that's something you do with someone special, someone you trust." I became sad thinking about the many times Black cheated on me. I looked to keep the game going. "Do you use drugs?"

"Nah. Well that's not's completely honest. I've never done any hard drugs, but I do occasionally smoke weed. It relaxes me and helps me think. Does that bother you?"

"No, actually Charmaine smokes. Every so often I take a puff or two with her then get real silly, want to raid the refrigerator, and eat up all the sweets."

He laughed. "Maybe one of these days we'll take a few tokes together."

"That would be cool. Just make sure you got something for me to munch on afterward!"

"Don't you worry. I always have something to satisfy your sweet tooth."

His response was full of lust, and I was starting to wonder if he just wanted to get me in bed. "Sin, what was it that attracted you to me at the Rucker game?"

"Now what was it? Was it those beautiful eyes, the pretty face, or your sexy shape? Maybe it was the long hair or those manicured toes. Nah, it was the smile! When you smiled it was as if it was made especially for me." I blushed. "But what really set you apart that day," he pointed to my temple, "was up there! I like a woman that's fine, but I love a woman that can bang with me mentally. That's what turned me on about you. I thought it was cute the way you tried to stump me with the Secretary of State question." He laughed. "Okay, it's my turn, Bright Eyes. Do you masturbate?"

I laughed then tried to be serious. "Nah, I don't masturbate. Do you?" I burst out laughing again then picked up the cup and drank the shot. The liquor burned going down. "Ugggghhhhh."

"See, that's why you shouldn't have lied. Let that be a lesson to you! And yes, I jerk my dick when necessary. Sometimes I just want to bust a nut and keep it moving. One last question, and then I'll tell you purpose of the game."

"If you could change one thing about yourself, Sin, what would it be?"

He thought long and hard before answering. He smirked then said, "Physically I'm more than blessed! Emotionally I could use some work."

"And why is that?"

"I've been told I have a cold heart and have trust issues. I personally don't see it as a flaw, but if more than one person tells you something, there's probably some truth to it. What about you?"

"I would change my height. I would like to be a little taller. You see how much you tower over me."

"Don't worry about that. It all evens out when we're in the bed. I'm not into tall women anyway. I think you're perfect just the way you are."

"Ahh, that was sweet! So now tell me what the purpose of your game was."

"The purpose is for us to have an avenue to share things about ourselves, get comfortable asking questions, receiving the answers, and building a level of trust ultimately reaching absolute honesty. If we're going to be friends, hang out, whatever it will be, there is one thing you have to do for me."

"And what is that?"

"You can never lie to me. I'll always keep it one hundred with you no matter what it is. All I ask of you is to do the same."

I bit into one the strawberries then said, "You got yourself a deal. I would actually prefer we be honest with each other instead having to deal with someone looking you in the face and lying through their teeth. Once you catch someone in a lie it's hard to believe anything they say after that."

He wasn't paying me any attention. He was too busy watching me suck the strawberry juice from my fingers.

"Is it sweet?"

I giggled then batted my eyelashes. "I already told you, it was. Do you want a taste?"

"I already told you I did!"

I smiled before gently placing a strawberry between his lips. He bit down then sucked the juices off my fingers.

"I'm hot. Do you want to get back in the pool?" he asked.

I was feeling nice and enjoying his company. We had been hanging out by ourselves the entire night. It felt like we were on a real date. At 3:30 in the morning I wasn't ready to end the night. "I wouldn't mind. Can you swim?"

"I can hold my own."

He got up, took my hand, and then pulled me up from the chaise. I lost my balance and fell in his arms. He held me, and his manhood became partially erect. He had to reposition himself in his shorts.

He looked down then jokingly spoke to his penis, "Yo, man, you better behave yourself!" We laughed as he escorted me over to the pool. "I'll be right back. I gotta go inside and get my trunks."

I dropped my dress and slid into the water. I rested my arms along the edge, leaned my head back, closed my eyes, and gently kicked my legs back and forth. The champagne and shot had taken affect, and I felt totally relaxed. After a few minutes I looked up to find him standing on the opposite end of the pool staring down at me. We studied each other as he tied his shorts. I smiled at him and wondered if he was thinking the same thing I was. He had made an impression on me and had me feeling a way I'd never felt before. It appeared as if he was contemplating his next move.

He dove in and swam under the water in my direction. Somehow he managed to ascend right in front of me, forcing me to either wrap my legs around him or pull them down. I chose the latter of the two. He rested his hands on the edge of the pool along the sides of my shoulders, and our bodies were bobbing inches apart. He lingered there in front of me and held a strong gaze. I wished he would kiss me. I wanted him to. I talked a good game, but had never actually acted on it before. Now here I was, damn near naked, in a pool with him, unsure if I would be able to fight temptation.

He looked delicious. I admired his thick eyebrows, his full lips, his cut up arms, and strong shoulders. The water made his eyelashes look longer. His grandmother was right—it must be a sin! His partially clad body all up on me was turning me on, and the champagne and vodka had me feeling extra warm inside. His erect penis bumping up against my thigh was making it difficult for me to think straight. I wanted to wrap my legs around his waist, let him pull my swimsuit bottom to the side, and give him some of my ravenous Kitty Cat. I knew I was going to have him all up inside of me one day.

Every woman knows which man she's going to give herself to, and I knew I was going to give myself to him in a special way. If Black could've seen me he would've killed me for sure. We continued to stare in silence. All of a sudden and before I could stop him, he leaned in and kissed me. I didn't resist. My mind said to push him back, make him stop, but my body was literally frozen in time. I accepted his tongue.

R. Kelly said it best in his song "Bump and Grind"—my mind was telling me no, but my body, my body was telling me yes! Next thing I knew my tongue was swirling around his mouth with such fever that I forgot for a second where I was. I gripped my arms around his neck and ran my hand over his bald head. He pulled me into him, and it started to get intense. We were making out right there in the pool. His erect penis was rubbing up against my clit. I raised one leg and wrapped it around his calf. Just as he reached under the water to pull my leg up to his waist, Charmaine and Miguel appeared.

Unbeknownst to us, they had been watching, and she suggested they come over. She asked with that "you're busted" look on her face, "Are we interrupting something?"

I looked up, embarrassed, out of breath, and feeling a little shaky from my Sin-high. I turned around and held onto the edge of the pool. Unfortunately for me, he didn't move. Sin held onto the edge of the pool and moved in. His long rod was now pressed between my butt cheeks.

"No, girl, actually you're right on time. I was just thinking how I need to get out."

"Uh-huh. You could have fooled me!"

He pressed himself deeper into me and my eyes fluttered. "Why don't you two get in? The water is great!" Sin was trying to give Miguel a hint, but before Miguel could catch on Charmaine responded, "We'll pass. I don't want to get my hair wet."

"I need to be looking to get out of here anyway," I said.

"Are you sure you want to get out?"

I twirled around then smiled. "Yeah, I'm sure."

He held his position then hesitantly lifted his arm. I swam off toward the steps while Charmaine walked over to the chairs and picked up my towel.

Sin huffed, "Damn, Miguel, you two got the worst fucking timing!"

Charmaine and I giggled.

"I told her to let ya'll live, but she insisted we come over. You know I'm not a blocker!" He leaned down to the edge then asked, "So what's good? You feeling her, or what?"

"Yeah, I'm feeling shorty."

"I told you she's a nice girl."

They stopped talking when Charmaine walked up although they were talking loud enough for us to hear them. Sin lifted himself out of the pool then walked over to me. I grabbed his towel then passed it to him.

"Sis, I'm spending the night here with Miguel, just in case you were waiting around for me."

"Where's Jaz?"

"She had to get up early for school, so Mitch drove her home."

"Okay cool, it's about that time for me to heading home too."

Sin shot Miguel a glare then elbowed him. He mumbled, "Motherfucker, you getting some pussy tonight and you let her fuck my shit up!"

Charmaine giggled.

"Charmaine, call me in the morning, and Miguel . . . do . . . not . . . even . . . think about trying any stupid shit with my girl! You know I will hunt you down and cut your thing off with a dull rusty knife!"

He laughed. "You crazy. Don't worry; I got your friend!"

Miguel pulled Sin by the arm and he looked over to me. "I'll be right back! Don't leave, okay?"

Charmaine grinned. "I see you two were getting awfully cozy in that pool. You said you were only going to test the waters, but it looked to me like you dove in headfirst. If I had known you were serious when you said you were tired of Black and looking for a new man, I wouldn't have interrupted. I thought you were just talking shit."

"I wasn't kidding, Cha! I am tired of his messing around—putting his hands on me and constantly lying. I'm done! I'm going let him stick around a little longer until I sort things out. Let him finish paying off my tuition in the meantime. Then I'm out!"

"You must really be feeling a brother to be so carefree. What if one of Black's boys would have seen you?"

"I guess I would be knee deep in some shit then, huh? You know I'm not crazy. Something just went off inside of me. On the real, I don't know what the hell happened."

"It seems like he really likes you too. You heard him admit to Miguel he's really feeling you. Go on with your bad self! See that's the right nigga to replace Black with. I ain't mad at you! He got it going on! If I were you, I'd give him some pussy."

"He got all close up on me, Cha, and next thing I know we were kissing. I know I shouldn't have drunk that second bottle of Moët or that shot."

"Yeah, yeah. Blame it on the liquor."

"Nah, I'm not blaming it on the alcohol. I'm definitely attracted to him! All I'm saying is the liquor impaired my judgment. Between you and me, I can see myself fucking the shit out of him! He's handsome, intellectual, assertive, and those lips. They're so soft and his dick, it's—oh my god—huge!" We both cracked up laughing.

"You know there are empty bedrooms upstairs if you want to spend the night."

"Girl, are you insane! I'm not trying to have sex with him tonight!"

"I would before someone steals him away. You got his attention. Now all you have to do is go in for the kill. You know how I do."

"Yeah, I know, and you know the two of us view relationships and sex in two different ways. I really like him, Cha. If I'm gonna have a chance at getting with him, it has to be done my way—not Charmaine's freak-him-and-flee way."

"At least I don't get hurt."

"Yeah, but you never fall in love either."

"Look at what loving Black has gotten you! You see me; I'm not looking for love. I'm going upstairs to indulge in some unadulterated sex with Miguel, and I don't care if he calls me tomorrow. If anything, Rico Suave will be looking for me."

"Well, have fun, because I'm taking my butt home."

"Just watch your back, and be careful with Mr. Sin. He's a player, and cats like him are heartbreakers. I deal with his type all the time. They got a bunch of bitches drooling over them and don't want a relationship. That's why I get what I can and bounce on their ass, but you're different. You believe in fairytales and love stories, and you're willing to put your all in to get it. I don't believe in soul mates or that happily ever after stuff your mother told you about. I didn't get that picture from mine. She showed me, up close and personal, that these men are only worth the dollar they spend."

She noted my change in expression. "Just take it slow. He could be legit. I'm not saying his intent is to dog you out. He seems like he's into you. I'm going to put my ear to the streets again and see what else I can dig up. He might just be all that and a bag of chips! Just be careful. You don't want Black to find out you messing around on him."

"I know!" I wasn't tripping on losing Black because I was ready to end the relationship. I was more concerned with getting caught and him trying to kick my ass. I looked over at Sin and Miguel talking at the bar. I waved to Sin then signaled that I was going in the house. I was ready to break out. Charmaine went over and told him I was taking a shower then leaving.

We met back up in front of the house. "It's late. Are you sure you want to leave? You can stay here if you want."

"Thanks, but I need to be getting home, Sin."

"Do you need a ride?"

"No, I drove my car."

He pulled me slightly into him and gave me a hug. He whispered in my ear, "I had a nice time with you tonight, and I would like to see you again." He caused yet more shivers to run down my spine and between my legs.

I studied him. "I would really like that, Sin."

"Where you parked at?"

I pointed. "It's the red car right over there." Black had recently bought me the Acura Legend coupe to make up for the Tamika thing, but I wasn't about to tell Sin that.

He walked me to my car then sat on the hood. "Nice car."

"Yeah, it's all right, but as soon as I get some money I'm gonna trade it in."

"Why? What's wrong with it? It looks new to me."

"It is, but it's a long story. Maybe I'll tell you about it another time."

"Are you okay to drive?"

"Yes, I'm fine. The shower woke me up."

He pulled me farther into him, and I leaned my body into his. He then planted the sweetest kiss on my lips. I clasped my arms around his neck and took in his tongue. He ran his hands down my back then rested them right above my butt. Our bodies began to slightly grind, and I could feel him getting hard through his shorts. I pulled away. I had to stop, regroup, and digest everything that had transpired.

"You sure you don't want to stay?"

"No, I have some things I need to do in the morning."

I could tell he was feeling me, but how much was still in question. Was he exposing his true self to me, or was it all a ploy to get in my pants? I gave him my house and pager number and told him to use code 155. I was happy he didn't press me to stay, because I might have given in and regretted it later. I kissed him one last time before getting in my car and heading home.

Years later, on one of my first visits to see Sin in jail, we swapped versions of what took place that night and our thoughts after we parted. He confessed that he was taking everything into serious consideration, and decided to take things slow with me. He didn't want to let on, but said he really liked me. He said there was an innocence about me that was refreshing. He said I had a magnetism that pulled him in, and you know when a live wire hits water—you're sure to see sparks!

He said as he watched me drive off he thought, *Honey's whipping a Legend, so her man must have invested a little paper in her.*

He also joked that if I had been his girl he would have had me driving around in the new C Class Benz, which he did eventually get for me. He said he knew based on the answers I gave to his questions it was going to be a bit of a challenge getting with me. My man was spending dough and I'd lost my virginity to him, but he wasn't intimidated. He said he just had to be patient.

Initially he wondered why I would take that kind of risk with him out in public, especially since Miguel had made it clear I wasn't a ho. He knew I wasn't that drunk. He deduced my actions as being a sign that I was willing to take a chance with him. He said some females are just no good and no matter what the situation they are going to mess it up, but he didn't sense that was the case with me. He figured two things: first, my man was really violating for me to jump out there like that, and second, I was ready to take that plunge and move on. He admitted he wouldn't have normally pursued me, but teased that my eyes hypnotized him.

He felt Black was slipping when he thought the money he gave would keep his girl faithful. He said he refused to be that nigga! He said his grandfather taught him money couldn't buy love. Black thought dropping paper on me was enough. I guess to a certain degree he was right. The average guy wouldn't have had a chance getting up in this. Too bad for Black, Sin wasn't the average man.

He said as he watched my taillights disappear into the night he thought how ol' boy was about to lose his girl. He said he let me get away that night.

He boasted that he was highly effective with his approach and was a master at getting a female to come out her panties. He prided himself on how quickly he could get a chick to give up the goods. I asked if that was the case why he didn't put his talent to work with me. He confessed that he couldn't understand why he let me get away either. He said he could have gone in for the kill, fucked the shit out of me, then sent me home, but didn't. When he saw I was hesitant he didn't push. I asked what made me so different considering he was the Houdini of hosiery, and he said he couldn't fully explain it, but he wanted to wait until I was ready.

He said my body in that bathing suit had his joint rock hard. I believed it when he said if Charmaine hadn't come over and interrupted us I would have gotten aired out in the pool. He said he wasn't concerned with shit getting back to Black, and he had a pack of wolves that would have gladly tore his ass up. Miguel didn't know it, but Sin had already done some research on the situation and heard good things about me. He heard my man was some ex-jock turned hustler who was chasing anything in a skirt. He weighed out the options and decided to go for it.

Black and Sin were cut from two different cloths. One was loud while the other was low-key. One wanted people to think he was the man while the other hid his worth. One had a block on smash in Texas while the other had crews running five different states. Sin said after his party he was going to leave me alone, but then reconsidered. He felt I could be an asset. He told me his plan around the time we met was to get out of the game, and he figured having a good girl by his side would be a solid move.

As I drove away from him that night I remember my thoughts like they were yesterday. Once I hit the end of the driveway I exhaled then thought, *That was close! Misty, you really let things go too far.*

I fought with myself all the way home. Charmaine talking about, "there's rooms upstairs." She must have really wanted to see me strangled by Black.

In the months leading up to me stepping out on him he had become extremely possessive, controlling, and domineering. Not being home when he called in the morning would have caused a serious problem. That was the main reason why I hadn't left him; I was scared of him.

I considered leaving Sin alone, but there was an electric force running through me in the pool. We clicked and I felt an instant connection, but I wasn't ready to give myself to him. He gave me butterflies in the stomach and the whole nine yards, but it would take more for me to have sex with him. I didn't know what he had going on in his life—if he had a girl, if he was in a serious relationship, or if he had children. All questions I should have asked during his game, but didn't. What type of girl would he think I was if I'd slept with him so soon? Some girls didn't care, but I did.

It's crazy how some men think. If a female gives it up too fast she's a whore, but if she holds out too long she's a Polly Puritan. You're damned if you do, and you're damned if you don't. Women have desires just like men. If a man turns her on, and she decides to have sex on the first night, that doesn't always equate to her being a tramp. Maybe the vibe was so right she broke all her rules.

At any rate, I couldn't afford to gamble on a real opportunity or risk getting caught out there. My good sense was saying, "Chill, cut Black off first," but Sin had me curious, and you know what they say—curiosity kills the Kitty Cat! It had been a month since I'd last had sex, and I was horny as hell. I had already given Black fair warning that if he kept the door wide open enough someone was bound to walk right in, and it appeared Sin was the perfect man to cum inside and lock it down.

# CHAPTER 6

## *Westside Highway*

My day off was slowly diminishing, and after running my errands I was beat. I still had a few hours to blow before meeting up with the girls. I made myself a grilled chicken Caesar salad, twisted the top off a bottled water, and sat down by the fireplace. The warmth of the fire was relaxing. I laid the empty plate on the coffee table then gazed at the burning logs. The bouncing flames brought down the sleep angels, and before I knew it, my eyes became heavy. I floated off into dream world. A world where I could relive the first time Sin and I had sex.

The day after the pool party, Sin paged me and invited me over to his grandparents' house for dinner. His grandmother—Grandma, as she lovingly preferred to be called,—was a petite woman who wore her hair in a long, neat ponytail that complimented her beautiful face. She looked like she could have been part Indian. His grandfather was more of a militant type and rarely spoke unless spoken to. From the very first moment, they made me feel welcome.

Sin's old bedroom looked as if it was still decorated the same way it was before he left to go off to college in Washington, D.C. He had basketball and football trophies on his dresser and walls plastered with posters of different professional athletes and rappers. I walked around the room examining all his trinkets. He had an array of sneakers neatly lined up against the wall and baseball caps in just about every color. As he was showing me his old stuff, he snuck a kiss and a handful of ass behind the door.

I helped Grandma set the table and assisted in serving the men dinner. The food was delicious. We ate dessert in the living room while she showed off tons of old pictures. I saw images of Sin as a baby, in kindergarten, all the way up to the present. He was a cute kid with his lopsided afro. She glowed as she told stories of his childhood antics. I could tell he was her pride and joy, and she adored him. She bid me a farewell and said for me to come back anytime. I felt honored that he would take me to meet them.

We spent the whole month of July together, and the sexual tension was mounting. Just being next to him set me on fire, but we were taking our time. After he took me to meet his grandparents I had him come over to meet my family. We went on dates to Rye Playland amusement park, the movies, and a museum. We shared countless meals. He took me with him when he went looking for furniture for his new three-bedroom condo in New Jersey and even let me pick out the bedroom set. Anything I had to do he was right there with me: food shopping, laundry, homework, studying.

I was still trying to figure out his motive. He was spending an awful lot of time with me considering I wasn't giving it up, and he wasn't pressing me for it either. He didn't seem like the type to wait around for some ass. I assumed after a week or two he would have stopped checking for me, but he didn't. We were just doing us, as he put it. He would come over to my father's apartment and watch the game with him while I cooked dinner for us. My father, Pop, as we all called him, told me he liked him, and had given Sin his blessing when he asked if it was okay to date me. My brother, Dyson, on the other hand, was a little leery when he first found out I was seeing him. Dyson was very protective of me, and didn't want to see me with another dealer. He hated Black.

Unlike my father, Dyson was very in tune with what was going on with me and Black, as well as what was going on in the streets. He heard things. Dyson already had beef with Black for slapping me and didn't want me seeing another street guy. He wanted better for me. Dyson told Black if he caught him at my father's place he was gonna beat his ass. He hadn't been back since, so I felt it was cool for me to have Sin there. When Dyson came home from California to visit I left him and Sin alone to talk. Once he saw that Sin was really checking for me, they knew a lot of the same people, and that he was a cool dude, Dyson felt more relaxed.

Things were going really well. When Sin was in New York he spent time with me, and when he wasn't he called. One night while we were on the phone he complained of pains. I suggested he come home, and he did. The next day he ended up having an emergency hernia operation. At the time he was having renovations done on his condo and decided instead of staying at the hotel to recover at his grandparents' house. I observed the way he got when he was around his grandmother. She pampered and catered to him, and he loved it. During his weeklong recovery we spent a lot of quality time together.

The first two days after his surgery I stopped by to see him before heading home from school. I would sit across his bed, reading or doing a class assignment while he watched television. He wanted me to stay, but as it got late I made up excuses to leave. The Friday following his surgery we sat on his bed watching a basketball game when my girls paged me. I used his house phone to call Charmaine back. She wanted to know if I wanted to go to a party Lavon was promoting. Sin sat back on the bed, pretending not to listen.

"No, sis, you go ahead. I'm chilling tonight. Yes, I'm with Sin." I giggled. "You're so nasty. No, we're not! He's still trying to heal from his surgery." I burst out laughing. "I don't need to test it! They didn't operate on that! Yes, I'm more than sure it's still working! Nah, I don't have any plans for the morning. Okay, I'll call you when I wake up, and have fun."

I hung up with her then excused myself to the bathroom. Upon returning to his room, I saw that Sin had changed positions and was now lying on his side. He instructed me to close the door behind me.

"Take your shoes off and act like you're staying for a while."

I stepped out of my Gucci loafers and sat down on the bed.

"Let me check out your toes." After a thorough examination he complimented, "You have pretty feet."

By eleven o'clock I began to yawn. This was normally the time I left. I got up.

"Why don't you grab one of my shirts out the drawer and spend the night with me? Don't worry, I won't try anything." He propped the pillows under his head then patted the space next to him indicating for me to lie next to him.

I retrieved one of his t-shirts, and instead of going into the bathroom I teased him and undressed in front of him. I slowly unfastened each button on my shirt then undid my pants. I pulled the shirt off then inched the tight jeans down my thighs before stepping out of them. I wore a pink and yellow bra with matching panties.

"Turn off the lights," Sin instructed.

While pulling the tee over my head I walked over to the lamp. The air conditioner gave the room a chill and I quickly slid under the covers and cuddled up next to him.

He wrapped his arm around my waist then whispered in my ear, "You really trying to hurt me."

I snuggled my back into his chest, and giggled when I felt his hardness between my butt cheeks. The following morning I woke with him spooning me. Our bodies fit so perfectly together. I felt so safe.

I got up early and left before his grandparents got up, but he asked that I come back later. I went home, freshened up, changed my clothes, and then returned that afternoon. His mother Theresa, Teri for short, was there. I was afraid of her. Grandma had warned me that her daughter was tough, didn't think any woman was good enough for her son, and didn't take crap from anyone.

I walked in the house, and the first thing Teri said from the kitchen was, "So where's this person at who has my son's nose wide open like a jar of Vicks?" I wanted to disappear. However, once she laid eyes on me she smiled then said, "Oh, you're pretty." We had a brief conversation before she yelled out to Sin, "We can keep her. She's much better than that last one," then walked back into the kitchen. We hit it off, and became very close. She eventually referred to me as her future daughter-in-law; which was a good sign.

Teri was beautiful. She had long brown hair, the biggest brown eyes, and long lashes like Sin's. She wore her nails long and loved hats just like me. She had tons of jewelry, dressed very stylishly, and had a large selection of designer handbags and shoes. We would go shopping together and people would ask if I was her daughter because we resembled so much. I looked more like her child than he did.

Once Sin started feeling a little better, he wanted to get out. He invited me to dinner in Manhattan. He was still taking pain medication and feeling tender in his midsection, but, like most men, he had that macho thing inside of him that wouldn't let him stay still. He was pushing himself to get well. He selected a lounge located on 43rd and 11th Avenue. It was a small, dimly lit, and intimate place. The restaurant was located on the main floor, and there was a club and live DJ tucked away on the lower level. The food was decent, and after dinner we went downstairs to listen to some music.

We chose a cozy table in the corner, but it was difficult hearing each other over the music. I noticed that he was getting tired.

"Are you ready to leave?"

"Yeah, we can get up out of here."

I purposely held his hand as we walked up the block to the car. I could tell he felt awkward, but he didn't pull his hand away. He opened the door for me, but before stepping in I ran my hands up his chest, leaned in, and passionately kissed him. It was a foreplay kiss. It was one of those kisses that led to other things. He smirked before walking around to the other side.

As we drove up 11th Avenue I turned down the radio. "So tell me more about your life, Sin. We've been spending a lot of time together and talked about all kinds of things, but I feel like there's a lot about you I don't know."

"What's there to know, beautiful? In a nutshell, I was raised by my grandparents in the Bronx and I'm an only child."

"So that's your resume?"

"Yup, that's about the size of it. How about you? Tell me something about yourself I don't already know."

"Well, you already know I was also born and raised in the Bronx. I'm in college, and I don't have any kids. You met my brother, Dyson, whom I am very close with. He's in LA permanently now. He works in the film industry. We're only two years apart; which comes in handy when I need advice on men. He taught me game, the good, the bad and the ugly so don't even think about trying it, mister."

"That's the easy stuff. Tell me something about Misty no one else knows. I want to know your dreams, your innermost thoughts, your fears, and your sexual fantasies."

I drifted off in thought. By that time Sin and I had come clean with each other. He knew about Black, and I knew he was dealing with someone in Washington. He admitted he cared about her, but said they weren't getting along lately. We were both in relationships that were failing. We discussed it and decided we would continue to date and see where it went.

I needed some more time before I cut Black off anyway. He was doing so much for me. The car wasn't fully paid for, I had two more installments on my tuition, and Sin and I had only been dating for about two months. It was technically a short period of time although we had been spending a lot of time together. Probably more time than I had spent with Black in six months.

The last time Black had come back home we got into a huge argument. I was cleaning out his duffle bag, and he had the nerve to have a box of condoms and two empty wrappers in it. That was the final straw! I was holding out on Sin because of him while he was out fucking anything he could. I swore to myself I would no longer hold back, and the next time the opportunity presented itself I was going to do it. I would no longer be a fool.

I yelled, "Black, are you serious? Condoms in your fucking bag! Now I know why you're not in no rush to get back here to me! One baby on the way isn't enough?"

"Nah, Misty, those condoms aren't even mine, and stop saying that shit! I'm not having no kid. That baby ain't mine and neither are those condoms. They must belong to my man, Pook."

"You're a lousy liar! Every time you get caught it's one of your friends. Mike-Mike, Sid, Art, Born, and now Pook! You've lied on your real friends so much you have to make people up. I guess the baby is Pook's too! Why don't you just let me go so you can do what you want? I'm tired of arguing and fighting with you. You're never going to change." I went to turn. "Fuck this, I'm out of here!"

He grabbed me up by my arm and tightly squeezed his fingers into it. "You ain't going nowhere! I told you those aren't mine now sit the fuck down and relax! Picture you leaving me. I told you that will never happen!"

"Fuck you! I'm done with you, Black!" I was way past the point of hurt. I was nauseated by his presence. I went to leave, but he pushed me back down hard on the bed.

"I'm telling you, don't fucking piss me off, Misty! Fuck you complaining about?"

"You think I'm gonna let you bully me into being with you and then sit by idly and let you disrespect me? You must be out of your mind!"

"As long as I'm taking care of you I should be able to do what the fuck I want, when I want. Now I said those ain't mine, handle it!"

I laughed through the tears. "Just don't act surprised when you find out I'm fucking somebody too!"

He rushed up and slammed his fist into my thigh. "If I ever find out you fucking somebody I'm gonna kill you and that nigga! You hear me?"

He made me sit there and wouldn't let me leave. I thanked God when his mother finally came home. I left and refused to come back or have sex with him after that.


I was now going on months without any loving, and I had plenty of pent up sexual energy. Sin had set off burning blaze within me that only he could extinguish. He made me laugh, he made me smile, and was interested in all aspects of me. It was becoming more and more difficult to think of anything other than giving myself to him. I put Black's threats in the back of my mind.

"Okay, something you don't know about me? I'm double jointed! That's something you don't know."

He smirked. "Nice. That can come in handy. You're going to have to show me that one of these days, but I was hoping for something more in line with your aspirations, long and short term goals, your innermost secrets, and sexual fantasies."

"Well, my dream is to one day open my own business. My innermost secrets, well, I think I'll keep them to myself for now, and my sexual fantasies are to make love on a beach, on an airplane, and on the highway."

"So you're an exhibitionist," he teased.

"No, but sex in a bed is so traditional. A fantasy should encompass something out of the norm. I do like uninhibited sex; spontaneity excites me!"

He confessed that he too secretly had a fantasy about making love on a beach.

We were parked in front of my building when he looked over and asked, "What do you think about the two of us fulfilling that beach fantasy together?"

I knew that was his way of indirectly asking me to have sex, and so I played along. "And on what island do you plan on making this happen?" I knew exactly what he meant, but I wanted to see his reaction.

He gulped. "I was thinking someplace a little more local. Like a beach we can drive to tonight."

*Good answer,* I thought, because if he would have said something slick like, "I'm not taking you to any island," the outcome of the evening would have been very different. It was time to go to the next level. I wanted him just as much as he wanted me.

"I'm down for sex on the beach, but are you up to it? You just had surgery and you're still in pain. You're not a hundred percent. I would hate for you to perform poorly and have to use that as an excuse later," I joked

I had been teasing him something terrible since he had the surgery. I'd spent the last two nights with him rubbing my ass on his crotch. There was an instant change in his demeanor and he got real conceited when talking about his private parts.

"I'll guarantee you the size of my tool alone will satisfy you."

Now, I had rubbed up on him and felt his penis, and, yes, he was holding, but could he work it, and how big was it really? I had been dreaming about a dick I hadn't even seen, and I wanted to satisfy my curiosity. I needed to see it up close and personal; which is what pushed me to give up my Kitty Cat before three months. When Charmaine told me about the conversation Sin and Miguel had, I decided to be safe and make him wait. I felt three months was a sufficient amount of time to hold out, but Sin making me so fucking hot, added with me suffering from dick deprivation, made me take a chance.

"Okay, let's do it, but we need a blanket. I don't want sand in my butt."

He looked at me like I was crazy. "Where are we going to get a blanket from at this time of night? All I got in here is towels."

I got insulted. "I'm not using any dirty towels!"

"Calm down. Those are brand new. I just bought them."

I thought then came up with an idea. Jasmine! I took a chance and called her knowing it was 3 o'clock in the morning. After what seems like a hundred rings she groggily answered. "Who is it!"

"It's me. Are you awake?"

"I was asleep! And now that you woke me up, this better be good." She must have looked over at the clock then yelled, "Don't you know it's three in the morning?"

"Sin and I are going to the beach and we need a blanket."

"What's happening at the beach at three in the morning?"

I paused too long, and then it hit her.

She sucked her teeth. "Why didn't you go to your own house?"

"Because I don't want my father to see me come in, get a blanket, and leave." Although I was grown and would be moving into my own place shortly, I still needed to respect his home.

"You're a pain in my ass! Come upstairs and get it!"

After retrieving the blanket Sin drove to the garage, parked his Benz, retrieved his Mazda MPV van then headed in the direction of Orchard Beach. The beach was a short distance away from my apartment complex; however, when we got there the road leading to it was closed.

"Shit! It's closed!" He refused to let the opportunity slip away. I had him waiting all that time, I finally said yes, and the damn beach was closed. He was quiet on the way back to my building. He later told me he was debating on which hotel he was going to take me to because he was getting some ass that night. He said he knew I was ready and he had to know what it felt like inside of me. As we merged onto the highway he came up with an alternate plan. "How about we change up the fantasy and do it on the highway?"

"I was down for the beach because it's isolated at night and no one would see us, but I'm not sure about the highway?"

"What's wrong with the highway?"

"People will be able to see in here."

"No one can see in this joint. I got tinted windows."

We went back and forth, and with a little persuasion I agreed to have sex on the highway. He jumped on the Cross Bronx and merged onto the Henry Hudson Parkway South. We continued down the Westside Highway looking for a good spot. About a mile past the 125th Street exit I saw an emergency parking area on the right, and suggested he pull over. The view of New Jersey across the water was the perfect backdrop.

He put the van in park, hit the lights, and then got out. He went around to the side of the van and adjusted the back seat so it would lay flat like a futon. He looked at me in the front seat. "Are you okay with doing this?"

I shyly nodded my head then turned the radio dial to 107.5 WBLS. I crawled over into the back seat while he entered from the side door. I had on a white sundress while he wore white linen shorts and a blue and white striped, short sleeved Ralph Lauren polo shirt with white uptown sneakers. He was having a hard time pulling his shorts down in the back of the van.

"Wait, Sin, let me help you."

He lifted his upper body up onto his elbows and raised his bottom just enough for me to slide the shorts completely down his legs. He had on burgundy silk boxers.

He watched as I pulled my sundress up and over my head exposing an orange La Perla bra and thong set.

He bit down on his bottom lip. "Damn, you sexy as hell!"

I was nervous because I didn't know what to expect. I laid down on my side, faced him, and waited for him to make the next move. He gently draped his arm over my waist, pulled me to him then kissed me. His kiss was soft, sweet, and deliberate. We explored each other's mouths while rubbing our hands across each other's bodies.

Our bodies were propped up against each other's and I could feel his erection growing beneath his boxers. He slowly ran his right hand up and down the crease of my back, giving me chills. Our kissing became more intense, and he began to roll me over onto my back. He gently laid the length of his body in between my legs.

"Are you okay?"

"Yeah, I'm fine," I shyly replied.

He lowered his mouth to mine and began to run his tongue over and around my lips. He massaged his shaft into my clitoris, and his manhood grew. The head was now laying somewhere above my navel. I held onto his face, kissing him with fever. I softly caressed his head and back. He ran his left hand up my thigh, and then gently pulled my leg up to his side. I wrapped it around his waist. I didn't know, but he had plans on giving me my first lesson; and it was that he was the one in control. He could have penetrated me right then and there. A little slip of the panties to the side would have been all it took, but that would have been too easy. He wanted to enjoy the moment and make sure I remembered it forever.

He kissed me from my forehead, to my nose, to my lips, to my neck, and down to my breasts. He unlatched my bra and took my breasts into his hands. I arched my back as I felt his hot tongue pass across my nipples. He sucked, licked, and then blew hot air, creating a wave of juices that began to freely flow from my Kitty Cat. My nipples felt like two ripe berries ready for the picking. I couldn't recall ever being so turned on.

He asked as he flicked his tongue over them, "How does that feel?"

Through half shut eyes I murmured, "Ooh . . . that feels nice."

He was talking shit in my ear, and driving me crazy with all the teasing he was doing. Black never did that.

"Your hair smells good. Did I tell you I'm going to make you pay for holding out on me for so long? The last time I wanted a piece this bad I didn't have hair on my balls. I am going to fuck the shit out of you. You ain't gonna want nothing or no one up in this when I'm done."

I didn't respond, but smiled. Men always talk shit about their size and skills.

He smirked. "Remember what I'm telling you. This is going to be my pussy."

I remained silent as my eyes flickered.

"Do you hear me?"

I could feel my hot sticky juices collecting within my thong. I had a puddle in my panties. He kept his eyes on me and waited for me to respond.

His sweeping the hair from my face caused my eyes to open fully.

"Yes, I hear you."

He stared down into my eyes, and they felt heavy as we kissed.

"I love your eyes. They have this glassed-over look like you smoked a joint, and the way they roll up into your head is turning me on. Did anyone ever tell you your eyes change colors?"

"When I was a kid my father said they did when I was really mad."

He smirked. "Well now you can tell Pop they also change when you're really turned on."

I chuckled. "You tell him."

He let his hand creep down in between my legs and I slightly jumped. "Don't worry. I told you I'm not gonna hurt you."

He laid on his side and made circular motions around my clit. I felt a warm sensation as he stuck his finger inside of me. He slid one, then two fingers in and out as he traced the lining of my walls. I was so wet I could hear sloshing noises. I was ready for him to fill my insides up with his anaconda. He pulled his fingers out, smelled them, and then smiled before sucked them clean.

He'd made it clear he wasn't big on performing oral sex. He said he didn't have to eat chicks out, and that his dick game was enough, however he admitted to wanting to savor mine. He used one hand to slide my thong off. "You ready to be turned out?"

The way he peered down into my soul told me I was in for a treat. He twirled his finger around my clit, and then stuck it back inside of me. He fingered my entry and played with my clit with his thumb. He was stimulating me in a way I had never been before. Black was a decent lover. I really couldn't complain, but I never had anyone to compare him to.

Sin took his time with me. His goal was to make sure I felt good, and he knew exactly where to start. He parted my neatly manicured lips, lowered his head, and began giving me oral pleasure. I reached down and grabbed hold of his bald head as he licked and sucked my clit while sliding his middle finger in and out of me. He began to maneuver his finger around as if he were looking for something then found it, my G-spot! When he hit it I moaned and bit down on my bottom lip. I threw my head back and clawed at the blanket. I was lost in the moment.

"Oh yes, yes, yes! That feels so good," I purred.

I was on fire and my body was craving more. I was in ecstasy without having to take the drug. He continued to glide his fingers in and out while lopping up my sweet nectar. The sensation of having my Kitty eaten while being finger fucked was driving me wild. It was becoming too much for me to handle. I gave forewarning. "You're going to make me cum!"

"That's what I want! I want you to cum for Daddy."

"Daddy?" I repeated more so as a question. I thought, *This boy is crazy. I got a father.*

"Yeah that's right. Say it again!" I looked at him as if he had two heads. "It's okay, get comfortable with it, Bright Eyes. By the time we finish, you'll be calling me Daddy in three different languages," he boasted.

He leaned up and began using both of his hands. One was working my clit while the other was finger fucking me. The way he spoke to me turned me the fuck on. This was an entirely new experience for me. He was confident, in charge, and had me right where he wanted. All Black ever did was breathe heavy in my ear and sweat out my hair.

"Daddy is going to have you cumming right in the palm of his hands." He added some pressure and increased his pace. His finger action was feeling better than Black's dick. "You want Daddy to stop?"

"Oh, no, Sin—No—it feels so good! Oh, yeah, right there!"

"Do you want Daddy to stop?"

"No, no, don't stop!"

He teased me like a spoiled child. "I can't hear you."

I begged with more intensity. "Please no, don't stop!"

"Then say my name," he demanded.

"Sin!"

"Nah, you know what I want to hear."

I refused to call him Daddy.

He smiled. "Have it your way. Fight it, but you will call me Daddy."

He went back down on me with those juicy lips of his. Like a teakettle brewing on the stove, I was on the verge of my boiling point. He suddenly stopped eating me, but continued playing with my Kitty Cat with a much slower pace. His fingers lightly ran over my now sensitive clit. I was feeling like a junkie in need of a fix. I leaned up and slid my hand over his head then down onto his shoulders. I tried to motion for him to come up to me. I wanted him inside of me, but he gently pushed me back down. He ran his hot tongue up and down my clit then sucked it every so often. He made me talk some shit of my own.

"Yeah, bad boy suck this Kitty. Suck it just like that!"

He picked my legs up and held my ankles together over my head. He continued to finger-fuck me while eating my pussy. "Oww, yeassssssss," I murmured. "You make me feel sooooooo good."

"Whose pussy is this?"

I whispered, "It's your pussy."

"I can't hear you! Whose pussy is this?" He was working my clit, and my legs began to shake uncontrollably. I was having an out of body experience. My breathing was heavy and my eyes were damn near rolled up in the back of my head. I threw my head back as he applied a little more pressure. I yelled, "It's your pussy!"

"No! Whose pussy is this?" He paused then started playing with it again. He was torturing me.

"It's Sin's pussy!" My insides began to constrict. I was on the verge of cumming.

"No! Whose pussy is this? Say it. Say my name!"

I couldn't take it. I shouted out, "It's Daddy's pussy! It's Daddy's pussy!"

He pushed his fingers deeper inside of me then licked and sucked until I had a powerful orgasm. Just as he stated, it was in the palm of his hand. I had never cum so hard in my life. Black needed to take a tutoring session in lovemaking from him. He let loose of my ankles, parted my legs, grabbed hold of my hips then slid my body closer to his. He reached into his shorts for a condom, rolled it down, and then situated himself to enter me. He pulled my legs and lifted them up over his chest and shoulders.

I believe him picking me up too fast put too much strain on his midsection because the worst thing that could have happened, happened. The hernia operation caught up with him, and a sharp pain hit him in his stomach. It was a pain he could not ignore. It was like a tearing sensation running up his midsection. It made him buckle over. He lowered me down, grabbed for his lower stomach then rolled over. I opened my eyes fully.

"Oh shit, are you okay?"

He cringed. "Yeah, I just need a minute. It was just a cramp. I'll be fine." He was trying to make light of the pain, but I wasn't falling for it. He carefully reclined all the way back on the seat and closed his eyes.

"Okay, let's stop before you burst a stitch."

"Are you crazy? I'm not walking around with blue balls! Only thing around here I'm going to burst tonight is a nut! Just give me a minute."

He was pissed. He took off the condom and threw it to the side. While he laid back I kneeled into the front seat to try to find something on the radio. I was turning the dial when he leaned up on his elbows to admire the view. Like a cat my entire tail was up in the air with remnants of my earlier orgasm still present around my soaked lips and holes. I had a perfect ass, no dimples or stretch marks. I could feel him staring at me. Holding my doggie style pose, I slightly turned my head and looked over my shoulder. His dick was hard again. He watched and licked his lips.

"What are you looking at?"

"A perfect picture! Where's a camera when a brother got a Kodak moment! Wait, stay just like that, I want to hit it from the back." He attempted to lean forward, but the pain in his stomach made him lie back down. "Isn't this some shit! First the beach and now the stitches."

I maneuvered myself back over to him with a mischievous look. "Maybe we can have some fun without you reinjuring yourself. You want Mommy to take care of Daddy and make him feel all better?"

He had no idea what I was up to, but he was down for anything as long as it resulted in him getting a nut. He smiled then nodded.

"Okay, just lay there and relax." He rested on his elbows as I pulled his boxers off.

My mouth actually watered. I couldn't help but marvel in the wonderment of his manhood. He was correct; I was overwhelmed with the size. I thought to myself, His dick is unreal! I was intimidated. There was no way he was going to put that whole thing inside of me. It looked to be as wide and as longer than a 16oz Poland Spring water bottle. It was humongous! The brother was certainly blessed with a dick that resembled an extra thick 10½-inch chocolate Snickers bar.

It had a narrow head then widened gradually as you descended down the shaft; which had thick veins snaking along it. I can't front, it was pretty enough to suck. Since that was not an option tonight, I softly pushed him down by his shoulders so he would lie flat then I straddled him. It was too late to turn back now. I placed my legs alongside him as he rested his hands around my hips. I planted soft kisses all over his cheeks, neck, lips and chest. He reached up and pulled me down so my breast was flush to his chest. His dick was at full attention and it positioned itself snuggly between my cheeks.

As we kissed he palmed my ass, and as I began to grind, his dick slid up and down between my butt cheeks. My juices lathered him. I lifted up, squatted, then hovered above him. The tip was right at the mouth of my vagina. I could feel my juices dripping down on him. I wanted him to feel the heat emitting from within me. I lowered myself just enough so I could dip the tip in. He moaned as I took the head in. I slid down an inch then hurriedly lifted back up when I felt my vagina clinch. We both knew going raw would be wrong although it was feeling so right.

"Do you have any more condoms?"

"Look in my shorts pocket."

I located the condom and put it on him. The wrapper said Magnum, but it only went half way down his shaft. After getting it on I slowly and methodically lowered my Kitty Cat back down onto the head. Since the tip was narrow and pointed we had no problem getting it in. As soon as he entered me we both let out a sighs of relief. I took my time descending to ensure I didn't hurt him or myself. About two inches down he let out another moan. I hurriedly lifted myself up, ready to jump off of him.

"Are you okay? Are you in pain? Are you hurt?"

"I'm good, real good, boo! Just enjoying the fit. Go ahead do your thing."

I twirled my hips as I lowered myself onto the head. As I gradually descended down his shaft it felt as if his dick was growing while inside of me. I thought I would do better than this. I didn't even make it half way down before I had to come right back up. It felt like I was a virgin all over again. It pulled at my walls, and stretched my insides. If I tried to bounce on it like I did on Black's I would surely wind up in the hospital. It would rip me apart if I wasn't careful.

My Kitty Cat had a death grip on him, and the farther I descended, the tighter the hold became. He was in heaven. I, however, was in a tight spot. I couldn't take any more in. The pressure was too much, and it was starting to hurt. I learned three things at that very moment. One, Black wasn't working with shit. Two, it was going to take me a whole lot of a time before I would be able to fuck Sin the way I wanted to, and three, once I did that dick would belong to me.

"What's the matter? Mommy can't handle Daddy's dick?" It was now his turn to poke fun. He knew damn well I wasn't going to be able to go any farther without needing sutures. Instead of continuing downward I came back up to the tip. This ride was going to be more like me riding a horse on a carousel as opposed to bucking a bronco at the rodeo.

"You want Daddy to help you out?" He thought it was funny and laughed.

"All right, I can't front, your thing is way too big for me! So unless you plan on taking me to the emergency room tonight, I'm only messing with the top half."

He laughed as I methodically ascended then descended, trying to loosen up the grip. I worked my way up and down at a slow pace.

He seemed surprised. "Damn, I thought you were fronting, but you really haven't been around. Your Kitty is super tight!"

"I told you I was only with one person."

After a few minutes I was able to comfortably get enough of him in without feeling like he was pulling my insides out along with his penis. I placed both hands on his chest and then picked up my pace. He held my ass cheeks and helped guide me. I rode him up, down, back, forth, left, and right. The pain mixed with pleasure reminded me of hitting my funny bone. I wanted to laugh and cry at the same time. I closed my eyes, and I began enjoying it. I know he got off more watching me then the actual ride itself.

"Oh Daddy, I'm cumming again!"

"Cum, baby, I'm gonna cum with you. Oh, shit! God Damn! Ugh . . . uhh . . . uhh . . . Aaahhh!"

I laid on his chest for a few moments catching my breath. I lifted myself off of him, grabbed a bottle of water out of the cooler, a towel from the bag, and cleaned up. I pulled the condom off and began wiping him down with the dampened towel. He laid back and folded his arms behind his head then grinned.

"Do you know the last time a woman cleaned me up it was my mother? This is the first time someone has ever done this."

After realizing what I was doing I giggled. "This is the first time I've cleaned somebody up after sex. I didn't think, I just did it. Do you want me to stop?"

He smiled and shook his head no.

"Do you like it?"

He grinned and jokingly nodded his head yes like a little boy.

"Then consider it my pleasure. A man should be treated like a king if he acts like royalty."

He smiled. "You know you're dangerous! If I'm not careful, you gonna have a nigga off his game. You holding some powerful shit right there! It's soft, super tight, and then it has its own unique wetness. It's creamy, but slick yet kind of sticky all at the same time. If I could sell that shit there in a bottle I would have niggas lined up around the corner like crackheads!" He burst out laughing. "Fifty dollar bottles of Sticky Icky!" He shook his head. "Nah, I'm gonna keep that all to myself! Give me a couple of weeks and I'm gonna mold that Cat to fit my joint like a surgeon's latex glove."

I silently thought, *if a chick was able to take his whole rod in right out the gate, she either had a real big pussy or was fucking around with farm animals.*

He leaned up as I slid the boxers up his thighs and then his shorts. "Thanks!" He slowly leaned up to kiss me. "You gonna have Daddy go broke fucking around with you!"

"Why would you say that?"

He laughed. "Because I can already see me wanting to be up inside you all day, and not out handling my business."

# CHAPTER 7

## *Celebration*

W hen I awakened from my dream it was dark outside and the fire
had died down. The clock on the cable box read 9:32PM, and
it was about time to start getting ready. Friday night traffic in Manhattan
could get crazy. Nickelle would never forgive me if I didn't show up to
celebrate with her. It had been a long week, and I was looking forward
to talking shit with my girls. Entirely too much time had lapsed since we
were all together at the same time.

I headed up to the bedroom to find an outfit, and after an hour of
destroying my closet I laid out a pair of black spandex and butter soft
leather pants, a light grey V-neck cashmere sweater, and a pair of dark gray
Christian Louboutin knee-high boots with matching handbag. The outfit
was perfect. It was sexy, but not too much.

I freshened up, applied a little make-up, retouched my hair, and called
Charmaine to confirm the time she was heading out.

On the second ring she picked up. "Hey, sister!"

"You got Nickelle's text, right? I hope you're getting dressed, Big Head."

"Yes, and I'm almost ready, but I need a favor. I had to put my car in
the shop this morning. Some idiot not paying attention talking on his cell
phone ran right into the back of me."

"Are you okay?"

"Yeah, I'm fine, but my Beamer is going to be out of commission for a little while. The dealer will have a loaner for me tomorrow morning."

"How are you going to get to the dealership in the morning?"

"I don't know? The train?"

"Pack an overnight bag. Marcus is in Detroit and won't be back until next week. You can spend the night, and I'll drive you in the morning."

"Ooh goodie, a sleepover. Just like old times! Isn't that cute?"

"Whatever, it's up to you. You can always take that iron horse if you prefer."

"I was just messing with you. What time are you going to get here?"

"I'll be in front within the hour, so please be ready, Charmaine."

"I will!" She ended the call, and I ran around tidying up a little before I left. I grabbed my car keys, cell phone, and Russian silver sable coat with matching hat then headed out the door. I started up the X5, connected the iPod to the stereo, and then selected "Sent from Heaven" by Keyshia Cole. I put the truck in drive then proceeded to the George Washington Bridge.

Charmaine and I lived together up until I moved to New Jersey with Marcus. She and I could have sold the brownstone and moved years ago, but it was our home. We'd had several offers, and the value was at its peak, but when we thought about the daily commute, we both decided it would be easier to stay. The location was central and convenient for two single women. We could jump in our car or on the train and be downtown in five minutes.

While driving down the avenue I noted how the look of Harlem was constantly changing. This was our playground years ago. It was a place you could drive up the avenue doing 90 miles per hour hoping you didn't hit a pothole, and the last thing you were worrying about was a cop stopping you. They were too busy chasing crackheads.

Now the police presence was greater due to 9-11. What were once abandoned lots, dilapidated, graffiti-ridden, and condemned buildings were now hotels, restaurants, lounges, condominiums, and apartment buildings with cameras everywhere. More schools were built, and with the establishment of charter schools, inner city kids have opportunity to a better education. Things were looking positive.

I was happy to see money finally going into the community, but did we really need to lose a whole generation of men to get it? There is opportunity today, but years ago the school system was failing, people were poor, and there was a sense of helplessness everywhere you looked. Then crack cocaine entered the hood; which was fine until the suburban kids got strung out too.

A simple combination of cocaine, water, baking soda, and heat turned into the worst epidemic since heroin. What most thought was a quick "come up" set us back decades. It was the best of times, yet the worst thing that happened to my generation. We were all naïve and couldn't see beyond our own needs and wants. I can only say it was good because like so many others, I reaped the rewards from it. But like so many, if given the chance and knowing what I know today, I would have done better. I would have known that nothing good comes from evil.

Most of my peers saw slinging crack as a quick way to escape their reality; a reality that consisted of poverty and other issues. I've seen the prettiest girl, the hardest man, and the smartest people all fall victim to crack in one way or the other. Some opted to use or abuse it while others chose to manufacture and distribute it. One took control, while the other lost it. We wanted instant wealth—the big chains, the fancy cars, and the latest gear—at any expense. At that time there were only a few jobs for young black or Hispanic men; supermarket, messenger service, or fast food, and all were paying $4.00 an hour.

If you had asked any healthy, young, and willful male living in poverty back then if he would sell something illegal or otherwise to a consenting party for profit, he would answer, "yes!" Was it wrong? Yes, but so was having a crackhead mother and three younger siblings to take care of with no food, clothing or means to get it. If you were extremely smart you got a scholarship. If you were exceptional in a sport a college recruited and, if you were lucky, someone financed you. Otherwise you had better know how to cut hair, rap, or sing. So many young men saw crack as a means of gaining success, achieving a level of comfort, and having an opportunity at the American dream. It was a doubled edged sword. It provided people with a means to eat, but destroyed lives at the same time.

The government began to investigate, and a decision was made that those selling crack, as opposed to the more expensive purer cocaine, should face harsher penalties. They felt the drug had a greater impact on society. They locked a large portion of my generation up and, in many cases, threw away the key. There are over 200,000 people in federal institutions and over 2 million housed in different state jails. That's more people than some third-world countries, and we call ourselves the land of the free. Now you know where a large chunk of our men are.

My phone started ringing and took me out of my thoughts. "Hello?"

"What's up, stranger?"

It was Jasmine. I was still a little salty about the way she came at me about Sin. The last time we were face to face, we almost came to blows. She had a bad habit of saying things without considering others' feelings. It got nasty, and the next thing I knew I was offering my foot to her ass. I hoped tonight turned out better.

"Are you on your way?" she asked.

"Yeah, I'm on my way to pick Charmaine up. We should be there shortly."

She said, "Okay, I'll see you there," then hung up.

One good thing about Harlem is you can find a store on every corner. I pulled over on 116th and 7th Avenue, where there was just enough room for me to legally park behind the fire hydrant. I made my way through the aisle and plucked a bottled water from the refrigerator case. I walked to the counter and pulled out a ten-dollar bill. I heard the bell chime on the back of the door and looked around. I smiled when I saw my old friend Smitty walking in.

Smitty was a kid I grew up with in the Bronx. He was getting paid at one time, and was wise enough to invest his money in a building and a bar on Lexington Avenue. He stood about 6'2", was built like a building, black as midnight, and had the strong features of a gorilla.

As soon as he noticed me he came over with open arms. "Misty, baby! Give me a hug!" He squeezed me so hard I thought I heard a few of my back bones crack. He leaned down and gave me brotherly kiss on the cheek. "What's good, sexy? Looks like you still driving these men crazy."

I gave him the innocent little girl look. "Who, me? I don't know what you're talking about." We both burst out laughing, "What have you been up to? I haven't seen you in years!"

"You know me; just keeping it low-key. How's everyone doing? Charmaine, your little sister, and what's the name of the mean one? Oh yeah, Jaz! Do you still keep in touch with them?"

"Yeah, everyone is doing wonderfully! I'm actually on my way to pick Charmaine up now. We are all going out tonight to celebrate with Nickelle. She's opening a new beauty salon."

"Tell her I said congratulations. Are you still doing the real estate thing?"

"Yeah, why?" I raised an eyebrow. "Are you in the market for something?"

He laughed. "Nah, I was just checking." He shook his head. "You sure don't skip a beat and still fly as ever." He eyed my coat. "It looks like somebody is taking care of you, and I mean real good care!"

I chuckled. "Ain't nothing changed, Smitty . . . only the year."

"I hear that! I run into a lot of the sisters who were fly back in the day. Some are doing their thing, but too many have fallen off. Those are the ones I call the terrible too's. They had too many kids, have too many issues, and gained too much damn weight! I ran into my old girl a couple of weeks ago. She's a grown-ass woman with five kids, but her way of thinking hasn't matured from when we were nineteen. She ain't did shit with herself."

"You see, I stayed in school and made sure I kept a job. I wasn't with that 'having a baby to keep a man' crap."

"What's up with your old man Sin? I heard he got slammed with a ton of time?"

"Yeah, you heard right."

"Damn, that's fucked up! He was a good dude. He don't deserve that kind of sentence. That man was getting paper, not flying around in airplanes and crashing them into fucking buildings. Then they'll turn around and give a child molester next to nothing! It's crazy how the system is ass backwards. Do you still keep in contact with him?"

"Yup, that's still my baby! I speak to him at least twice a week. He's doing fine, trying to make something happen and work his way out of there."

"Damn, you two still together?"

"Yeah, as much as we can be."

"I can't believe you two still speak after all this time! You've been with him as long as I can remember. How many years has it been, like a hundred?"

I laughed. "Wow, has it been that long? Time flies when you're in love!"

"That's a beautiful thing, and I'm happy to see you standing by that man. I'm trying to find me a good one like you. These females spend up your money, and when shit hits the fan, they're out! There aren't too many sisters out here down for a brother after the game is over."

"True, but let's be honest. A lot of brothers weren't worthy of being held down or waiting for. They dog their girls out, and long before the game was over for them, their girls were through. There aren't many men built to sit up in a cell for years, nor are there a lot of women built to do the time with them. Shit, a nigga's boy will abandon him after a few years. It's sad because there are a lot of intelligent, handsome, and caring men in prison who would love and appreciate having a positive woman by their side."

"You're right about that!" Smitty went into his pocket and pulled out a few hundred dollars. "Put this on my man's books for me."

Now, if he was someone else I would have been insulted, but I knew he meant well. I didn't want to offend him, but I had to politely decline.

"Smitty, you should know the last thing my man needs is money, but thanks for the offer. I will definitely tell him about your kind gesture and that you asked about him. When I start up the 'Get Sin the fuck out of jail' campaign I'll be certain to hit you up for a donation."

"You do that!"

We hugged and parted ways. It was always nice seeing him. I got back in my ride and headed over to the brownstone. Just as I pulled up Charmaine called my cell to see how far I was away.

"Come outside. I'm pulling up now," I stated.

She descended the steps decked out in red. She was draped in a red three-quarter shearling, 3½-inch red suede boots, and black pants. She looked cute. She jumped in the truck then leaned over and kissed my cheek.

"What's good, girlfriend?"

"Guess who I just ran into?"

"Who?"

"Smitty!"

"Get out of here! What's he up to?"

"The same."

Charmaine joked, "Still ugly as a bear's bottom!" I frowned at her and she giggled. "All right, sis, I'll be nice. Does he still own the bar on Lexington Avenue?"

"Yup! One of these days we're going to have to stop by his place for a drink."

"Let's make that a date. I miss talking shit with him. Back in the days he was good for a couple of bucks."

"You should know! You were always in his pockets. You should have given him some play Charmaine."

"Hell fucking no! He didn't want me." She smirked. "He had a crush on you!"

"So what? That didn't stop you from asking him for money every time you saw him."

"He liked giving me money. He was paying me to get close to you. Just think, if you would have gotten with him, you'd be the proud mother of a chimpanzee right now."

We both cracked up. "Cha, you stupid!"

She pulled out a joint and searched her bag for a light. "Do you want some?" I wasn't a big smoker, but every now and again I would partake.

"Yeah, let me take two puffs." As we pulled up in front of the restaurant, Butter, my eyes were burning and I was high as hell. "What type of weed was that you gave me? It got my heart pounding in my chest and it stinks."

She laughed. "Oh, I forgot you don't smoke like that. It's called Kush."

"Kush? What kind of shit you got me smoking? It sounds like some back yard bullshit."

In her best Jamaican accent she replied, "Nah, mon, me only smoke the good ganja. Tis the real deal! Get ya supa high"

She took one last pull and started choking. I cracked up.

Nickelle, Jasmine, and Toya were sitting in Jasmine's car when we pulled up. I flashed my headlights at them, and Nickelle signaled that they were ready. I pulled into a parking space then met them out front.

"Nickelle, did you make and confirm the reservations?"

She smiled then replied like an annoyed child, "Yes, Mother. I took care of it earlier."

Butter was packed. We were told our table wouldn't be ready for another twenty minutes. We sat at the bar and ordered drinks. I knew everyone's drink, so I took the liberty of ordering for us. "Let me get five shots of Patrón now and then bring a cosmo, a watermelon margarita, a mudslide, a strawberry daiquiri, and a piña colada over to the table."

The bartender gave us the shots.

I cheered out, "To Nickelle's new salon!"

We clanked glasses then gulped down the Patrón.

"That coat is hot, Misty!"

I smiled. "Thanks, Nick."

"Is that the fur Sin got you for your birthday?"

I took the coat off and turned it inside out before draping it over the back of the chair. "Yeah, this is it."

"It's bad! A brother got to be in love to be buying coats like that!"

I didn't tell them that Sin did a favor for a friend who was a fur manufacturer. The guy's kid got locked up for selling ecstasy pills and was having some problems. Sin helped the kid out and made sure he was safe. The furrier wanted to show his gratitude and offered Sin money, but he refused. Instead, as a token of his appreciation he had Sin send me down to his showroom so I could pick out whatever I wanted for my birthday.

I looked to change the subject. "He is indeed in love. So have you thought of a location for the new place, Nick?"

"Definitely midtown Manhattan!"

The waitress came over and informed us that our table was ready. We gathered up our coats and handbags then headed downstairs. Our drinks arrived shortly afterward.

I looked over at Toya. "So what's new with you? I haven't seen you in weeks!"

"Girl, between work, the kids, and my husband, I don't have time for anything."

"How are the kids?"

"They're bad as hell! Last week Malik, Jr. decided he wanted to play with matches and set the area rug in his room on fire. Thank goodness I was home and able to put it out, otherwise that little terror would have burned my damn house down! I told Big Malik in hopes of him tearing his son's butt up and he tells me I'm being too hard on him. He's a boy. I feel like I'm the only one in my house who has any damn sense. And that Ky'elle, she's a whole different story. She thinks because she's a teenager she's grown. I had to slap her two days ago!

"What did she do to merit a slap?" Jasmine asked.

"I caught that little heifer on the phone with some little dirt bag from her school talking about she would let him eat her thing-thing, but she wasn't ready to let anyone stick it in yet! I went to talk to her, she got slick with the lip, I lost it, and I slapped her."

"Maybe one of us should have a talk with her," I suggested.

"What's the big deal? She's in the eleventh grade. At least she's not giving up the cookies with the milk," Charmaine joked.

We all looked over at her.

"Don't ask why you're not the one we send in when counseling is needed," Jasmine snapped.

"I thought I was going to lose my whole entire mind! I don't know what I'm going to do with her, but I know the very next day I set up an appointment with the Gyn for her to get some birth control."

"What did Malik have to say?" Nickelle asked.

"He didn't say a word. Once I slapped her he just walked out the room."

"So what did he have to say about it?" I asked.

"All he said was he was glad it was me who picked up the phone, and not him, because he would be in jail for killing somebody's son." We all fell out laughing. "My life is boring and all about Malik and our kids. Charmaine, you always have something interesting going on. What's new with you?"

"Well . . . I just got back from a weekend getaway in Bahamas with Shawn."

We looked around at each other then asked in unison, "Who's Shawn?"

We all burst out laughing before she casually continued. "He's a gentleman I met a few months back who I'm seriously dating."

"Girl, you change men like some women change their shoes," Nickelle teased.

"Don't hate the player, hate the game! It's not my fault you don't get out!"

Nickelle replied, "I get out. I just don't meet any good men, and I don't have the courage to just up and travel with a stranger."

"I did know him before I went, Nickelle. Your problem is you never had the liberty to just up and go before. You always had Trey, but pretty soon he'll be off in college and you won't have any excuses. There's no better place to get to know someone than at a neutral location, and the free sun and sand doesn't hurt. Plus, I always get a separate room just in case."

Jasmine interrupted. "Wait a minute. Whatever happened to Derrick? I thought the two of you were hitting it off."

"We were, for a minute, but he's old news. He wanted a commitment, and he's not husband material. He's a nice guy and all, but he's too clingy."

"You need to grow up, Charmaine, and stop searching for someone that doesn't exist," Jasmine stated.

Charmaine ignored and rolled her eyes. "As I was saying, he's not the one."

"If it means anything to you, I thought he was a nice guy," Toya admitted.

"He is nice, but he's not Mr. Right. I want the kind of relationship Misty has with Sin."

Jasmine cut her eyes. "What does she have with him?"

"She has a friendship, a bond, and an unconditional love; that's what she has! She has a relationship based on honesty and a love so pure it goes beyond aesthetics or worldly possessions. What she has is real!"

They debated back and forth as if I wasn't at the table.

"That's your opinion. I think what she has is another sad story."

Nickelle interjected, "That's not true, Jaz! We all know they have loved each other for a long time, and through it all they always remained true to each other, and that's not sad. It's nice to know you have someone in your corner no matter what."

"Well, it's sad to me. He surely picked a convenient time to profess his eternal love now that he's got all that time," she spat.

It was time for me to step in and put an end to this discussion. "What are you trying to say, Jaz? That he only loves me now that he's in jail?" She didn't reply, but rolled her eyes up into the air. "You need to go ahead with that bullshit. He knew he loved me long before that."

"If he didn't run off and leave you, I might believe it."

"Jaz, you're like a sister and all, but you're out of line, and you don't know shit about our situation. I trust what's in his heart, and that's what matters. It's a shame you're still hating on us after all this time."

"I'm not hating. I'm giving you my opinion."

"But did I ask for it? I could have sworn the last time you tried to give me your opinion on my relationship and my man I advised you to mind your business and worry about getting one of your own!"

"For your information, I am dating someone, and even if I wasn't, anyone is better than wasting my time on a loser."

"Okay, Jasmine, you're getting a little bit beside yourself," Toya stated.

My mouth dropped, and my eyes narrowed. No one—and I mean no one—gets away with disrespecting Sin. Not in front of me! "Loser? Loser? Who the fuck do you think you're calling a loser? Look at the tired-ass men you deal with!"

"Ladies, we need to end this now before someone's feelings get hurt," Toya stated.

I glared at Toya. "It's too late for that shit!" I looked back to Jasmine with fire in my eyes. "Let me make something clear to you for once and for all. Sin is handsome, intelligent, sexy, rich, suave, and has the dick of a god! He took and still takes great care of me—emotionally, spiritually, and if need be, financially. He gives me more than any of your men collectively give you. Loser! Your tired ass couldn't get a man like Sin to pay you some attention or stay focused whether he was locked up or not!"

I sat steaming mad. "How dare you call him a loser? People get punched in the mouth for saying disrespectful shit like that, Jaz! Deep down inside I know why you say ignorant things. It's because you're miserable. You finally got a man to stick around long enough to claim him, and he's a fucking bum. He borrows money from you, and then dips you! I'd take my loser over three of your bums any day!"

Sin had been called a lot of things, but loser was never one of them. I was heated! You could see flames bouncing around in my eyes. We all sat quiet before I couldn't take it anymore. "Why you always do that?"

"Do what?" she asked as if she had no idea what I was talking about.

"Always have something smart or negative to say about him knowing how I'm going to react. We've been dealing with each other for years, and I would think by now you'd learn some tact as well as have some respect for the fact that I love him. Don't you get it? I want him to be a part of my life, I enjoy loving him, and he's not going anywhere!"

She snickered under her breath. "Yeah, I know, Misty . . . he's in jail."

"You know what? Fuck you Jaz! I'm personally tired, and way over my limit with your bullshit! Seems like all you do when we get together is fuck up my mood. You're miserable, and misery loves company. I refuse to have the 'J' zapped out of my joy, so do us both a favor and stay the hell away from me until you learn what to say out your mouth!"

"I'm just saying if the shoe was on the other foot I don't think Sin would be there for you. You claim to be so down for Sin, but you're still with Marcus? It appears to me that you two are playing a game and you're merely having your cake and eating it too."

"That's where you're wrong! You have no idea of the internal struggles I've faced to get to this point of clarity—a point of being confident in him again. I do know Sin would be there for me. If you knew anything you would know Sin has, and will always be the motherfucking cake, the frosting, and the god damn candles sitting on top. You just mad you couldn't get you a slice!"

"Okay, ladies, we're supposed to be here to celebrate," Nickelle interjected, trying to defuse the situation.

"I don't want to argue with you. I'm simply saying I feel you're wasting your time and can do better."

She was attempting to diminish her role in the disagreement; which made me even hotter under the collar. "Did it dawn on you I might be at my happiest with him regardless where he's at?" I shook my head. "Why am I even bothering trying to explain it to you? You wouldn't understand because you never had a serious relationship to know what it takes to keep one together. You never had someone make you feel the way he makes me feel."

My comments hit a nerve, and she got an attitude. "I understood when he left you high and dry!"

We all knew the story, so she was playing herself by even bring it back up.

"What was he supposed to do, Jaz? Take me on the run with him? Put me at risk and possibly locked up with him? I'll be the first to admit my heart was broken when he left. I was depressed and angry. I thank all of you for pulling me through the rough times, but let's get something straight. I was never suicidal. What matters is that he did the best thing for the both of us at the time. He thought enough of me and my future not to put me in harm's way, and I have a great respect and love for him for that. He made an unselfish decision and put my well-being first, and now that I fully understand the scope of the consequences had I left with him, I truly thank him."

"Was he thinking of your well-being when he was out making that baby?"

Charmaine leaned back in the chair and crossed her arms over her chest. "Oh, no you didn't go there!"

Her words hit me like an unexpected punch to the gut. I wanted to grab her up by the roots of her hair. "So fucking what if he had a kid! Things happen! It doesn't matter what the fuck happened in the past! We've worked through our issues and plan on being together, so watch what the fuck you say about him, and stay the fuck out of our business!"

"But I thought Marcus was your business. Remember him?"

"What about him? Why are you so concerned about him all of a sudden? You got a crush on him too? One minute you hate Sin, and the next you like Marcus. I think you're jealous and I stay on your radar. I have two men who love me, you don't have any, and that bothers you. It bothers you that they both chose me over you, and they both take care of me while you struggle. If it makes you feel any better, when Sin gets out of jail I'm leaving Marcus. Now you won't have to worry about what I plan to do with him! I'm going to be with Sin no matter what, and the sooner he gets his ass out of jail, the better!"

"Well, that may be your loss."

I sat back in the chair then chuckled. "Jaz, I'm winning! You're the only one who doesn't see it. This is what I'll do for you. Since you're so concerned about Marcus, I'll hook you up. I'll do you a solid if that's what it will take to get you off my back and Sin's dick!" She rolled her eyes at my sarcasm. "I'm looking forward to when my Daddy comes home, and yes, I did say when! I read all of his court papers and believe wholeheartedly that his wrongful conviction will be overturned, and so do those brilliant attorneys we hired. Let me know when you're ready for me to drop Marcus's tired ass over at your place. You shouldn't mind him dry humping you to death. It's not like you know the difference between great dick and run of the mill cock!"

Nickelle's eyes could have popped out of her head. Charmaine burst out laughing, and Toya sadly shook her head. The waiter walked over and took our orders. Nickelle kept looking over at me with a plea for mercy in her eyes. Charmaine didn't care either way and would have loved to see me go batty on Jasmine, who put her face down in the menu. I got up from the table and headed to the ladies' room. I needed to cool down. If I sat there a minute longer I might have slapped the shit out of her.

The nerve of her telling me what I should do with my heart like she was the fucking love doctor. Lonely bitch! Sin and I sacrificed a lot over the years, and to still be in love after all the shit we went through is a blessing. Somehow we managed to find each other again, and now that we were both on the same page I wasn't going to let no man or woman take us under!

I heard Charmaine from the other side of the bathroom stall.

"Sis, are you okay?"

I waited until the ladies' room was cleared before I replied. "I'm good, Cha. She kills me with this vendetta she has against Sin. She acts like he did something to her."

"Don't pay her any attention. She hates on all of us. That's her personality. Don't sweat it. I see what you have with him, and believe me, I'm out here searching for it every day, and it's not easy. I meet men all the time. Good looking, rich and available men, but something is always missing. He's either attractive with limited income potential or rich and boring. I envy what you have with Sin, and if I was you I wouldn't give up. It's worth fighting for."

"I love you, Big Head, and thanks for understanding."

We exited the restroom and joined the girls at the table. Toya and Nickelle must have said something to Jasmine because by the time we got back she was trying to apologize, but spoken words could not be unsaid. The plates came, and the rest of the night went pretty smooth, but I was quiet. We left the restaurant and went to a lounge a few blocks away for a couple of hours and called it a night.

On the ride home Sin was heavily on my mind. I wished I could call him and hear him tell me everything was going to be all right. Hearing him say, "Fuck Jasmine," would've made me feel better. That's the part of this bullshit jail thing that drives me crazy. Charmaine knew the conversation at the restaurant was bothering me, but didn't bother to bring it back up on the ride to my house. As soon as I hit the door I went straight for the shower. I needed to clear my head.

In the beginning I questioned myself, and a war waged within me for a long time. I was torn between doing the right thing and my happiness. I knew Marcus wasn't a bad catch. If he were, I wouldn't be in this predicament. I couldn't comprehend why I loved, wanted, and needed Sin so much. How could a person penetrate another's heart so deeply that no one else could infiltrate it? He said it was divine intervention that keeps us together. I joked that he secretly stuck a magnet in my chest then put his magnetic force field on in overdrive.

As the hot water ran down my back, I thought about Jasmine's comments. Since the internal battle was long won and I surrendered to my heart, I no longer fought myself for loving him. A heart knows not who it loves, but was she partially right? Was I being unfair? Should I have been honest with Marcus a long time ago instead of being selfish and staying because I was unsure what I really needed and what I was willing to give up to have it? What would he think if he ever found out about Sin and I? He had a very turbulent relationship with his ex, and I heard he chased her off the road. I was told not to let the suit and tie fool me because he was like Dr. Jekyll and Mr. Hyde.

I knew deep down inside my actions were unscrupulous, but how could something so wrong feel so right? I was torn. Marcus had never given me any reason to doubt his love or his loyalty, but my heart wouldn't love him the way I loved Sin. Was I risking everything for a man who might not deserve another chance?

The first couple of years Sin and I dated were magic. After having sex on the highway I was spending more time with him than Black, and he was spending more time with me than with his so-called girlfriend. If we weren't together, we were on the phone. Even when he went out of town he made it his business to check in on me at least twice a day, and that was big for him!

He wasn't the average man. Within the first two years of dealing with him I watched him drive a selection of vehicles: Range Rover, Acura NSX, Porsche, Lexus, Benzes, BMW's, SUV's, and various motorcycles. He would often buy cars according to his mood and then give them away to his boys shortly afterward. He also had several apartments and houses in and out of state. He was an official baller, and part of the job required him to be away a lot, so the time he spent with me became precious.

He gave me furs and a collection of jewelry, but I valued the simple things like cuddling on the sofa, watching sporting events, playing video games, watching movies, taking walks, talking, or making love. This is why I loved him so much. He took time out just for me. We spent our time creating our own little reality. He would say spending time with me felt so natural, and I totally agreed. It was as if the world stopped when we were together, and nothing else mattered. It was priceless.

On a humble I happened to have baited and snagged one of New York's most eligible hustlers. His name was ringing bells in the streets, and the women were coming out of the woodwork. They saw the possibility of a come-up, which is why he would say, "A chick couldn't get a dime out of me." He was paid and rumored to have a big dick, but they weren't going to get a chance to try it if I had anything to do with it! I was the number-one Queen Cock Blocker, and he would have a problem if I even thought about sliding off with someone else.

When we first got together I believe he thought it was cute when I got jealous of all the attention females gave him. I would walk right up on him and shut them down quick. He would tease me and say, "You know you got a little crazy lady living inside your head."

He talked crap, but he did his share of blocking too. He couldn't stand to see me somewhere and someone playing me close. He just handled the situation a little smoother than I did. His approach was subtler. He would wait for the perfect moment, make his presence known, and give me that face that said, "You better bring your ass over here!"

Initially we were both with other people, but shortly after becoming intimate the rules changed. Whether he wanted to admit it, I had penetrated his heart. Over the years we learned to trust, and depend on one another. The relationship matured and evolved into something so much greater than either one of us could have ever anticipated. The carefree lives we once valued filled with the hottest parties, the flashiest cars, and the most expensive outfits became a life filled with dreams of family and building a foundation. I still believed in that dream.

# CHAPTER 8

## *Father*

Although it was late when we arrived back to my house, I wasn't tired and couldn't sleep. I checked in on Charmaine, and she was still awake as well.

"Hey, Big Head, want to watch a movie?"

"Sure, what you got?"

We headed down to the family room and she selected a movie. I popped some popcorn, threw on the DVD, and she began to fill me in on her latest conquest. We stayed up until 5:00 in the morning, and she still hadn't finished telling me all the stuff she had done lately.

We fell asleep right there on the leather sectional and didn't start moving until 1:00 in the afternoon. We got up, and I made breakfast while she called the dealer to make arrangements to pick up the loaner car.

She walked in the kitchen and asked, "When did you say Marcus was coming back?"

"He'll be back on Tuesday. Why, what's up?"

"I was just thinking we should do something fun and spontaneous."

"Like what? It's cold outside!"

"Like maybe drive out to Foxwoods Resort, do a little gambling. I feel lucky! You know they have a shopping outlet right next door," she added, trying to make the invitation more enticing.

I thought about it and decided to go. "Okay, but two things. I need to stop by the post office first, and I got to be back home by tomorrow afternoon. I have some paperwork I have to take care of."

She agreed, and within an hour we were dressed and heading out the door.

"Did you hear that CD *Love's Crazy* from the artist Slim formerly of the group 112?"

"I only heard one or two tracks. Is it good?"

She went into her bag and pulled out the CD. "Here, put this in and put on track number nine, 'Bedtime Stories.'" She increased the volume and reclined back in her seat. We jammed the same song all the way to the post office. I ran inside and was happy to see I'd gotten mail.

"This is a good sex song," I stated upon getting back in the jeep.

"That's what I'm trying to tell you." She grinned. "Shawn played this CD the whole time we were in the Bahamas."

When we pulled up to the dealership she jumped out, took care of the paperwork, and pulled in front of me in a pearl white 650i convertible BMW. A handsome man walked out of the dealership and leaned into the car. They spoke for a few minutes, and then she escorted him over to my jeep.

"Misty, I want you to meet my dear friend, Shawn Jones."

I lifted my hand to his. "It's a pleasure to meet you."

He smiled. "The pleasure is all mines. I've heard nice things about you."

We exchanged pleasantries before he kissed her on the lips and told her he would call her later. She was giddy like a schoolgirl. It had been a long time since I'd seen her like that, and I decided to mess with her. I picked up my cell phone and called her as soon as we pulled off. She answered the phone laughing.

"So that's the infamous Shawn?"

She giggled in my ear. "Yup, that's my Mr. Bahamas."

"It must be nice to have a hook-up with the dealer. You got upgraded to a 650i when you only drive a three series."

"Brains will get you a job, body will get you a man, but some good pussy will get a mean upgrade." She laughed. "It does have its benefits," she added with conceit.

*Beep.*

"Cha, that's Marcus on the other line. I'll call you right back."

"What time are you trying to go to Foxwoods tonight?"

"I don't care; just call me when you get home."

*Click.*

"Hello?"

"Hey sweetheart, are you missing me yet?"

"Hey, Marcus, how are things going down there in Detroit? Did you have a good flight?"

"It was on time and there was very little turbulence."

"That's good. So how did your meeting go?"

"I think I wowed them, but I won't be certain until next month when my firm presents the final figures. I still have to meet with the marketing and advertising departments this week."

"Well, good luck! Oh yeah, before I forget to tell you I'm going with Charmaine to Foxwoods tonight."

"Okay that sounds like fun, but try not to spend too much money."

"I won't."

"Okay then. I'll call you tomorrow."

I disconnected the call, turned up the volume on the stereo, and sang along with "No One" by Alicia Keys. I loved her voice and thought she was super talented. There wasn't a song she performed I didn't like.

The weather wasn't as cold as it was the day before, and the sun was trying to peek through the clouds. I reminded myself to make sure I packed something nice to wear to the casino just in case. When you were rolling with Charmaine you could never be too sure. I needed to be prepared for anything. She was not going all the way to Foxwoods to sit up in a room.

I remember a time when we all went down to Atlantic City for the weekend; I didn't sleep for two days straight. In forty-eight hours I shopped, gambled, ate, partied, walked the boardwalk, swam, and got my hair done twice, and I wasn't even tired. I was younger then and had the energy for that type of running around.

Pulling into my driveway, my thoughts were on my father. I had not spoken to him in a while, and didn't want him to start worrying about me. Growing up, Pop was everything to me. When my mother died he stepped up and did everything she would have, including teaching me how to use a sanitary napkin. It was hard for a long time not having her around, but we all learned to adjust. My parents adored each other, and were very affectionate. I would catch them all the time hugging or kissing or slow dancing in our living room to Teddy Pendergrass's "Turn Off The Lights."

My mother would tell me, "Misty, when I met your father I knew he was the man for me. When you get older you may kiss a frog or two before you get to your Prince Charming, but when you find him you'll know."

"But how will I know?" I asked.

"There will be a connection. He'll touch your soul and you'll feel it in your heart, baby."

I was so young. "But what will it feel like, Momma?"

She laughed. "It's hard to explain, but it will be a feeling you can't shake or replace. It's kind of like thunder and lightning or fireworks going off inside of you. It's something like the feeling you get when you're on a rollercoaster. It will be a feeling he'll give you almost every time you see him, and that man, pumpkin, is what you call your soul mate."

I loved my mom. Everything she did was about my father and us. He came first, and her job was to take care of home. We were a happy family who did things together. She would make pancakes for us every Saturday morning, place our plate at the table, cut on the cartoons, and then serve my father his breakfast in bed. It was as if she could read his mind. She would just bring him a beer from the refrigerator then plop down on his lap and watch the game with us. I wanted to be just like her; so feminine and ladylike.

She always smelled good too! She said, "Misty, you have to make sure you keep your body clean. No boy likes a dirty little girl."

I would laugh because I was a tomboy and didn't mind a little dirt. She was very meticulous about her appearance and made sure she looked great for my dad. She also made sure my hair and clothes were neat. She kept me fly. I was wearing silk blouses by the age of twelve.

She also kept our apartment immaculate. From young she taught me how to clean up behind myself and maintain my things.

She would joke and say, "You better marry yourself a rich man, little girl, so you can have a maid, but until then go in your room and pick up your things. You know where they belong."

She never yelled or beat us. She used to say she liked peace in her house. I don't even recall seeing my parents really argue. We knew when she was upset because she would get quiet.

My dad said I reminded him a lot of her. He said we had the same shape, disposition, and smile. I sometimes wonder how different my life would have been had she not been hit by that cab. My life was perfect until that fatal day. I left for school, came home, and she was gone forever. I was twelve at the time. I knew what death was because my father's mother died, but I didn't feel the impact of her passing. When my mother died it was as if my world was turned upside down.

It was tragic. I can remember reading the newspaper captions. "Mother of two plowed down by runaway cab." I had so many questions I wanted and needed her to answer. I was mad at God; I was mad at her, and mad at the cab driver. I wanted to blame someone!

There was a big turnout at her funeral. She had a lot of friends. Her family came, but my father kicked them out of the reception. He told them to never come back around, ever! At the time I didn't know it, but they came to the funeral with intentions on taking me and my brother from him. He would hear none of it. He told them it would be over his dead body then dismissed them.

I wrote down all the little stories and advice my mother shared with me after her death so that I would never forget them. Sin couldn't believe I still had the journal. When I showed him, he couldn't get over my twelve-year-old penmanship. The first page was titled "Mommy Said" and had a list of things she said to me.

Boys don't like dirty girls, girls should smell nice, there is nothing wrong with being smart and pretty, take care of your things, and find a good guy who treats you right. The list went on and on.

I'm more than sure over the years there would have been a lot more she would have taught me about dating, relationships, and sex. I missed out on all those things. At least I was blessed to have her for twelve years.

My father decided to move down to New Orleans four years ago to be closer to his brother, Billy. Even though multiple sclerosis had taken away almost all of the mobility in his legs, my father was a proud man. There was a real nice assisted living facility a mile away from his brother, and he felt it would be better for him to be there. He didn't want to rely on strangers to take care of him. When I told him I wanted him to stay with me, he told me he didn't want to be a burden and I was too young to be bogged down tending to him. I tried to make him change his mind, but he was as headstrong as me.

I checked it out, and the place was modern, the staff was super friendly, and they had medical staff on call twenty-four hours a day. The facility had everything you could imagine—gym, heated pool, movie room, tennis and basketball courts, and room service.

I picked up the phone and dialed him. He answered on the second ring. "This is Mr. Bishop speaking."

"Hi, Pop!"

"Misty, *mi chica favorita*! I was just thinking about you! What took you so long to call me back?"

"I've been doing a lot of running around, Pop. How are you?"

"I'm okay. Tired of this wheelchair, but fine otherwise." There was a long pause. "Do you remember when I told you I thought something was wrong with Ms. Presley?" She was my father's next-door neighbor.

"Yeah, isn't she the lady you told me was always forgetting her keys?"

"That's her! The doctors detected early stages of Alzheimer's."

"That's so sad. Is she going to be able to remain there or will they have to place her in a more secured setting?"

"I'm not sure, but her daughter came and picked her up yesterday."

There was a brief silence. "Dad, is there anything you need?" I was very particular when it came to him.

"No, I have everything I need. Your uncle was over here this morning." There was another pause. "Are you okay, Chica? Is there something you want to talk to me about?"

There was another pause before I sighed. "Well, yeah. Pop, I'm thinking about moving back into the brownstone with Charmaine."

"What's going on? Have you finally figured out what you're going to do about your situation?"

I was always close with my father, but after my mother's death we became thick as thieves. My brother would tease us and say I was his favorite son. I had told him everything, so he was pretty much up to speed on the things going on in my life. I told him when Sin and I started speaking again and how I was feeling. A few months later while visiting Pop, Sin called my cell and I let them talk. The next thing I knew the two of them were communicating on their own.

He respected my decision, but didn't like it, and told us both just that. He told me to leave Marcus if I wasn't fulfilled, be with Sin if that made me happy, or find somebody new. He told Sin he raised me to be an honest person and didn't agree with the love triangle we'd created. He told Sin he expected more from him after all this time, but understood his rationale after their heart-to-heart. My father and Marcus had spoken on the phone, but never met. My father decided he didn't want to meet him until I made a choice because he refused to be a hypocrite.

"I think I almost have it figured out. You know I care about Marcus, but the truth is I don't like him. I'm content, but I feel like I'm cheating myself out of true happiness. With him I feel like a painter being told they can only use black and white, or a musician being told they can only play in one key. I feel like I'm being held back."

He knew how Sin and I felt about each other. We talked regularly and he pulled no punches when he gave me advice. Ideally Sin was his guy; however, he did express his desire to have a grandchild and maybe one day see me walk down the aisle. He told me to figure out which one I wanted more.

"Does your moving back to Harlem have anything to do with Sin?"

"Not really. My concerns with Marcus have little to do with him. I want kids and to get married, but we're not compatible, and I refuse to settle with someone who I know has a totally different outlook on life than I do. That would just add more confusion."

"You're right about that! And I don't want any confused grandkids or conflicts around them. I think you know what to do. Why are you having a hard time making it happen? What's holding you back? Why are you procrastinating?"

"Honestly, I'm scared. Pop, I feel like Sin and I are so close, but yet at times I feel like we're so far apart. I'm in love with him, and I know he's the one, but I'm scared he may never get out and scared I may never find another man to replace him. I don't want to wind up alone with no one to love me."

"How could you ever be alone when you will always have him?"

"Pop, Sin doesn't want to marry me—"

"Nonsense! He told me himself he can't wait to marry you."

"He wants to marry me, but not while he's in there. What if he doesn't get out for another ten, twenty years? I love him, Pop, with all my heart, but I want a baby. I want a family. What am I to do? Am I supposed to leave him and settle?"

"I named you Misty, not Misery! I would rather see you alone and happy than with someone and sad. I raised you to follow your own mind and heart. You have to live your life for you and according to your rules. People told me I needed to remarry because I had two young kids who needed a mother figure. You see I never remarried, I never regretted it, and we did just fine! I'm very much alone, and very happy. I have a full life, and that's what matters. You want a baby, go to a sperm bank. I don't care. I'll love it just the same. If you want something you have to go get it! You only have one life, Chica. Do what you need to do for your own happiness, and if waiting for him is it then do that. You have always made me proud, and I know you'll make the right decision for you."

"Thanks for the support, Pop. I'll let you know how the move works out. So what are your plans for the weekend? A handsome guy like you should be going somewhere with someone."

He laughed. "The only place your tired father is going is to the bed, and I'm going there alone. What about you? What are your plans for the weekend?"

"I'm going to Foxwoods Resort with Charmaine tonight."

"Foxwoods! I love the casino! Tell her I said she better call me. I haven't heard from her in a month. How's she doing?"

"She's fine, and I'll tell her to call you. We're only going for the night."

"Is Marcus going with you?"

"No, he went away on business. It's just me and Charmaine on this trip."

"Maybe that's the problem with you two; he's always gone," he joked.

"I'll call you sometime this week. Oh yeah, Pop. Sin said he got the magazines you sent to him and said to say thank you."

"Perfect. You have fun, be safe, and don't forget to tell that Charmaine and Nickelle to call. Love you, Chica!"

"I love you too!"

# CHAPTER 9

## *Foxwoods*

When I arrived at the brownstone Charmaine was still getting dressed.

"I should be ready in a few," she yelled as she walked into the back room.

I removed my coat and plopped down on the sofa. I reached into my bag, retrieved the envelope from Sin, and then ran my fingernail under the flap. It was a greeting card, and on the front was a half moon hugging a star.

The inside read, *I love you so much . . . I think God invented hugs just for us.* I smiled. There was also a letter enclosed. It started reading it, but stopped in midsentence when he started talking some nasty stuff. I placed it back in the envelope. This was the type of letter I preferred to read when I was alone.

"Misty, can you answer the phone, and if it's Shawn tell him I'll call him back!"

"Hello?"

A tense masculine voice spoke. "May I speak with Charmaine?"

"She's not available right now. May I ask who is calling?"

"Can you tell her Derrick called again, and I would appreciate a call back?" He sounded annoyed.

"Oh hey, Derrick. It's me, Misty."

"Hi, Misty," he replied in a dejected tone. He sounded as if he had just lost his best friend.

"Is everything all right?"

"Yeah, yeah, I'm fine, but your partner has been dipping my calls and treating me like a punk."

"I see. Well she's in the shower right now, but I will tell her you called." I was not going feed into this conversation. Poor guy didn't know he had been cut off weeks ago.

"Are you two going to be in the house for a while? I'm in the area! I can stop by."

"Actually, we're on our way out the door. I'll tell her you called once she gets out the shower."

"What are you two getting into tonight?"

I thought, *Desperate*. He wasn't getting any information out of me, so I kept it simple. "Nothing much, just getting something to eat."

"That sounds cool. Where you two heading? I haven't eaten. Maybe we can all meet up."

*Charmaine must have thrown some voodoo pussy on this one because he was hard up to see her. She might have a stalker on her hands.* I pulled out my cell phone and proceeded to dial her house number. As soon as I heard the beep breaking in on the other line I said, "Derrick, I need to take this call. It was nice talking to you and I'll let her know you called."

He let out a long sigh. "Okay. Take care, and don't forget."

"I won't."

Charmaine walked into the living room. "Who was that?"

"Girl, that was Derrick! What did you do to him? He sounds like a lost puppy."

"What he say?"

"He said you were treating him like a punk and not returning his calls."

"You would think he would have gotten the hint when I stopped taking his calls."

"Well, maybe if you told him you were no longer interested, he would stop."

"Believe me, I tried that already, but he won't give up! I'll call him tomorrow because he's starting to get on my nerves. He has to stop this popping up at my job and my house unannounced bullshit. Last week I was having a late lunch with a male colleague, and he walked up on our table. He began questioning me about what was going on between the two of us. I was so humiliated. The shit is getting crazy with him. Picture if that had been me and Shawn. I can't have that."

"If he keeps acting stupid we'll just have to make a call to Smitty and have him pay him a little visit," I joked.

"And I will call him too!" She laughed then sighed like a true diva. "It's so difficult having the four B's."

Both of us sang out in unison like it was a slogan, "Brains, Body, Beauty, and that Bomb."

We both laughed. "Beauty will attract him, a body will entice him, brains will help you snag him, but it's that bomb that will keep him coming back!"

I left my car at a nearby parking garage then jumped in the convertible with her. Even though it was too cold outside to appreciate the drop top, the car was still hot. The ride there was smooth, and her heavy foot got us there in record time.

We had a double occupancy suite reserved at Foxwoods MGM Grand. After checking in we freshened up then hit the casino floor. I personally wasn't much of a poker player, but I did know how to drop a few coins in a slot and pull the handle.

Charmaine was the gambler, and once I'd lost a hundred and fifty dollars in quarters, I made my way over to her table. She was hot so I gave her five hundred dollars and told her to win some for me. I grabbed the cocktail waitress and ordered us both a drink. Charmaine gambled for two hours while I looked on. She was ready to call it quits after she won $6,700. She peeled off fifteen hundred-dollar bills and handed them to me. I thought that was cool since I hadn't done anything except cheer her on. I noticed a group of men gambling across the room. I pointed. "They look like they're having a ball!"

She looked over in their direction and suggested we go over to see what all the commotion was about. Upon reaching the table I noticed all four men looked like professional athletes. They were all tall and muscular with broad shoulders. They were playing Black Jack and making a killing. One of the gentlemen gave me the onceover as we approached their table. He tried to gain my attention.

"How are you ladies doing tonight?"

"We're fine, and yourself?" Charmaine replied.

He answered wearing a bright player's smile. "I'm doing much better now that you two came over. Let me introduce you to my teammates."

*Yup, they're players.*

"My name is Trevor Taylor, and this is William Banks, Harrison Adams, and Damon Young."

We told them our names and exchanged handshakes.

"What are you ladies getting into tonight?" the one named Damon asked.

"We just finished gambling and were thinking about getting something to eat."

"If you like, you can join us. A few of the players are having a party upstairs, and we have plenty of food and drinks."

"Is this a real party or just the two of us and the four of you? Because I'm not about to go up to anyone's suite for a little private party," I stated matter-of-factly.

"Nah, nah, sweetheart. My boy Seth rented out the penthouse, and he's hosting a big party upstairs."

"So why are the four of you down here gambling and not up there?"

"We wanted to play a couple of hands."

"I see, but we'll need to go to our room and change into something more appropriate," Charmaine said.

"Okay, just come on up when you're ready and tell the person at the door I invited you."

We decide to attend the function, and as soon as we hit our room we transformed into divas. Charmaine wore a royal blue spaghetti strapped number while I wore a red long-sleeve, back-out dress with a pair of heels I'd purchased in Brooklyn from Je T'aime shoe boutique on Flatbush Avenue. My girl Jiton always had the hottest look.

We made our way up to the penthouse, and as soon as we stepped foot off the elevator, security was there. He checked our bags and ran a metal detecting wand over our bodies before letting us pass. The party was packed mainly with women, but there were enough men to go around.

Charmaine smiled. "I think I'm going to collect me a few numbers tonight!"

"You go ahead. I'm good."

We surveyed the room, and over in the corner I thought I saw a familiar face.

"Cha, is that Mitch over there?"

She couldn't see through the crowd, so we walked over to get a better look. Mitchell "Sweet Feet" Seth had made a name for himself in baseball, and was now on the final leg of his career. It had been many years since we'd seen each other.

I slowly approached. "Excuse me . . . Mitch?"

He looked up and there was that same million-dollar smile. "Misty, is that you? Charmaine!" He got up and gave us both a bear hug. "What a surprise, you here in Connecticut at the same time as me! What brought you ladies to Foxwoods?"

"We just decided to get away for the night," she replied as she tossed her hair.

"Well come over, grab a seat, and let's catch up!"

There were two women sitting on the half-moon sofa with him. He looked over and politely as possible told them to move. "What's up with your girl Jasmine?"

I wanted to say, "She's still the same miserable ass she was back when you dated her," but instead I answered, "She's doing well. I know she would have loved to see you."

"Tell her I said hello! So what have you been doing with yourselves?"

"Just working and maintaining."

He then peered over at Charmaine. It was obvious he was attracted to her by the way he was looking at her. "And what about you, sexy?"

She smiled. "Same for me. I'm fine."

He smirked. "I didn't ask how you looked. I asked what you've been doing."

He was definitely flirting. She laughed it off as she took a seat. We hung out with him and his boys for the rest of the night. I hadn't laughed so much in a long time. Mitch grabbed Charmaine up and had her dancing until her feet hurt.

"Do you still play cards?" I asked. When we were younger Mitch would come over to the house and play spades all night.

"Yeah, I still play." He got one of his boys to join us.

Mitch hadn't changed a bit. He talked crap every time he won a book. The first game they won, but the second game they lost because he was so busy talking shit he reneged.

He leaned back into the sofa, stretched out his legs then placed his arm behind Charmaine's head. "So Charmaine, are you married yet?"

She seemed surprised by his question. "No, not married, but dating."

"That means it ain't serious."

"We haven't been dating long enough for it to be serious."

"Then there's room for competition."

She smiled. "You talk as if you have a friend you're trying to introduce me to? You didn't seem too interested in hooking me up with anybody when your buddy asked about me earlier."

"Damn right! I was thinking of us two getting together, maybe dinner?"

Charmaine didn't know how to respond, so I broke the silence. "Are you trying to get with all of my friends, Mitch?"

"You got to be kidding! I messed with Jasmine years ago, and that didn't amount to anything. That was kiddy stuff." He looked back over to Charmaine. "So are you down for dinner?" If he was anyone else she would have jumped at the offer, but I knew she didn't feel comfortable messing around with someone who her friend dated, regardless if they dated over ten years ago.

She finally responded, "Mitch, you're crazy! I can't get with you!"

"And why not?"

"Because I would have to sneak around behind Jaz's back, and I'm not the sneaking around type of woman."

"Who said anything about sneaking around? She wouldn't be upset about us going out on one date."

We both responded, "Yeah, she would!"

He let it go, but had the determined look of a hungry lion waiting at a gazelle crossing. She was his prey, and he was going to pursue her.

I pulled out my digital camera and asked his friend to take a picture of us. We posed for a few shots.

"You should send this one to Sin," Charmaine stated.

"Oh, shit! What's up with my man Sin? I haven't seen him in years!"

"Unfortunately, he's locked up."

"Damn, I didn't know that. How long he got?"

I shook my head. "He got too much time."

"You got to give me his information so I can get at him."

I gave him the information as we finished off the last bottle of champagne. My head started spinning. I went to the bathroom and threw some water on my face. When I returned I gave Charmaine the eye that said I'm ready to leave.

She stood. "It's about time we get out of here. It's been a long night."

"I got an early flight myself. I'm not even gonna bother going to sleep. I'll sleep on the plane. I'll be in New York very soon and will be calling for my dinner date." He then joked, "And I won't not take no for an answer."

We exchanged phone numbers.


The following morning we ate breakfast then went straight to the outlet. We spent four hours trudging through the stores and snatching up deals. We brought our bags back to the room then headed back to the casino to hit up the slot machines and poker table before we left. I won $750 on the slots, and Charmaine lost $300 at the table.

I wanted to test drive the car, so I drove back home. The 650i drove like a baby! It hugged the turns and accelerated as soon as my foot tapped the gas pedal. I had that bad boy doing well over 100 miles per hour.

My cell phone rang and I hit the earpiece to take the call. "Hello!"

"Hey, sweetie! What are you up to?"

"Hey, Marcus. We're on our way home."

"How was it? Did you win any money or did you spend it all shopping?" he asked jokingly.

"A little of both," I admitted.

"Tell Charmaine I say hello."

"Marcus said to tell you hello."

She responded very drearily, "Tell him hi," then looked back out the window.

"She said hello."

"What time do you think you'll be back in the city?"

"The way I'm driving I should be there shortly."

"You better stop speeding. You already have points on your license."

"Yeah, I know, but this car she's got is so fast!"

"What type of car is it?"

"It's the new 650i BMW!"

"Where did Charmaine get a car like that from? One of her men?"

I ignored his sarcasm. "I love it!"

"Well maybe if you're a good girl, Santa will bring you one for Christmas."

We talked a few more minutes before my earpiece died. I told him I would call him back then ended the call.

"So what did Mr. Marcus have to say?"

"Nothing much. He said if I'm a good girl I may be getting me one of these for Christmas."

"Your car is only two years old. Do you think he'll trade it in so soon?"

"I hope not. I would hate to give it back when I leave him."

"If he bought me this car I wouldn't give his ass back shit!" She laughed.

My phone rang again. I turned down the stereo, pressed the talk button, and then placed the phone to my ear.

"Hello?"

Pause.

"You have a prepaid call and will not be charged for this call. This call is from Garrett Butler, an inmate at a federal penitentiary. Hang up to decline the call, to accept dial 5 now."

I hit 5 then waited to hear his voice. I didn't want to get caught talking on the phone by the police so I slowed down and moved into the center lane.

When Charmaine saw my bright smile, she said, "That must be Sin!"

"Yes, it's my baby!"

I spoke seductively into the receiver, "Hey, Daddy!"

"What's happening, Bright Eyes?"

"I'm on our way back home from Foxwoods Casino."

"Foxwoods? The last time we spoke you were on your way out to eat with the girls."

"I did go eat! Charmaine spent the night and we decided to drive up to Foxwoods yesterday."

"Is she there with you now?"

"Yeah."

"Let me holla at her real quick?"

"Hold on; let me put you on speaker." I looked over at Charmaine, hit the speaker then said, "He wants to talk to you."

She purposely stretched out his name, "What's up, Siiiiin?"

"Chillin', what's good with you?"

"Taking it easy!" She imitated Wendy Williams, "So how you doing?"

He laughed. "I'm good. You guys have fun last night?"

"We had a ball! Guess who we ran into?"

"Who?"

"Your boy Mitch Seth!"

"Get the fuck out of here! I haven't seen him in a long time. How's he doing?"

"He's doing F.I.N.E! Misty gave him your information. He had us at a private party in the penthouse, drinking champagne with him and some of his teammates."

"I hope you didn't have my lady mixed up in any of your funny business," he teased.

"You know your lady has a mind of her own, and I, for your information, was on my best behavior, considering your boy Mitch was the one pushing up on me!"

"Get out of here, but that's a good look for you. He must be trying to have you rumbling with the head case."

We laughed. "That's what we said! He did say the next time he's in New York he was coming to take me to dinner. We left it at that, although I should have given him some play just to get some pay back for Jaz talking shit to Misty at the restaurant."

"Baby Girl?"

"Yeah, Daddy?"

"What did she say this time?"

"Nothing. She was making comments about stuff she don't know anything about."

His tone got serious. "What did she say, Misty?"

I didn't like telling him about the arguments we had because I didn't want him to totally hate her. Nevertheless, Charmaine had no problem with it, and before I could answer she butted in with her two cents in.

"She was talking shit about you, Misty loving you, and you being in there. She said you only love Misty now that you're in jail."

He sat quiet.

I hit her in her arm, and then mouthed, "Why you tell him that!"

I knew he felt a certain kind of way about the choices he made in the past, but it was too late to change them, and for that he felt culpable.

"I hope you checked her for me, Cha."

"I didn't need to! Your girl checked her! She handled her business and made me proud. She handed Jaz her ass on a platter! She told her to mind her fucking business and stop worrying about what's going on between her and her man!"

"That Jasmine is something else."

"She can't get past the fact that you bounced out and then had a kid with someone else. She's always trying to make Misty feel bad for that. Don't take it personal; she messes with all of us about something. I know she got one more time to come at me crossways."

"I don't appreciate her fucking with Misty; especially about my choices. I think I need to have a talk with her. Give her a chance to say directly to me whatever it is she needs to say."

"It's okay. I can handle her all by myself," I interjected.

"Nah, she dead wrong, boo! I didn't do everything right, but to question my feelings for you is way out of line."

"Well, maybe if you didn't go and have a baby with somebody else she wouldn't have the ammunition to use against me!"

All that could be heard after my comment was the engine purring in the car. I don't know where that came from, but it had already escaped my lips.

"You all right?"

"Don't pay her any mind, Sin. That's Jasmine talking."

His tone got firm. "How long before you get home, Misty?"

"About an hour."

"I'll call you back at 5:00. Answer your phone. Yo, Cha, as always it was nice talking with you, and take care."

"You too, and talk to you soon."

He immediately hung up. I knew he was pissed because he disconnected without saying anything to me. I knew better than to stress him out over such trivial matters. We had bigger fish to fry, but every now and again that green monster reared its ugly little head.

Charmaine muted the volume on the radio then looked over at me. "Misty, can I ask you a question?"

"Huh?"

"Why are you letting what Jasmine said get to you?"

"I don't know. Sometimes I get so frustrated with our situation, and I want to blame him."

"Do yourself a favor, and let it go. I haven't seen you this happy in years. I can remember that time when you were heartbroken. You lost your sparkle. It's only since Sin came back in your life the glow returned. I've seen what the power of love can do through you, and it's an inspiration to me. I applaud you for having the courage to follow your heart. I've always been more of the opportunist myself—really, a coward. I was too afraid to even try my hand at love. I didn't have the fortitude for all of that, but I am working on it. It's because of you two that I believe in love. Things are moving forward for you even if it's not at the place or pace you want them. You got your whole life ahead of you to figure it out."

She was right. Out of all the people in the world, he made me feel whole. Everything seemed meaninglessness without him. I literally felt dejected if I didn't hear from him for long periods of time. He loved me. He told me, he showed me, and I felt it. There was no question about that, but because he hurt me I was sometimes cautious. The physical abuse I suffered from Black was nothing to compare to the pain and despair I felt as a result of Sin's actions.

"It's amazing, Cha, how the same person who fills your heart with so much love can deflate it with one single blow. Like a pin to a balloon."

"Do you believe in him?"

"Of course I do! I wouldn't be bothered if I didn't."

"Then go with your heart, sis! We all have regrets and have made mistakes. I've made decisions I wish I could go back and change, but in the moment I did what I felt was best—the same thing you're doing now. When you set out to please yourself you often hurt others, but that's the price of self-gratification. You know I'm the first one to say fuck a nigga, but that would be a tragedy in this case. So when I say it's okay, it is okay!"

"Cha, sometimes I start to remember that pain, and all the negative emotions come back. I think about going through that all over again, and I become frightened. I panic. I can't love him a little bit. He's such a big part of me. With him it's all or nothing. I'm completely in and totally exposed. He has my heart and it's wrapped in a glass bow, which makes me vulnerable. Could you imagine?"

"At one time in my life, hell no! I couldn't picture being that wrapped up into anybody, but today I can. I'm looking forward to loving a man that much. You've shown me that two people can love each other without all the strings, grow old together, and be happy."

"I see myself spending the rest of my life with him, Cha, but what if things don't work out that way? What if we missed our window of opportunity?"

"He's a good man, and eventually something is going to have to give. The type of sentences those people gave him is inhumane. Yeah, some deserve to be exactly where they are for the rest of their lives—trust me I've dated a few—but not him. You have to have faith in yourself, in him, the lawyers, and over all, in God. Don't allow Jasmine, his child, her mother, Marcus or anyone else to interfere with that. Stay focused on the ultimate goal and make that your motivation."

"I'm just scared that he may never get out."

She smiled. "If he never gets out then you will just have to go in there and get him! You can still have him in your life, but in a different way. If you have faith in your heart there can't be room for fear. If you truly believe like you say in 'us,' then you need to support 'Him' while he works on a way back to 'You.' He can't put everything he's got into that if he's distracted with bullshit."

"Whose friend are you anyway, mine or his, Big Head?"

She laughed. "Both! It will work itself out. You'll see!"

"What do you think about me moving back in?"

"I think it would be a great idea! I miss having you around."

"You know I love you, right?"

"I love you too, sis!"

Charmaine laid back and listened to music until she dozed off. I used the time to reflect on the inspirational words she shared with me. I felt much better, and was now wondering how upset Sin was and what he was thinking.

I picked my car up from the garage and made my way home. Half hour after reaching my house the cell rang. I knew it was him.

"Hey, Daddy."

"You okay now?"

"Yeah, I'm good."

"Did you get that all out of your system?" he asked sarcastically.

I wearily replied, "Yeah."

"Are you sure? Because you don't sound like it."

"Yes, I'm sure! Charmaine gave me a good talking to, and I'm sorry for how I reacted."

"Good, because I'm not in the mood to be arguing with you over nothing."

"I did apologize."

"Yeah, you did, but you shouldn't have gone there in the first place. You know better. We're a strong front and we have to be on the same page at all times. I'm only entering into this conversation because I love you, and it's my job to make sure you don't have any uncertainties.

"You're either going to forgive me and trust, or you're going to give up and walk away. I made the decision to walk away once. I did what was in your best interest, and although we both know deep down it was the right thing to do, I still repeatedly apologized for it. I shouldn't be made to keep doing that. I'd take a bullet for you and die trying to save you, and I felt that was what I was doing then. I got a lot riding on things working out. There's enough bullshit happening around me every day, and I won't be stressed out in here unnecessarily."

"You can poke you chest back in, Mister Man. I heard you!"

He chuckled. "And I love you too! I don't want you to have doubts, Misty. Doubts are like a virus, and if we don't catch it early it will spread and kill everything we've built. You can't let anyone place doubt in your mind and have you questioning something you know to be fact. Especially someone you know deep down inside is envious of what you have. As for my daughter's mother, I told you before how we hooked up. What you and I share is nothing to compare—period and end of story. I keep it decent with her so we can have peace. I do what I have to in here to survive, and you're doing what have to do out there. Do I question you about your man?"

I sucked my teeth. "No."

"I don't because I don't want to put any added pressure on you. You don't think it bothers me knowing at night while I lay in a cold cell he's right there next to you with access to your warm body? You don't think it bothers me when I pick up the phone and call you, and you can't answer because you're with him? It bothers me, Misty! It bothers me you call his house your home, and it's him you go home to at night. There are a lot of things that bother me, but I'm a man, and I deal with the hand I've been dealt.

"I want you all to myself, Baby Girl, but I also don't want to be selfish. I want you to be my wife and bear my children. It bothers me that may never happen. I want you out of that man's house, but I don't tell you that because it wouldn't be fair. The choice has to be yours. As long as I know when I come home you'll jump into my arms, walk right out of whatever situation you are in, without any hesitation, and never look back, I'm good.

"I don't stress you because I know you're human and you have needs. I don't trip because no matter what you're doing out there on the physical level, I know your heart, mind, and soul belongs to me. You need to know when I get out it's you I'm coming for; you and no one else."

"What if I told you, Sin, my emotional needs trump any physical need? What if I told you I was ready to leave that man's house, understood the sacrifices I would be making, and was still willing to give it all up for us? What would you say then?"

"I would say I want you to really think about that over and over again because once we make that move there's no turning back! In here I still have control over three things, and that's my mind, my balls, and my heart, and I plan on keeping all of them intact. I'm hopeful yet petrified of failure. However, if I don't try then I will not succeed. If anyone can make a marriage in here work it would be you, and because I know the strength of your heart I am willing to discuss it. I love you that much."

"For real?" I smiled brightly. "I love you, Daddy! I guess I just needed some reassurance today."

"What you need is for me to spank that ass! Now give Daddy kisses!"

I puckered my lips up and made a loud kissing sound, "Uummaahhaa! So are you gonna take my panties down when you spank me?"

"See now, that's the shit I like to hear! That's the shit that gets my joint hard. I might have to get my man later as I visualize that bare ass bent down over my knee jiggling every time I slap it." He laughed. "Did you get my letter?"

"Yeah, I got it, but I didn't finish reading it yet."

"Let me find out Daddy isn't important anymore. I asked you to come see me, you haven't gotten here yet, and now you're treating my letter like second-class mail?"

"Cut it out. It will never be that! I started reading it, but you had some freaky stuff in there that I preferred to read alone. I want to get my girl later." I giggled.

*Click.*

"Ugh!" I yelled into the phone when I realized it went dead.

I hate that damn 15-minute time limit. As soon as you get good into the conversation—*bang*—the damn phone hangs up!

I unpacked, showered, and made something to eat. I had a big week ahead of me. I was going to be meeting with a major client who was looking to buy a house, and I was determined to close the deal. The commission was going to look nice in my bank account, and the deal had to the potential to turn into something that was advantageous.

I pulled out Sin's letter and began reading.

*Misty,*

*I received your card, pictures, and letter today, as well as the copies of the documents I requested. Thanks, baby! Hearing from you is hands down the best part of my day. I just got out of the shower, and I'm laying here with my feet crossed, relaxing, listening to some music, and looking at your pictures. Damn, you look good! Looking at these visuals got me thinking of all kinds of depraved sex acts. I feel like I'm being tortured. If they don't let me out or you up in here soon, I think I'm going to die! I know you feel me. All I need is one hour with my baby and I'd make that shit last forever.*

*What I wouldn't have given to be the one behind the lens of the camera clicking these sexy images. They could later serve as evidence of motive in my 1st degree murder trial, because I'd definitely be catching a body for killing that pussy! If I could jump into one of these pictures I'd wrap you up in my arms and get lost in the beauty of your eyes and the intoxication of your smile.*

*Feeling the heat from your skin would make me want to head straight for those juicy lips for a taste of your tongue. See, now I'm getting hard. I'm visualizing your face, and how those sexy eyes would be looking up at me as this big dick grew hard and inched up your tight stomach.*

*I wouldn't be able to resist lifting you into the air and lowering you down on my hardness. I'd grip that luscious ass, part that Kitty Cat then pump you so full of this Sin Stick until it's completely coated. Then I'd bend you over the closest thing I could find, slide it deep inside from the back,* and hit it until you're in a state of confusion. I'd have you crying for me to stop and begging for more all in the same breath (LOL).

Do you know how I would fuck the shit out you right now? This dick is a monster! There's no way you can't tell me this shit hasn't gotten bigger since I've been down. For real, this shit is so big we might not be able to get it out once we get it in. They may have to throw cold water on us like they do dogs that are stuck together.

All this talk about fucking got my shit standing up at full attention. Since I'm not going to be able to bust off and write at the same time, so I'm going to enjoy the rest of this experience with you on my mind. I'm sure this nut will be incredible thanks to you.


P.S. I jotted down some reasons why I love you and decided to share them with you. I'll call you tomorrow.



Love you 4-ever & a day,
Garret (Sin) Butler

# WHY I LOVE YOU!

I love you because you complement me in ways that make me strong.

I love you because you make me laugh in the midst of an environment that makes a grown man want to cry.

I love you because I truly believe your love was a divine gift given to me straight from God.

I love you because after all this time you still have faith in me, and in us.

I love you because I know without a doubt you got my back.

I love you because you have made it possible for me to know what truly being loved feels like.

I love you because you stood by my side not only in the warm, glowing sun, but in those coldest, darkest hours.

I love you because you are kind, gentle, and considerate. My happiness brings you joy.

I love you because I can comfortably say these things and know I won't appear weak or be judged.

I love you because you bring out the best in me!

These are just a few reasons why I love you!

# CHAPTER 10

## *Black Rain*

I walked into the office on Monday morning and was greeted by my assistant Stephanie. Three years ago she walked into my office and asked if I need clerical help. Her resume was bare; however, after she offered to work for free to gain some experience, I agreed and ended up hiring her after two weeks. I found her to be a diligent worker. She came in early and never complained if she needed to stay late. She was a fast learner and very humble. We instantly hit it off, and she turned out to be a great asset. She recently obtained her real estate license and would be working directly with me on my next contract.

I came in to look over the file for my meeting with Jeremy Whittaker of Introntel. This contract had the potential to turn into so much more. I sat at my desk, unlocked the drawer, and inside hidden in the back was a folder containing some pictures. I had buried years of memories in the back of my desk. I had pictures of Sin and me at parties, on vacations, or just hanging out. I picked up a handful of the photos and reminisced. As I looked at the images I admired how nice we looked together. One picture in particular drew my attention. We had taken it back in the 90's at a party in the Ramada in New Jersey. We took it right after we had sex outside on top of a car. I smiled and thought back to that warm September night.

Jasmine, Charmaine, and I decided to go to the private party at the hotel. I was still dealing with Black and sneaking around with Sin. The last time we spoke, Black told me he wouldn't be back from Texas for another week. When I spoke to Sin that morning he said he would be returning in a day or two. Sin and I had been dating for four months, and the big question my girls kept asking was what I planned to do about Black. I knew what I wanted to do, but wasn't sure how to go about it. Financially, he was taking great care of me. He gave me an allowance as well as paid my tuition and car note. It was hard to walk away from that. In addition he left me with a lot of idle time; which I gladly spent with Sin. Just two weeks prior to this party, Charmaine, Nickelle, Trey, and I had moved into the brownstone on 134th Street & St. Nicolas, and Black didn't even know about it.

Sin and some of his boys helped us move. Since I was technically still Black's girl, Sin didn't offer and I didn't ask him, so the move put a big dent in my savings. Back then I wasn't only taking care of myself, but Nickelle and Trey as well, which meant I had to buy three bedroom sets. My goal was to stash some cash before I left Black's ass!

Sin didn't sweat the fact that I was still dealing with Black, but I knew he didn't like it. I saw the effect it started to have on him right after he went with me to get the bedroom sets. There was this really nice set I couldn't afford. Sin started to tell the salesperson he would pay the difference, but stopped himself and walked out the store.

I asked him in the car what that was all about and he admitted he had to catch himself. He said he wasn't about to spend no money on a bed the next man was gonna be lying in.

Shortly after that he began to distance himself from me, and I took notice. It was hard not to since he was so on point at first. He suddenly started to not show up after saying he was coming over. He wasn't returning my calls as fast, and he even had the nerve to excuse himself from dinner one night to call someone back. My intuition told me it was a female, and I was heated, but refrained from commenting.

We had an understanding, but somewhere along the line we both caught feelings. What started out as a summer fling quickly turned into a steamy love affair. We remained in the trenches, too afraid to pop our heads up out the foxhole. We were afraid to admit our true feelings. I knew the day I gave myself to him it was more than just a fuck for me. I was long over Black, but was playing it safe because I wasn't sure of Sin's intentions. He would never tell the next man's woman how he really felt about her. He was too macho for that. Plus he still had a girl in D.C.

Sin took me to nice places, and he did thoughtful things like buying me a leather binder and Gucci book bag for school. He was not however taking care of me, taking me shopping, or giving me cash. He made it clear he was no trick, and he stuck to his rule! I didn't bother to try my luck. In part that's why I continued to see them both. Black was handling the financial aspect, and giving me money like I was on his payroll. Every two weeks like clockwork money was dropped off. The only problem was sometimes he brought it to NY himself and then wanted to have sex. I had no intention of ever sleeping with him again, and when he tried I made up excuses. I told him I was still mad, I heard he was messing with some girl, the baby with Tamika, and if that didn't work, I said it was that time of the month. I even wore sanitary napkins so he wouldn't try to get some.

With Sin it didn't matter if he gave me large sums of money or bought me things. He knew what he was doing when he spent all that time with me. He was setting me up to fall in love. Many nights he would pick me up on his bike and take me for a ride upstate. He would find a scenic location, pull over, and park. We'd walk, talk, then sit and watch the sunrise. He'd show up at my school or send flowers to my job with sexy notes. It was those small things that made me fall for him.

On this night I decided to go out with the girls. I had been flaking out on them, and they were starting to complain that I was spending all my free time with Sin. Upon entering the party Jasmine spotted Black.

"Ah, Misty, did you know Black was in town?"

When I looked in the direction she was pointing, sure enough there was Black in all his glory surrounded by his dirty cronies. They were drinking champagne out the bottles and pouring it on girls. He was laughing and acting his normal boastful self.

"Obviously he's drunk. I'm getting up out of here before he sees me. I'm not in the mood to be around his stupid ass! He's such a fucking liar. He told me he wasn't coming back until next week."

Just as we turned toward the door to leave, Sin came walking in with his boys. "Oh shit, Sin!" I was smack dab in between the both of them. "I got to get the hell up out of here before shit hits the fan!"

Black spotted me and sent his friend Sidney over to get me. Sin hadn't seen me yet, so I walked over to Black. I could use the fact that he lied to my advantage.

I gave him much attitude. "What you calling me over here for!"

"What's the matter with you?"

"You told me you weren't coming back to New York until next week, and here I find you in Jersey at a party!"

He thought he was going to sneak up to New York and bring his side chick and her friend without me finding out. I knew off the rip which of the two girls he was fucking. She was the one who kept looking over at me with an attitude.

He tried to talk low. "At the last minute my boys was flying up for this party and I decided to roll. I was going to call you."

I pointed in his face. "So why didn't you?"

"I was going to when I left here," he said, smiling through lying teeth.

I noticed Sin looking over in my direction.

"You are so full of shit! The only way you would have called me tonight is if you couldn't get one of these skeezers to leave with you." I smirked then looked over at her. "But that won't be the case since you imported your own ho tonight. I just hope you're ready when it catches up to you."

Instead of causing a scene, I walked away from him. "Have fun, Black, because like a half-fare bus pass . . . your time is limited!"

He was so out of it he didn't even try to protest. He yelled back at me, "I'm going to page you when I leave here, and you better call me right back!"

I yelled back over my shoulder, "Don't bother to call with your slick ass. I'll be busy," I laughed, "And make sure you use a condom this time, asshole!"

He should have known something was wrong right there. The old Misty would have cursed him out and made him leave. Not anymore. I headed toward the door. When I reached where Sin was standing he had a slick grin on his face. He had watched the whole exchange.

He grabbed my hand on the low. "What's up for tonight, sexy?"

I lustfully looked at him then sucked my bottom lip. "What you got in mind, handsome?"

"You tell me. Your man's over there?"

"No, my man is right here!" I inconspicuously rubbed my hand that he was still holding across his crotch.

"Let's go outside," he suggested.

I told the girls I would be back then walked outside into the block-long parking lot. The parking lot sat in between two hotels and was lined with rows of trees. The night was calm and warm, and although the temperature was in the mid 80's you could feel the moisture in the air. We walked through the parking lot toward the middle where we could have some privacy. I selected a random car to prop up against. I could see the balconies of the hotel between the branches, but the trees prevented the guests from looking down on us. Sin pressed himself into me and tried to kiss me. I gave him my cheek.

He held my hands. "What's up with that? Daddy can't get no sugar?"

I brought my face up to his and gave him a gentle kiss on the lips. After studying his eyes, I broke the silence.

"What's happening with us, Sin? You've been acting different lately."

"What are you talking about? We're good." He read my body language and knew I was looking for more. "We're cool, Misty. I've been busy, on my grind, and trying to get that paper."

"I think it's more than that, Sin. What's up with the no-shows? You tell me you're coming over and then don't come. You may not know it, but I sit up and wait for you. I get worried. That's real inconsiderate, you know. You could call. How come you told me you were coming back in two days, but you're here?" I was now wondering if he was no better than Black. He could see the disappointment in my face as I lowered my eyes.

He picked my face up by my chin. "Don't do that to me. Don't give me that face. My plans were to be back in two days, but I was able to get somebody to take care of some things for me. Maybe if your butt was at home, instead of here, you would have known I was trying to see you tonight. I even left a message on your machine, and you know I don't do that! Where's your pager?"

My face lit up. "You left me a message?"

"What difference does it make what I'm doing? You look like you were chillin' with your boy." He leaned his back onto the driver's window, folded his arms across his chest, and remained stone-faced.

I went in my bag and handed him my pager. "The battery is dead, and I did not come here with him. I only got here a few minutes before you walked in, and would have left if you didn't stop me. I'm tired, and I'm ready to move on."

I decided to ask the question that had been weighing heavily on my mind. The question if asked to soon in a relationship could scare someone off. I took a deep breath. "Are we going somewhere with this relationship? I mean, are you really cool with the way things are between us?"

I paused and gave him a chance to think before I continued.

"You asked me to always be honest with you. The truth is, I didn't mean to, but I've fallen hard for you. I didn't question you about it before, but you've been spotted on occasions in some questionable situations. You said you had someone in D.C., but I'm hearing about you and females in New York. I'm caught up, but I can get my feelings in proper perspective if I have to. I need to know what's on your mind."

He smiled. "So you're feeling a brother like that?"

I blushed and his smile grew bright.

"Don't act like you don't know how I feel about you, Sin. I call you Daddy. I got a lot to lose messing with you, and I could get seriously hurt in more ways than one."

He pushed himself off the car then stood in front of me and smiled. "I'm really digging you too, shorty. You don't have to worry about me playing with your feelings. Since we started messing with each other I've always been up front with you about the way I move. If we had nothing else then I wanted us to have that honesty thing between us. As far as these little sightings you're referring to, it's no secret I have lots of friends. Talking to a female doesn't mean I'm sleeping with her. These hoes don't mean shit to me, and they would never come between us unless you let them. I do a lot of moving around, and there's no telling where I might be from day to day, but it feels like I'm home when I'm here with you. When I'm in town I spend my time with you. Want to know why?"

"Yeah, why?"

"Because you're special to me, and I enjoy your company."

I cheered up. "You do?"

"Yeah, Bright Eyes, I do! I have to fall back sometimes and check myself because you're not mine. You have a man. If you're telling me you ready to leave him, that's a different story. We'll need to discuss that. Just because you're ready to leave doesn't mean he's going to be ready to let you. Anytime you allow a man to take care of you on the level he is, he may feel like he owns you. You're right; you do have a lot to lose. You never know how he's going to react once his pride and ego are hurt."

"I am ready. I just need to tie up some loose ends."

"Well, make it happen if that's what you want to do. What I got going on with you is not my style. It's dangerous, unnecessary, and potentially bad for business. The truth is, I'm taking the kind of risks I don't normally take dealing with you. I would hate to be put in a position to have to pop that nigga's top over his girl! You've been saying you leaving him for a while now. Just know he's not just gonna let you just walk away as long as you're sleeping with him and taking his money. When you're actually ready to leave that alone, let me know. I'll give you your time to keep fucking, I mean to tie up your loose ends, and in the meantime I'll continue to do me."

His last comment pissed me off. I placed my hands on my hip then rolled my eyes. "For your information, I haven't fucked Black since I started sleeping with you! Maybe I should just start off fresh and stop messing with the both of you! It seems like the only thing you two are concerned with, is doing you!" I began to walk away.

He ran up behind me and playfully wrapped his arms around by body then picked me up.

"You must be crazy if you think I'm letting you go anywhere! That's my pussy now, and I'm never gonna stop hitting that! You better not give him any if you're smart. Once he get up in that Kitty Cat he's gonna know somebody been in it, remodeled, and upgraded the spot." He laughed.

"There isn't enough hot baths with Epsom salts for me to hide the presence of that big-ass dick of yours." I giggled. "And we have been fucking like rabbits."

He kissed me. "Don't worry, I got you. Do what you need to do, and we can make it happen."

The long, sleeveless dress I wore that night had two long splits running up the legs, exposing the front of my thighs. The dress also had a plunging neckline, which hung low, showing cleavage. He placed me down on my feet then rested his hands around my waist. I tongued him down.

As I pulled away he held me then asked, "What color panties do you have on?"

"Stop playing. I'm trying to be serious here. What about your girl?"

"I'm dead serious, and don't worry about her. When you figure out what you gonna do then we can discuss her. What's the color?"

"I'm not wearing any."

"Say word! Let me see," he demanded, pulling at the material. He bent down and tried to pull the material between the two splits up so he could get a peek.

I pushed the material back down and leaned back on the side of the hood. He stepped up, pinned his body up against mine, and started kissing me. I could feel his dick getting hard.

"Stop, you know I can't take that thing rubbing up against me," I teased.

Kissing down my neck he whispered, "If you want me to stop then let me see if you have on panties."

I chuckled. "I was only playing! I have on panties."

He tried to run his hand between my thighs, but I squeezed and shut them then grabbed his wrist with my two hands.

"What color are they?"

I could hear the sky rumbling above, and it was about to rain.

"Okay, I'll let you have a peek if you move your hand."

He agreed and took two steps backwards. I parted my legs, lifted the front flap, and raised the material enough for him to see the pastel pink lace panties. He reached to touch my Kitty Cat, but I hurriedly dropped the flap then closed the split. He lifted me up, sat me on the hood, and then stood between my legs. He slowly ran his thumb down my breast. He knew I had super sensitive nipples, and that was the easiest way to get me wet. He tried again to slide his hand between my legs. "Come on, you know you want me to touch it."

I playfully swatted his hand away. "Nope!" My feet dangled along with side of the front tire. He tried again. "What do you think you're doing, Sin?" I asked, hitting his hand away. My shoe fell off.

He replied with a sinister grin, as he pulled the other shoe off, "I wanna see if you're wet."

I honestly tried to stop him, but he was determined, and I was beginning to get turned on. He managed to get his hand between my legs and his fingers into my panties.

"Stop before someone comes and sees us."

"I don't care! It's mine! You see, boo, the Kitty is wet! Let me play with her."

His fingers touching my clit were turning me on. It started to feel good, but I squeezed my thighs together on his hand. "You have to stop!"

We both knew I was only playing hard to get, which made him want it even more. He pulled his hand out of my panties then smirked. "Okay, now take them off. I want to smell them."

"What! Are you some kind of freak? Get out of here! I'm not giving you my panties!"

His body was wedged in between my legs, and he wouldn't budge. He unbuckled his belt then unzipped his pants.

"You need to cut it out, Sin. I told you I wasn't giving you my panties!"

He winked. "I thought about it, and I don't want your panties anymore. You got my joint hard, so now you gonna give me some pussy!"

I waved my hand at him. "You had a better shot at smelling the panties."

"I'll put money on me fucking the shit out of you right here on top this car!"

I took the bet since I knew I wasn't giving it up, but was interesting in seeing him try. It started slightly drizzling, but the leaves from the trees were blocking most of the drops.

"What if you don't get the Kitty? What do I get out of it?"

"We can do whatever you want tomorrow." This was his way of indirectly keeping me away from Black. "But if I win, after I fuck the shit out of you, you're gonna give up those panties, and I want some head later!"

I hadn't done that to him yet, but secretly wanted to. I thought about it. "You did say anything I want to do tomorrow, right?"

"Yeah, anything."

"Okay, you got yourself a bet!"

I figured as long as I remained seated on the hood of the car he couldn't get it. Wrong! He kept his body between my legs then pulled my torso into his. He held my back tight then picked me up off the car. He bent his knee and leaned my body backwards, causing my legs to fly up in the air. I gripped my arms around his neck to stop myself from falling backwards. He then swung my legs over his arm and used his free hand to snake up my dress and inch my panties down my ass. Once the panties were at the middle of my thigh he laid me back on top the hood.

"Okay, you've proven your point. Now let me up before someone reports us."

"Let them!"

"Come on, stop. What if someone from the party sees us?"

He ignored my last question. I tried to lift up, but he used his one hand to hold me down while the other tugged two more times on each side before the thong was completely off. He smiled as he twirled it around his pointer finger. He leaned down and gently kissed me. He lowered the top of my dress, pulled my breasts out of my bra, pushed them together, and slowly ran his tongue back and forth over the nipples.

"Why are you giving Daddy such a hard time, Misty? You must have missed me."

I moaned. "You know I did."

He continued to suck my breast as the drizzle pierced through the branches and droplets fell on us.

He smiled. "I know you did, because I missed you too."

His upper body weight had my back pinned to the hood as my legs dangled off the side panel. His kisses were sweet and I stopped pretending to fight. It was on! I wrapped my legs around his back as the drizzle turned into a light rain. Our soft kisses became more intense, and I clawed at his lower back.

"Put it in, Daddy. Give it to me."

He hurriedly pulled his pants down until they fell around his knees. I wanted him inside of me, outside in the rain, on top of that car, and really didn't care who saw us. He placed the back of my knee in the creases of his arms, pulled me into him, and without hesitation buried himself inside of me. We both moaned and the relief was like cold water to hot coals.

We always used condoms. During a discussion he said chicks were trifling, looking for a payday, and would try to use a kid to trap him off. I personally didn't care who the father was or how much he had to give; I wasn't ready for a baby. Every single time I had sex with Black we used condoms. It was my mother's desire that I be married before I had children, and I wanted to grant her that wish in death. That night we threw caution to wind.

I was fighting myself to tell him to pull out, but the natural feeling of our bodies was so much better than the latex condoms. Feeling his shaft stroking in and out of me, mixed with my body fluids, was out of this world. I stopped debating with myself, wrapped my legs tighter around his waist, and let him have his way with me.

I could hear voices. It was Black and his entourage leaving the hotel. Sin and I were too far off in the distance for them to see us, and too far into things to stop. I braced my feet on the other car and he stroked deeper in me. We fucked like we were in the house and didn't stop until he blasted off.

"Yeah motherfucker, take this pussy!"

He pulled me off the car then had me turn around. He lifted my dress, bent me over the hood, then slowly inched himself back into me. Over time and with each stroke, my body had become acclimated to his size, and I was now able to take more of him in.

"Take this dick!" He braced his palm on the hood, gripped me up by my waist, and pressed his body into mine. My torso slid back and forth as he pumped and grinded. He worked himself up, and pulled out right before he came. He jerked his dick and his load shot out like a rocket onto the ground.

His legs seemed wobbly as he pulled his pants up to his thighs. He gave me the juiciest kiss then pulled his shirt over his head. We used his undershirt to clean ourselves up. He threw the undershirt under the car, buckled his pants, and put the polo back on. I stepped into my thong.

We hadn't realized while we were fucking it had started raining hard and our clothes and my hair were wet. I smoothed the lose strands back so it could look neat, but I needed a restroom in the worst way. Sin wanted to just break out, but I wanted to let my girls know I was leaving. As we began to walk back to the hotel Sin stopped. "Wait, aren't you forgetting something?"

I looked back at the top of the car, "No, I got everything."

He pointed down between my legs. "Pass me the panties."

"Are you serious?"

He wore a stupid Kool-Aid smile. "Did I or did I not fuck the shit out of you on top of that car? A deal is a deal."

I grinned. "You did, and the dick was extra good too!" I went under my dress, pulled the panties down, and stepped out of them. I gave him a quick kiss before handed them to him.

He stuck them in his pocket. "I might have made a big mistake hitting that raw. The pussy felt so good it make me wanna cut that nigga Black off for you," he joked.

Upon locating the girls, Charmaine informed me that Black was asking where I was, but she told him I left. I told her I was breaking out and was spending the night with Sin. As we were leaving the lobby I noticed a man taking pictures for $5.00. I asked Sin if he would take one with me and to my surprise he did. As we cruised out of the parking lot I said, "I know we should have used protection, but do you think we can do that just one more time, but in slow motion? That dick felt so good, Daddy."

He threw the car in gear then grinned. "Sure, but only after you finish paying off your debt."

"What debt?"

"What, you forgot already? You owe me some head."

He noticed I turned red. "Don't worry, Baby Girl. Daddy's gonna show you how to make love with your mouth, then I'm gonna give it to you as slow as you want for as long as you can take it."

He took me to his condo in New Jersey and I spent the next two nights with him. Something was different; it felt like he was making love to me. He held me tight, worked it slow, and didn't use a condom the whole weekend. Although I lost the bet, the next day he treated me to the spa and dinner. I remember the events surrounding that night because I almost got busted.

Black's man happened to be leaving the restaurant as Sin and I were coming in. He immediately called Black and reported he saw us together. Black had been trying to reach me the after the party, but I wasn't returning his calls. At some point that day he must have gone back to Texas because he started paging me from a 214 area code. I was having so much fun with Sin I figured I would deal with Black another time.

Black knew exactly who Sin was. If you were in the streets you had at least heard his name or about his wild-ass crew's antics. Everyone knew he was getting mad paper and was not to be fucked with. They didn't know each other personally, but Black knew Sin was an official nigga.

The same way the key players knew Black was a liability. He was loud, obnoxious, flashy, and grimy. He would bully people out of their work and then take his time paying them back, if he did at all. He was making a name as a shady businessman. Sin was on a completely different caliber of person. He was amongst New York City's elite group of hustlers who had successfully achieved five-star dining.

I knew he had money, but had no idea just how much. I later found out after he was locked up that by the time we had started dating he was a millionaire a few times over. He was one of the few who were smart enough to invest and have an exit plan.

Black's mentality was "Ball till you fall!" He loved to be in the spotlight and wanted nothing more than to be the man. From the outside looking in you would have thought he was getting it, but the truth was he was nothing more than a block boy, spending it as he got it. His plans consisted of which club he would go to, how many bottles he would pop, and what farce he would front. He had a few dudes on the block slinging rock for him, but his money was a piggy bank compared to Sin's vault.

I could hear the rage in Black's voice when I finally called him back. "Why the hell you ain't answering any of my calls?"

My stomach flipped. I got scared, but played it cool. I wasn't about to confess to anything. "Call you back? For what? So you can lie about that girl you brought to the party?"

"Don't worry about that bitch! What the fuck is up with this shit I'm hearing about you and Sin? What the fuck is going on between you and that nigga?"

"What you hear?"

"Don't be fucking cute with me! My man told me he saw you and that nigga in One Fish Two Fish together!"

"Who told you that? I was at restaurant, but I wasn't with Sin. I was with Charmaine and Nick."

"Yo, Misty, don't fucking play with me! This ain't the first motherfucking time I heard some shit about you and him. My man said he saw you two walking in together. I know you ain't playing yourself because I'll kick your fucking ass!"

"I saw him there, but we weren't together. I went outside to put change in the meter and happened to see him on my way in. We had our own table before him and his wild-ass boys walked in the door." I threw that in there so he would know that I knew what time it was. He sat quiet and analyzed what I said.

"I'm going to look into this, but I swear if I find out anything different from what you told me on my unborn children I'm gonna beat fire out your ass!"

"Don't you mean unborn child, cheater? That's who you need to be worrying about. Isn't she about due? Either way if you don't believe me go ask Charmaine. Better yet, why don't you ask Sin?"

"Misty I will send somebody over there and when you look through the peephole they'll put a bullet in your brain!"

"I'm tired of you threatening me, Black. I'm tired of you putting your hands on me, and so tired of you fucking around! I'm done! I'm leaving you. You can keep on with your shenanigans because two can play this game, but understand I'm playing for keeps."

He was mad, but hearing me say I was leaving quieted him down. I could hear a female's voice in the background. "Listen, I got to go take care of some business, but I'm coming back tomorrow. We can talk then." He abruptly hung up in my ear.

As soon as I hung up with him I called Charmaine to make sure we had our stories straight. He was slick and I wouldn't put it past him to call her. I also called Sin to give him a heads up that Black had questioned me about him.

His question was icy cold. "So what you gonna do?"

"I am not going to do anything? I told him it wasn't true."

He got an attitude. "So what are you telling me for?"

"So you would know!"

"Nah, you're telling me just in case he starts asking questions. I thought you said you were ready to leave him?" He paused. "You know what? I'll go along with this little game you got going on. You won't have to worry about me blowing up your spot. It's not like he'll step to me anyway. He's neither stupid nor crazy." His saying game made it appear as if the last four months with him weren't special to me. Like what we were doing didn't mean anything; like it wasn't real.

"This is not a game to me, Sin! I just thought it would be best to let you know!"

You could hear the sarcasm drip from his tongue. "I got your message loud and clear, and I'm busy so I'll holla at you another time."

*Click.*

He didn't return my pages or messages for two weeks. I was being punished, and the change in him was for the worse. He started acting real carefree with other females in public and spending a lot of time out of town. When he was in New York he was partying and didn't have time for me. The fact that Black was on my heels put a damper on my flow. Black made me attend a function with him and I had it sit all night watching female's up in Sin faces, him taking numbers, or letting someone grind their ass on him while they danced. He was purposely doing shit in my face, pushing my buttons, and it was working!

I couldn't get close because Black had all of eyes on me and was up underneath me for the two weeks he was home. I had to stay at my father's place seeing that Black still thought I lived there. The fool actually tried to blackmail me into giving him some pussy before he left to go back to Texas.

"I don't care if you're mad. If you don't give me some, I'm not paying your tuition!"

Little did he know my tuition was already paid! I told him I didn't want to be with him anymore, and he flipped out then chocked me out. When he calmed down and tried to say sorry and kiss me I damn near threw up all over him. I lied and said I didn't feel well, but in truth he made me sick.

I was happy to see him go back to Texas because it gave me the time I needed to get back in Sin's good graces as well as get him back in line. He felt he didn't need to use discretion because I was Black's girl. At the same time he couldn't take it when he saw another man trying to get with me. It was my turn to push his buttons. I'd flirt right in his face. Initially he acted as if it didn't bother him, but his act came to an abrupt halt when one of his boys from out of town seriously tried to push up. Checkmate, and by the end of that night we were leaving together. Our friends teased and said we were junkies for each other because we just couldn't stay away for long.

From the time I moved into my own place Sin and I were going at it hard. He had clothes at my house, underclothes in my drawer, and a toothbrush in my bathroom. The physical relationship still had its magic, but the emotional connection was taking a severe beating. The obstacles were becoming too big to ignore, and as the weeks progressed he backed off more and more. He was doing a lot of partying and drinking, which didn't suit him well because it made him loose. With the amount of females coming at him I could feel him slipping further and further out of my grasp.

It started becoming an ongoing project for me to keep his ass in line, especially since we were still hiding the fact that we were together in public. Some serious action had to be taken otherwise I was going to lose him. I finally took matters into my own hands and solidified my place in his life.

I placed the pictures back in their hiding place and pulled out a legal pad and began writing down all the things I needed to address this week. I jotted down five things and first on the list was book a flight to Arizona. Sin had asked me to come see him and I had yet to get the ticket. I needed to feel his warm kiss upon my lips just as bad as he needed mine. What I wouldn't give for a conjugal. In some state facilities like California, Connecticut, Mississippi, New Mexico, New York, and Washington, if the inmate is married, they permit conjugal visits, but not in the Feds.

I don't understand why a petition for conjugal visits in federal facilities hasn't been signed off on. Federal inmates are doing long sentences, and in the majority of cases are based in a state where they don't have family to receive a weekly or monthly visit. With proper policy, regulations, and restrictions I think it could be instituted. I knew Sin would give anything to be wrapped in my embrace for a weekend.

There would be an incentive for inmates to comply with the rules and avoid infringement. They wouldn't want to lose their privileges. You wouldn't hear a peep out of Sin if he could have some of this every now and again. Shit, they wouldn't hear a peep out of 90% of the eligible inmates. Who would screw up something that would assist them in maintaining a family connection, ease tension, and probably reduce some of the sexually deviant behavior that's going on around them?

# CHAPTER 11

## Work, Work, Work

On this particular Tuesday morning it was more hectic than usual getting into Manhattan. I figured some political figure might have been in town. The melee of school buses, garbage trucks, pedestrians, and delivery trucks brought traffic to a crawl. It would normally take me less than thirty minutes from my house, but today it was an hour-long commute from hell. By the time I got to my meeting my skirt was twisted and half of my lipstick was gone.

My client, Jeremy Whittaker was a powerful businessman, who owned a few internet-based businesses, and had a net worth well over $100 million. My brokerage firm was being given the opportunity to purchase a house for his soon-to-be ex-wife. One of the divorce stipulations mandated Jeremy to purchase a home for her and the children since he refused to give her one of the residences he already owned. The couple had only been married for three years, but with the birth of their two sons and no prenuptial agreement, she was looking forward to a hefty settlement. She had retained one of New York's best divorce attorneys, and Jeremy was advised by his lawyer to make an offer before it got ugly.

I sat in my car for a few minutes freshening up my makeup. I opted to wear a blue pinstriped suit, three and a half inch pumps, and a white blouse. My hair was swept up and held by a large hair clip. I looked smart yet sexy; which was the look I was going for. I had met Jeremy a few times over the years and felt comfortable going into the meeting. I quickly ran over the advice Sin gave me. I could hear his voice in my head saying, "You can do it, Baby Girl!" I was ready.

I pushed open the glass doors of Jeremy's office and was greeted by a little woman with a friendly face. "Good Morning, may I help you?"

"Yes, my name is Misty Bishop, and I have a meeting with Mr. Whittaker."

"Of course. He's expecting you."

She turned to the intercom and advised Jeremy that I had arrived. I heard his baritone voice reply, "Send her in!"

As soon as I entered his office he rose from behind a long computer desk, came around, and extended his hand. He stood six feet tall and weighed about two hundred and fifty pounds. He was a large Caucasian man with skin the color of vanilla with a tint of pink around the cheeks. His wore his dirty blond hair finger combed back, and unlike most businessmen clad in a three-piece suit, Jeremy sported a wrinkled blue collared shirt, blue jeans, and rundown tennis shoes.

His stature was of a football player although he never played a sport in his life. He was a computer geek, and well connected. He was definitely a person you wanted to have as an ally. I looked around and could tell he spent a lot of time in his office. On top of the black desk were three 30-inch monitors, empty soda cans, takeout containers, candy wrappers, and an ashtray spilling over with cigarette butts. He had an expensive leather sofa, but thrown on it were a pillow and blanket.

"Welcome, Misty. It's nice seeing you again!"

I reached for his hand. "The pleasure is all mine."

He escorted me to the other side of the room, where he had a beautifully hand carved mahogany desk. On it was a picture of his sons, a Montblanc fountain pen, notepad, a 27-inch monitor, and two thick books held by a set of bronze *The Thinker* bookends. We chatted about business then family, which eventually led to us getting down to the nitty-gritty.

"So I understand you're in the market to purchase a new home?"

"I wouldn't call it that. I'm in the market to buy a house for that kleptomaniac ex-wife of mine. Have you ever heard of someone stealing from their own home?"

I laughed and he shook his head.

"I'll give it three months before my paintings pop up. She'll be in jail and I'll get custody." He went into his desk and pulled out a folder then tossed it across the desk. It contained the divorce settlement. "I'm being ordered to purchase her a house, and I don't like it one bit."

"What type of house and price range are we talking about?

"Moderate. I don't want her to have anything too excessive, just enough to keep her quiet. When I met her she had nothing, and now I'm being told I have to keep her in a certain kind of lifestyle. Isn't that something?"

I could tell he was becoming upset. I picked up the folder and began scanning through the documents. Based on the language of the contract, he was required to maintain a residence for his children.

"Did your lawyer tell you that you had to purchase a house for her or maintain a residence for the children?"

"What's the difference?"

"The terms of the contract, as I interpret them, state you must maintain residence for your children; that does not mean buy her a house. You can buy the house in your name and allow her and the children to reside there. Nowhere in this contract does it state the house must be purchased in her name or for her."

He reached over the desk and grabbed the folder out of my hand.

"Let me see that!" He read the line then instantly picked up his phone. He told his receptionist to get his attorney, Ian Davenport, on the phone. He needed to verify the terms. Two minutes later the receptionist announced that she had him on the line. "Hey, Ian. How's it going?"

I had been told that Ian was one of the coolest Jewish people you could meet. He grew up in Brooklyn, loved Jay-Z's music, and knew his way around the law. I'd never personally met him, but I'd heard a lot of good things about him.

He sounded congested and spoke in a nasal tone, "What can I do for you, Jeremy?"

"I'm here in my office with Misty Bishop of B&B Real Estate."

"Hello, Misty."

"Hi, Ian."

"Misty's company is going to be handling the purchasing of the house for the divorce settlement. She just pointed out that the contract does not state the house has to be purchased in Trisha's name. Is that true?"

We could hear him shuffling papers back and forth for a minute or two. "She's right! A small oversight we will be taking advantage of. The contract states you have to maintain residence, but it does not detail whose name the house must be in."

A huge smile spread across Jeremy's face, and he beamed like a kid who won first place and was just handed a big prize. "So you're saying I can purchase the house in my name?"

"Yes, that is what I'm telling you. But if I were you, I would play it safe and purchase the house in your name and list the children as the second owners."

Jeremy came around the desk and grabbed me out my chair and swung me around. "Misty, you're the best!"

Ian was still on speakerphone. He called out my name as I fixed my suit.

"Yes, I'm here, Ian."

"Maybe you should look into a career change. I think you may have a future in law. My company can always sponsor you."

"I handle contracts, and I know a little something about reading the fine print, but that's as good as it gets. Thanks for the offer, and I will keep that in mind if I ever decide to try my hand at law." They completed the call and hung up.

"Misty, this is superb! I owe you big time for this!"

I smiled. "Well, when you're ready to move your headquarters, keep my company in mind to broker that deal."

"I certainly will!"

Jeremy explained what he was trying to accomplish and the size of the space he would need to do it. He then gave me his accountant and attorney's contact information. "I will definitely be calling once I'm ready to relocate unless you find something before then that I can't turn down. In the meantime, I want you to find a modest home for them and make sure mine and the children's names are the only ones on the paperwork. If either of my sons want to take care of their mother when they turn twenty-one, that's their problem. I also want you to sell the house she's currently living in. I won't be going back there. Use the proceeds from that as a deposit on that $7 million dollar estate out on the island. You can help with that purchase as well. You snuck pictures of that place in with the other houses you sent me to review for the divorce, but I'm glad you did. I love it! The view of the lake is fabulous!"

At the sound of $7 million I gulped. I hoped I heard him right. "Okay then. I'll draw up the Exclusive Right to Sell, Listing Agreement for the current residence, and the Exclusive Agency Agreement for the eventual purchase of two properties. I'll need to do a walkthrough of the current residence and compile a complete list of available yet modest homes for her. If that all sounds good, then I'll be in touch very soon."

We said our parting words and I left. The meeting had gone better than expected. On the drive back to my office I was elated! My personal assistant, Stephanie, had been working her tail off, and to show her my appreciation I was going to give her the task of selling the wife's primary residence. Stephanie had recently obtained her real estate license, and as the listing agent she would be entitled to a 3% commission. If I listed the house for what I felt it was worth, $3.5 million, she would make $105,000. I knew the money would help, being that she was now a single mother of a three-year-old.

Upon reaching my office I noticed a police car with flashing lights outside. I slowly pushed the front door open.

"What's going on?"

Donald, my very gay friend and employee, walked in my direction and began telling me the business. "Girl, we had an incident up in here this morning! Stephanie's ex was here."

"What happened?"

"He came in here yelling about the child support that's being taken out of his check. He grabbed her up and then tried to pull her outside."

"So what did you do?"

"I called the police! You know his punk ass would love for me to hit him so he could have me locked up. I'm too pretty to be sitting up in a jail cell, you know. The last time I snatched him up he tried to press charges. Somebody ran next door to Pauley's, and he came over with a bat, and Bernard left."

I had been through a violent relationship myself and knew firsthand how those assholes could be. I walked over to Stephanie, who was sitting with the police.

"Are you okay?"

With big wet eyes she looked up at me. "I'll be okay, but I don't want to go home tonight."

"You can stay at my house."

"Thanks, but I'm going to my grandmother's. He doesn't know where she lives anymore." She sighed. "I tried to work with him, but he refused to pay anything. He says if we can't be together then I need to take care of myself. He can be such a jerk! The child support isn't for me! It's for his daughter! I could see if I wasn't contributing, but I work hard and do ninety-five percent of it by myself. The little money he gives isn't enough for her snacks at the end of the week. It was the court who decided to take it directly out of his paycheck due to his refusal to pay."

"Then he brought it on himself. Samantha's well being comes first."

The police officer informed Stephanie she would need to go down to Family Court for an order of protection. She gathered up her purse, but before leaving I told her there was something I wanted to discuss when she got back.

I proceeded to my office then closed the door. I unscrewed the top of my water, pulled out a bottle of Aleve, popped two pills in my mouth, and looked through the mail Stephanie left on my desk. She must have stopped at the post office on Saturday before I did. She was the only person other than me who had access to my P.O. Box. I shuffled through the mail and found an envelope addressed from Sin. My spirit was instantly lifted. I cleared my voice mail and my emails and addressed all the items I needed to.

When Stephanie returned to the office around one o'clock I was heading out for the day. "Stephanie, do you have a minute before I leave?"

She gave me a hesitant look. "Umm sure, let me put my bag down."

I noticed her breakfast was still sitting on her desk. "Have you eaten anything since you left this morning?"

"No, I didn't get a chance. It took so long over there I decided it would be better if I ordered a sandwich when I got back."

"Come on, I can kill two birds with one stone. I need to talk to you and we're both hungry. We can go next door."

We walked to deli and I greeted Pauley. "Thanks for helping out earlier."

He replied with a heavy Italian accent, "No problem, Misty. He's lucky I didn't break his face for pulling on this lady!"

We placed our order, took a seat, and I got right to the matter at hand. "I have a proposition for you."

"I hope it includes erasing my ex-husband off the face of the earth."

"I don't think so, darling. Unless it's to see Sin, I don't plan on going to jail anytime soon, especially for helping you dispose of Bernard's remains." I laughed. "What I got is better! It's a business proposal; something that could perhaps help you get farther away from Bernard. I met with Jeremy today, and I got the deal. B&B is going to do the closing!"

Her face instantly lit up. "Congratulations! This is great! I'll get the contracts together for you as soon as I get next door."

"That's not it. For all your hard work I would like you to be the listing agent on his primary residence."

She seemed surprised. "Listing agent? Thank you! I thought you were going to fire me earlier."

"Fire you? Why would you think something like that?"

"When you said you wanted to talk to me I just knew Bernard had done it this time and got me fired."

"I'm not going to fire you. You're my best employee!"

"Since that's the case, I am ready when you are!"

"This is a three-part deal. We'll be listing his primary residence, and then closing on a residence for his ex-wife. Now are you ready for part three? Drum roll . . . he also wants me to close on that seven million dollar mansion."

She sat blinking.

"Are you okay?"

"Seven million dollars? You're too good to me. You gave me a job when no one else would look at my resume. You patiently taught me the business then sponsored me to get my real estate license. Now you're helping me with my first listing and giving me the commission." Her eyes got watery. "No one has ever been this generous to me. I don't know what to say, but thank you."

"No, thank you. I truly appreciate all you do for me personally and professionally. You're more than my assistant; you're my confidant. We all need a break sometimes, and you deserve this opportunity. I know you will get that house sold then you can move your family into that gated community we were talking about." She reached across the table and hugged me tightly.

"I won't let you down!"

I walked away from lunch feeling like a million bucks, and on the way home I decided to call Marcus and share my good news.

He answered on the third ring. "Hi sweetie, what do I owe the pleasure of this call?"

"I'm calling to tell you about my day!"

"I was going to call you too. I have good news and bad news; which would you like first?"

"Give me the good. I don't want to ruin my day just yet."

"The good news is business is going great! I believe I'm going to get these guys to sign off on the contract."

"That's wonderful, Marcus! It looks like we're both having a very productive day. Mr. Whittaker agreed to let me list his primary residence and purchase two new houses for him!"

My excitement was short lived, for he acted as if he hadn't heard me, and continued talking. "If this thing goes the way I want, Misty, I'll be certain to get that corner office! Now are you ready for my bad news?"

I wearily replied. "Yeah, sure. Go right ahead." I couldn't believe he just totally brushed me off.

"I'm going to have to stay out here until next Monday."

"But I thought you said you'll be back today."

"I know, but they're having some department heads fly in to meet me, and I need to be prepared. I need to go over these numbers this week and make sure they match up."

"But I was hoping to celebrate the Whittaker deal tonight."

"What I'm doing here is much more important. We can celebrate your little closing some other time."

I pulled the phone from my ear then stared at it. What did he mean by "little closing"? Did he just minimize my accomplishment? Jeremy had more money than Marcus could ever imagine, and here he was referring to his closing as little. Did he not care that this meant a lot to me, and could turn into something very lucrative for my company? Did he not realize if Jeremy liked my work he could hire me as his personal real estate broker and refer me to all his clients and friends? When I told Sin about my pending meeting he was encouraging and supportive. He told me how he read somewhere that Jeremy was looking to relocate his main headquarters. The article said he was tossing around the idea of centralizing his operations and buying a building or some land. Sin thought it would be good if I tried to get in on that opportunity.

"Yeah, okay, Marcus. I'll see you when you get back." After letting him ramble on for a few more minutes I interrupted him. "I'm going to have to call you back. I need to take care of something important."

"No problem. I'll talk to you this evening."

This fool had no idea how upset he'd just made me. He was so self absorbed. Days like this confirmed why I loved Sin so much. He kept me balanced. He had faith in my abilities and respected the work I put in. It was sad to admit, but Marcus didn't value my mind. There were households where the two incomes didn't equal the amount of money I netted in a year, but that wasn't good enough for him.

People would believe he was this educated, wonderful man who worked hard and had it all together, but he had a selfish heart. What was hidden behind closed doors was an insensitive, hypocritical, narcissistic who could drive anyone mad! I spent the rest of the day trying to shake it off.

Around six o'clock my phone started ringing. I looked over at the caller ID and it was Toya. I thought it was strange that she was calling so early in the evening. She normally called during her down hours; which were after she got the kids settled and finished cooking.

"Hey, what's up?"

"I need to talk!" She sounded as if she was about to explode.

"What's going on?"

"Are you sitting down?"

I started to get nervous. I felt like she was getting ready to tell me bad news like someone died or was seriously injured. "Is everything okay?"

She paused for a long time. "No! I think Malik is cheating on me again."

"Why would you think that?" They had been together forever, and had their share of problems over the years, but I thought that was in the past.

"I was going over his credit card statement and on last month's bill I found some peculiar transactions. I dug a little deeper, and over the last six months there were charges for flowers and Victoria's Secret. He's cheating, and probably with one of those women he works with over there at the elementary school."

"Did you confront him with this?"

"No, I need to gather some more evidence. You know he'll lie. I sensed something was wrong. It began a few months ago when he started acting like he didn't want to touch me. He started coming in later and later from work, and lately he's been going out with his boys a little too frequently for my taste."

"Damn, Toya. I'm sorry to hear this."

"That bastard! I told him the last time he cheated on me, Misty, it would be his last, and I meant it! What kind of example would I be setting for my daughter if I keep letting him disrespect me and our marriage?"

Malik was a real bow-wow, but it wasn't my place to tell Toya to leave, stay, or work it out. I can't count the amount of times she's caught him lying and cheating. She'd confront him, but would take him back. He had been on his best behavior lately, but like they say, a donkey never stops being an ass—or is it a zebra never changes its stripes? "Do you have any idea who he's messing with?"

"I'm not a hundred percent sure, but I think I know who it is. I checked his cell phone log, and one number stood out. When I called it was his co-worker Michelle voicemail. My gut is telling me it's her. When I was at his job two weeks ago she couldn't look me in the face. I got her home address, and I wanna stake out her house. He already told me he's going out this Friday with the boys. This is where I'll need you."

"You want me to watch the kids?"

"No, I need you to ride with me over there. If I find that son of a bitch at her house I might completely lose it and kill him."

"I'm down to roll, but I'm letting you know right now I'm not with the bullshit. You better know what you're doing before you go over there looking for trouble."

"Hoping for the best, but prepared for the worst. I'll call you with all the details this week."

"Stay strong."

What women go through for love. I personally didn't believe it was a good idea for Toya to marry Malik. She was pregnant in her fifth month when she found out he was cheating. She left him. When Ky'elle was born he begged for another chance, her mother convinced her to take him back for the sake of the baby, and she did. She thought it was the right thing to do. In my opinion a happy, loving, single parent home is better than a dysfunctional two-parent home any day. The children who grow up in dysfunctional homes often have emotional and psychological issues.

As soon as we hung up I called Charmaine.

"Hey, Big Head, have you spoken to Toya yet?"

"No, Why?"

"Girl, I just got off the phone with her, and Malik is cheating again."

"That tail-wagger is back up to his old tricks again?" She sucked her teeth. "He's such a fleabag."

"She wants me to ride out to the woman's house with her on Friday to confront them."

"How does she know he'll be there?"

"She doesn't but he told her he's going out with the boys."

"Why is she wasting her time trying to catch him? Every couple of years he pulls the same shit and she takes him right the fuck back. Why bother?"

"I totally agree, but that's our girl, so we have to support her. Maybe this time she'll really leave him. Who knows?"

"I'll support her, but I think it's a complete waste of time. First she wants to catch him, then she kicks him out, and then lets him back in. Not once, not twice, but time after time. That shit is old already! She needs to just let that man fuck around and turn a blind eye like the rich women do instead of going through all these changes for nothing! I got better things to do on a Friday night."

"You don't think I have better things to do? I feel the same way, but I'm going! I'm not gonna let her ride go out there by herself."

"Calm down. You know I got her too. I'm gonna ride. I love Toya! I just want it to be put on record that I think it's pointless. If she dumps his ass this time for more than three months I'll be pleasantly surprised. Anyway, what's up with you? Did you and Sin make up?"

"Yeah, he called me back, we cleared the air, and we're good now."

"I bet you are. I can see you cheesing through the phone!"

I giggled. "Oh, be quiet. How's Shawn doing?"

"He's fine! He's actually on his way over here now, and I need to get off this phone and clean up."

"Why don't you just hire a cleaning person? That way you won't have to throw everything in the closets whenever company comes over."

"Shut your mouth, neat freak. I'll call you tomorrow from the office."

"Have fun, and smooches!"

I reclined back and analyzed Toya's situation. Here we all thought she had it together and on track; marriage, two healthy children, a house, and running her own business. She was holding it down while her louse of a husband slung meat around town like a butcher in Manhattan's Meatpacking District. The last time he got caught she cut up his coats, piled his clothes in big black bags, and poured bleach all over them. She called and cancelled his car insurance then took a crowbar to his headlights, rearview mirrors, and windshield. She also punctured the rear tires. They worked it out, and this buffoon had the audacity to be at it again.

# CHAPTER 12

## Phone Sex

Wednesday was pretty smooth at the office. Stephanie's ex-husband had not returned, and things were getting back to normal for her. She decided not to hide out at her grandmother's house. Bernard knew where she worked, lived, and where their daughter went to school. She felt if he really wanted to hurt her he knew where to find her. She was hoping the order of protection would scare him off.

I noticed Donald singing and dancing around the office. The singing and dancing was normal, but the tidying up part was strange. He always argued when it came time to get his hands dirty and was not the domestic diva type. I wondered what had him in such a bubbly mood.

I walked up behind him and playfully poked him in the side. "What's gotten into you today?"

He dramatically turned around with a dazzling smile, clutched his chest, then replied in his most feminine voice, "Oooow, Misty child, I've been keeping secrets!"

"Oh, no you haven't! I'm hurt. I thought I was your peoples," I teased.

"You know I tell you everything! I would have told you sooner, but the other day," he looked over at Stephanie and cut his eyes, "with the production going on around this place, I didn't get a chance."

She waved her hand at him.

"Sit down and let me give you the 411!"

I grabbed the first available seat and gave him my full attention.

"You see, a friend of mine set me up with a nice guy a few weeks ago, and we're really hitting it off."

"Get out of here!"

"Yes, girl! I wasn't down with the blind date thing at first, but once I saw him and that watch he was wearing, I decided to give him a chance, let him try his luck. I figured the least I could do was give him the opportunity to impress—and if lucky—undress me."

We all laughed before I waved him off. "You don't even know if his watch was real."

"Oh, yes I do, sweetheart! Real recognizes real!"

"Uh-huh. Real fake," I taunted, hoping to rile him up.

"Listen, little Miss Prissy. I know the difference between genuine and bootlegged shit! If I even look at a knockoff too long my eyes start to burn!"

We burst out laughing, and he was now on stage.

"Anyway, as I was saying before you rudely interrupted me. We spoke on the phone a few times and he invited me to join him at the mall. He hit up Gucci, Kenneth Cole, Armani, and Ralph Lauren and he even purchased me a couple of things. We've been hanging tight, and so far everything is cool."

"So you done went and finally got yourself a baller?"

He grabbed me by the shoulder and pretended to shake me. "Who are you, and who stole my friend? You have got to be an imposter acting brand new with me today." I giggled as he released me. He twisted his head then put his hand on his hip. "Get it together, lovely, because my Misty would know I keeps me a baller!" He snapped his fingers. "And don't let me have to remind you again, Boo-Boo!"

Stephanie passed him some papers. "I know if it's hard for a straight woman to find a good man, it's got to be difficult for a gay man. Why didn't your friend snag him first?"

"Because my friend is a she and snagging them isn't hard; at least not for me. When they see me, Steph, they see the truth, and they come running."

"You are too much!" I loved the fact that he was so comfortable in his own skin. "So tell us what he's like."

"His name is Wesley. He's tall, handsome, works with cars, and has a son."

"How old is his s—" My question was stopped by a potential client walking into the office. We all got back to business.

"Misty, you have a call on line two," Stephanie announced.

"Who is it?"

"It's an important client."

I knew what that meant. Sin! I walked into my office, closed the door, and picked up the receiver. "Hi, Daddy! I was hoping to hear from you today!"

"Were you busy? I can call back if it's not a good time."

"It's always a good time for my baby! How you doing?"

"I was feeling a little under the weather today. I needed to hear your voice."

"What's the matter? Are you sick?"

He chuckled, "Yeah, lovesick over you."

"Tell me anything, lover man."

"Real talk! Speaking to you helps me escape all this misery that surrounds me."

"Well, I'm here whenever you need to get away."

"And that's one of the reasons I love you so much. I can always count on you."

"I don't like the way you sound, Sin. You sure nothing else is bothering you?"

"I just need to relieve some of this stress; my nuts have been killing me lately."

I giggled. "Balls got the blues, huh? You need me to hook you up?"

"Baby Girl, you're about the only one who could hook me up, and it's a whole lot of hooking up to do to! This thing feels awfully heavy."

"Why don't you call me tonight so we can get away together? Help each other relieve some of our stress. It's been a while since we had a phone date."

"Now that's what I'm talking about! What time should I call?"

"I should be home around five-thirty, but you need to give me an idea what time you'll be calling otherwise you'll be mad again!"

The last time we decided to have phone sex the call ended right before he was able to hear me cum, and by the time he called back I was already marinating in my juices. He was pissed that he missed the best part.

"You know you were wrong for that! You should have waited for me to call back instead of going for self."

"Man, please. I was too far gone to try and stop that!"

"Yeah, all right. I'll hit you around eight, but if the phone hangs up you better hold that, or pretend you did when I call back," he joked.

"I'll be waiting just the way you like me . . . butt naked."

"Perfect! I'll talk to you then. Wait, how did things go with that meeting with Jeremy Whittaker?"

"Oh, it went fine."

"Fine? That's it? I know you've been working real hard on this, so fine ain't gonna cut it. What happened?"

I dryly replied, "I got the contract." I caught myself and remembered I wasn't dealing with Marcus. "I'm sorry, Daddy; it went great! Not only did B&B Real Estate get the listing on one house, but we'll also be the selling agent on two other properties, including a seven million dollar mansion out on Long Island. He also agreed to let me broker the headquarters deal."

Sin started clapping. "That's my girl! Awesome, but why didn't you sound excited at first?"

"I made the mistake of trying to tell Marcus earlier, and he made me feel like it was no big thing."

"It is a big thing! You've come a long way in this business, and I know how much this means to you. Don't let anyone lessen your accomplishments."

"I know, and you're right. I walked out of that meeting feeling like a million bucks, Sin. I found a loophole in the settlement and even impressed Jeremy's lawyer. When I write you I'll give you all of the details."

"That's my baby! You did a great job!"

"Thank you! That information you shared with me came in handy. I want to give Stephanie the listing. What do you think?"

"Sounds like a solid thing to do. She'll appreciate the gesture. I hate to cut this convo short, but I got to run to the law library. I'll hit you back tonight around eight o'clock."

"Okay. Love you."

"I love you too, and Misty . . ."

"Yeah?"

"I'm proud of you, baby!"

*Click.*


I got home around 5:30 and had plenty of time. I entered the house, went straight to my office, dropped my briefcase on the desk then retrieved the DVD of me and Sin making love. The scenes were originally on VHS tapes, but I had them converted to DVD. I played the videos on those days when I needed to see him, or hear his voice, and couldn't. We amassed a nice collection of home movies throughout our relationship. We often filmed ourselves at different outings, on vacations, or just chilling in the house.

The first time Sin and I had phone sex was years ago, and it was by accident. He had been away for a few days and we were missing each other. He called in the middle of the night and was expressing what he wanted to do to me when he got home. I began telling him how horny he was making me and how I wished he was there. He told me to close my eyes, listen to his voice, and follow his directions. He asked me to play with my Kitty. I felt uncomfortable at first, but once I allowed myself to relax we had fun.

It would amaze a lot of people to realize the intense level of pleasure that can be reached by two individuals whose mental and emotional connection has ascended to a plain that virtually renders the physical obsolete. A place where two people can exist in an almost spiritual zone. Where passion dipped words and the vibration of a voice causes an animalistic desire that awakens the senses. Where fantasy blurs into reality and the brain unleashes a flow of sexual gratification triggered by the feel of one's own caress. After an experience so true I had a greater appreciation of that old saying *"A mind is a terrible thing to waste."*

I used up an hour setting the mood for our date. I forwarded my calls from my cell to the house phone, stripped off my clothing, and laid my dildo on the bed. I turned on the stereo and let the sounds of Ne-Yo fill the air.

Federal inmates were only given one fifteen-minute call per hour, so I needed to be ready when he called. I showered then popped the DVD in and pressed play. I retrieved the Johnson & Johnson lavender body gel and began oiling my skin.

Sin recorded this video on our first vacation together. He was always busy taking care of his business, so when he offered to take me away for a weeklong vacation I jumped at the chance. We had a great time. We jet skied, parasailed, rented mopeds, and as promised, he made love to me on the beach. I can recall the powdery white sand beneath us as he rode the waves into me. We remained on the beach all night wrapped in a blanket listening to the sounds of the surf crashing up against the rocks. We gazed out into the blackish blue sky lit up with twinkling stars. We watched the moon's reflection bounce off the ocean then disappeared, allowing the sun's orange glow to cast rays across the water. It made for a perfect vacation.

I gently messaged the oil into my thighs as the television came alive. There on the flat screen we appeared in our suite back in Barbados. We had gone to a concert earlier that night and were feeling irie from the rum punch. Sin had been playing around with the camcorder in our room and decided to videotape us making love. The tape started off with his face right up in the lens. He was trying to focus the camera and place it in a good position. As he put it, he wanted to get the perfect shot. We had both been drinking, so the tape started off with us being real silly.

He removed his shirt then crawled up the bed to me. He removed my red heels, and threw them over his shoulder. He started sucking on my toes and I giggled. He had the three toes between the big toe and pinkie toe in his mouth. I kept trying to pull my foot back from him, but he wouldn't let it go. He put my foot down then tried to crawl his way headfirst up my dress. I was kept pulling it down over his head. We were cracking up.

He got hold of the dress and pulled it up to my waist, revealing my black thong. He turned, looked at the camera, and gave a thumbs-up while licking his lips. He kissed his way up my legs while slowly pulling the thong down my thighs. He brought my panties up to his face and sniffed.

He smiled. "Smells like coconut."

I returned his smile then slowly ran my hand down my stomach and between my thighs. I plunged my finger inside it then placed it to his mouth. "And it taste like pineapples."

Every so often he would look over at the camera to make sure the red light was still on. The drinks had me feeling light, and he was about to have me floating on cloud nine.

He threw my thong in the direction of the camera, leaned over me, and began kissing my neck and licking the edges of my ears. All of my giggling subsided and was replaced by light moans. He rolled off me and leaned his back up against the pillows.

"Take off the dress," he commanded.

I knelt on the bed, undid the few buttons then pulled the dress over my head. It got stuck and he had to help me. I started laughing.

"Stand up," he instructed.

I threw the dress to the floor then stood up on the bed with my legs spread wide open to keep my balance.

He sat up then ran his hand up my thigh, along my hip, and rested it on my stomach. "You got a mean shape!"

I combed my fingers through my hair then rested my hands around my waist. I smirked. "You think so?"

"Damn right I do! You're sexy as hell!"

He rose to his knees, knelt in front of me, then kissed up my thighs.

"I know life with me isn't always easy, but know that I love you, and one of these days it's gonna all pay off, and when it does I'm going lock you down!"

He ran his hand over my taut stomach then kissed it.

"One day you're gonna carry my seed in here."

I wasn't sure if it was the liquor talking, but he'd never said anything like that to me before so I took it seriously. He gently pulled me down to him and we kneeled facing each other. He ran his hand up my back then took hold of the nape of my neck. He peered into my eyes, gripped my hair, then started kissing me.

Watching this video always got the juices flowing. It was one of the best sexual experiences we ever shared on tape. I got comfortable on the bed, picked up the dildo, and resumed watching us make love.

My arms were wrapped around his neck as his hands held my back. Our tongues twirled slowly in, out, and around each other's mouths. We kissed like that for a long time before he took off my bra and laid me down on the bed. He reached over to the nightstand and grabbed some ice from the ice bucket. He placed a cube on my nipple, and I jumped from the chill. He put a few cubes in his mouth, and then pushed them into my vagina. I could feel the ice melting within my cavity. He reached over to the fruit salad sitting next to the bed and popped a strawberry in his mouth.

I turned my vibrator on low and began stimulating myself. After a few minutes I eased up. I didn't want to get too excited just yet. I wanted Sin to be a part of this and help me cum.

As he ate on the strawberry, he took his fingers and played with my freshly shaved Kitty Cat. He ran the half-eaten berry across my clit then bent down and sucked the flavor off of it. He did this a few times. I could see my chest rise each time he did it. He reached into the fruit tray, grabbed a piece of orange, and began squeezing the juice down onto my breasts and stomach. He grabbed both breasts and began lopping up the liquid. I was fully aroused. He got up and removed his pants and boxers.

You could clearly see his erection in the video as it bounced across the screen. His dick looked like a long, thick chocolate bar. He got back in the bed and rested on his back. I stuck my fingers in the whipped cream then spread it across his stomach. I began licking my way down . . .

The house phone rang, and I looked over at the caller ID. It was my baby! I grabbed the phone off the receiver and waited for the prerecorded announcement. I hit five, and put the phone on speaker. I was good and stimulated already, so a little nasty talking from him was all I needed to make this happen.

"Sin?"

"Yeah, I'm here, Baby Girl."

"I got Daddy's pussy ready for him, and it's nice and wet the way you like it."

"Ummmm! I'm visualizing that. What do you got on, and what are you doing right now?"

"I'm naked, lying in the bed, playing with my dildo. I'm watching the video we made in Barbados."

"What position are you in?"

"I have my legs spread apart, knees pointed to the sky, and I'm running the vibrator across my clit. Ummmmm . . ."

"What part of the movie are you up to?"

"I'm watching myself lick whipped cream off your stomach. Now I'm sucking it off your Sin-namon stick, and you look like you're really enjoying it."

"Yeah, I remember that scene."

"My Kitty Cat is calling you, Daddy." I started rolling the vibrator over my clit again and became aroused knowing he was on the other line. I was making slight moaning noises into the phone, and his breathing was become heavy.

"Tell me how that feels."

"It's feels good, baby. Tell me how bad you want me cum for you. Tell me. Tell me what you would do with me if you were here."

"If I was there I would be hitting it from the back while I tug on your hair. I'd be spanking that ass and flipping you from left to right. I'd have you riding this dick backwards screaming my name. I want to fuck you so bad."

"How hard is your dick?"

"My dick is hard like . . ." He paused as other inmates were walking past.

"Daddy?"

"I'm here, Baby Girl. Don't worry; you got my full attention."

I purred, "I wish you could feel how hot and wet this Kitty is right now."

"You got me about to bite a hole in my bottom lip. My dick is throbbing in my pants."

"I'm looking at your dick right now and what I wouldn't give to jump through the screen and wrap my mouth around it. How slow would you want me to suck it?"

"Slow like honey dripping off a spoon, and I'd stroke in and out of you even slower."

"My cat is hungry for you, Daddy. Should I feed her now?"

"Yeah, take care of that for me."

I slowly penetrated myself, and let out a long soft sigh. "Yeeeaaaah, baby."

"I see your face so clearly in my head, boo. I can see all those sex faces you make. I can see you biting down on your bottom lip." This was something that turned him on when we made love. "Baby Girl, fuck that pussy and let me hear you cum hard for Daddy."

My eyes were closed as I pictured every inch of his thickness inside of me. I was visualizing him being right there with me. I pictured him standing over me; watching me, smiling down on me. While pumping the dildo in and out, I raised one hand and began sucking on my middle finger, pretending it was him. My moans became groans and my sighs became cries. My juices dripped down my hand.

I yelled, "Daddy . . . I could cum right now!"

He whispered, "Yeah baby, cum for daddy."

"But I don't want to cum yet," I whined.

"Baby Girl, we ain't at no hotel," he said jokingly. "We only have a few more minutes left to make this happen, and I don't want to miss this. I need it."

I continued masturbating while he listened. He could hear the murmuring sound of the vibrator as well as my moans. I know if he could have stuck his dick through the receiver and fucked the horseshit out of my eardrum he would have. The sound effects were doing something to him, because he started talking nasty.

I let out a squeal and screamed. "I'm cumming, Daddy! I'm cumming for you!" He listened as I climaxed then caught my breath.

"Damn, my bitch is bad!" He laughed, "You was about to have me nut in my sweat pants. I got a wet spot on the right leg!" We heard the beep indicating we had one minute left before the call terminated. "Give me kisses!"

I placed my lips close to the receiver and blew him a kiss "Umah!"

"I love you, Bright Eyes!"

"I love you too, Daddy. Now make sure you hook my man up. We can't have him singing the blues."

He laughed. "You don't have to worry about that, superstar. I'm on my way to take care of that right now! I'll call you in the morning."

*Click.*

The phone went dead. I erased the unknown caller from the caller ID, and remained in bed thinking about him. When we first met, our goal was to get into each other's pants, but I now know God sent him to get into my heart. I finally got up and walked into the bathroom smiling. I looked in the mirror then said to my reflection, "Even behind bars that man can make me cum hard!"

Some people needed physical contact in order for them to feel loved. I've learned you don't always need the physical if you allow your other senses to take over. The mind is a powerful tool, and when the senses—taste, touch, scent, sight and sound—are stimulated, the images in your mind become clearer, realer, and truer. If you ever had a fantasy or found yourself having a wet dream then you are capable of being what Sin and I call, "Brain Fucked." Humans have the ability to imagine, fantasize, and use our brains in so many ways, to accomplish so many things. Why not explore alternate ways of stimulation? Why not mental gratification?

# CHAPTER 13

## Two Birds with One Stone

I awoke thinking of Toya and her situation with Malik. In my opinion he was a weak excuse for a husband. I don't know how she dealt with it time after time. It was enough to destroy a person's self esteem. You would think he'd figure out he's no good at cheating. He screws around and gets caught each and every time. To add insult to injury, he has the nerve to try and wine and dine the women.

Sin never had to spend to get a woman. They naturally gravitated to him. He didn't have to pursue; they came. If a female got a sit-down dinner at a real restaurant with him she was lucky, and an outfit was out of the question. Trust me, I know!

He could give two duck clucks about any of the women who tried to get with him or their feelings. Don't get me wrong; he was far from an angel. I got to see him in action when we first got together. He could work a room without even moving. They swarmed to him like bees to honey, but it was me he was leaving with. Women would try to inconspicuously get his attention or pass him their number on the sly, but he had too much respect to give them bitches a one up on me.

I had my share of drama with him over the years, but it was rarely over a female. If I complained it was only for more of his time. I didn't worry about him fucking around, tricking his money, or catching feelings. Either he rocked me to sleep, and had me so blinded that I couldn't see, or

I was keeping him content, and he was happy.

There wasn't much a woman could offer him that he didn't already have. He was getting everything he wanted or needed from me, and I made sure I took care of my man. He was getting treated like royalty just like I watched my mother do for my father. I catered to his every desire and enjoyed doing things for him. It made me feel good when I cooked and served him meals, ran his bath then washed him, oiled him down, and gave him full body massages. I even had an L rolled for him when he came home. What more could a man ask for? Pussy?

He had that. I was serving up platinum pussy that was perfectly manicured, waiting in his bed, and enthusiastically anticipating his return. The last thing on his mind when he walked out the door should have been sex. We were fucking like it was going out of style. On any given day as he sat on the sofa playing the video game I would walk up, kneel before him, release his manhood, and taste him. I would be in the kitchen cooking and he'd step up behind me, lift my robe, and hit it from the back. We burned plenty of meals that way. It was all about him, me, and us. It didn't take him years like dumb-ass Malik to realize what he had. Sin cut his shenanigans out the first time he got caught up and I was going to leave him. . . .

Black was completely out of the picture, and Sin and I were seeing each other exclusively. It was a Saturday, and I had spoken to Sin that morning. He said he would be catching an afternoon flight and wanted me to meet him at his place. It had been a week since we'd seen each other, and I wanted to plan a special evening for him. I got my hair and nails done, stopped at the liquor store and the supermarket, then headed to his place. I used my key to get in and got busy setting the mood. As dinner cooked I placed candles all around the condo, put fresh linens on the bed, and tossed rose petals. I took a shower, oiled my body, slid on a sheer red tube top and matching boy shorts then applied some red lipstick.

As the time passed I started to wonder what was taking him so long to come in. I tried to reach him at ten then again at twelve, but got no answer. Nickelle paged me 911 around 1:30 in the morning. My heart jumped. I thought something was wrong with Trey. I called her back and she informed me that she had just saw Sin at a party in New Jersey, and he and his crew were drunk and acting stupid. She said they were wilding out. I was heated. Without even thinking I threw on my full length mink, slid on my heels, snatched up my pocketbook and keys then sped to the club.

I thanked God I knew the bouncers at the door and was able to walk right in. If he had asked to search me it would have been a slight problem since I hadn't put on any clothes before leaving the house. If I opened my coat he would have gotten an eyeful. I looked around the dark, noisy, smoke-filled club trying to find him. I saw some of his associates in the VIP section. It appeared as if they were celebrating something. The club was extremely crowded, and it took me some time to get to the other side.

I made my way across the dance floor, up the five steps, and past Big Stan, who was guarding the entrance. Sin's boys were making a bunch of noise as I approached their table. I noticed they had empty bottles of champagne on the table, fresh bottles in the buckets, and hoards of females hovering around like flies to shit. His boys hooting and hollering made me want to see what all the commotion was about. Through their bodies I could see a female in a little-ass skirt simulating a lap dance. I stepped further through the crowd and realized she was gyrating her almost bare vagina up and down on Sin's crotch! Like a cartoon character my eyes damn near popped out of my head.

I tapped his man Danny on the shoulder. He turned around, and when he saw me he spit out his drink. The rest of his boys looked up and immediately got quiet then started moving out of the way.

Someone yelled, "Yo, Sin. Your wifey is here!"

He looked up and when our eyes met he quickly pushed her off his lap, sending her tumbling backward. He tried to play it cool as he got up and fixed himself then smiled. He walked over, grabbed me up in a hug, and then kissed me.

"What's good, Bright Eyes?"

I looked from him, to his friends, over to her, and then cut my eyes back at him. My demeanor was cool, but there was fire in my eyes as he put me down.

"You tell me, Daddy?"

The girl stood there looking on, not sure what to do. I turned to her, and said "Your little show is over. You can go now."

I shooed her off, but she didn't budge. She acted as if I wasn't talking to her. She couldn't have possibly been waiting for Sin. To make sure she wasn't, and to ensure she knew I was directing my statement to her, I turned then asked, "Why you still here? I know you don't think you getting up with him tonight or any night for that matter! You better go jump on one of these other niggas' jocks! This one here belongs to me!"

One of his friends cracked a joke, "She waiting for her tip!" They all snickered.

I sucked my teeth. "A tip! Shiiiiit, she better be glad I'm not asking her to pay me for that free ride she just took on my dick!"

They all cracked up laughing—even Sin—but I was dead serious.

Little Tyke turned her by the shoulder then pulled a wad of money out of his pocket. "Come with me, shorty. I'll tip you all night long if you ride mine like that!"

Like a bunch of drunken hyenas they all laughed. She giggled, not realizing the joke was on her. They were wasted. They went back to partying as I glared at Sin.

Once their attention was off of us he asked, "Why you keep looking at me like that? She was just dancing."

I pulled him to the side then got in his ass. "What's the deal with you up in here acting like you don't have a woman?"

He stood with a deadpan stare. "Misty, we were just having fun. It's no big deal. It's not what it looked like."

"Don't tell me what my eyes didn't see! You think I'm stupid? I guess that wasn't your dick that was hard when you hugged me either!" He stood quiet with his hands folded over his chest. "You giving out free samples to these hoes?"

He peered out into the crowd of people and acted like he didn't want to hear what I had to say. I loosened the belt on my fur then tapped him in his chest. When he looked down I opened it enough for him to see.

"I was sitting at your place waiting for you to come home so I could give you this!"

He got a nice view of the sexy outfit I had on. The sheer material holding my breasts was so transparent he could see my nipples poking straight through it.

"Yo, what are you doing?" He quickly grabbed the coat and pulled the collar closed, and I retied the belt.

"I'm showing you what you could be at home having right now; instead you up in here letting some two-dollar trick ride my dick!"

He smirked and tried to make light of the situation. "I like what you got on. We may have to find us a private corner up in here," he teased. He tried to pull me into him, but I stopped him.

"Nah, you not gonna sex me up in here after the next bitch got you hard!"

He became annoyed. "Why you tripping!"

I was holding it in, but was outraged. "I'm not tripping! You're playing yourself!"

He glared down at me then turned his head in disgust. He looked over to see if his boys were watching. He wasn't used to someone checking his actions, especially a female.

"You know what, Sin? You stay here with your friends and have fun, and I'll leave!"

He was embarrassed. He didn't say a word or follow after me when I walked off and left him standing there, but he was fuming.

I got back to his place, grabbed a garbage bag, and immediately started gathering my things. He walked in the door twenty minutes after me. He stepped into the living room and noticed the candles and rose petals on the coffee table. He threw his jacket over the back of the kitchen chair and saw the table was set and I had a bottle of Moët sitting in a bucket of now melted ice. He walked into the kitchen and peeked in the pots. I'd made his favorite meal. I watched him take a taste off the spoon and his eyes rolled up into his head. He smacked his lips, and I sucked my teeth.

He knew he messed up, but his ego wouldn't let him admit it. We tried to talk, but he said everything except the right things; I'm sorry, my bad, or it wouldn't happen again. He insulted me when he said it was only a lap dance.

That's when it went downhill. "I'll remember that the next time I feel like rubbing this Kitty Cat up on someone else!"

"Go ahead and play yourself if you want to, Misty! I ain't fucking no body. What time do I have to fuck around? You need to trust me!"

"Trust! Aren't you the one that said trust has to be earned? How am I supposed to trust you when you're doing reckless shit right here in New Jersey, at a club you clearly knew Nickelle was at! I could have walked up in there at any time, just like I did."

"Why would you be walking up in there when you were supposed to be here, at my home, waiting for me?" he snapped.

"So that's what makes your behavior okay? Knowing I'm here waiting for you?"

It was getting ugly. He walked in the kitchen, got some juice, and then plopped back down on the sofa. I continued to gather my things as he pretended to not care. It was way too soon for me to be dealing with that same bullshit. It was like déjà vu. I would not tolerate him taking over where Black left off, no matter how much I cared for him.

"I see where this is going, and I won't be going down this path again! If you don't respect me no one else will, especially your boys."

He got up from the sofa. "I don't feel like talking about this! I'm tired. I'm gonna take a shower, get me something to eat, then I'm going to bed." He kicked off his boots then walked into the bedroom. He got undressed down to his boxers, grabbed a towel out of the linen closet, and then walked into the bathroom. My feelings were hurt. I felt as if he was dismissing me. What was supposed to be a romantic evening was ruined.

I finished getting dressed, picked up the black garbage bad, my purse, shoes, and coat, placed his key on the entertainment center then walked out the door. He happened to come out of the bathroom as I was pulling the front door closed.

He opened the door with the towel wrapped around his waist then shouted, "Yo, where you think you going?"

"I'm out of here Sin! I'm going home!" I turned my back to him and began frantically pressing the down button for the elevator. I was on the verge of tears and trying my best not to cry.

"Stop playing and get back in here, Misty! It's too late for you to be going anywhere." He thought I was just trying to get his attention, but it was more than that. I held my stance, and when he saw I wasn't moving he put the slam lock on the door then walked to the elevator. "Damn, why you acting like this? It was nothing! You know a nigga got you!"

"You having me has nothing to do with this, and you know it! Your actions tonight were too familiar to me. Maybe the way our relationship started got you thinking that type of stuff is cool, but it's not. I'm not going to stick around and wait for you to play me out."

"You're really bugging. Damn! Nobody is trying to play you out!"

I could no longer hold my tears as they trickled down my face. The elevator came; I stepped in, and pressed 'L' for lobby. As the door began to close he stuck his hand in and stopped it. He recognized that I was really going to leave.

He grabbed my hand. "Don't go."

"Just let me leave; no hard feelings, Sin." I was sniveling. He pulled me off the elevator, and the door closed behind me. "I didn't get with you for this. There's no reason for me to stay."

"Yes, there is . . . I don't want you to go."

"I love you too much to stay, and know I'll have to share you. I'd rather not have you at all. I don't want to play that game anymore. I thought I proved that to you already. I'm here thinking I'm doing everything right to make you happy, and I'm dead wrong."

"You're not wrong!"

"It sure feels like it!" I laid it all out. "You weren't at a strip joint where that type of behavior is somewhat to be expected. You up in a regular club getting cheap thrills with some skeezer. That could have easily have been someone with a gun who walked up on you instead of me. I was the one who missed you while you were gone. I was the one who planned a special night just for you." He didn't respond. "How would you feel if you saw me out somewhere acting out of character, letting somebody rub themselves all up on me?"

"I would cut your ass off!"

"Exactly! So why should it be any different for me?" He stood quiet. "Have I ever tried to get over on you?"

He was smug. "You wouldn't have gotten this far if you did."

"Have I not been good to you, Sin? Are you not happy?"

"Yeah, I'm happy!"

I stood quiet trying to hold in the emotions. I wiped my face with the back of my hand, but the tears wouldn't stop.

He reached out and pulled me to him. "Come here."

I looked up at him. "Is this what happy men do? Is this what you and your boys do when I'm not around? Is this what I am to expect out of you?" I lowered my head feeling defeated. "I could only imagine what happens when you're out of town. I think I might have given you too much credit. I thought you were more selective and above the rest. You're no better." I began to picture the countless times he went away and what he could have been doing. I now had a clear vision to hold onto in my head. "Your boys must really think you're the man, huh?"

"Actually, they don't. Lately it's been just the opposite. They think I spend too much time with you and you got me pussy whipped. They rag on me every chance they get."

"So you were trying to prove a point to them at my expense? You don't need to be torn between being 'The Man' and being 'My Man.' I'll help you out. I'll leave." I turned toward the elevator door and pressed the button. I wanted to avoid his stare as the tears streamed down my cheeks.

He turned me around. "Okay, stop it! You're a hundred percent right. I was dead wrong. I care a lot about you, and I don't want you to go." Admitting he was wrong was big for him considering he didn't like to ever acknowledge it. He pulled me into his chest and held me there as I wept. I bawled like a baby. "Please stop. You're killing me, Baby Girl. I can't take seeing you cry. I'm sorry."

There was no way to front or play it off because I was hurt. I was prepared to leave him, and he knew it. He held me tight and rocked me as his head rested on top of mine. He did that for a long time, and eventually I calmed down.

He lifted my face, took his thumbs and gently wiped the tears away, and apologized. "I didn't realize how much I hurt you, and I am really sorry . . . okay? Don't leave. Not like this." There was a long silence. "I don't want any of these bitches out here. I got who I want, and I'm happy with you! If you walk out on me now, you'll regret it. I'll regret it. You're my boo. Come back inside."

I reflected on the evening's events, and visualizing that woman rubbing herself on him made me upset all over again. I dropped my head. "I think it's best if I go."

He grabbed my hand. "Are you going to come back inside?" When I didn't respond he tried to make me laugh. "If you don't come inside I'm going to follow you downstairs wearing just this towel."

I continued to look down at the floor then sighed. I was at a crossroads. I wanted to be with him more than anything, but not at any price.

He lifted my face with his two fingers. "You know I'm not letting you go, right? You're stuck with me, Bright Eyes. How you just gonna walk out on me? I thought you said you love me?"

I finally looked up. "I do love you! I tell you it all the time! You're the one who has a problem with the words."

He wrapped his arms tightly around my waist and started yelling for all to hear. "I love you, Misty Bishop! I love your beautiful eyes! I love your generous heart! I love your bright smile! I love your astute mind! I love the way you smell! I love the way you taste! I love your succulent breasts and your juicy ass! I love the way you take care of me and how you make me feel. I love your Kitty Cat and the way it grips me, and I love your tongue and the way you've learned to work it on my—"

I put my hand over his mouth. Two of his neighbors had opened their doors and were listening to him profess his love to me. They didn't need to hear how well I worked my tongue and what I worked it on. I turned around so my back was on to his chest. I didn't want them to see the bulge in the front of his towel. He wrapped his hands around my waist, and I placed my hands on top of his. I apologized for the noise, they said no problem, and then went back inside. He actually made me smile.

He kissed the side of my face then whispered in my ear. "I meant it when I said I love you, and was serious—I am sorry."

I looked over my shoulder at him. "And it won't happen again?"

He smiled then replied, "And it won't happen again." He nudged me toward the door. "Now come on. Let's go back inside and have make-up sex."

The events of that evening were a milestone in our relationship. It was the last time I had any kind of woman drama with him, the first time he told me he loved me, and the first time he called me Baby Girl.

It was a shame after all these years Malik still hadn't learned anything. He was still pulling the same stunts. One time Toya actually busted him in the bed with another woman. It was a year or two after Lil Malik was born. If I would have ever caught my man in the bed with another woman, and didn't die from a heart attack or killing him, I would have to leave him. I was not having some woman all up in his face, and I damn sure wasn't going to have her in his bed!

I didn't want to share my man, period, point blank. When I first got with Sin I thought I could handle that, but I was wrong. I was too jealous and selfish for that. It's was one thing to know about the other woman, but it's another thing to have her raiding your space or flaunted in your face. The night he decided to bring his girl to New York for one of his parties was the night that point was proven.

This event occurred a few weeks after Sin and I were spotted in the restaurant by Black's man. I had told Sin I was going to cut Black off, but hadn't done it yet. I didn't know if he was trying to get a reaction out of me or had just lost faith in us, but he decided to bring the female he was dating from D.C. to New York for his party. When he told me, I played if off like it didn't bother me, but it did. I didn't like it one little bit! Since I had yet to cut Black off, I was left to basically handle it, so we all thought.

I know him bringing her was in part to spite me. What other reason would he go out of his way to invite me too? Didn't he know bringing her to New York was a car collision waiting to happen? Didn't he know inviting me was like driving down a steep hill with no lights on black ice? Didn't he know the likelihood of me having an attitude and getting jealous was great? I took it as his way of sending me a clear message—either get rid of Black, or be prepared to see him with other females, especially this one.

The week of the function I saw him like regular, and the Friday night of the party I was prepared to play my position. I was dipped from head to toe. My whole crews, and a few females we were rolling with, were in attendance. Early in the night I spotted him with her. She had a light brown complexion, short haircut, and a banging body, but was plain in the face. She was dressed nice and had on some jewels. I couldn't front; she had it going on, but I wasn't intimidated. I had it going on too, and in my mind I was the baddest bitch!

At first I chilled, but as the night progressed and the alcohol took effect, the green monster appeared. I was okay up until I saw him whispering something in her ear. I knew he was messing with me, because while he talked to her he winked at me.

Charmaine caught it too, and laughed. "You want me to go punch that bitch in her face?"

"Nah, sis, I got this! He wants to play and make people jealous; I got something for his ass. I'm getting ready to blow his spot up!"

"You better chill before you blow your own spot up."

"Fuck that! Everybody up in this club before the night is over is gonna know me and him got something going on! All night I've been quietly watching, and I've had enough! His girl and every other ho in here are about to know who's running this show! They're all about to be mad!"

"You for real or do I need to take your drunken ass home?"

"I might be under the influence, but I'm far from drunk! I know exactly what I'm doing." I got up from the booth. "I'll be back. I'm going to get my man!"

"What about Black?"

"Fuck Black! It's time for me shake his ass and stake my claim. I'm over here while bitches claw at Sin, and this out of town chick think she got him, but not after tonight. Sweetheart's feelings are getting ready to get hurt. This is my town, that's my man, and I'm about to turn it up!" The alcohol had me on some shit.

She giggled as I walked away. "You know I'm always down for some action!"

There were a few females I had seen him with, but the one from D.C. was holding the title. In my eyes that was my spot, and it was time to knock her ass off that pedestal. If they all made up a body, she was the head, and if you remove the head then the rest of the body will crumble. In one clean sweep, she was about to be dethroned and beheaded.

The first chance I got I started messing with him. I asked him to dance. I rubbed up on him and whispered sweet shit in his ear. I was all over him with a purpose, and could feel him getting hard. I wanted her and everybody else to see us together. I wanted her to step to me about him so I could tell her about us then cut her ass off for him. I was in rare form and being real careless.

Charmaine was at the bar when she overheard Sin's girl asking his man, Coco, about the female he was dancing with and what was up with me. She was complaining about the way I was dancing on him, and wanted to know why every time she turned around I was up in his face. Of course, Coco pretended to not know what she was talking about. She then said something smart about me.

Charmaine was good and tipsy, and back then she loved to stir up shit. She didn't need alcohol to get shit poppin'. Since I told her I was going for mine she decided to instigate. Once Coco got up and walked away, she turned to girlfriend, and slurred, "If you need to know who that is, that's my sister, Misty. Why don't you go ask Sin about her?" She giggled.

"I don't need to ask him anything about anyone, but you need to tell your sister to back up off him! Why is she all up in my man's face?" Girlfriend had too much attitude to be talking to Charmaine. She didn't know that at any point she could be punched out her shirt.

"You really don't want to know the answer to that question. It might burst your bubble when you find out he's not gonna be your man for much longer." They all fell out laughing. Girlfriend got mad and rolled her eyes.

"She's ain't nothing but another bamma on his shit. I ain't worried about her!"

"Bamma? What the fuck is that?" They all chuckled. "We in New York and we say ho, skeezer, skank, or trick here, bitch! You got it confused. They're on each other's shit! I bet you he figures out a way to dip your ass later so he can be with her."

To save face, girlfriend replied, with a little too much confidence, "I don't think so! I'll be the one sleeping in his bed tonight!"

"You probably will . . . but I bet it will be alone!"

"I bet you I won't!"

Charmaine shuffled through her pocketbook then located her wallet. She scanned through the money until she found a hundred dollar bill. She slapped the bill on top of the bar counter in front of girlfriend. "I'll take you up on that bet! I bet you one hundred dollars he'll dip your ass, and you'll be sleeping alone tonight!"

Girlfriend got up in a huff and started walking away.

Charmaine yelled behind her, waving the money, "Don't forget to have my money tomorrow!"

I could hear my crew and they sounded like a bunch of cackling hens when they burst out laughing. I watched from the distance as girlfriend stormed off. She was steaming, but not stupid. She knew she was in our town, and there was too many of us for her to even think she had any wins. She would have gotten chased up out of there. I was later informed of the little conversation with Sin's soon to be ex, and was determined to win my girl's wager. He was going home with me—no if's, and's, or but's about it.

Every chance I got I was tugging on his dick. He finally said sarcastically, "You better be easy. You don't want your man stepping to you again."

I wasn't hearing any of it. "You want me to stop because of Black or because of her?"

"I can handle her! She's been getting on my nerves anyway. Do you think I would ever let you carry on the way you were tonight if I gave a fuck about her? I give my woman more respect than that. I told you before no one can come between us unless you let them."

I threw my arms around his neck then surprised him by kissing him square on the mouth.

He smirked. "I hope you know what you're doing."

"I do! So are you coming over after you leave here?"

"I don't know about that."

"If you break out with her I swear I'm never messing with you again, Sin! All my friends are here. They know we're seeing each other. How would that look?"

He nonchalantly looked down at me then replied, "The same way it looks to my people when they see you with Black knowing I'm fucking you. The best I can do is try to meet up with you after I drop her off at my place."

"You gonna sleep with her in the same bed you sleep with me in? I picked out that bed, Sin!" I was heated. "You should have never brought her here!"

"Yeah, I should have. You got a man, and I ain't gonna play myself waiting on you to one day leave him. There's a bunch of females that want to get with me."

I noticed girlfriend trying to come back into the VIP, but the bouncer held her at the ropes. Charmaine had already given him fair warning if honey said something slick, we were going to mop the floor with her.

Girlfriend started yelling, "I'm with Sin! I only went to use the phone."

He yelled back, "I understand, but I was given strict orders, no wristband, no entry, and that includes you! I'm not losing my job. Just wait here while I have someone find him."

"But you already saw that I was in there!" She looked around and located Sin over by the bar with my arms draped around his neck. She started carrying on.

Sin looked over and saw her arguing with the bouncer. He pulled away from me, and went to step away, but I stopped him. "Daddy, I don't want to do this anymore. I want to be with you, and only you."

"Are you sure? You've been saying that for a while now." At that point it was do or die.

"I'm emphatically, unequivocally, one-hundred percent sure!"

"When you plan on making a move so that can happen?"

"Right now! Don't you think my actions have made that blatantly clear? Now the question is are you ready to leave all these other females alone? You got a lot of admirers in here."

"I told you these bitches don't mean shit to me. They're only pressing their luck."

I pointed in the direction of the bouncer. "And what about her?"

He looked over. "I'll take care of that later. She's only here because she heard about the party from my Coco's girl and begged me come. We haven't been good for a while, and I haven't seen her in months. This was the perfect opportunity for me to kill two birds with one stone. I was planning on using this weekend to get rid of her and let you see just how many other chicks are standing in line eager to replace her." I frowned and he chuckled. "I knew you wouldn't be able to take it. There's a method to my madness and a reason why your eyes are green—you're jealous!"

I smirked. "So it's over with you two?"

"Bright Eyes, you did a pretty good job seeing to that all by yourself. It's not like you were trying to be discreet tonight. I think it's safe to say her and every other female in here know we fucking around, as well as Black's peoples!"

"So where are you sleeping tonight?"

"I don't think I'll be getting much sleep. She's gonna have me up arguing about you. To be honest with you I ain't in the mood for that shit."

I smiled then pressed my body into his. "Wouldn't you rather be up in some hot Sticky Icky?"

He kissed me on the forehead as one of the bouncers came over to ask about the wristband for girlfriend. He passed him a band as she stared over at us. Before the bouncer walked away I threw my arms around his neck, stretched up on my tippy toes, and tongued him down right there for all to see. It was official! Charmaine and the rest of the girls started clapping and cheering when they saw us making out. Girlfriend was seething, but she didn't approach.

Later on, as me and my girls sat on the other side of the VIP, we saw her yelling and arguing with Sin. We watched the whole thing and laughed. Toward the end of the night he snuck me in the back office, and I hooked him up with some head, but refused to let him cum. He pulled Coco to the side and asked him to drop girlfriend off. He told him to tell her he had to stay back and count the money. She agreed only after being told Sin would meet her there after he finished.

Once she was gone he came over and grabbed my hand. "How you get here?"

"Charmaine drove."

"Come on, you riding with me! You gonna finish what you started back there. The shit you've been doing all night got me horny as hell, and I'm ready for some pussy!"

Some of Black boys were still outside when I jumped in Sin's latest toy; a brand new black on black Acura NSX. He put on a show for them before pulling off. He made the tires smoke and chirped the gears, all while blasting the music. They wasted no time telling Black everything they saw, including me leaving in Sin's car.

He spent the night with me then went back to his place the following morning. He said as soon as he walked in the door she started beefing. Bad move! He called me two hours after he left to see what I was doing. I told him I was laying in the bed with nothing on but his t-shirt. A half an hour later he popped up at my place unexpectedly.

We went to the movies in Manhattan, and as soon as the theater went dark I stuck my hand in his pants. After the movie we went straight back to my place and fucked until dark. His girl was blowing up his pager and mobile phone. While he slept, I went in Charmaine's room to fill her in. We were so immature back then, and I let Charmaine convince me to dial his house number so she could fuck with his girl.

As soon as girlfriend picked up Charmaine yelled, "I know he told you don't answer his fucking phone, ho!"

"Who is this?"

"The same person who tried to tell your dumb ass he was gonna dip you last night ! How was it sleeping alone in that big old bed?"

"Who is this?"

Charmaine put on a spooky voice. "It's the debt collector bitch!"

"Grow up! I hate a rancid-ass ho! I can't believe you're calling here like this for a measly hundred dollars!"

"A hundred dollars? You really thought I was serious, trick? A hundred dollars ain't gonna break me. I was actually calling to give you some more free advice."

"You lunching! Wait to Sin hears about this!"

"Well, when he wakes the fuck up I'll be sure to have my sister tell him! He'll be pissed, but he'll get over this just like he's over you. Now back to that free advice. Don't sit up and wait BECAUSE HE WON'T BE BACK TONIGHT EITHER, BEEOTCH!"

I covered my mouth and fell out laughing.

"Fuck you!"

"No fuck you! And STOP PAGING HIM! He's fucking sleep, HO!"

# CHAPTER 14

## *Two Dogs and One Bone*

After girlfriend slammed the phone down in Charmaine's ear, I crept back in my room, and fell asleep in Sin's arms. Around 9:30 that evening, his pager started going off. He ignored it, but after two more pages he decided to see who it was. He put the remote control down on the bed then reached around me for his phone.

His moving woke me.

"What's the matter, baby?"

"It's nothing. Somebody's paging me 911 from an out of town number." He directed me to go back to sleep as he dialed the number. "Who's this?"

I could hear Black's loud, deep voice bark through the receiver, "Nigga, this Black!" My eyes opened wide and I watched a smile spread across Sin's face. My natural reaction was to get up and run, but I quickly remembered whose arms I was laying in, and remained in my laying position.

Fucking with him Sin barked back, "Black who, and just how did you come by this number?"

"Don't worry how I got your fucking number! Why am I hearing you fucking with my bitch?"

Sin was menacingly calm. "First of all, you better start talking with a little less bass in your voice." He looked down at me, "And to answer your question, no I'm not fucking your bitch."

I looked up at Sin, surprised he didn't claim me to Black, but didn't say anything.

"Nigga, don't play wit' me! I heard you been fucking with my bitch, and don't try to deny the shit!"

Sin pulled the phone away from his mouth and laughed hard. He whispered in my ear. "It's Black. That little show you put on last night finally got back to him."

Sin had just fucked me damn near into a coma, had me lying on his chest, and this clown ass was on the other line calling me bitch. Yeah. Okay. I smiled then mouthed back, "I know. I hear him yelling through the phone. Tell him we're 'sleep, and we'll call him back in the morning."

"Yo, give me a number so I can hit you right back, man. My battery is low." Dumb ass Black gave Sin the hotel phone number and his room before hanging up. "Pass me the house phone, Boo."

I rolled over on my side and he turned then spooned me. I laid the phone on the bed in front of me then snuggled my body deeper into his. He hit the orange speaker button, dialed the number then wrapped his arm around my waist. I chuckled as he pressed his dick into my butt.

When the front desk answered, Sin asked to be switched to room service. He ordered a steak dinner and a bottle of expensive red wine to the room. He then asked to be transferred to room 111. Black picked up on the first ring. "Yo!"

"I'm back. Now where were we? Oh yeah, me and fucking with your bitch?"

"Motherfucker, are you fucking with Misty or what!"

"Now that's two totally different questions, Black." He winked at me. "Fucking with your bitch, no, fucking with Misty, yeah I am seeing Misty."

"So that's how you gonna play it?" Black challenged.

Not wanting to see them go at it, I interrupted. "Black, that's how I played it. I'm over you and it's over between us."

Sin almost looked surprised. "I guess that's it. You heard it for yourself out of her own mouth. Ain't nothing left for me to say. Your bitch chose me, player."

"You trying to disrespect me!"

"Disrespect? You acting like this shit here is personal!" Sin calmed down. "Listen, dawg, I'm beat. I've been fucking for damn near two days straight, and I'm laid up with my shorty. I ain't got time for the bullshit, so I'm gonna give it to you straight with no chaser. Broads change hands every day. You ain't the first to lose his, and you won't be the last. Accept it, playboy. She chose up, and she's wants me."

"Just like that, huh? I made her! Everything she is, I made!"

"You might have made her, but you couldn't keep her! You left her to run around the city with nothing but free time on her hands. You gave every nigga in town who about anything an opportunity to take a shot at her."

"Ain't nobody taking shots? Niggas know that's my girl! Like them you were supposed to respect that!"

"You talking respect then respect the game you playing! How many nigga's bitches you knocked down? You probably fucking some nigga's girl right now and laughing at that man. Shit ain't so funny when it's happening to you! You should have shown your bitch some respect and not left her vulnerable. How you gonna leave a beautiful woman alone, neglected, and in need of affection, and not think she's gonna turn on you? It was a matter of time before a thoroughbred like myself came along and snatched her up. Shit, she's bad! Seem like you didn't know what the fuck to do with her, so I took her off your hands." Sin pinched my ass, and I had to hold in my laughter.

"So you gonna try and school me on my bitch? Get the fuck out of here." He chuckled, "She must got you open. My girl is far from neglected dawg. If you seeing her then you know I take good care of her!"

"Taking good care and your so called girl ain't fucked you in months? Stop and ask yourself why your so called girl was giving up all those excuses." Black sat silent as Sin grinned, knowing he had him. "It's me why that pussy has been off limits to you, idiot. Damn, dawg where you been? Too busy chasing the next bitch."

Black breathed heavily into the phone. He was beyond mad. "When I catch up to that bitch I'm gonna slap the shit out of her!"

"And any finger you lay on her I'm gonna break! I heard about your little hand problem. Putting the fear of God in a woman isn't gonna stop her from fucking with the next man? If you thought that, you were dead wrong. It's like this, if you got a problem with her messing with me then come see me about it. I'll take full responsibility for this, but don't lay a hand on her. That's all I got to say. I would hate for this shit here to get out of hand to the point where lives could be lost. I know you understand what I'm saying to you."

"Is that a threat?" Black fumed.

Sin laughed. "Nah dawg, I don't need to threaten you. I think you already know what time it is. That was a plea for you to keep breathing. The bottom line is this, Misty is fucking with me now, I'm feeling shorty, and I'm gonna continue to rock with her. Two dogs can share the same bone so go dig another one up. We good, or do we have a problem?"

It took a long time before Black responded. He wasn't crazy. Going to war with Sin was a death sentence. "I'll see you around, nigga!"

*Click.*

Sin got up and went to the bathroom and made a phone call. A half an hour later two of his boys were stationed downstairs in the living room. He knew Black wasn't going to wear this well. The following morning when we woke, he told me he was expecting for him and Black to bump heads, but for me not to worry about it.

I made sure I fucked him until his nuts were sore then fed him breakfast. I walked him downstairs and gave him the longest tongue kiss on the front steps before he and his boys left.

When Sin got to his place he called and said old girl was good and angry when he got in, and I loved it! He said she went off when she saw the hickey I put on his neck. He laughed because he didn't remember me putting it there, but I did. He also thought what Charmaine did was fucked up, but laughed it off. I joked that she won the bet, wanted her money, and called to see if girlfriend was ready to pay up. He said he would be over later then hung up.

Some hours passed and the intercom rang. Nickelle had a bad habit of just buzzing people in. Without looking she buzzed the person in, opened the front door, and then walked into the kitchen. Seconds later in stepped Black. He left the front door wide open and stomped into the living room. At the point she realized it was him, it was too late.

I could hear her yelling, "Wait, Black! Does Misty know you're here? Where do you think you're going? You can't go upstairs! I'll go get her!" She called up the steps to me as she tried to direct him back toward the door.

He strolled past her. "Where's Misty at? Is she up there?"

"Oh, shit," I said as I gently closed my bedroom door and locked it. I paged Sin 155-911-911. I tried his mobile phone, but it was off. I had just hung up with him minutes before and he said he was on his way. Thank God he called right back.

"What you need me to pick up before I get there," he joked.

I was trembling, and trying to talk low. "Daddy?"

"What's the matter, boo? Is everything all right?"

By then Black had seen that all the other room doors were open and begun to bang on mine. "Hurry the fuck up and open this door, bitch!"

213

I held the receiver as close to my mouth as possible then whispered, "B
here. Nickelle accidently let him in. He's acting crazy, and banging on my be
door. It's locked, but I'm scared what he'll do if he gets in here."

*BANG! BANG! BANG!*

Black roared from the other side of the door, "Yo, Misty if you don't o|
this fucking door, I swear I'm gonna to kick it down!"

Nickelle was talking to him, but he wasn't trying to hear her. "Fuck th
I ain't going anywhere! This bitch running around fucking with the nex|
behind my back like I'm a joke or something! I'm gonna teach her some f
manners. She needs her teeth punched in and some sense kicked into her a|
banged again. "Open this fucking door!"

I was repeating what Black said to Sin. He had heard enough. "Tha|
better not put his hands on you! I'm on my way. I should be there in less th
minutes. Just stay in your room with the door locked."

I thought I would just sit on the bed and wait it out, but after what s
like a few seconds my bedroom door came crashing in. When Black ente|
room I was cowering on the corner of the bed with my arms wrapped |
my head. Nickelle ran up behind him and started pulling at his shirt in h|
getting him to retreat. He was not a small guy, so her tugging was in vain. |
foaming at the mouth with nostrils flaring as he approached.

As he reached for me, I yelled, "No, Black. Get out!"

"I ain't going a fucking place!" He hovered over me with piercing ey
looked around, and the next thing I know he started tearing up my room. H|
as he ripped clothes from the hangers and dumped clothes out of the draw

"All this shit you got up in here, I bought! I don't give a fuck wha|
doing, you were supposed to sit your fucking ass still and wait for me. N|
fucking around with the next nigga!" He knocked everything off the dres|
sent perfume bottles crashing to the floor. "How long has your slick ass bee|
up in here anyway?"

He ripped picture frames from off the walls then smashed them bene|
feet. He shattered every single piece of glass and mirror I had before runn|
of steam. He stood panting trying to catch his breath. "All your little sec

coming out! My man saw that nigga's car parked out front last night. Where's his bitch ass now?"

I barely heard him as I looked around in disbelief. It was like a tsunami had hit my room. He rested his elbow on top of the new 55-inch projection television Sin had bought me as a house-warming present and waited for me to respond. When Black looked over and saw a picture of me and Sin his anger resurfaced. He grabbed the back of the television and sent it crashing to the floor. I was now crying and scared to death. There was nothing left to tear, rip, or break in the room except for me. I knew it was a matter of time before his rage would be directed at me.

Nickelle came over to me. "I'm gonna call the police, Black, if you don't leave!"

He pulled his shirt up and showed her his gun. "And by the time they get here, you'll both be dead!"

I was disgusted with him, and as I blew my nose we caught eye contact. I rolled my eyes at him, and he lunged and slapped the horseshit out of me.

I flew backwards over the bed and slammed into the wall. He came around the bed, and grabbed me up off of the floor by the neck with one hand. My feet dangled as he slammed my back up against the wall, and he began choking me. It felt like he was trying to squeeze the life out of me as Nickelle punched and screamed for him to let me go. He just swatted her off and sent her flying into the now empty closet. Seeing that I was turning blue, he loosened his grip and I fell to the floor. I held my throat as I coughed and gasped for air. Nickelle sat on the bottom of the closet next to the safe. I thought about the three guns in there, but I wouldn't be able to unlock the safe in time.

Pointing his finger in my face he said, "So you really fucking with that nigga."

I just wanted it over and done with. "Yes, Black. I'm seeing him."

"You gold digging bitch!" He hocked up and spat in my face. His thick saliva dripped from the side of my face and hair. I used the bottom of my nightshirt to wipe my face. To spit on someone was degrading, and I wanted to kill him..

"Get the fuck out!"

"You're auctioning off pussy to the highest bidder now, trick?"

"Fuck you, Black. You know that's not true!"

"As much as I do for you why would you give that nigga some pussy, Misty?"

He slapped me again. I didn't respond. I had no emotions. I simply wanted him to go, but he stayed and continued to belittle me.

"I know why you gave him some. You're a fucking ho, a fucking slut, a fucking worthless bitch!"

I couldn't take it anymore, and without thinking I yelled, "I gave him some because I fell in love with him. What you think I've been doing all summer? I've been with him doing all the things I should have been doing with you. I wouldn't have minded sitting my ass here and waiting if you weren't such a fucking dog. You messed up, not me! I let you know I was tired of your bullshit, I damn near begged you to stop, and I warned you this would happen. I said I wasn't going to take it anymore. I even told you I was going to leave you, but you thought I was kidding! Well, you see I wasn't."

He began laughing like a lunatic, then hauled off and slapped me, causing me to accidently bite my tongue.

"Bitch, you crazy! He got a girl! I heard she got a fat ass too! My man told me he saw him up in the club with her, and you were the one playing yourself chasing after him like a groupie!"

"Like a groupie? Your man told you wrong!"

I looked over at Nickelle, and she shook her head no. She mouthed, "Don't say anything." She had no idea just how much I despised him. I hated everything about him, but instead of saying what I really wanted to, I spit blood at his feet.

"Whatever, Black."

"You're a stupid ass! I was getting ready to get you an engagement ring. I was gonna ask you to marry me. You went and fucked that up for a nigga who's gonna treat you just like any other ho! I heard after someone in his crew fucks a bitch they get passed off. You'll be the next one they pass around like a peace pipe!"

He had already beaten me up with his fist, and was now using his mouth as a gun to shoot me down. There was but so much more of his verbal thrashing I could take.

"You're just another piece of ass to him, Misty! That nigga is going dog you out and toss you to the side! You think he's gonna wife you? You think he's different or better than me? He got ten times more, so expect him to be one hundred times worse! Give him a month, and he'll be done with you, and you'll be crawling back to me."

I was a good girl to Black outside of this, and he had no right to make me out to be a whore. That was the last straw!

"Go to hell, Black! Not a single word of what you're saying is true, and I'm glad you didn't get me a ring. I wouldn't have married your tired ass anyway. You're nothing more than an abusive womanizer. Why would I want to spend the rest of my life with that? I don't know why you even bothered to come over here. Why don't you just go back to Texas and play with all those females you've been down there cheating on me with? Better yet, why don't you fly your baby mother down there? What happened? Tamika busy this weekend, or is her belly getting in the way?"

He got quiet and for once realized the result of his actions. He had pushed me too far. "You came over here to find out what it is. Well now you know, and you can go, Black!"

"I don't know anything!"

"You're so full of shit! Forget what anybody else told you, you know I'm fucking with him because I just told, and he told you last night!!"

He stared at me as I boldly stared back.

"We were in bed together when he called you back. I heard everything he said to you, especially the part about me being his girl, and for you to stay clear of me!" I chuckled. "How was that steak dinner?"

"That nigga was just talking tuff shit trying to impress you. You're probably fucking around on him too? How many other niggas been sneaking up in this secret love nest?"

"Black, regardless of what you think, I never fucked around on you until now, and I'm not sleeping with a bunch of men. I'm making love to one!"

"Making love?" He laughed. "That nigga ain't got no love for you!"

"Yes he does!"

"Today it belong to him, tomorrow it'll belong to ten niggas in his crew."

Nickelle shook her head as I smirked. "Nah, this will only belong to him. I'm gonna keep that one! He knows how to take exceptional good care of my Kitty. His sex is mind-blowing, and he fucks me so good I be calling him Daddy while I'm cumming!" The whites of Black's eyes turned red as he seethed with anger. I smirked because I had wanted to tell him that for a while.

"What did you say?" he asked over and over again. "What the fuck did you just say to me?"

"You heard me!"

Nickelle jumped up as he grabbed me up off the floor by my nightshirt.

He poked me in my forehead with his middle finger. "Since it was my pussy first you gonna have to pay up! It's time you pay me back for all the shit I gave you! All the shit I did for your little trifling ass. I'm gonna recoup it in pussy payments. I don't care whose pussy you think it is now, but every time I want it, you're gonna give it to me! I might take that asshole too! I never got a chance to get that!" He grabbed me between my legs.

I screamed, "Get off of me, Black! You can take all your shit with you. I didn't ask for it, I don't want it, and I don't need! Most of it was guilt gifts anyway! Get the hell out, and do us both a favor and never come back! Leave!"

"I said you are gonna pay me back!" We started tussling.

Nickelle jumped on his back, but he threw her over his shoulder. She got up and started punching him as he tore the whole left side of my lounge pants. The only thing holding the right leg up was the elastic waist. I threw wild punches as he ripped open my pajama shirt, sending buttons flying. I scratched his cheek and caught him with a solid right. I refused to go out without a fight. Nickelle came back at him, but he pushed her to the floor, and she bumped her head hard.

I wasn't sure if it was a slap or half-punch he hit me with, but it dazed me. Blood trickled from my nose. He grabbed me around the neck, balled his hand into a fist, and then placed it to the side of my face. "You must have lost your fucking mind! You're my fucking girl! Mine, you hear me? And you can't tell me no. You got the nerve to tell me you love that nigga. I know I've been fucking up, but we gonna fix this shit, Misty!"

I thought to myself, fix this? He must have lost his entire mind. Black picked up the phone from off the floor, mushed it in my face then said, "You gonna call that nigga right now and tell him you ain't fucking with him no more, and we're back together. There is no leaving me!"

"You can beat me until you kill me, Black, but I won't tell him it's over, nor will I ever get back with you again! I told you I love him. It's over. Now get the fuck out!"

Just as Black lifted his fist to punch me in the face, Sin and his man, Rock, appeared behind him. Sin ran up directly behind Black and like a heat seeking missile he found his target. He cracked him in the back of his head real hard with a big-ass 45. Black released his grip from my throat, and crumbled to the floor. I scrambled away before his weight pinned me down.

My shredded shirt and pants were barely covering me. Nickelle threw my robe to me while Sin and Rock grabbed Black up by his jacket. They flung him to the other side of the room, where he bounced off the wall and slid to the floor. Rock patted Black down, took his gun then caught him with a timberland boot to the chest. Black keeled over like a fish fresh out of water gasping for air.

Sin walked over and stomped his foot down on Black's right hand. You could hear the bones crushing as he smashed and twisted his boot into his finger. Black hollered out in harrowing pain and begged for mercy. Sin reached into his waistband, and pulled out a 357 Magnum then stuck both of his guns under Black's chin.

"Motherfucker, what the fuck is your problem?"

Black began crying and screaming like a bitch. He knew shit was serious when a nigga like Sin was holding two loaded guns at his head.

"Wait, wait, this doesn't have anything to do with you, man! This is me and Misty's business."

It appeared as if Sin was looking straight through Black's soul. His face was tight and his brow creased. The eyes I loved and knew as soft and warm were now cold and void of emotion. It was like the Grim Reaper had taken possession of his body. The normally suave Sin had turned into a beast right before my eyes.

"My peoples hipped me to your card after I was spotted going into that restaurant with her, Black. They told me you were asking questions about us. I started chilling out, slowing down, and falling back from spending so much time with her. I did take into consideration she was your girl. I admit I was wrong for fucking with her, but when you didn't step your game up, I did. What's puzzling to me is why you would prefer to come over here and beat her up as opposed to talking to me man to man. You would have at least earned yourself some respect."

The way Sin's eyes were fixated on Black, I could tell he was debating on what to do with him. Whether he would kill him now or later? He finally stood, keeping one gun pointed at Black. He placed the other into the small of his back then looked over at Rock. It was as if the two had a silent conversation with their eyes. Rock walked over and aimed his gun at Black's head, who sat motionless on the floor. When he cocked the gun Black cowered, and cried out, "Please, no!"

Rock looked to Sin and waited for the order. Sin looked around the room. He looked at Nickelle, who was still rubbing the lump on the side of her head. He glanced at me as I tightened the robe around my body. "Are you all right?"

When I looked up he was finally able to see just how badly Black had beaten me up. I had blood all over my face. He clinched his jaw then looked over to Black. "This shit is real fucked up, chief! This ain't about business, this is about me!" Sin pointed to me and Nickelle then said, "You two get some shit and get out of here and don't come back until I say it's okay."

"Nah, Sin, chill. This is all about me and her," Black begged.

"Anything pertaining to her is about me, nigga! I specifically told you she's with me now and to not put your fucking hands on her!" He stomped on his right hand again. "Didn't I make myself clear last night? That was you I was talking to, right? I know I wasn't high or drunk when I spoke to you, motherfucker!"

There was no response.

"This some straight sucker shit, dawg!" He looked around the room and took in the destruction. His face tightened when he saw the picture of us on the floor in a broken frame. He walked up and punched Black in his mouth before picking up the picture and shaking out the glass. He took the picture from the frame and put it in his back pocket. "I know you heard what the fuck I said last night!"

Black's ego had pushed him to come see me. He wasn't thinking of the possible repercussions of his actions. He never did. He was always blinded by emotion. He tried to play stupid. "What you talking about?"

"You heard when I told your bitch ass if you had a problem with me dealing with her to come see me and we could talk man to man!"

"I wanted to talk to her."

Sin's eyes grew wide. "She was right there the whole time we spoke, and I didn't have a gun to her head when she was talking to you! I think she made it very clear." He wanted to hurt Black so bad his left eye was jumping. It took great discipline not to splatter Black's brains all over the wall. "So now that you did all this, did she tell you anything different?"

Black took a little too long to answer.

"Bright Eyes, get over here!"

I got up off the bed, walked over, and stood behind him. He turned slightly and took in my bruised face. My lips and nose were bloodied, and my left cheek and eyelid was bruised and swelling. I even had fingerprints around my throat the next morning. I looked like I tripped and rolled down a hill face first.

Looking at me infuriated him. "What did you tell this nigga?"

I was angry Black tore my room apart, kicked my ass, and tried to rape me, but I was no longer afraid. "He asked me if I was fucking with you, and I told him yes!"

"And what did he say?"

"He said I was just another piece of ass to you."

Sin tightened the grip on his gun then looked Black dead in his face. "Did she have to tell you she was with me?"

Black started to lie. "She ain't told me shit about—"

Nickelle cut him off. "He's lying! She did tell him!"

222

Sin bent down and stared Black dead in the eyes. "Did she or did she not tell you she was with me?"

"Yeah, she told me . . ."

*BAM!*

Sin smacked him across the side of the face with his gun. Black tumbled sideways as a combination of blood and saliva dribbled from the side of his mouth. He waved the gun in his face like a mad man. "You must have a death wish, motherfucka! When I told you she was my girl you had to know shit was serious between us! You were supposed to fall back, and if you had an issue with it, come see me—not come over here and fuck with her! I gave you the open invitation."

Sin paced the room and talked out loud to himself. "I told this motherfucka I was gonna take shit personally. He can't think shit's a game. He's got to know how me and my crew get down! Everybody know we seen niggas dead for less, so why would he decide to cross me? That crack pussy must got him tripping the fuck out!" He shook his head. "Yo Bright Eyes, what else did this pussy-whipped ass motherfucker have to say?"

"Daddy, he called me a whore and said I was auctioning off my Kitty to you."

"Daddy?" Black repeated dumbfounded.

"Yes, Daddy! If you were listening to me earlier, with your dumb ass, you would have heard when I said Sin dicks me down so good I call him Daddy!" Rock snickered. "I also told him I love you. He called me a groupie and said you would be passing me off to your boys next."

Nickelle sat not believing the scene that had just unfolded in front of her. She was in shock. All the girls knew I was playing with fire and had warned me, but none of us ever imaged Black flipping out like that.

"I told him I'm your girl, this Kitty belongs to you, and it's over!"

Sin smirked. I knew inside he was smiling because his ego was inflated hearing me talk aloud about my vagina belonging to him.

"He said I was going to repay him in pussy, and that's when he tried to rape me! He wanted me to call and cut you off, but I refused, and . . ." I started crying.

Sin wiped my tears then bent down and slapped the shit out of Black on the other side of his face. Nickelle covered her eyes.

"I can take care of this for you, Sin! Let me murk this nigga," Rock zealously offered.

There was no response as Sin stared down at Black, contemplating his next move. "How you look just trying to take the pussy? Now that's not playing by the rules. I didn't take the pussy when it belonged to you! She gave it to me, and made a nigga wait good and long for that shit too! I mean, I can understand how you feel." Sin laughed. "She does have the sweetest pussy I've ever been in. Shit, I'm a little whipped my damn self." Then he got dead serious. "But that doesn't mean you can touch it. It belongs to me now—every fucking pubic hair on it! And just so we don't have any confusion in the future, Yo Misty tell this nigga what he came over here to hear before he meet his maker!"

"Whatever you heard, Black, it's true. It's over between you and me! After what you did we can never speak. Don't call me or come over here ever again! I hate you, and for the record you're a wack-ass fuck! As much dick you slinging about town I would think you'd know how to work it."

"Fuck you, you ungrateful bitch! You gonna remember this day when he dogs your ass out! A thousand other females would love to be in your shoes! You look real good to him now driving my shit, wearing my clothes, and rocking my jewels. You'll be back! He can have my leftovers." He snickered. "I had that first."

I couldn't believe this penny ante nigga was sitting in my face talking shit about the things he bought me. Like Sin was some scrub who couldn't replace it all in one shot. He was insulted. "Yo, boo, give me those fucking car keys?" I went searching around the room and located the keys in my pocketbook. "Give me all your jewelry too!" I went into my closet, opened the safe, and pulled out the black velour bags and boxes. I located the cross my Mother gave me when I was ten then passed it to Nickelle. I put the rest of the jewelry in one bag. He pointed to my earlobe. "Take those shits out your ear too!" I unscrewed the backs off the diamond studs, placed them in the bag, and then handed it to Sin. He threw the bag and keys to Black.

"The only reason you're not dead right now is because she got legitimate connections to this place, but if you ever come near her or attempt to contact her in any way again I promise I'm gonna show you what suffering really feels like. You got lucky tonight; you got a pass, but know you won't get it again. You got your car and the jewelry. Have that car out of her name by Tuesday morning, or I'll have it set on fire. I should be a petty-ass nigga like you, and make you pay me for the fucking TV you broke, but I'll charge that to the game. I'll get her another one. Make arrangements to have someone come over here to get these fucking clothes and furniture up out of here too! You fuck with a bunch of bum-ass bitches. I'm more than sure one of them could put use some slightly used shit. Whatever you don't get by the weekend I'll have thrown out!"

Sin turned, went into his wallet, pulled out one of his credit cards then passed it to me. "Here, take this!" I looked down at the American Express Black card that read the name Garrett Butler. "Hold on to that! Tomorrow we'll go get you new stuff." He glared down at Black. "You're right, I can't have my girl walking or driving around in your old shit! She's my lady, and although you had her first best believe she won't be back. I spent many nights, taking my time, long stroking that pussy and molding it to fit my dick just right. She was a virgin when you got her, but it was Daddy who popped that cherry, and trusts me; you wouldn't want it after me. The amount of time it took for me to get my joint up in there I know your little dick would be swimming in it now."

Rock had a contagious laugh, so when he started Nickelle giggled, and everyone started laughing except Black.

"Fuck you, Sin, that's my—"

WHAM!

Sin backhanded him, and the huge diamond ring he wore on his pinky sliced into the skin under Black's eye. Sin grabbed him up roughly by the front of his jacket then placed the nozzle of his gun to his temple right next to his birthmark.

"You want a hole to match that spot on the side of your head?"

When Black went to speak, Sin stuffed the gun in his mouth. "Man, you just don't know when to quit. You don't know how bad I wanna fucking kill your ass right now! My dick is hard."

"No, Sin, please!" Nickelle yelled.

I also begged. "Please don't!" I pleaded with Sin to leave it alone and to let him go. "My conscience would haunt me if you killed him and ended up in jail for it."

Sin threw him back down to the floor. "You're one fortunate motherfucker! Get the fuck out of here before I change my mind."

Black was defeated, but not counted out. As he staggered out of the room he said, "You got this one, Sin."

Rock followed him down the stairs, locked the door then ran back up the stairs. "Yo, boss man, you should have let me body that nigga for you. It ain't too late. I can still catch up with him."

"Nah, let him go."

I knew the only reason he didn't kill Black was because me and Nickelle was there to witness it. We could all see in Black's eyes it wasn't over, and that the two of them would eventually meet again.

Rock went downstairs with Nickelle to the kitchen to get some ice for her head, and she came back and handed me a wet washcloth before leaving.

Sin sat down next to me on the bed. "You okay?"

"I've seen better days, but I'm alive, and it's finally over. I must look like shit."

He took the washcloth from me and started wiping my nose and mouth. He smiled then kissed me on the cheek. "You're still beautiful to me."

I smiled, and had to grab my jaw because it hurt. "Thanks, but I know you're only trying to be nice. I'm really sorry I got you involved in this mess, Sin."

"We're both to blame, Misty. I knew what I was getting myself into when I started dealing with you. I really didn't think he would have come at me, though." He pulled me up onto his lap. "You know I got you, right?"

I half smiled. "Yeah, I know."

He could see my uncertainty. "For real, Misty, you stole my heart, Baby Girl, and from right underneath my nose."

"So it's really going to be you and me? No more sneaking around?"

"Just me and you, boo!" He pushed me up off his lap then gave me a light tap on the ass. "Grab something to put on. You're going with me back to my place. I'll take you to the mall in morning and get you some stuff, then have my man come over here and fix the door."

"Okay." I grabbed a pair of jeans off the floor and shook them out. "Wait a minute. Isn't that girl still at your place?"

"Oh shit, I totally forgot about her. Damn! Her flight leaves in the morning."

I frowned then pouted. "It's okay, I'll just stay here. I need to clean up anyway. I doubt he'll be back." I sat back down on the bed dejected. My eyes filled with tears.

"Don't cry. We can stay at a hotel."

"Nah, Sin, you need to go handle your business with your girl. I'll take care of this."

He smiled. "I am handling my business with my girl! Now get dressed.
stay at a hotel, I'll talk to her tomorrow while I drive her to the airport, and
I get back I'll take you shopping. How's that sound?"

Sin ended things with his girl and pampered me at his place for a week st
I looked worse the next day and I chose to stay in until my bruises went awa
stayed with me the whole time, only going out to make quick runs. When
better he took me shopping and gave me one of his cars to drive.

I did have the unfortunate experience of running into Black like a month
the incident on 125th Street. He tried to speak, but I walked past him and
as if I didn't know him. He got mad and went to putting on a show for his
He got loud and started throwing pennies at me. Sin found out and was p
didn't tell him. Word also got back to him that Black had been trying to ass
a little team to get at him, but no one would bite. Black's revenge was short

Weeks had passed and I didn't see or hear from Black. It was pouring o
and I had just left school. I ran to my new Benz and threw my book bag in th
seat. The next thing I knew a hand grabbed me from behind, and a handk
was placed over my mouth and nose. I struggled, but the substance on the
knocked me out cold.

Shortly after Black and I broke up it was rumored that he came into
money, but the truth was he conned a Mexican kid from Texas out of a larg
of drugs. He took the bricks of cocaine on consignment, but instead of fl
them and paying up; he kept the cash, came back to New York and started b
He bought a new car, clothes, and jewelry. Alacrán, the guy he robbed,
several attempts to collect on the debt, but his calls went unanswered, so
was sent out in search of Black.

Alacrán was small in stature and quiet. The short, frail young man v
match for Black physically; which is why he didn't take him as a serious
However, his entire family being part of the Mexican Mafia made him
powerful person.

When I woke, I was in a basement that smelled of old, molded wood.

was one small window, which provided a single stream of light. There was a single orange work light dangling above my head which was connected to a generator by a gray extension cord. I could hear my pager going off in my book bag, but my hands and feet were tied to an old metal chair, and a scarf was wrapped around my mouth. I had no idea who had taken me, where I was, or how long I had been there.

The door at the top of the steps cracked open and I could hear footsteps on the wooden steps behind me. Two men appeared. They had stocking caps over their faces. One spoke to me in English, but with a heavy Latin accent. He took off my gag.

"Me no want to hurt you, *señorita*. Me want your boyfriend."

I was scared beyond words. "But I don't know where he is."

"Me so sorry you say that. We must talk to him, and if you no tell me where he is," he shook his head from side to side, "you be very sorry."

"He is not here! He left this morning, and he's not due back until next week. Please let me go!"

"You call him, he come for you, and we let you go."

"I only have his pager number. He just got a new phone."

The one speaking looked to the second man then said, "*Subir escaleras y obtener el teléfono.*" He trotted up the steps and came back with a phone. He plugged the cord into the jack.

"*¿Qué es el número?*" I read off the number and told him to put in 155-911-911 after the number. Within minutes the phone started ringing. The man answered the phone and placed it on speaker. He had already given me strict instructions what not to say.

"Sin! Somebody has me and they want you to come here!"

"What! Who is it?"

"I don't know," I cried, "but I'm scared."

"Don't worry, I'm coming for you."

"Please hurry!"

The man spoke. "Black we've been looking for you!"

"This is not Black! My name is Sin! Who is this, and why did you take her?"

He seemed puzzled. "You no Black girlfriend?"

"No! I don't date Black anymore, and I don't know where he is! Now please, let me go!"

He spoke to Sin. "Who is this?"

"Listen, I don't know who you are or what this is all about, but I assure you, she doesn't have anything to do with Black anymore. Who you have there is my girl, and my name is Sin—*Pecado*. I'm sure we can resolve this matter. I'm willing to give you whatever you want to get her back safely. Call your people and see what we can do. "

The Spaniard's eyes swept back and forth as he pulled at his pointed beard. He was searching his mind. "Sin? *Pecado*? I call you back in ten minutes." He abruptly hung up.

The two men walked back up the stairs speaking in Spanish. They didn't know I understood some Spanish, but didn't speak it. They said something about calling the boss. Minutes later the door opened and they removed my blindfold, untied my hands, said they would be back, and then left again. The stream of light from the window shrank and dimmed until it became completely dark outside. It felt like hours had passed and rats began to scurry around. I never wanted to be home so badly.

I heard footsteps upstairs then the sound of something heavy being dragging. There was a heavy thud like a sack of potatoes being dropped on the ground. The door swung open, and the Spanish man from earlier told me he needed to retie the scarf over my eyes. I could hear fumbling with a chair and tape being ripped. A few seconds later I heard plastic being placed over the window.

Two Latin men descended the steps then removed the cover from my eyes. Someone else was in the basement behind me. I couldn't see them, but I could smell weed and cigarette smoke. I glanced over, and beside me sat an unconscious Black. He had a knot the size of a golf ball protruding from his forehead.

He was abruptly awakened by a hard slap from a wet washcloth to the face. He looked around frantically, trying to figure out where he was. He soon realized he was tied up in the basement. His mouth, hands, and feet were duct taped.

"Mr. Black, we've been looking for you. I'm so glad you could finally drop in." The tape was ripped from his mouth. "This girl here tells us she's not your girlfriend. Do you think I should let her go since she has nothing to do with this?"

"I don't care if you kill that trifling bitch!"

A tear dropped from my eye. I couldn't believe I was getting ready to die alongside this orangutan.

"I hear her new friend has lots of money. Maybe you help us get him and whatever we get we'll apply it to your debt?"

"Deal! I hate that pretty boy, punk ass motherfucker anyway!"

The man looked at me. "How about you? Are you willing to help us set your new boyfriend up? All you have to do is show me where he lives and I'll release you."

I knew he would kill me either way, so I shook my head no. "I can't do that."

"You can't. And why not?"

I looked right at Black then said, "Because he's been good to me, I love him, and I'd rather die than set him up." I began crying. "Just do me one favor before you kill me?" I glared over at Black. "Please give me the satisfaction of watching you kill him first?"

Black squirmed and rocked in his chair trying to get to me. Since my hands were free I slapped the shit out of him.

The man laughed. "You see, Black, you could learn something about principles from this girl. She's more honorable and got bigger balls than you! Now I can see why a man would go to such great lengths to secure her safety. I'm personally glad he was able to locate you for us, because I'm going to enjoy killing you slowly. I'm sorry for the terrible mixup, Misty. You're free to go."

I sat there for a second, not sure what had just happened. Was he serious or going to put a bullet in my back as I ran away?

I could see a figure, hidden within the darkness, far off in the corner. I bolted toward the steps, but before I could climb them a hand grabbed me. I screamed and started swinging. Sin held his arms out then raised the hood from over his face.

"Daddy?" I broke down as he held me tight. I trembled in his arms as Buddy stood close by with an AK 47 in hand.

A nicely dressed, middle-aged Latin man descended the steps, and they shook hands. "Alvaro, my friend, it's good to see you again. I only wish it was under better terms," Sin stated.

"Yes, I agree. You should call more often. Last time we spoke was at Johnnie's wedding in Bahamas. Alacrán sends his personal regards and thanks you for handling this situation for him. We've been looking for this *puta* for weeks. You have our sincere apologizes for the confusion."

"It's no problem. I'm just glad my peoples here didn't accidently get caught up."

"It's a good thing you reached out to me when you did, because she was first on the list to go. So did your Bright Eyes pass the test?"

Sin smiled. "Yeah, with flying colors!"

"I'm happy for you! Make sure you bring her to the house to meet my wife."

They had a brief conversation before Alvaro walked over and picked up a pair of hedge trimmers off a milk crate. He then grinned. *"Hola carbron, hoy aprenderas una leccion!"* He snapped the blades open and closed in front of Black's face.

Sin looked over at me. "What he say?"

I whispered, "Today you will learn a lesson."

*"A mí nadie me roba, pendejo! Y menos a mi familia!"* (No one steals from me and definitely not from my family!) *"Primero, te cortare los dedos…uno por uno y luego las manos. Igual no te haran falta en el infierno carbron!"* (First, I'll cut off your fingers one by one, and then your hands. You won't be needing them in hell, motherfucker!) *"¿Ves esta tijeras? Son Para cortarte el guevo maricon!"* (You see these scissors? They're to cut off your dick, fucking pussy!)

All the men began laughing. Black had no idea what was being said.

I turned to Sin. "What test did I pass?"

"You could have given me up, but you didn't, and that was admirable. Although I didn't have to, I would have paid a nice penny to get you back, and I wanted to make sure you were worth it." He grabbed my hand. "Let's get the fuck out of here before we witness a murder."

We walked up the stairs, and as we got to the top I heard the slicing of the sheers then Black scream. The men laughed.

Someone joked, "Look, he peed on himself!"

Weeks later Black's body was found tortured. His penis, both of his hands, and all ten of his fingers had been hacked off. He was also set on fire. I asked Sin how he and Black ended up in the basement with me. He said I was lucky he knew the man the guys in the basement worked for, some calls were made, and arrangements were made for my release.

Before getting on a flight to New York, Sin called Buddy and gave him strict instructions to locate Black and have him snatched up. They located him at the first placed they checked, his apartment. I found out I wasn't the only one with a secret pad. Black had moved out of his mother's house months before and had a one bedroom in Mount Vernon.

Sin joked that Black was so predictable. He said he had Buddy tap

Black's new Nissan 300ZX causing the alarm to sound, and when he came down to check on the car they hit him over the head with a tire iron and threw his limp body in the back of a cargo van. They brought him to the address, and rest is history. Sin and I never spoke about that evening again. I learned from that night to stay out of his business and to let him handle things they way he saw fit. He was right, and I should have let him kill Black's ass at brownstone.

# CHAPTER 15

## *Stake Out*

I decided to work from home on Friday. Toya and Malik had been on my mind since she informed me of her suspicions. She had called me six times since, and I was hoping for his sake she was mistaken.

I went online and checked Corrlinks.com, and had a new message from Sin.

He wrote, "Misty, I woke up with you heavily on my mind. Last night you danced all through my dreams, and I wanted to be the first to tell you good morning and have a great day! Love you!"

I responded, and then shut down my computer. The phone rang.

"Hey, Misty, are we still on for tonight?"

"How many times do I need to tell you, yes I'm going with you, Toya. I'm down as long as you're sure this is what you want to do."

"I am positive! I need to know if my husband is laying the pipe to another woman. You just don't understand how I feel right now." She sighed. "I feel violated beyond words. I thought at this point in my marriage we would be past this type of crap. I've been busting my butt to keep our family together, financially above water, and this man is out there tricking the little bit of money he makes on the next woman! If that bastard is cheating on me again, I'm divorcing him. I swear this time! He must not recognize that there are men who make passes at me. I could have gotten with any one of them behind his back. We both could have been out there getting our groove on! He don't think I get tired of that same old dick year after year?"

We both laughed.

"It's settled then. We'll go out there and see what's going on. Hopefully he won't even show up. Have you spoken to Charmaine yet?"

"No, but I left a message on her voicemail. I did speak with Malik this morning, though. I tried to get him to take me out to dinner tonight, but he said maybe tomorrow, and that he had plans. He claims he'll be hanging out with his boys."

"What time do you want to go over there?"

"He normally leaves our house around nine o'clock. Since he said he was going out I told him you, Charmaine, and I were going to the movies and that the kids would be spending the night at my aunt's house. He knows when I go out with the girls I come home late. I think I should leave my house right before he does; that way we'll already be there when he pulls up."

"We're gonna have to take another car. He might see yours."

"And what if he does? By the time he sees us, it'll be too late for him!"

"Alrighty then. It seems like you've got your mind made up."

"I do, but we'll have to finish this conversation later because I have to get some work done. I'll call you as soon as I get off."

I had a bad feeling about this. I was rolling with her, but my sixth sense was telling me it wasn't going to turn out good. People act like they want to know until the infidelity hits them smack dab in the face. I went through my share of drama with Sin, but we were young, weren't married, didn't have kids, and there was never a question as to who held his heart. He either had his game tight, his bitches in check, or didn't fuck around. On a few occasions I had to check a female who had gotten beside herself. I didn't blame them for trying, but it wasn't happening.

I placed all my papers back in the briefcase then tried to reach

Charmaine. I also got her voicemail. I left a message. I got myself dressed, went to the post office, and made a few stops. I needed to mail a box of transcripts from Sin's case to the lawyer and send him a letter I had written regarding some legal matters he wanted me to look up. The weather finally broke and was back up in the 40's. I threw on a jogging suit, my Ugg boots, and a North Face jacket then headed out the door. I was able to get everything done and was back in the house by 4:30.

I was making myself a sandwich when I heard the doorbell ring. I wasn't expecting anyone or any deliveries. I looked through the peephole and saw Nickelle. I pulled the door open wide and greeted her with open arms.

"Nickie, what brings you around to these parts?"

She walked into my embrace. "I was a couple minutes from here and thought to put these pictures of Trey in your mailbox, but saw your car and decided to ring the bell."

"Come on in! I was just about to make myself a sandwich. Do you want one?"

"Yeah, I'm hungry. I haven't eaten since breakfast." She pulled off her coat and followed me into the kitchen.

I prepared sandwiches with soup and salad. "Have you spoken to Toya?"

"No, I haven't seen her since we went out to Butter. I've been so busy with Trey and the salon. I've been meaning to stop by her shop. She left me a message, but I didn't get a chance to call her back. What up with her?"

"Malik may be up to his old tricks again."

"Are you serious? You've got to be kidding. He's got to have one of those sex disorders or something. Maybe he's a nymphomaniac or a sex addict. He just can't be that conniving and stupid!"

"Well, we're going to stake out this woman's house tonight."

"Who's going?"

"Me, Toya, and Charmaine. Do you want to come?"

"Yeah, why not? Trey is staying over his friend's house, and I don't have any plans. It may be fun!"

"Nick, you're the only person I know who could make fun out of going to stake out the next woman's house."

"You got to get your fun in where you can! We can get us some food and make a night out of it. It may even get interesting."

We continued talking as we ate our lunch. I admired the pictures of Trey. He was so handsome and growing up to be a real nice young man. He never gave her any problems and had plans to go off to college soon. They had a good relationship and were able to relate since they were close in age. He told her everything. They talked about girls, clothes, his basketball games, and his sexual experiences—and he was very sexually active. Unlike most teens he felt comfortable talking with his mother about anything, and he didn't hold back either.

The ringing of the house phone interrupted our conversation.

"Hello."

"Hey, girlie! What's up?" Toya sounded as if she'd just drunk a few cups of coffee.

"I'm sitting here talking with Nickelle."

"Let me talk to her for a second."

I passed Nickelle the phone.

"Toya, I've been meaning to get back to you. I was running around like a mad lady. How are you doing?"

I could hear Toya going off about Malik. Nickelle played dumb. "What's going on over there tonight?"

Nickelle nodded and then smiled, "Eight o'clock. I'll be there!"

Charmaine was cheery when I arrived at the brownstone. She had prepared a pitcher of peach margaritas for us. Nickelle was already there and had the music pumping. She was the type of person you wanted to be around when she was tipsy. She would crack jokes and have you laughing all night long. I grabbed me a glass and kicked off my shoes. She was playing my jam. I started dancing and singing along to "Party" by Beyoncé.

"Okay, let's get this party started" Nickelle cheered as she swayed to the music.

We all sang in unison. "'Cause we like to parta…Ha…Ha….ha…ha… hay!"

Charmaine was dancing by herself in front of the mirror. She took a good look at herself then said, "I do look good! I could give some of these twenty-year-olds a run for their money!"

Nickelle burst out laughing.

Charmaine swung around with her hand on her hip. "What you laughing at?"

"You may have the body of a twenty-something-year-old, but those ashy ass feet are showing your years!"

We all looked down at her feet and burst out laughing. They were super ashy.

"Oh, shut up! I just got out the shower."

"It's called lotion! Try some, don't be afraid, and let's not stop at the ankles."

Toya arrived shortly after we finished our first drink. Surprisingly, she too was in a good spirits. You would have thought the four of us were getting ready to celebrate something instead of preparing to stake out some woman's house in an attempt to catch Malik cheating.

"Here Toya, have a drink before we leave." Nickelle passed her a glass. "I want you to listen to the words of this song and dedicate it to Malik if we catch him tonight." Nick put on a track by Jazmine Sullivan, "Bust Your Windows," and we all laughed.

"Girl, I've been there and done that," Toya joked.

I proposed a toast. "To great friends, stakeouts, and possible new beginnings!"

We clanked glasses and drank up.

When we piled up into Nickelle's Range Rover, we were all laughing and joking. Charmaine packed a thermos of margaritas to go, and Toya had potato salad and fried chicken for the ride.

"I want to get something sweet to munch on before we hit the road," Charmaine stated.

Nickelle complained, "You have a refrigerator full of stuff, and Toya brought food. I ready to hit the road and do some investigating."

"Slow down, Inspector Gadget. I'm gonna need some chocolate for after we smoke this." Charmaine pulled out and dangled a bag full of weed in Nick's face.

Nickelle quickly shut up.

Charmaine unsealed the bag, put it up to my nose then giggled. "Misty, I got some more of that Kush you liked so much."

I laughed then moved her hand. "I'm not messing with you! The last time I smoked with you I was all messed up!"

Nickelle snatch the bag from her hand. "Good, that means more for me!" She put the clear bag to her nose then sniffed. "Damn! We got to get something to roll this up in."

I fanned my hand in front of my face. "That shit stinks!"

I remained in the car while the attendant pumped the gas. It looked like they spent fifty dollars on junk food. The woman, Michelle, whose house we were going to stake out, lived about forty minutes away from Harlem, so we had a nice ride ahead of us.

Directly after merging onto the highway Charmaine lit up a joint. She took two puffs then passed it Nickelle. She took two puffs and then passed it to Toya. I felt like an outsider because all three of them were smoking, and Toya almost never smokes.

I stuck my hand out. "All right, all right, I'll take a pull." I sighed. "Peer pressure is a motherfucker!" We all chuckled.

Nickelle lit another joint then pretended not to want to pass it to me. "Did you put in on this, man?"

I sucked my teeth. "And neither did you, so pass me the joint."

She took one last pull then passed it to me.

I took a pull, started coughing, and instantly started feeling silly. Within the forty-minute drive we smoked and sang along to a dozen songs.

The street Michelle lived on was a typical neighborhood in Long Island lined with private houses. Her house was completely dark inside, so we knew no one was home. We parked four houses up then cut off the engine.

"I'm hungry! Toya, can you hook me up with some of that potato salad and a piece of chicken?" She grabbed the bag of food then passed it to me in the front seat. I smirked. "I guess that means no and to help myself."

She chuckled. "That's exactly what it meant, Misty."

I made everyone a plate and we got to munching. "Pour me some margarita, Cha."

Nickelle broke the silence with another one of her comical stories. "Listen, the funniest thing happened to me the other day!"

"What happened to you, Nick?"

"I was walking up 44th Street and this drunken, dirty bum in a wheelchair tried to get his rap on. I ignored him, but every time I tried to pass him he'd roll his wheelchair up and blocked my path. I made a few attempts to get around him, but he was pretty good maneuvering that thing. I slipped between two cars and started walking in the middle of the street. He started following me and cursing me out. He was saying some crazy shit too! He said I needed to go home and take care of our kids.

People actually thought I knew him! He was yelling that I was fucked up for leaving him in his condition."

"So what did you do?" Toya inquired.

"I finally stopped and told him to go fuck off! I went into the bank. You wouldn't believe it, but that maniac waited. He pulled off his prosthetic leg, and when I came out the door he threw it at me!"

Charmaine covered her mouth. "What?"

"You heard me right! He threw his fucking fake leg at me! You already know I don't have any sense. So I picked the leg up and threw that bitch right back at him! Everyone on the street was looking at me like I was the lunatic. They don't know I've learned living in New York you can't let these crazy people mess with you."

I couldn't help but giggle. "You're dead wrong, Nick."

"Hey, I could have left the fucking leg in the middle of the street. Let a truck run over it, but I didn't. I do have a heart."

"You always seem to attract the craziest people. I don't know anyone who has the kind of strange encounters you do."

"It didn't stop there, Toya! That only got him started! He took the shoe that was attached to the leg off then threw that at me! I was so pissed! He almost hit me in the head!" We all started laughing again. "Did you know in some countries to throw or hit someone with a shoe is a sign of disrespect? He must, not have known who he was dealing with!"

Charmaine was laughing so hard she was holding her stomach. "What happened next? What did you do?"

"I picked the shoe up and hurled that motherfucka like a football over a fence!"

I couldn't stop laughing. Toya had tears running down her face.

"He'll think about that the next time he thinks to throw a shoe at someone!"

"Oh, no, you, didn't?" I couldn't breathe.

"Oh, yes, the fuck, I did! Wheelchair bandit chased me for another two blocks before I was able to dip into the train station."

She was so animated. We sat in that car eating and drinking until about 11:30.

Charmaine couldn't take it anymore. "How much longer are we going to sit out here? I'm high as hell, and if I eat another piece of candy I'm going to throw up!"

"Let's give it a little more time. He said he wasn't leaving our house until after nine."

Charmaine instantly changed her attitude. "Turn that up! That's my jam!"

Nickelle reached for the dial and turned up the volume. "Remember this song?" The radio was playing some throwback hip-hop and had on Naughty by Nature's "OPP".

"That was the shit! This song brings back so many memories. Do you remember the crazy shit we used to do?"

"How could I forget? Other People's Property was everybody's slogan when this first came out," I added.

"Especially yours, Charmaine!" Nickelle teased.

"You damn right! I was the OPP queen! I liked other people's penises." She laughed. "Did I say that? I meant to say property. The only guys who were off limits were my crew's men. Anybody else's man was up for grabs. Life was all about traveling, sex, dough, and a new outfit for me. I had no time or interest in settling down. I was having too much fun!"

"Well, I'm glad you had fun. All OPP got me was my ass kicked by Black."

"That's not completely true. OPP got you with Sin, and that turned out to be one of the best move you ever made."

"You're right, Cha. We were doing it big!"

"Yes, you were! When I look back we were living it up! When most females were trying to get sneaker money, Misty was whipping a Benz, and I had a Land Cruiser! We was wearing full-length minks and nothing but designer gear by the time we were twenty! We were rolling with the high rollers and partying with celebrities! I felt like a movie star flying from state to state. We were living in the fast lane, driving hot cars and fucking with rich, influential, and powerful young men."

"I know I had an exceptional life with Sin. I had one of the hottest brothers on the East Coast, and he was in love with me. Most women my age could only imagine doing half the shit I've done or going to half the places I've been. It was VIP all the way with all-access passes!"

"I missed out on loads of stuff," Nickelle whined.

I jabbed, "That's because your fast ass had a baby, and no ID."

"But we sure did do it up for you, girl," Charmaine teased. "The All Star games, championship boxing matches, Super Bowl weekend, NBA playoffs, all of the music awards, BET, Source, MTV and Soul Train. We were there in Miami, Cali, VA, DC, Vegas, Atlanta, LA, Chicago, and the Carolinas just to name a few and countless vacations to the islands."

"What was your favorite trip?" Nickelle asked.

We all started thinking, but Charmaine answered first. "I got it! I would say my favorite trip was to the Soul Train Music Awards out in Cali. LA had a different vibe than New York. People from all over came out for the awards, and we lived it up to the fullest. We partied for four days straight and met so many people! I even got to smoke some chronic with some of Snoop's people!"

"Wow! Now that's hot! I would have liked to do that," Nickelle confessed. "What about you, Toya?"

"Don't even bother to ask me. Broke-ass Malik could never afford to take me anywhere! Thanks to Misty and Sin I did get to go to the Super Bowl once."

"What about you, Misty? What was your favorite trip?"

"The same as Charmaine's, but I'll tell you about the craziest trip I was ever on. Our girlfriend, Marisol, was messing with this guy, and he invited her down to Miami for his birthday party. He asked her to bring some friends and he would foot the bill. He had rented out a huge penthouse apartment. It had an outdoor balcony running along the entire perimeter of the building, a private patio on the roof, and a fat Jacuzzi. Sin and I got into a debate over me going. He said, "No man was gonna pay for some chicks to fly down unless he was getting something out of it!"

"I felt like he just didn't want me to go. Charmaine was going, and it was Marisol's man's party, so he reluctantly agreed. I got my ticket, but he had me purchase a return flight to Alabama. He wanted to see me before I went home.

We get to Miami around seven o'clock. It turns out Marisol's man was a dealer slash pimp. As soon as we walked in the place all we saw were naked girls running around. They were giving lap dances and blowjobs at request. Marisol had no idea dude invited us with the intent to recruit us, and her too!"

"Get the hell out of here!"

"Yeah Toya, there were three or four women and two men having sex right there in the middle of the living room. I never saw anything like it in my life. One big, gigantic orgy! The shit was bananas! It was way too freaky for me. Charmaine and I got the hell up out of Dodge. We caught a cab and went straight to the airport. She came back home and I had Sin pick me up in Alabama that night. He thought the whole thing was amusing."

"What was your most fun trip?"

"With my girls I would say when we all flew to Hawaii for the Pro Bowl. With Sin it was the time I went to see him out of town and he took me to Dave & Buster's. You know the both of us were video game junkies. We spent the whole afternoon playing games." I giggled as I thought back.

"There was this driving game that actually looked like the front half of a car. It had everything including doors that closed. While he's playing I got to fucking with him. I got him all worked up. My man gave the kid waiting next in line some money and told him to scram. Sin put like $20.00 in the machine, and had me ride him while he played. By the time we got out a line had formed."

"You two could find a hole to fuck in," Charmaine joked.

"Damn right! My most romantic trip was to Europe. It was beautiful, but Barbados will always be my favorite vacation. It holds a special place in my heart. We got to fulfill our fantasy of making love on the beach."

Toya huffed. "It's a damn shame! Malik and I have been together longer than you and Sin, you two have been apart for many years, and I still don't have half the memories you two share. The last time Malik and I took a vacation was over five years ago. It was to Disney World with the kids, and I had to pay for it! I didn't even get a honeymoon."

We all sat quietly listening as she brought the mood down.

She looked at her watch. "It's twelve-sixteen. Where the hell is my husband at?"

Just as she finished her sentence Nickelle who had been checking the rearview mirror looked over into the back seat and said, "Everybody, be quiet, I see headlights coming up the street!"

"Nick, what does you seeing lights have to do with us being quiet? They can't hear us, dummy!"

"Okay, okay, okay! Cut me some slack. I'm new to this!" We all giggled at her silliness. "Do you know what they're in?"

"He should be driving his jeep."

"I see a jeep and a small red car coming," she announced with childlike excitement.

I thought to myself that Nickelle was enjoying this stake out just a tad too much considering what we were really there for. Toya tried to turn in her seat, "What color is the jeep?"

"It's a dark color, maybe blue or black?"

She sat straight up. It was as if she smelled him coming up the road. We broke our necks trying to see the approaching vehicles. As they neared we crunched down low so we wouldn't be noticed. The red car pulled up and parked outside the garage. The blue jeep parked adjacent to the house. We all sat in suspense waiting for him to exit the jeep. Michelle walked into the house, but left the front door open.

"That's her right there." Toya pointed.

I grew inpatient. Malik was taking forever to get out of the vehicle. I wanted to walk up to the door and pull his ass out! Finally the light from his cell phone illuminated the interior of the jeep. Shortly afterward Toya's cell started ringing. We all looked at her as she pulled the phone from her bag.

"Misty, turn the volume up on the radio." Once that was done she said, "Watch this," as she slid her finger across the screen of her iPhone. "Hi Malik. I'm surprised you're calling. What's up, darling?"

Charmaine looked up at me; I looked over at Nickelle who looked back at Toya, who looked around at all of us. She was cool, calm, and collected while talking to him. "So, you're going to be in late? I see uhh-huh . . . no, it's fine. Yeah, I'm out with the girls. So where are you? Oh, having a couple of beers with the boys."

She rolled her eyes, twisted her mouth and shook her head in disgust. "Tell your boys I said hello."

"So what time should I expect you home tonight? Yeah, okay . . . all right . . . sure and you have fun too. Huh? Oh yeah, I love you too Malik." She hung up and after what seemed like five minutes the truck door swung open, and out stepped Malik carrying a bouquet of flowers and a bottle of wine. She reached for the door handle, but Charmaine stopped her. "Wait, Toya!"

"What are you doing? Let her get out!" Nickelle was obviously just as upset as Toya, and ready to kick some ass. However we knew to wait it out a little longer. Malik needed to be caught with his hand in the cookie jar; otherwise, he would have opportunity to lie his way out of it.

"I can't believe him trying to throw me off! That fool had the nerve to actually say out loud, to no one in his car, 'Toya said what's up, man!' If he would've answered himself I would've jumped out this car. He's a good for nothing cheating bastard!"

"I'm sorry, Toya," Charmaine whispered.

I reached around the front seat and rubbed her shoulder. "You deserve better! He's not worthy. He's a piece of shit!"

Our support calmed her down. We sat silently and watched as the lights went on and off in different rooms. We watched as they kissed passionately at the kitchen window. We watched as they made their way upstairs. Her blinds were partly drawn, and we could see their silhouettes.

Once it got still in the room I said, "Let's go get this motherfucker!"

We marched up to the front of the house, but before the rest of us could step up on the porch Toya was kicking on the door.

"What are you doing? Are you trying to get us all locked up?"

She continued to bang. "Misty, I advise all of you to not step on this porch because I'm about to fuck him up, and I may need somebody to bail me out!" The lights in the house came on as well as the porch light. Stupid Malik swung open the door in his boxers with a bat in hand. She stared at him and asked with ice in her voice, "What you plan on doing with that, motherfucker? Save your whore?"

All we heard was, "Oh shit!" before Malik tried to slam the door shut. She wedged her foot between the door and the frame then used her body weight to hold it open. She eventually won the struggle and pushed her way in. He took off running up the stairs, but tripped. She tackled him as he tried to get up and they toppled onto the steps. The bat flew as she came crashing down atop his back. I was recording the whole thing on my cell phone.

Michelle was at the top of the stairs in a towel screaming, "I'm going to call the police!"

Nickelle picked up the bat from the floor and pointed it at her. "If you even think about picking up that phone, I'm going to fly your fucking head!"

Charmaine and I looked at each other and snickered. We had been through this before, just never at the mistress's house. It was new to Nickelle which is why she was so hyped up.

Malik squirmed beneath Toya's weight. "Get off of me, Toya!" She threw wild punches at his back and head. "Would you stop, and let me get up!"

"You dirty son of a bitch! You couldn't take me out tonight because you wanted to come here!" She battered him with her two fists.

"Let me up so I can put on my clothes, and then we can go home and talk."

She slapped him in the back of his head. "What's there to talk about? You want to talk about that phone call you just made to me from outside! Where are your boys at, Malik?"

She pounded his back with her fist one last time before a sudden wave of calm came over her. She rose to her feet, stepped over him, then straightened out her clothes. She descended the three steps and walked toward the door.

"Wait, Toya. Where are you going?"

She spun around and stared at him with revulsion. "Away from you! I don't want to hear you lie, and you're not worth me staying here to fight for. I want a divorce Malik. You have brought me shame for the last time. I'm going to take you for every fucking dollar—pardon me—cent you have in alimony and child support! I will have no mercy, and by the time

I'm done you won't have anything left to buy flowers and wine with!"

She looked up at Michelle. "I hope you got some money, tootsie. You're definitely gonna need it to take care of him when I'm finished! Let's see how good his sex is when you have to pay for it, whore!"

Malik sat on the steps holding his neck as Toya turned for the door. "I'm sorry, Tee."

She stopped then looked down at him.

"Fuck you, Malik! And you're right; you are sorry. You're one sorry ass motherfucker! I should have never married you, and I damn sure should have left you a long time ago. I stayed, but not another day. Not one more fucking day! You hear me! I kill myself trying to keep our shit together. I struggle all because of you, because of your shortcomings, and your inability to contribute. You're my husband so instead of treating myself to something nice or traveling, I put the money into our family. I don't complain or make you out to be less of a man. I just get things done so we can be okay. That's the sacrifice superwoman over here has made to be with you. What have you given up?"

Her eyes welled up, but she held it in. "Outside of dick, you haven't given up a fucking thing! I like wine, Malik! I like flowers! Do you not see the woman who stands before you? I'm not your momma. I'm your wife! I'm cutting corners, clipping coupons, and shopping for deals so you can come over here with presents? You just told Ky'elle this morning you didn't have any money to get her hair done, but you're buying gifts? It's a few weeks before Christmas for God's sake, but you're not worried. Superwoman over here has already handled that. She ran out and made sure the kids had everything they wanted."

She gazed down at the floor lost in thought. "Matter of fact, what did you get them for Christmas? Does it matter to you that I had to borrow money from my girls to stop a foreclosure on our home six months ago? You're so used to things just getting done that you don't even see that I'm the locomotive, the coal, and the steam that keeps this train moving down the tracks."

She waved her hand dismissing him. "You are such a big disappointment. I put my destiny in the hands of a momma's boy. I can't blame it all on you. It's partially her fault you're the way you are . . . an ungrateful jackass! And by the way, thanks for spoiling my holidays and derailing my life yet once again." She looked up the steps. "And you can go to hell, Michelle! As soon as I can I'm going to tell every single person I know you're a whore who knowingly sleeps with married men! I'm gonna warn every parent and teacher at your school about you, Miss Michelle Moore!" Toya picked up her pocketbook. "And Malik, please don't bother trying to call or come to my house."

"What about my stuff?"

"The kids will help me pack your things while I explain to them why you won't be coming back ever again!"

"Don't try to turn my kids against me, Toya! That's not fair!"

"Turn your kids against you? I don't play those kinds of games. You are their father, and I would never try to keep you away from them. If they're going to hate you it will be all on their own. When you cheated tonight you didn't just cheat on me; you cheated on all of us! You have Charmaine and Misty's phone numbers. Call them when you're ready to pick up your stuff, but don't, and I mean don't fucking call my house ever again!"

"Toya—" Michelle started to call out, but was cut off.

"Bitch, the best thing you can do for yourself right now is to not say a fucking word to me! Not one! I'm trying really hard not to blame this on you, but I swear to God if you say one fucking word I will run up those steps and lose my shoe all up in your adulteress ass! And give me my goddamn flowers!" Toya snatched the flowers out of the vase on the ledge then slapped Malik across the head with them. She took one last look down at him then shook her head. Nickelle handed her the unopened bottle of wine that was sitting on the kitchen counter before we walked out of the door.

A few of Michelle's neighbors had come out of their homes when they heard the ruckus. Toya turned to the nosy neighbors and said for everyone to hear, "I want you all to know the lady who lives in that house is a home-wrecker! She likes sleeping with married men, so you better watch your husband when she's around! Mine is in there with her now, and once she pulls his dick out her mouth you'll never know whose husband's will be in there next!" We jumped up into the Range Rover and headed back to the city.

"Please someone roll me a joint! My nerves are shot." As she lit the joint Nickelle couldn't help but to keep peeking over at Toya. "What is it, Nickelle? I know you want to say something."

"Are you okay? I've never seen you like that. You looked demonic then all of a sudden you got up. I was sure you were gonna kick him. Thank God that woman didn't come down the stairs. She would have got that ass whooped for sure! Seriously, though, I'm really sorry you had to go through that, but if it makes you feel any better that woman was wack with her big-ass teeth!"

Toya chuckled. "I thought the same thing, but I didn't want you guys to think I was hating on her."

"Nah, that wouldn't have been hating," Charmaine chimed in. "That would have been you being super honest. She did have some big-ass teeth sticking out of that big-ass camel face of hers!"

"Thanks for coming with me. I couldn't have done that by myself. I really appreciate your support. Especially you, Nickelle! When Michelle said she was going to call the cops I was about to haul ass," Toya joked. "But she dropped that idea quick when you threatened her with the bat."

"Hey, I can get a little gully when I need to. I'd fight for any of you before I'd fight for myself. You didn't do so bad yourself. He's gonna have one hell of a headache come tomorrow morning." Nickelle laughed.

"He may need a chiropractor after that beating he took." Nickelle passed Charmaine the bat. "Here, put that in the back."

"You know Nick there was a small part of me that was hoping Malik wouldn't show up. The last time I went through this with him I distinctly remember asking myself, when is it enough? Tonight I found out." She paused. "I'm emotionally exhausted. I don't have anything left to give, and I feel for my kids. Ky'elle and Lil Malik are going to be devastated behind this. What do I tell them? Your father won't be coming back home because I caught him in his draws at his mistress house? The last thing I ever want is for them to be affected. That's one of the main reasons I stayed all this time. They didn't need to know just how much of a moron their father really is, but I can't lie to them or remain in a marriage for them anymore."

She turned and looked out of the window. We rode the rest of the ride in silence. When we got back to the brownstone Charmaine made something for us to eat and we all crashed. Nickelle and I slept in our old rooms while Toya took Trey's bedroom. She appeared to be handling the situation a lot better than I expected. She was pretty good considering she just caught her husband with another woman. In the next few weeks she would go through the full gamut of emotions then have a moment of clarity. It would be then that she would know her next move. In the past her next move usually ended with her taking him back.

I've watched many of my girlfriends struggle in relationships that are not fulfilling, loving, or stable. Many are more concerned with holding on and keeping dick in their bed opposed to letting go and finding a good man. Many fight to preserve and retain relationships with men who haven't the slightest idea what it takes to be a man. It's crazy how the roles in a relationship have changed so much over the years. The man's understood role as head of the household has diminished while the woman's role has increased. Women are now the wife, mother, employee, chef, sex machine, nurse, teacher, chauffeur, accountant, and, in some cases, the father. No one told Malik a man's mere presence in the house is not enough. Interaction and participation is required.

The obstacles our great-grandmothers went through are completely different than what today's modern women are facing. It's not only expected for women to cook, clean, and take care of the kids. They're expected to bring something to the table like an income. She's challenged with balancing it all—checkbook, career, husband, household, and motherhood. Way too often she walks that tightrope balancing everything across her shoulders while her partner sits back and watches. Was it Malik's mother who ruined him—spoiled him and left him with no idea how to be a man, a father, and a husband? Was he so accustomed to Mommy catering to his every need when it came time for him to man up he had no inkling how to do it?

Most women have simple needs. They want to feel secure, be encouraged, supported, nurtured, loved, respected, and held down. Should those basic needs become secondary to everything else going on? It's insisted that she remain sexy, sensitive, and selfless, but that becomes laborious when she's made to wear the pants in the relationship. Just because Toya wears both the pants and the skirt well doesn't mean she likes it. Malik forgot a real man holds down his family regardless of his income.

# CHAPTER 16

## The Holidays

Monday evening when I heard the garage door opening I knew it could only be Marcus returning from his business trip. I walked over and unlocked the door connecting the garage to the house. I was actually happy to see him. I got a chance to miss him during the week apart. It was sad to say, but one of the major reasons we lasted as long as we did was because he was always gone.

He grabbed his bag from the back seat then greeted me with a peck-kiss to the cheek.

"How was your trip?"

"Everything went well! Thank God I was able to make it home in time for Christmas."

I followed him into the house and upstairs to the bedroom where he placed his bags down. "Do you have anything to eat? I'm starving. All they gave us was pretzels and a free beverage."

"Look in the refrigerator. There's a plate of food you can warm up in the microwave."

He went downstairs. I unpacked his suitcase then went and joined him on the sofa.

"So how was your week without me around?"

"It started off quiet, but then Toya had some drama with Malik, and it ended with a bang."

"What's going on with Malik?"

"He got caught cheating again." I watched to see his reaction.

"That's terrible he got caught. He should have been more careful." Marcus's reply sounded like he was okay with the cheating, but upset Malik got caught.

"So you don't think anything is wrong with him cheating on her?"

"Yeah, I think it's messed up, but you know how it goes. How did he get caught anyway?"

"I deduce it to him being careless." I decided to bring up the lipstick stain I saw on his shirt. "Did you know you have lipstick on your collar?" He started looking at his shirt.

"I don't see any lipstick."

"I'm not talking about the shirt you have on. I'm talking about the light blue shirt in your suitcase."

"I have the slightest idea. Maybe when I hugged the Marketing Director goodbye it got on there." He turned back to the television.

I didn't push the issue. I was planning on leaving him anyway. Over the weekend I'd started moving some things back into the brownstone. My plan was to be completely moved out sometime after the New Year.

I left him to watch the game and I went about my normal Sunday chores. I swept the wood floors, mopped, did laundry, and then cooked baked chicken, macaroni and cheese, and cabbage.

I was extra quiet while we sat at the table and ate dinner together. I had a lot weighing on my mind.

"Those meetings can be quite stressful. I was looking forward to unwinding with you."

I half smiled. I already knew where this conversation was going. He wanted to have sex. We continued a light conversation, and after dinner he put the dishes in the dishwasher as I washed out the pots.

"I'm going to take a quick shower. When you finish come on up to the room and join me."

I forged a smile. "No problem, I'll be up in a minute."

I took my shower then joined him in the bedroom. He had the lights dimmed and soft jazz playing in the background. "What is that you have on? It smells good!"

"It's Issey Miyake," I replied.

"It smells nice!"

"That's funny because I wear it all the time. I'm surprised you never noticed before."

"Tomorrow throw away the rest of the junk on your dresser. I want you to wear only that. I love it!"

I didn't say anything, but thought, *Junk?* He leaned over and kissed me. His kiss was a little wet, but soft and warm. We kissed for a few minutes before he put on a condom and positioned his body on top of mine. He lifted my nightie to my waist. He intensifying his kissing and did some fondling of my breasts, just enough to get my nipples to perk. There was limited foreplay, and the little he did do was so routine that it felt scripted. There was no conversation, and I was barely moist when he made an attempt to jam himself inside of me.

I wasn't the slightest bit aroused. "Marcus, I'm not even wet yet."

He reached over into the end table and grabbed the bottle of lubricant. He squeezed some into his palm then rubbed it onto the condom. I could see this was going to be one of those nights. The best sex I had with him was when he was drunk. Under the influence I was able to control the momentum. He passed me the lubricant and I squirted some on my two fingers then rubbed it around my entryway. He tried again this time with less resistance.

He started pumping himself in and out with no particular rhythm, and I didn't like it one little bit. As I lay there stared up at the ceiling I thought of the scene in the movie *The Color Purple* where Celie described sex with Albert aka Mister as him just climbing on top of her and handling his business.

I thought, *What I would give for an hour with Sin.* I closed my eyes and visualized his face. I saw his chest with my name tattooed on it, and then his entire body appeared in my head. I escaped reality and allowed myself to fantasize about him and it actually helped a little. I was at least able to get wet.

It didn't matter because within ten minutes Marcus was cumming. I got up and went to the bathroom. I looked at myself in the mirror as a tear rolled down my face. In my heart I knew something had to give. Is this really what I was to expect from him if I stayed? I thought to myself, You can't go on like this, Misty.

By the time I came out of the bathroom Marcus was sound asleep. I went down to my office and started wrapping Christmas presents. It was only a few days away and I needed to get the stuff in boxes and under the tree. I made myself a cup of hot chocolate, then sat on the sofa, and listened to Whitney Houston's holiday CD. I reminisced on past holidays.

Christmas was always my favorite holiday, and I always got nice things. As a kid I got the hottest toys, and as an adult the gifts got better—leather, jewelry, furs, designer handbags, and trips. This Christmas the gift I really wanted couldn't be bought in a store, although I would spend every single penny I had to have it. The ultimate gift would be for Sin to be home, making love to me, under the tree like old times.

Every year we were together we christened the tree, and knowing that he was all alone during the holidays bothered me. He tended to be down during this time of year knowing everyone was with their loved ones and he was trapped in there.

I could feel myself becoming sad. I needed to see my man in the worst way. My thoughts switched to Toya. What a time to find out your husband was cheating on you. I decided to give her a call to make sure she was okay.

"Hello?"

"Hi, Ky! It's Auntie Misty. Is your mom around?"

"Yeah, she in her room! I'll go get her."

"Hey Ky'elle, before you go get her, you and I need to have a little talk."

"What's up?"

"There are two things I need to discuss with you. First, you need to focus on school and stop worrying about getting your little pussy eaten."

"Oh my god, Auntie!"

"Don't 'oh my god' me! If you're old enough to consider it then you're old enough to discuss it. Your mother told me about your phone conversation with that boy from your school, and I was very disappointed in you. There is nothing wrong with sex when you're ready for it, but I know you're not ready. You don't even have a steady boyfriend yet! Tell that little snot nose your auntie said go find somebody else's Kitty Cat to nibble on." Ky'elle thought what I said was the funniest thing and started giggling. "I'm not trying to be funny, Ky. I'm dead serious! I expect more of you. Cut the crap out and get your head right! Do you hear me?"

"Yes, Auntie. I hear you."

"Always remember what I am about to tell you and never forget it! The one thing you have that will stay with you forever is that Kitty Cat. Your face will wrinkle, your hips will spread, your tits will sag, and your belly will bulge, but if you keep your Kitty tight you'll have it for the rest of your life. Think about that the next time you consider letting someone have a taste; especially someone you don't even love."

"I wasn't going to have sex with him" she admitted.

"Did you know you can contract a number of sexually transmitted diseases from oral sex like HIV/AIDS, gonorrhea, herpes, syphilis, HPV, and chlamydia? In addition you're exposing your private parts to him. You don't want to get labeled a whore. That label will stick like funk on a skunk. Trust me, once you get that tag it's hard to shake, and boys will not take you seriously. Respect yourself and these boys will have no choice but to follow suit. Do you understand?"

"Yeah, I got it, and thanks!"

"Anytime, my love! The second thing I wanted to talk to you about is your mother. How's she doing?"

"She's been moping around, but she says she's okay. My father keeps calling my cell phone, but I won't answer him."

"So you know what's going on?"

"Yeah, I kind of overheard her yelling at him on the phone."

"So why aren't you accepting his calls?"

"Because, I'm really upset with him. He messed up our family!"

"Regardless, Ky, that's your father, and I suggest you talk to him. If for nothing else it should be to let him know how you're feeling."

"I'll think about it."

"Your mom is going through a rough time right now. She's going to need your help, so try not to stress her out with the foolishness please."

"I won't."

"Thanks, baby, now put your mother on the phone. Hey, Ky?"

"Yeah, Auntie?"

"I want you to know you can always talk to me about anything— boys, sex, pregnancy, birth control, drugs. I don't care what it is. You can always come to me, and I can keep a secret. I love you, kiddo!"

"I love you too! Did you get my Christmas present yet?"

"Yes, and I'm not telling you what it is or giving you any hints, so pass your mother the phone, thank you."

She giggled. I could hear her talking to her mother before passing her the phone. "Hey."

"What's up girlfriend? How are you doing?"

"I'm okay; just going through the motions."

"Yeah, I hear that. I was just checking in on you. You know when you hurt we all hurt."

"That's exactly what Charmaine told me when I spoke to her earlier."

"Then you know it's the truth!" I could feel her smiling through the phone. "I wasn't really planning anything big, but I've decided to have a get together at my house for New Year's, and I'm not taking no for an answer."

"You know what? I think that would be a good idea for me to get out of this house. These kids have got to be sick of me by now," she giggled. "I'm trying to show face for them, but it's hard. Every time I look around this house all I see is memories of him. I need to pack some of his stuff up."

"Do what you have to do. New Year's at my place, and don't bring anything, but you and the kids."

We continued talking for a few more minutes before she had another call.

The following morning, I spoke with Marcus about the party, and he loved the idea. I called Charmaine, Nickelle, Jasmine, and a few other people and invited them. I also had Marcus invite his co-workers. Everyone said they would attend. I only had a few days to plan.

When I got to my office I invited Donald and the rest of my staff.

"Is there anything you want me to bring?" Donald asked.

"No, Dee, just bring your new boyfriend and a bottle of bubbly!"

"I don't think I'll be able to make it," Stephanie advised. "I don't have a babysitter."

"You can bring Samantha!"

"Are you sure?"

"I'm positive! There will be plenty of kids for her to play with. My house has a basement, and all the kids can run amuck down there."

She cheerfully confirmed.

I headed into my office and called the caterer. I decided to go with Two Son's cooking. The owner, Josephine, was a tall West Indian sister who specialized in southern and Caribbean cuisine. I got lucky. She had planned to go to St. Thomas for the holidays, but had to cancel her trip. After a brief discussion we had the menu all picked out: fried chicken, oxtails, stewed fish, collard greens, macaroni and cheese, rice and peas, cornbread, and for desert red velvet cake, strawberry cheesecake, and apple pie.

Next I called the liquor warehouse and placed my order, which would be delivered the next day. I was actually getting into the holiday spirit! For the past few weeks I just wasn't into it. With the economy in such turmoil I wasn't really feeling Christmassy. Gas prices were up, the market was down, the cost of food increased, and people were losing their jobs left and right. I figured a party was exactly what we all needed to start off the New Year!

On Christmas Eve, I had a small office party. All the staff showed up and a few brought dates. I normally gave my staff a big party for Christmas, but this year I decided to have something small at the office and split the money between them. I believed they would appreciate the monetary gift much more.

Donald had Wesley, his new beau, meet him at the office. He was in seventh heaven as his lover was being very attentive. This was perfect because he loved to be showered with affection. Wesley was a very handsome man just as Donald had described. He stood about 6'4" and was dressed immaculately. I thought to myself, *I know he doesn't have a problem attracting a female or male for that matter.*

I watched Stephanie who appeared to be distracted. I empathized with her plight. You could see how much the harassment was affecting her. She told me earlier in the day that her ex-husband, Bernard, was back threatening her, and she felt helpless. She didn't have any family to help her out, and her grandmother was just too old. She said he called her day in and night out. I told her the next time he called the office to let me speak with him because I was not about to have him interfering with my business.

As the night winded down, and before closing I made sure to tell everyone to have a Merry Christmas and gave them their presents. I invited Marcus, but he couldn't make it. He was waiting for me when I got home. He was resting on the sofa next to the fireplace and had a bottle of champagne chilling on ice. I took a quick shower and joined him on the sofa. I threw my feet up in his lap, and he massaged them. We relaxed there for the rest of the night, drinking champagne and watching movies. I dozed off, and when I woke it was 6:30 AM.

"Wake up, Marcus! It's Christmas!"

I was excited like a big kid. I wanted to open my gifts as soon as I got up. He preferred to sleep late, eat breakfast, drink a cup of coffee, watch the news, and then open his presents. No sir, it was gift-getting time! I shook him until he finally lifted his head from the sofa. "All right . . . I'm up! Go ahead and open up your stuff so I can go back to sleep."

I ran over to the tree and started pulling boxes out. "Okay, this one is for you. Open it, open it!"

He reached for the box and pretended to shake then sniff it. He ripped the paper off and fell in love with his Armani suit. "Wow, this is a sharp suit! I'm going to look like a million bucks in this!" He tried the jacket on.

"If you want to close those million-dollar deals you got to dress for part."

"Thanks, sweets! I know you'll like what I got you!"

He passed me a long rectangular box. I instantly knew it was jewelry by the shape. I eagerly grabbed the box from him and began tearing off the paper. Inside was a black velvet box and inside that was a diamond necklace. It was stunning. I could tell he spent a pretty penny on it.

"Thank you! Thank you!" I yelled as I kissed him a few times. "It's beautiful!"

"Wait, there's more."

I was ecstatic. I kneeled in the sofa anticipating the next box. He brought back four beautifully wrapped boxes. In the first box were the matching diamond earrings. In the second box was the matching diamond bracelet. In the third box there was lingerie, and the fourth box held an emerald green dress I saw in a store in Queens.

After cleaning up all the wrapping paper I headed to the kitchen to make breakfast. We were scheduled to have dinner over at his Aunt Pat's house, and were expected at two o'clock sharp.

His family was cool, but his two sisters and three female cousins were very resentful. They were envious and scornful. They had a bunch of deadbeat baby daddies and nothing going for themselves. They were insecure, and anytime a man in their family was doing something for anyone other than them, they had an attitude about it.

When we arrived at Aunt Pat's house everyone was in the Christmas spirit. The older females including his mother were in the kitchen cooking while the men sat around the living room drinking, playing dominos, and talking sports. The kids were running around and playing with their new toys.

All the platters were laid out, grace was said, and dinner was served. Aunt Pat could throw down, and made everything from scratch. I had never seen so much food in my life. She made red rice, dirty rice, rice with black eyed peas, cabbage, collard greens, roast pork, turkey, honey ham, macaroni and cheese, yams, mashed potatoes, squash, lasagna, and a variety of deserts; including my favorite red velvet cake. I was stuffed when I pushed myself from the table. I felt as if I was going to burst.

After dinner everyone sat around the living room telling stories. I had an incoming call. I answered and heard the automated message. I pretended I couldn't hear and excused myself before pressing the number 5. I went into the bathroom so I could have some privacy.

"Can you talk?"

"Yeah, Daddy, I'm at his Aunt's house. We just finished eating dinner. Everyone is in the living room talking. How you doing?"

"You know me. I wanted to wish you a Merry Christmas and let you know I was thinking about you." There was a silence. "I miss you, Baby Girl." He sounded despondent.

"I miss you too, Daddy, and Merry Christmas."

"I'm not going to keep you. I don't have much time left on my account, but I will call you back after the first of the month."

"Okay. I love you, Sin, and I'll be down there to see you very soon."

"Cool, and I Love you too."

He hung up and I went into the kitchen to help clean up. Marcus came up behind me and wrapped his arms around my waist. He had been drinking with the men and smelled of alcohol.

He leaned in and whispered. "Are you ready to go home and work off some of those calories?"

His Aunt Clara started laughing as he grew embarrassed. He hadn't realized his other aunt overheard him too.

"I remember when your nasty uncle used to do that same thing to me."

I blushed. "Let me finish off in here, and then we can head on home."

"No, baby," his aunt said, "I can handle this by myself. You two go on ahead and have some fun for me. This old lady can't remember the last time she had some."

I was determined to end the night on a good note, so when we made it to our bedroom I put on the new lingerie he got me, and seduced him. Instead of letting him take the lead, I controlled the mood. I slid the condom on him and gave it to him real slow and with great intensity.

Instead of ten minutes it lasted twenty.

"This was the best Christmas I ever had. What got into you tonight, Misty?"

I frowned. "What are you talking about? Nothing got into me. You could be getting it like that and better if you would just slow down."

He got defensive. "What are you talking about?"

"I don't want to hurt your feelings, but let me be frank with you. Our sex life is suffering. You don't take your time or try to please me. For the last year I've been feeling like you don't care if I'm into it or not. It's like it's all about you in the bed."

He became agitated. "Well, I'm sorry you feel that way. I wasn't aware you were so displeased with my performance. No one has ever complained about my lovemaking skills before," he added very smugly. "Maybe you're the one with the problem."

I sucked my teeth. "I don't have a problem whatsoever, especially in the sex department. Maybe you need to time yourself the next time we have sex then we'll see who has the issue."

He was pissed. He got up and grabbed his robe. "You really need to do something about that attitude of yours!" He went into the shower.

I didn't mean to upset him, but I felt that was the opportunity to express how I was feeling. I thought he would have been more receptive and understanding—maybe even listened, took in what I had to say, and agree to work on it. Not look to point the finger back at me. It was a shame I came harder from Sin's voice and a toy than I did from Marcus's penis.

One of the things I loved most about Sin was the fact that he was so in tune with me. Marcus and I had been living together for a while and he couldn't tell you my favorite flower, color, ice cream flavor or fruit. A man should know basic things about his woman. He should want to learn and discover the little things that make her smile. Often that's all a woman wants—a man who's willing to try to understand her needs. Since Marcus was a know-it-all and determined to dictate what he thought I should like, we were destined for doom. We might have lived together, but were miles apart. I got up and slept in the guest room.

The day had finally come—New Years Eve, and it was party time! The caterer had all of the hot and cold hors d'oeuvres laid out, and the house was looking very festive. We had about thirty people attending, and I wanted everything to go as planned. Marcus and I hadn't been on the best of terms, but agreed to put our differences aside and enjoy the night. I asked the guests to get there by nine o'clock sharp, because black folks always arrived late. I asked my close friends to come earlier to help out.

The first to arrive was Toya and her kids. This was perfect because I wanted Ky'elle to childproof the basement and connect the Wii game system to the flat screen television.

Charmaine, Shawn, and his son, Justin, arrived, then Donald, his boyfriend Wesley, along with Stephanie and Samantha. Nickelle came with Trey, and Jasmine, who I hadn't seen in a while, came with her latest boyfriend and his three bad-ass kids. If their momma picked up and left them, why Jaz would want to take on that headache was beyond me. She went from one pathetic man to the next. I introduced everyone and told them to help themselves to the food and the fully stocked bar.

Wesley kept looking at Shawn with a questioning look. Finally he said, "Your face looks familiar. Do I know you from somewhere?"

"I don't know. I own a BMW dealership. Maybe you've seen me there?"

"I do order parts from different places. Maybe that's where I saw you." He left it at that.

Donald and Wesley looked good together. I was delighted he found someone he could possibly build something with. He truly appeared happy. Stephanie was another story.

Donald pulled me to the side. "Did you take a good look at Stephanie's right eye?"

"No, what happened to it?"

"When I got to her house to pick her up I noticed she had packed on the makeup. When I looked closely I noticed she was trying to cover up a black eye. I think you should talk to her."

I approached her and asked her to help me in the kitchen. Charmaine and Toya were in there, but weren't paying us any attention.

I pulled her to the side. "What happened to your eye?"

She lowered her head. "Is it that noticeable? I tried to cover it up."

"It's fine. Did Bernard do that to you?"

"Yeah, he came to drop presents off on Christmas day. I made the mistake of letting him come in. He got caught up in the moment, watching Samantha open her presents, and asked if he could come back home."

"What did you say?"

"I said no! He said he wanted his family back and how trying to maintain bills in two households was killing him. You would think the sixty dollars he pays a week is breaking him. When I said I didn't think it was a good idea, he started yelling. He was accusing me of sleeping with someone. He said I better not have his daughter around any men, and if he thought I did he'd kill him. I told him it wasn't about another man and that I simply didn't want to be with him anymore."

She sighed. "Misty, he lost his mind and got to pushing and shoving me. He grabbed me by my arm and threw me into the loveseat. When I started yelling for help he punched me in my face. If it wasn't for the couple next door calling the police I don't know what would have happened."

"Did the police arrest him?"

"Yes, but he's out on bail. He called and said I ruined his life. I told him it's his abusive ways and lack of anger management that has his life in turmoil. He has a problem with rejection. I'm pressing charges this time.

He's beaten me so many times I've lost count. I'm afraid and he hasn't left me with a choice. I have a daughter to think about, and I need to do what I have to do to protect us. Something in his voice told me he was serious this time, so instead of ignoring him I've decided to try the legal route. I have to appear in court in two weeks. I'm not going to drop the charges either. He's going to learn to keep his hands off of me!"

"Be careful, and if you need anything just let me know." Nickelle walked into the kitchen. "Nick, come over here for a second."

"What's up?"

"I need your help." I pointed to Stephanie's eye. "Can you work your magic on that?"

She checked it out. "I sure can! I'll take her up to the guest room and have her looking like America's next top model in no time! Come on." She took Stephanie by the hand. "I have to get my bag out the truck."

I walked over to Toya and Charmaine then pulled out a stool and sat at the island.

"What's up with your assistant?"

"Domestic violence."

"Malik might be a lot of things, but at least he wasn't kicking my ass."

"Toya, abuse comes in many forms, and physical is not the only type. Malik might not have been kicking your ass, but he sure as hell was beating up your spirit. Those mental scars can last a lot longer than the physical ones," Charmaine added.

Toya grew quiet and mulled over what Charmaine had just said.

Donald and Wesley entered the kitchen.

"Do you need any help in here, ladies?"

We all secretly eyed Wesley.

"No, we're okay," I replied.

"Did you get a chance to talk with Stephanie?" Donald asked.

"Yeah, we'll talk about that later. Are you enjoying yourself, Wesley?"

"Oh, yes! And thanks for having me!"

"Donald was telling me you work in the automobile industry. Are you a mechanic?"

He smiled. "Something like that. I own a body and detailing shop. I specialize in customizing foreign cars; BMW, Volvo, Saab, Audi, and Mercedes."

"That's nice to know! I got a BMW truck, and you never know when you're going to need a good body man," I joked.

"Don't be flirting with my man, hussy," Donald teased.

I laughed then playfully poked him in the side. We joined the rest of the guests into the living room, and shortly afterward Nickelle brought Stephanie down looking like a new woman.

When 10:30 rolled around the house was packed. People were dancing, mingling, eating, and drinking. I noticed Donald and Wesley over in the corner exchanging words, which was strange because they seemed okay when we were in the kitchen.

Marcus and I made our way around the room, socializing with our guests. I left him talking with his co-workers and walked over to Donald who was now standing alone.

"Is everything all right with you?"

"Yeah, I just had to check Wesley! I notice he keeps eyeing Shawn and I wanted to know what was up with that."

"What did he say?"

"He said he wasn't checking him out, but merely trying to figure out where he knew him from."

"Dee, I don't think he would try to get with him tonight, especially with you and Charmaine here. Maybe he does know him from somewhere and is trying to put the pieces together."

"He better, because I don't play that shit! I will not be disrespected!"

"Calm down, it's New Year's Eve. Relax. The ball will be dropping soon. Don't ruin your night with that crap. He seems like a real nice person and he appears to be genuinely into you. You got to trust him. Plus Shawn is not gay, so you don't have to worry about him trying to take your little boyfriend away from you," I teased.

Stephanie came over and grabbed his hand. "Let's dance!"

I walked back over to Marcus. I noticed Wesley taking pictures of Shawn with his cell phone. I thought . . . *he better not let Donald catch him doing that because it will be on and poppin' in the middle of my living room!* Lucky for him, Donald wasn't looking.

I looked around the room and everyone was having a good time. Stephanie was shaking her tail feather with Marcus's co-worker, Evan, who had taken a liking to her.

I heard someone yell, "Five minutes till midnight!"

I hurriedly passed everyone a champagne flute while Marcus filled their glasses with bubbly. Charmaine and Donald passed out the horns and crazy hats. Nickelle turned the Sony 65-inch 3D HDTV to channel 2 so we all could watch the ball drop. Jasmine ran downstairs and brought all the kids up then poured them apple cider in Dixie cups.

Marcus came over to me and took my hand.

Charmaine yelled, "One minute until countdown, people!"

We started the countdown as we lifted our glasses. "Ten, nine, eight, seven, six, five, four, three, two, one," we sang out in unison, "HAPPY NEW YEAR!"

Marcus turned to me and we kissed. I don't know if it was the alcohol, but I think I felt a tingle. We exchanged hugs and wished each other the best for the upcoming year.

I signaled for Toya, Nickelle, Jasmine, and Charmaine to meet me in my office where we could have some privacy. I had a Christmas present for each of them, but wanted to wait until we were all together before I gave it to them. Once they were seated I started.

"We met as girls, but have grown into women together." I then looked over at Jasmine in particular. "We haven't always seen eye to eye, but I love each and every one of you like sisters." I looked over at Toya. "This year has been challenging for all of us—some more than others, but we made it and we will survive." I looked at Nickelle. "Sometimes we need a little encouragement when we doubt our own potential." I finally looked at Charmaine. "Sometime we need to slow down, make time, and follow our hearts." I walked over to my desk and pulled out four envelopes.

"What's in the envelopes?" Toya asked.

"I hope it's a check," Nickelle joked as she reached her hand out first. "I don't care if anthrax in there; as long as it's a gift for me. I didn't get shit this year for Christmas!" We all laughed.

I handed each of them their envelope. Jasmine was the first to open hers then gasp. Nickelle saw her facial expression and ripped hers open and started jumping up and down while Charmaine and Toya both screamed. All the commotion caused Marcus to come into the room. "Is everything okay in here?"

"Yes, we're fine. I just gave them their Christmas presents."

He smiled. "It sounds like they liked it! Enjoy, ladies." He backed out of the room and closed the door.

I had given each one of them a weekend spa retreat. We would have unlimited access to massages, facials, hair, manicures, pedicures, waxing, and sauna. They were getting the works for a whole weekend.

"Girl, you're the best big sister a girl could have! I've been so stressed trying to get this new salon up and running. I can sure use this!"

Toya placed her hand on her hip. "Who you telling? Stress is my middle name lately." She scanned down the pamphlet then twisted her lips. "Too bad they don't have dick listed as one of the services in this brochure because I would be making me an appointment for some of that!" We all fell out.

I was having a hard time finding the perfect gift for them, and Sin suggested the spa. He said he remembered how much I enjoyed going and thought we were all due for some R&R.

"We'll be leaving tomorrow morning, so be ready to leave some stress behind, ladies! I already made arrangements for your mother to watch the kids, Toya, and she offered to keep an eye on Trey too, Nick."

We all hugged and went back into the living room. We did the soul train line, the electric slide, and stepped in the name of love. Charmaine had my camcorder recording the evening's events and planned to send everyone a copy of the disc. Donald come over to me around 3:30 AM and said he was getting ready to leave.

"You better let Stephanie know you're ready. She's over there with Evan."

"I told her I was ready, but Evan said he would drop her off."

"Why are you guys leaving so early?"

"Wesley has to get up early, so we're going to head back to my place and get some sleep."

"Is that what you call it nowadays? Sleep?"

He smiled. "I'll see you on Monday, and Happy New Year, Miss Misty!" I gave him a hug and kissed him on the cheek. "Happy New Year to you too, Dee!"

I watched Charmaine with Shawn as they slow danced. She had her arms draped around his neck as he held her softly around her waist. They slowly swayed to the music. I couldn't hear what they were talking about, but they were engrossed in their own conversation. I grabbed Marcus by the hand and led him upstairs.

"Where are we going?"

"Shush . . . just follow me," I instructed. I led him into our private bathroom. "I'm horny, and I want some!"

"Misty, we have guests downstairs."

"Oh come on, they won't miss us."

He was apprehensive, but quickly got with the program when I started undoing his pants. The alcohol had me frisky as hell. I sat on the sink in the master bathroom, pulled off my thongs, then reached down in the drawer and pulled out a condom. I spread my legs and played with myself as he slid on the condom. Marcus was so excited he came after ten quick strokes. I freshened up then flushed the used tissue down the toilet. As I checked my make-up in the mirror I laughed out loud. Marcus smiled as if he knew what I was thinking, but if he only knew. I was giggling because he simply couldn't handle the pussy. It was too much for him. He was a ten stroker joker.

# CHAPTER 17

## Relief Retreat

When I woke up New Year's Day I noticed I had a few missed calls on my cell. I checked my messages and Donald had called stating he needed to speak with me right away. I hoped he and Wesley hadn't gotten into an argument the night before over Shawn.

"Hey Dee, I just got your message. Did you have a nice time last night?"

"Oh yes honey! You sure know how to throw a party! We had a great time!"

"Good! I thought you and Wesley got into it for a second."

"We got into it, all right, but not in that way." He chuckled. "Honey, it was the complete opposite. You had so much liquor everybody was shit faced by the time they left. We went straight back to my place and fucked all night!"

"TMI, Dee, too much info. So what did you need to talk to me about?"

"I don't know how to say this, but Wesley figured out where he knows Shawn from."

"Okay, so where does he know him from? I hope he's not married or no stupid shit like that. Charmaine is really feeling him."

"That would be simple," he mumbled under his breath. "I don't know how much she's going to be feeling him once she finds this out."

"What? Spit it out already!"

"There's no easy way to say this, so here it goes. Shawn is bisexual."

"What! Did I just hear you right? Repeat yourself so I can make sure I heard you correctly." My heart was racing, and although he sounded serious this had to be a joke.

"I said Shawn is bisexual, and in case you didn't hear me this time let me spell it out for you, B-I- S- E- X- U- A- L!"

"But he's not gay! He was married and has a son! Tell me you're playing."

"I wish I were. Last night Wesley took a picture of Shawn with his phone. He sent it to a few people, and his friend Chandler confirmed that he was seeing Shawn like eight months ago."

"How long did they mess around? Was it serious?"

"I would say so. They dated for about a year."

"Dated? Oh my God, this is terrible! Did you get confirmation because I'm not saying anything to her until we have some proof?"

"Go check your emails. I sent you the pictures Chandler sent to us this morning. It sure looks like Shawn to me," he added.

"Hold on. Let me sign on and check this out!"

I turned on my laptop, went online, and opened the attachment he sent. I carefully reviewed the pictures. "Fuck! That's him, all right!" I contemplated, *How am I supposed to tell my best friend that the man she is falling head over heels for is or was sleeping with men?*

I said out loud not realizing what I said, "Damn, so he's a homo?" As quick as it exited my mouth I apologized. "I'm sorry, Dee, you know I didn't mean it like that."

"I understand, and nothing personal taken." He chuckled. "Honey, I said the same thing. Do you want me to tell her?"

"No, this is something I need to handle."

I stared at the pictures and shook my head. Shawn was very masculine.

I would have never thought he messed around with men, but these days you could never tell which men were on the down low. What does a down low brother look like? You can never really know. They're in hiding and blend in with the straight men. There is no distinguishing characteristic. They look, smell, and act like straight men. They will even crack jokes about homosexuality, but it's a different story behind closed doors.

"Thanks for the heads up, Dee. We're going away this weekend, so I'll try to figure out a way to tell her then. Be on standby in case she wants to talk to you."

"Okay, I'm here."

How can a woman sexually compete with man? They don't have the same parts, and a man would have the advantage. Who better to know what makes a man feel good, but another man? I respect gay and openly bisexual people. They don't engage in recreational games of hide and sneak. Donald is one of my best friends. He's very gay and at peace with his sexuality. You will never see him messing around with a woman. He knows what he wants, and like straight people, he and many other gays are searching for love and monogamy.

It's those who choose to indulge in secret relations with both sexes who cause all the confusion. They're either unsure of what they want or selfishly trying to have the best of both worlds.

I was no longer looking forward to this retreat. How do you tell a woman her man was having intercourse with a man? This weekend certainly wasn't the appropriate place to divulge this information; however, the sooner Charmaine found out, the better. I'd think of something. I printed out the pictures and packed my weekend bag. I literally had knots in my stomach.

Marcus came in the bedroom and noticed I was upset. "What's wrong with you?"

"I just heard something crazy."

"What's going on?"

"I was just told Shawn is bisexual."

"Are you talking about Charmaine's latest fling? I don't believe it."

I let his comment about latest fling slide. "I just got off the phone with Donald, and he emailed me these." I passed him the copies I printed. "They're of Shawn and his ex-lover on vacation." As he examined each pictures thoroughly I asked, "So what do you think now?"

He looked at me appalled. "This is preposterous!" He pointed to one picture in particular. "Look at this! He's got a guy sitting on his lap and they're kissing in the mouth! Disgusting!" He passed the pictures back and I slid them into a big envelope.

"She's going to freak when she sees these! What do you think I should do?"

"Tell her of course, but I would at least speak with him first. Give him a chance to clear his good name. This might be an attempt to defame his character. You never know in this day and age what a person can do with a camera, a computer, and Photoshop."

"I didn't think about that. Talking to him first sounds like a good idea." I actually felt a little better.

As planned, we all met up at the brownstone. When I walked in the door Charmaine was on the phone. I poured myself a shot of Patrón. It was early, but I needed to take the edge off. She hung up and told me Shawn said he was going to miss her.

I thought, *If he only knew just how much.*

While Charmaine got ready and Toya moved about the kitchen Sin came to mind. I hadn't spoken to him since Christmas, and I was missing his voice. Speaking to him just made my day a little brighter. Toya yelled, "Misty, get the door!" She was washing a huge pot and had soap all over her hands.

I walked over to the front door and welcomed in Nickelle. "So glad you could finally join us."

"I'm not late!"

"For once in your life," Charmaine sarcastically replied walking past her. "And why didn't you use your key?"

"I don't carry it anymore. Is everyone here?"

"No, Jaz is stuck in traffic, but said she'll be here in five. And please put that key back on your ring in case I ever get locked out I can run to the shop and get yours."

Nickelle ignored her and walked over to the bar and poured herself a glass of coconut Ciroc with pineapple juice.

"Why every time you come over here the first thing you do is go to my bar?"

"Don't you buy this stuff for your guest?"

"Yeah, and?"

"Do I still live here?"

"No, but—"

"But nothing! If I don't live here then I'm a guest, and this particular guest likes to drink. So expect me to drink up all your shit whenever I come!"

"Well excuse the fuck out of me. If that's the case at least make me one with your fresh ass!" We all laughed.

Toya walked into the living room drying her hands with a paper towel. She threw the wrinkled tissue down on the table. "Where the heck is Jasmine? When I spoke to her last she said she would be here in five minutes, and that was over a half an hour ago! I'm ready to go!" She sighed. "If I'm going to be subjected to waiting I might as well have a drink too. I wasn't trying to be a lush like the rest of you doing cocktails so early in the day."

"Toya, please! It's a holiday weekend. Chill out and live a little," Nickelle joked.

Fifteen minutes passed and I started getting antsy. "Can somebody call Jaz's cell and see where she's at?" The doorbell rang as I finished my sentence. "Perfect timing! Now we can get out of here," I said as Toya walked over to let her in.

Jaz started apologizing as soon as she entered. "Sorry I'm late. I had to make a quick stop. Is everybody ready to go?"

I got up from the sofa. "Yeah, we're ready. Let's hit the road."

We got our bags and headed out the door. We had to drive two vehicles. Charmaine, Nickelle, and I drove in my jeep while Jasmine and all of the bags rode with Toya. We hadn't even gotten on the highway before Nickelle started complaining about the radio being too loud and our talking keeping her awake.

"I'm not in the mood to hear you complain for an hour, Nickelle! No one told you to jump your butt in the back of my jeep! When we stop for gas, get out, and get in the other car with Toya." I snickered. "She got plenty of room in that caravan."

When we got to the gas station Toya and I filled up while Nickelle jumped in her back seat. She stuck her middle finger up at me as we pulled off.

"What's the first thing you're going to have done when we get there, Sis?"

"I'm not sure, Big Head. Probably a massage. What about you?"

"Shawn suggested a Swedish massage. He told me he had one done when his sales team went away to the Caribbean."

The pictures of him on the beach with the man appeared in my mind, but I kept quiet. I drove while she ran on about Shawn. For the last three months she was seeing him exclusively. She cut off all her male suitors and was focusing solely on him. This made what I had to tell her five times more difficult. I didn't want to be the bearer of bad news nor see her hurt. I decided as soon as we got to spa I would make that call.

Toya and Jasmine opted on facials. Nickelle got a pedicure and Charmaine went to the Jacuzzi. I stayed back in the room and called Donald. He answered on the second ring. "Dee?"

"What's popping boo?"

"I need a favor. Can you see if Wesley still has Shawn business card? I need his cell number. He wrote it on the back of his business card at my party."

"Hold on, let me see if Wes still has it." Donald placed the phone down, and luckily the card was still in his wallet. He gave me both Shawn's cell and office numbers.

"Smooches!"

I called, but got his voice mail. I left my number and a message that I needed to speak with him immediately. I scheduled all my appointments for the next day and a half then met up with Charmaine in the Jacuzzi. Nickelle joined us once her nails dried. We sipped wine and nibbled on coconut shrimp as the warm water relaxed our bodies. After an hour I was pruned and ready for some real food. Toya and Jasmine were in the lobby and also ready to eat. We changed and met up with them in the dining area. Since we agreed not to discuss our men dinner was pleasant.

Around 11:30 PM my cell phone rang and startled me out of my sleep. I answered and on the other end was a man's voice I didn't recognize. "Hello, may I speak with Misty?"

When I realized it was Shawn my stomach turned. I had prepared what I was going to say to him earlier, but now, half asleep and a few drinks later, my mind was blank. "Uhh, this is her?"

"Hey Misty, it's Shawn! I was checking my voice mail and heard your message. Did I disturb you?"

"No."

"So what's going on? Was your call related to buying a new car or something?

"No, not at all."

"Okay, so to what do I owe the pleasure of your call?" I sighed, and he noted my seriousness. "Is everything okay?"

"Yes, but maybe no. I need to talk to you about something."

"Is something wrong with Charmaine?"

"She's fine. It's not about her. It's about you. Can you talk now?"

"Yeah, what's this about?" He sounded concerned.

There was no right or wrong way to ask it, so I took a deep breath and just went ahead with my question. "Shawn, are you bisexual?" My question threw him for a loop, and he was taken aback. I could hear him fumbling around with the phone.

"What made you ask me that?"

"Some photos of you and an old lover on an island were brought to my attention by a friend."

He didn't deny it and instead became annoyed. "Who is this friend and why are they talking my business?" He acted like he was ready to step to someone. Little did he know Donald thumped! He was a fighter. Many let the feminine disposition fool them, but he could turn into a man real quick when he wanted.

"The friend is irrelevant. What we need to clear up is, are you also into men?"

His reply came with much resentment. "I believe this is a conversation I need to be having with the person I'm dating, not you! It is none of your concern what I'm into."

"It sounds like you have a problem with me questioning you about your sexuality!"

"What I did or do has nothing to do with you or her!"

"What you did or do in your sexual relationships has everything to do with her, and because she's my sister, it has everything to do with me! You two have been dating for months! When were you planning on having that conversation with her? I don't know what kind of sick, twisted game you're playing, but you give real bisexual men a bad rap! You weren't even up front with her!" I was mad at him like I was the one dating him. Who the hell did he think he was getting an attitude because he got exposed?

"Charmaine means everything to me, and I won't stand by watching your confused ass pull her down, Shawn! If she wants to continue dating you, that's her business, she's grown, but she has a right to know who she's dealing with, and I'm going to make sure that happens."

"She knows who she is dealing with! I love her and she loves me!"

"You don't love her! If you did, you would have told her! You may care, but you also care for men, and that leaves room for backsliding. You're selfish!"

"You're passing judgment on me, and you don't know me or my situation!"

"I personally don't give a fuck about you or your situation, Shawn! Charmaine is my only concern. Were you raped? If not, you consented, and that makes you a willing participant! She wasn't given that opportunity."

"She's special to me, and I care about her a great deal. I didn't want to hurt her."

I could feel my blood boiling, and I had heard enough. "Save the explanation, justification, or rationalizations for when you get around to talking to her. I've personally heard enough!"

I hung up on him, but couldn't fall back asleep. Normally when I was upset I would call Charmaine, but I was on my own with this one. I decided to try Marcus instead. When he answered I could tell he was asleep.

"Hello," he said groggily.

"Marcus?"

"Misty, what time is it?"

"Umm, it's twelve."

"Are you okay?"

"Yeah, I'm fine. I just spoke with Shawn and . . ."

"You woke me up for that! I don't care about him, your friends or their men problems! This is foolishness! I'm going back to get some sleep."

He hung up on me. What did I expect? Why would I think this time would be any different? He was never available, and my concerns were always secondary to his. If we had four good days, there were twelve bad ones to follow. Just as I was about to question my actions, the selfish Marcus reappeared.

The following morning, as we all ate breakfast, I felt uncomfortable, like I was keeping a secret. I needed to speak with Charmaine alone. I needed to tell her ASAP. Once I found out what she had planned for the day I scheduled to use the sauna at the same time as her. I went to my room, took a nap, and around two o'clock went to her room. She opened the door and continued to cheerfully talk on her cell. I sat on the edge of the bed and waited. She hung up and announced, "That was Shawn!"

I gulped. "Really? What did he have to say?"

"He said he can't wait to see me and had something to tell me when I got back."

"Did he say what it was?"

"No."

"Did he give you a clue?"

"No, but he did ask me if I spoke to you." She gave me a sly grin. "What do you two have cooking up?" She giggled, "Am I getting ready to get a new car? Maybe a marriage proposal?" she joked.

I rolled my head. "I hope not!" I caught myself. "I mean, it's a little too early for that, don't you think? You don't even really know him yet." She gave me a peculiar look, which I ignored, but she knew something was amiss because I was normally more positive.

We went to the sauna, and the whole way there I tried to figure out how to tell her. She looked as worried as I was when we took off our robes and got in the water.

"What you thinking about, Big Head?"

"What Shawn wants to talk to me about? I know you know something."

I took a deep breath. This was as good a time as any. "I know, Cha."

She got excited. "I knew you were in on this! Tell me, what did he get me?"

She really thought she was about to hear something positive. It was painful to see her so enthralled in a man who deceived her. I swallowed and then chose my words carefully. "Cha, Shawn is . . . umm, well he is . . ." I played with my hands, which was something I did when I was nervous. "Let's just say he's not the man you think he is."

She stared at me defiantly then shot back, "What do you mean he's not the man I think he is? What the fuck does that supposed to mean, Misty? You got to come better than that, sistah! That makes no sense."

"I got some pictures of him I think you should see."

"Pictures of him doing what!"

I remained calm although she was on flip mode. Charmaine was a hot head and I knew how she could fly off the handle. "I would rather you look at them, draw your own conclusion, and then we can talk about it."

She grew frustrated. "Why you playing games, and what do these pictures have to do with him not being the man I think he is?" She tried to make a joke. "Was he once an exotic dancer or something?"

I remained silent with a dismal expression. "The pictures are in my room, but before we go up to look at them you should brace yourself."

She angrily got out of the sauna, grabbed up her terrycloth robe then turned to me. "Well come on! I want to see these pictures!"

She had an attitude; which was understandable. A woman will flip out on you about her man, and I was no exception. Blood is thicker than water, but sperm is thicker than them both.

The elevator ride to my room took forever. She pressed the button like ten times as if that was going to get us there faster. I unlocked my door with the key card. We stepped in, and she plopped down on the bed. I went through my bag, pulled out the manila envelope, and passed it to her. She snatched it then dumped the contents on the bed.

In total there were ten photos. She picked them up, looked at them then dropped her mouth. She looked up at me with a perplexed look then said before turning to the next picture, "Tell me this is some kind of joke?"

I shook my head then sat down next to her. She flipped to the next picture, and by the time she was looking at picture number six she was crying.

"What the hell are these, and where did you get'em from?"

I passed her the box of tissues. "Do you remember Donald's boyfriend, Wesley? At my New Year's party he thought he knew Shawn from somewhere. It turns out Shawn was dating one of his friends not too long ago. The pictures were taken when the two of them were on vacation."

She looked at the pictures over and over again in disbelief. She was confused, hurt, and pissed.

"So you're telling me Shawn's a fucking faggot? He fucks around with men!"

"It appears so." She ran to the garbage can and threw up. "I'm sorry, Cha. I spoke with him last night, and I asked him."

She wiped her mouth with the back of her hand. "And what did he say?"

"He didn't deny or admit to it. He said it was a conversation he wanted to have with you."

"So this is what he wanted to talk to me about? He sounded all cool on the phone, like he had good news. Stinking motherfucka! I'm gonna cut his bitch ass!"

"I told him I was going to tell you, so I assumed that's what his call was all about."

"I want to go home now!"

"Cha, I don't think you need to be alone right now or around him. I think you should stay. I just hit you with some unbelievable information. You need to digest it, think it through then figure out what you're going to do. You can't just run up on him with your knife."

"You're right, a knife won't suffice. Let me borrow your gun? I'm gonna pop a cap in that niggah's ass!"

"You need to calm down. You got too much to lose to be out there reacting strictly off of emotion. And I don't lend out my gun, sweetheart. Could you see yourself still dating him knowing he had a relationship with a man?"

"It's weird because I would want to based off what I know about him, but I know me, and I can't, Sis. Knowing what he did tarnishes that whole image I had of him being a perfect partner."

"I'm not trying to be funny, but most gay men are the perfect partner. They're into the same things we are, and they love shopping just as much us or more."

She sat on the floor holding her head in disbelief. She finally got up. "I am going to get a massage. Hopefully that will help get my head right. I can't believe this shit is happening to me."

"I'm going to get my hair done. By the time we finish everyone should be ready for dinner. We can talk more later on."

When she left I called and made dinner reservations then called the front desk and left messages for everyone, telling them we would be meeting for dinner at 8:30 sharp.

Everyone's skin was glowing when they came down to eat. Pampering yourself did pay off.

"So is everyone having a good time so far?"

"I am having a great time! I could really get used to this type of treatment! It beats sitting in that flower shop all day. I feel like a new woman. Thanks again, Misty!"

"It was my pleasure, Toya!"

It was obvious Charmaine was detached from the conversation and already drunk. She was there physically, but her mind was off in space. The waiter walked up and took our orders.

Nickelle looked over at her then playfully asked, "So who peed in your corn flakes?"

Charmaine cut her eyes at her but remained silent.

"What bug crawled up your ass?"

"Nothing crawled up my ass! I'm just not in a very social mood."

Nickelle didn't know what was going on between her and Shawn; no one did. They always played around, so she continued messing with Charmaine hoping to loosen her up. "So why didn't you just stay your unsocial butt in your room then?"

"Because I didn't fucking feel like it, that's why! Mind your business."

Nickelle looked around baffled. "Wait a minute? What's wrong with you?"

Charmaine placed her elbows on the table, brought her two palms to her face then ran her hands up her forehead. We watched as her eyes became watery. She knew talking about it, and getting feedback would help. She looked over at me, "You fill them in. I'll be right back. I'm going to the ladies room." Once she was gone I told them about Shawn's questionable sexuality.

"Who would have ever thought he got down like that, Charmaine? I would have never known. He appeared straight to me," Toya commented.

"I can spot a gay man like Donald a mile away, but those undercover brothers are tricky," Nickelle admitted.

"This whole thing is scary to me. If it wasn't for Donald telling me we might not have ever found out. Thank God it's a small world."

Jasmine jumped in. "I hope you used condoms every time you slept with him." Charmaine sat quiet and gulped down her second double. "Please tell me you used condoms!" When she didn't respond Jaz went in for the kill. "I mean to say in this day and age I would think you would be more responsible and protect yourself! I told you your lifestyle was going to catch up with you one of these days. Running around being so carefree, now look at you! You could have AIDS!"

"Okay Jasmine, you're going all the way to the left. She don't need a lecture right now."

"That's the problem, Nickelle! No one wants to hear anything I have to say until it's too late!" Jaz looked back over to Charmaine. "Have you even had an HIV test?"

Charmaine's eyes shrunk to slits. "For your information, I use protection and I go to the gynecologist twice a year, and that exam includes an HIV test, thank you very much! My last exam was right before I started dating Shawn. You don't think I know how serious HIV and AIDS are? He's one of the first men in years I trusted enough to sleep with unprotected. I only slept with him without a condom maybe twice, and that's enough to kill me!" She shut her eyes tight. "If he gave me something, there will be nowhere on this earth that man can hide from my revenge!"

"HIV is not something you can just get rid of with some ointment or a pill, Charmaine!"

Charmaine's eyes flew open, "Jaz you are such an insensitive bitch! I'm here dealing with a life crisis and the only input you can give is more negativity. I don't need your bullshit right now!" She looked up toward the ceiling. "Lord, please give me strength. I'm already on edge, and drunk. If Jaz goes there tonight I don't know what I am capable of doing." The two double shots Charmaine had downed had taken full effect.

Seeing that things were getting ready to get ugly, Toya attempted to play the peacemaker, and tried to squash it before it escalated into a fistfight. "Come on, ladies, let it go! Why every time we get together an argument breaks out?"

"An argument breaks out because she's miserable!" Charmaine stated.

"I am not, and I resent that! What I am is a realist. I call it like I see it."

"No, you put us under your microscope and inspect us! It's like you get some kind of joy out of trying to make others feel bad. You're a fucking hater!"

"What do any of you have that would make me want to hate on you?"

"You hate on Nickelle's talent, you hate on Toya's marriage, you hate on my lifestyle, and you hate on Misty's relationship with Sin. The truth is you're jealous! Jealous that Nickelle makes more money than you without all the college degrees, you're jealous that Toya got married before you, you're jealous that I continue to live a fabulous life you only wish you had the courage to live, and you're jealous of Misty because you always wanted her man!"

"That's a lie!" Jasmine defensively replied.

"Ask anyone at this table if I'm lying!" I don't know why, but she looked over at me first. I personally would have been the last person at the table she asked about her hating ways. "Misty, do I hate on you?"

I had some thoughts on the topic, and since we were, as she put it, calling it as we saw it, I let it rip.

"Yeah, you do. You do a whole lot of hating, especially on me. Look how you acted at the restaurant when we took Nickelle out. You were very insulting. You called Sin a loser; threw his child up in my face, and said it's only now that he's in jail he loves me. How could you say that to me? Sin is an exceptional man who I love dearly. And his love for me unquestionably. I just can't understand why, if you're my friend, you would say such things knowing it would hurt my feelings."

Charmaine slurred, "I'll tell you why! It's because Miss Killjoy over here tried to push up on him years ago, and he shut her ass down!" Charmaine started laughing.

Nickelle, Toya, and I all looked at Charmaine as she giggled like a drunken monkey.

"What are you talking about, Cha?" I asked.

"Shut up, Charmaine! You're always running your mouth!"

"No, please continue, because I would really like to know when she tried to push up on my man."

"I promised her I would never tell you, but since we're calling it as we see it, it's time to pull her card. Do you remember the party Peter Shue threw down at the pier?"

"Yeah, I remember that night. It was a black tie affair."

"Exactly," Charmaine slurred. "Do you remember she was drunk and Sin offered to give her a ride home because he had to leave to meet up with someone uptown?"

"Yeah, and?"

"Well, Killjoy over here tried to swing an episode with him. When they pulled up Sin had to use the bathroom. She let him up to her apartment, and when he came out of the bathroom she made her move. He thought she was playing until she grabbed his crotch. She told him how she always liked him, how great she heard his sex game was, and she wanted to try it."

My mouth dropped. "What!" I was ready to slap the shit out of her. "Did they fuck?"

"Nah, Sin wouldn't dare touch that. He told her he wasn't a grimy dude who fucked his girl's friends, and he would never play you like that. She told me what she did and I asked him about it. He told me he was shocked and thought she was trying to set him up. He told me he was going to forget about it, and suggested she do the same. He asked me not to tell you for obvious reasons."

Jasmine was so embarrassed. She just kept looking around the room to prevent direct eye contact with me.

"You sneaky bitch! I couldn't figure out for the life of me why you disliked him so much, but now I know why, ho! He wouldn't fuck you, and you couldn't take it! I would hate him too if I offered him some free snatch and he turned it down like stale bread." I thought to myself, *Wait till I speak to Sin about this.* I burst out laughing.

When the waiter walked up with our meals he had no idea what had just transpired. It appeared as if we were having a good time because I was laughing hard and Charmaine and I both had tears running down our face, but for different reasons. We ate in silence. Not even Nickelle cracked a joke. The tension was thick.

Directly after dinner I went straight to my room. I didn't want to be bothered with anyone. Exiting the shower, I heard a light tap on the door. I wrapped myself in a towel. "Who is it?"

"It's me." I sighed before opening the door. Charmaine's eyes were bloodshot from crying. "Sis, I'm scared. What if he gave me something? What am I going to do?"

"The first thing we're going to do is make you an appointment for an HIV test. I don't think you've been infected or anything like that, but it's better to be safe than sorry. They have all kinds of medications now to help people with HIV live long normal lives." She started crying again.

"I'm not ready to die."

I walked over to her and hugged her. "Don't worry; you're not going anywhere no time soon. HIV is not a death sentence, Big Head. We're going to handle this together, no matter what the outcome is, okay?"

She cried hard on my shoulder. I grabbed the tissue box off the end table and passed her a few. "You can hang out in here with me if you want. I was just going to watch television."

She blew her nose and wiped her face. "Yeah, that sounds good. I swear Misty, if Shawn fucked around and gave me something I'm gonna kill him."

I went to the bathroom to put on my nightclothes, and when I came out Nickelle was in her pajamas lying across my bed too. I looked at the two of them and smiled. It reminded me of when we were younger. The three of us piled up in someone's bed, watching movies, and playing cards.

Charmaine and I decided to head out directly after breakfast. She lit her joint as soon as we hit the highway. "Do you think I was wrong for telling you what Jasmine did after all this time?"

"No, what you're wrong for is not telling me sooner!"

"I couldn't tell you back then when it went down. You would have killed her, and probably never forgiven her like I know you will now."

"How do you know I'm going to forgive her?"

"Because it happened so long ago, and it's in your nature to be forgiving." Charmaine laughed. "There was really no harm done except to her ego."

"On a serious note if you need to talk or to get away you know where I'm at."

"Thanks. It's going to take me forever to get an appointment with my doctor."

"I have a friend who runs a private women's clinic. I'll call her and get an appointment for you. You focus on what you're going to do about Shawn."

"He called me like nine times and left three messages last night, but I don't want to talk to him. What can he say? That it was a onetime thing, a thing of the past? I don't want to hear that shit! I could never trust he wasn't secretly lusting after Marcus, Malik, Donald, Wesley, or any other man that was around. Two kids and a house down the line and I find out he's sneaking around with the fucking pool boy. I care more about myself. I know what I can deal with, and a bisexual man ain't it! I'll take a stone cold thug who's doing life over that any day." She reclined back in the seat.

"I totally understand how you feel."

"Do you? I feel violated, like he raped me with someone else's dick, Misty. He kept relevant information from me. I should have been given the opportunity to decide whether I wanted to deal with that. Maybe in his eyes it wasn't important, but it is to me. I let my guard down which was a big mistake. We all know HIV doesn't have a face, so I should have been more responsible, used protection every time, and when that time came, got tested together."

"We've all lived dangerously before. Back in the day all you had to worry about was an unwanted pregnancy or an STD; which was nothing an abortion or some penicillin couldn't cure. Now you can get some shit that they don't have a cure for. What's sad is so many women are walking around unaware they are infected, because their husbands, baby daddies, or boyfriends are indulging in high-risk activities. The statistics are frightening. The blessing is society now understands it's not a gay disease, but a people disease. When we get back I'll talk to my friend about you taking the test over at her clinic, and you figure out how you are going to deal with Shawn."

"I'll deal with Shawn, all right! I'm gonna snip his fucking balls off with a pair of toenail clippers!

# CHAPTER 17

## *Domestic Violence*

When I walked in the house on Sunday the aroma of food pierced my nose. Marcus was a pretty good cook, and I could smell what I thought was a roast in the oven. I dropped my bag at the door then moseyed into the kitchen.

"Hey there! You're home early. How was the spa?"

I was still irked because of the way he acted on the phone. "We had a nice time."

"I assume you told Charmaine? So how did that go?"

Since he didn't have time to speak to me when I needed him, I was brief. "She took it well."

"Is she okay?"

I started to walk away. "Yup! She's just fine."

I appreciated the fact that he was now trying to show concern, but it was a little too late. He should have shown interest when I needed it. I didn't really want to discuss her feelings with him anyway. He was too opinionated. It wasn't like he was genuinely concerned.

"Wait, are you hungry?"

I turned back to him. "Yes, I'm starved! What did you cook?"

"Chicken, but it's not ready yet. Do you want a sandwich in the meantime?"

"Sure, let me go unpack my suitcase."

I ate then caught up on paperwork while Marcus sat on the sofa watching television. For once my phone wasn't ringing off the hook, and I was able to get a lot accomplished. I checked all my emails and out of fifty messages, only ten were worth opening. The rest were junk mail. I replied to everyone then went on the FTD website to order some flowers for Charmaine. I knew from experience the next month was going to be hard, and I hoped they would cheer her up.

I went on Corrlinks.com to see if Sin had sent me an email. He'd sent a brief love note and a reminder that he wanted to see me. I replied before shutting down my computer. I headed up to my bedroom for a nap. When I roused it was 7 o'clock, and I was hungry again. I went to the bathroom, washed my face, brushed my teeth, and then headed downstairs.

"Perfect timing, sleepy head! I was just about to come up and get you. Dinner is ready." Marcus carried two plates over to the table while I grabbed the bottle of wine and two glasses. We sat and had a quiet dinner.

The following morning I had two things on my agenda. The first was to place a call to my friend, Yvonne. She was the Director of an upscale women's clinic on the upper east side of Manhattan. She was going to be my go-to person for Charmaine's HIV test. I explained that the matter needed to be handled with the strictest of confidentiality. She checked the schedule, called back, and said they had an opening at 11:00 AM on Wednesday. We made the appointment under an alias name. I called and informed Charmaine of the appointment then headed to my office. The second item on my to-do-list was to reserve a plane ticket to see Sin.

Donald entered my office. "Morning, Misty!"

"Morning, Dee! How was your weekend?"

"It was pretty quiet. Wesley and I went to the movies last night, and then chilled over his place. How did things work out with your girl?"

"Oh, Charmaine? She's okay."

He raised his hand then placed it over his chest. "So, how did she take it?" He was looking for me to gossip, but there were certain people who were off limits, and she was number one on that list.

"She handled it like a trooper! Whatever happens in the end, it will be his loss."

"I hear that. I know she was upset though."

"Of course she was upset. Anyone would be upset, but she's a resilient woman. She'll get over it, and will have a new man in no time."

"I hear that!"

I looked around the office and noticed Stephanie hadn't arrived. "Did you speak with Stephanie today?"

"No, I just got in myself. Maybe she got stuck in traffic?"

"I remember her mentioning something about going to court with her ex-husband. Let me check the messages and turn off the answering machine."

"Talk to you later."

He took off in the other direction. There was no message from her.

My client arrived at 10:30 on the dot, which was good because I wanted to stop by the post office. There was a lot of mail in the box, but nothing from Sin. It felt like forever since the last time we spoke.

I walked to my car disappointed. I pulled down the visor and applied a fresh coat of MAC's Oh Baby lip-gloss. I said aloud before placing everything back in my bag, "I miss my Sin. God, I wish he would call."

I placed the key in the ignition, and just as the engine turned over my cell phone rang. "Shit!" I went searching and was able to locate the phone before it went to voicemail.

"Hello?"

"You have a prepaid call and will not be charged for this call. This call is from Garrett Butler, an inmate at a federal penitentiary. Hang up to decline the call or to accept this call dial five now."

I couldn't believe his timing! I wondered if he could possibly feel my soul calling out to him. This wasn't the first time he just happened to call at the very moment when I wanted him or needed him. At one time I thought it was just a coincidence, but I was starting to believe it was more. I hastily pressed "5" and waited for him to speak.

He greeted me trying to sound annoyed, as if he had been put on hold for a long time.

"Helloooooo?"

I started giggling.

"What's so funny?"

"Whenever you say hello like that, too much time has elapsed since you spoke to your Baby Girl."

"It has! It feels like months! When am I going to see your face? Come to think about it, didn't I ask you to get your ass down here like a month ago? Let me find out you're slipping."

"I started to look for a flight earlier, but didn't get a chance to book it. I promise I'll definitely do that as soon as I get back to the office."

"How many times do I have to tell you I want to see you, Misty? I want to see you this month! It's important, so the next time I ask you that question, I hope you got a different answer for me! Make it happen already."

I grinned. He didn't know how much he turned me on when he got pushy. I'm not a weak woman, so I needed a strong man who knew exactly when to be aggressive, when to apply pressure, and when to ease up, all while knowing how to not tick me off or turn me off.

"Say no more. You got it, Daddy!"

"This month, Misty! I also spoke to the lawyer you got."

I got excited. "So did you like him? I know you don't trust lawyers, but I got a good vibe from him, and he came highly recommended. Did he have good news?"

"He said he has some information for me pertaining to an appeal, but we would go over it in detail next week when he comes to see me."

"I pray it's something that will get you home real soon."

"I don't know about that real soon stuff, but yeah, I agree, the sooner the better! I want four things and that's to come home, cum inside of you, marry you, and for us to make some babies, and they don't have to happen in that order."

"You know all four would make me happy, but there are some serious obstacles in our way. You better hurry up before I'm too old and one of them is not an option."

"I'm trying, but we can't rush this thing. It's due process, baby."

"Due process sucks! The court's backlog got you backed up, and due process is preventing me from doing you."

"Baby Girl, I don't want some judge just rubber-stamping my shit. I need them to see the injustice and do something about it! I lost faith in the system a long time ago. People spend plenty of money, and when it comes time to fight those lawyers lie down and sell people out. I may only get one chance at freedom, and we don't want to waste it."

"I know you don't trust the system and feel lawyers are the biggest crooks, but I have to have faith. At least in the ones I hired. These guys are fighters and have a major disdain for the injustices taking place in the judicial system. They are going to make sure when you get that date we're prepared."

He laughed. "You know you're my baby, right?"

"I better be!"

"So how's everything else going?"

"You missed a lot since we last spoke. The holidays were fine except Malik got caught cheating, again. And Charmaine found out her new boyfriend goes both ways."

"Get the hell out of here! How did Cha not see that, and why the hell is Malik still fucking around?"

"Honey, Shawn is just as masculine as you. I wouldn't have seen it either."

"You knew I was straight as an arrow."

"Yes, I did. You also came to me with a reference from a reliable friend. I never had to worry about you having sugar in your tank. If anything, it's the complete opposite. You got too much testosterone, but this is not about you, sweetheart. When I first told her—"

"Wait a minute. How did you find out her man was into men before she did?"

"Long story made short, a friend of mine gave me some pictures of Shawn and his ex-lover on vacation together."

"Damn, you got spies like that? They come with pictures! Now I see how you were able to keep such close tabs on me."

"Not close enough, my dear. You did slip off my radar once, and we see where that got you."

He laughed. "Go ahead with that! How's Charmaine doing?"

"She's hurt. She was really getting into him. She feels out of all people she should have been able to see the signs. It's just going to take her some time to get over it. That reminds me, I haven't called her since we got back."

"Got back? Where did you go?"

It was moments like this that reminded a person behind bars just how limited their access was to loved ones.

"We went to the spa for the weekend. Remember the Christmas presents?"

He sat quiet on the other end. He didn't respond. It was obvious he was displeased with the fact that he knew nothing about me going away. When we lived together we had an agreement to tell each other any time we were going somewhere. I told him it was common courtesy. I made it my business to tell him everywhere I went because I wanted to know where he was going. In spite of writing, sending email, and calling there were still days where we had no contact. "What's the matter?"

"Nothing. Go ahead. Finish your story," he replied flatly.

I thought back to what my mother told me when I was little. She said a woman needs to learn her man; his moods, his needs, and his dislikes. She said once she did that she would have learned how to keep him happy. She said don't focus on his wants. She said men want it all, but only have a few needs. I realized what caused the sudden change in his disposition.

"Before you think anything I didn't tell you when I was going because I didn't speak to you since Christmas. I reserved our rooms right after Christmas and decided to leave on New Year's Day because everyone was off and Toya's mom agreed to watch the kids. You know I would have told you in advance."

To make sure he was okay I added, "I sent you an email. It may be a different playing field, but the rules haven't changed. You know I always keep you in the loop."

He acted as if what I said didn't matter, but we both knew it did because his mood instantly changed. He went right back to his vain self.

"I know something must have happened for you to forget to tell Daddy. We were on lock down all this time, so I didn't have access to the phones or computer until today."

I smiled because his ego was back intact. "And guess what else happened? It got nasty between Jaz and Cha at the spa."

"Jasmine strikes again, huh?"

"Pretty much! She put her foot in her mouth, and Cha pulled it out and beat her with it! I found out some very interesting information during their argument too."

"What?"

"I learned that Jasmine tried to sleep with you behind my back, and you failed to mention it to me."

"Damn, who told?"

"Did she actually get a feel on my Sin-namon stick?"

"Huh?"

"Don't answer that. All I have to say is she better be glad it's been some years. You know I don't play that shit! I'm surprised you never told me, but I do understand why you held onto that one. That could have started a war."

"I keep telling you, your Daddy got it going on, and the ladies can't help themselves!"

"Oh, please. You ain't even all that. Those jump-offs have your head all swollen!"

"You know I'm the man, Baby Girl." He snickered. "And, yes, it's in part due to my swollen head."

"Oh, yeah? Well, you better watch where you stick your swollen head before you have two swollen eyes to match it. You won't be so irresistible then."

We both laughed.

"Let me stop playing with you. How did your doctor's appointment go?"

"Everything went fine. The doctor did say I am way overdue for an exam with my specialist. So when can you schedule me in, Dr. Butler?"

He laughed. "As soon as you get your butt down here! You know I'll be happy to stick my thermometer in your mouth and take your temperature. Other than that, is there anything you need or want?"

"No, I don't need anything except for you to come on home, and I got what I wanted when you called. I feel much better now that I've heard your voice. I was missing you something terrible. I was actually thinking about you right before you called. I put it out there in the universe and, bang, I'm talking to you!"

"I was walking past the phone and decided to hit you before I went to work out. Hold on a second my man is calling me."

"You go ahead. I need to get back to the office."

"I'm going to call you back."

A big smile spread across my face. "What time?"

"I'll hit you back in like two hours. Is that good?"

"Yup, I'll be waiting."

We hung up and I was beaming from the inside out. He touched my heart in the sweetest ways. I put the car in drive and drove back to the office.

As soon as I entered the reception area I asked if anyone had seen Stephanie. We were to discuss the Jeremy Whittaker file today. No one had heard from her, and that was strange. She was normally the first person at the office, rarely called out, and when she did, she always left a message. Today there was no message, and she wasn't answering her BlackBerry. I wondered if she was okay.

Donald walked into my office. "Hey, Misty!"

"What's up?"

"My friend is showing at an art exhibit tonight in Manhattan, and I thought you might want to come. She's the one who painted that picture hanging in my living room. The one you love so much."

"I'd definitely like to go! What time are you leaving?"

"I figure we can head over there after work. I want to get there early enough to get some free food," he joked.

"It sounds good to me! Let me call Marcus and let him know I'll be home late."

I called Marcus's office and spoke with his secretary. She told me he was in a meeting and according to his schedule wouldn't be free for another two hours. I told her to let him know I called.

When he got a break later he returned my call. "What's up sweets? I see you left a message."

"Yes, Donald's friend is showing her paintings tonight at an exhibit in Manhattan. I wanted to let you know I was going with him. Do you want to come?"

"What time does it start? You know I don't really feel comfortable hanging out with your gay friend."

"That's on you. I'm going, and it starts around six o'clock."

"The time is good. Text me the address, and I'll call you when I'm on my way."

"Fine." I hung up and thought, *for someone so smart he was just plain ignorant.*

I went into my office and booked my flight and would be going to see Sin in two weeks. I tried Stephanie's house and cell again, but got no answer. I even called her grandmother's house, but she hadn't seen or heard from her either. She said she was also starting to worry. Something wasn't right. I got an eerie feeling; an omen that something was terribly wrong. I had the phone number for her daughter's school and tried there, but was told Samantha hadn't shown up today. Stephanie kept a spare key in her desk, and I planned on using it once I left the exhibit.

Around 4 o'clock my cell rang, and it was Sin! "Hi, Daddy!"

"Hey Boo! That shit with Charmaine been bugging me out. Do me a favor the next time she's with you tell her I want to talk to her. Now, what's up with Malik?"

"Toya had a feeling he was messing around. She had us ride with her over to the co-worker's house she suspected him of messing with, and sure enough he got busted."

"So he was at the lady's house?"

"Yup! Opened up the woman's front door in his boxers and Toya was on the other side."

"Ouch! He really got busted! How did she handle it?"

"Honey, she whipped his ass! It wasn't funny, but she tackled him onto the steps and began punching him in his back and head. I taped the whole thing on my cell phone. I thought she was going to punch her fist right through his skull. She told him she's filing for a divorce."

"Malik is cool, but he was always a jerk. She's a good person, and he's dead wrong. I can see that going on when we were younger, but not now. People got too much at stake; too much to lose. It sounds like we're the only two who don't having drama this week."

"I thought the same thing. You know Jaz would say, 'That's because you're in jail,' but we know better. It's because we got a good thing going on! A lot of the crap other people are going through we've been there and done that—except the bisexual thing. Is there anything you want to tell me?" I chuckled.

"Woman, don't even joke like that!"

"I was just teasing. I know you're all man! How was your workout?"

"I ran three miles and did some lifting."

"Don't go too crazy. I don't want to have to walk around with a bat to beat these women off of you when you get out."

"I got those pictures of you in the green bikini. Shit, I may need to get me a burner to back off the hounds. Your man should be thanking me for keeping that heart of yours on lockdown. If it wasn't for me someone would've been come along and took you from his tight ass." He laughed, but noticed I wasn't laughing with him. "What's the matter? You don't like it when I poke fun at your little boyfriend?"

"When we first started talking again I didn't intend to fall back in love with you, Sin, but I did. I'm in a very compromising position. I don't want to hurt him, but my heart belongs to you, and I can't let you go."

"I need you too, Misty. I don't know what I would do without you in my life. My heart would stop beating. You're what keeps me pushing. He got one up on me right now because he got my woman, but not for long. Daddy's getting ready to make some power moves to bring us closer together. I got big plans for us. Matter of fact I got to get off this phone. I have an appointment with my case manager in a few minutes. I also need to swing by the law library. I'll hit you back tomorrow."

"Okay, I'll talk to you then. Love you."

"And I love you too!"

Time must have gotten away from me, because the next thing I knew Donald was knocking at my office door to see if I was ready to go. I called Marcus and he confirmed he was coming, so I left my car at the office. There was no sense in paying to park two cars.

I rode in Donald's cranberry colored Audi to the exhibit. To my surprise Marcus actually beat us there and was pleasant. The exhibit was nice, and I selected an abstract piece to match the living room.

I pulled Donald to the side and informed him I was getting ready to leave and was heading over to Stephanie's house.

"It's not like her to not show up or call. I'm a little worried about her, Dee."

"Me too. Do you want me to follow you over there?"

"No, that's okay. I know you're supposed to meet up with Wesley later. We don't want to keep him waiting, now do we?"

He smiled. "No, we don't. Call me if you need me." He kissed me on the cheek and shook Marcus's hand.

We stopped and got a quick bite to eat before driving to her place. The drive was quiet. I tried reaching her once again, but nothing. When we pulled up to her townhouse, all the lights were off. We walked up to the front door and knocked, but there was no response. I reached into my pocketbook and retrieved the spare key.

Marcus looked at me like I was crazy. "What are you getting ready to do?"

"I'm about to open the door and make sure she's okay. Her ex-husband was over here the other day, and he hit her. She could be in there tied up for all we know!"

He shook his head. "You watch too much *Criminal Minds* and *CSI*."

I stuck the key in the door, but it wasn't locked. I slowly pushed the door then stepped aside and let Marcus walk in before me. It was pitch black. We bumped into things until I finally found the light switch. It looked like someone had been fighting.

"Do you think we should call the police?"

"What's the crime? A messy apartment! Let's get out of here."

"What's that smell?"

"Probably the garbage she didn't throw out."

The stale smell became more pungent as we made our way up the stairs to the bedrooms. The first bedroom belonged to Samantha, and the light was on. It was pink and white with a neat row of dolls and books on the shelves.

"See, nobody is home. We should get out of here," Marcus suggested.

"Okay, let me just check her room and then we can go."

The door to the master bedroom was closed. Marcus turned the knob then cracked the door. He knocked then reached his hand in and felt the wall for the switch. He hit the light then pushed the door completely open. I quickly scanned the room then screamed at the top of my lungs. The overwhelming smell of blood and decay made me gag. My stomach jumped, and up came everything I had just eaten. I had never seen such carnage. The gore reminded me of a scene from a horror movie.

There were bloody handprints crawling up the walls. The nightstand and lamp was knocked over, and sprawled across the mattress, that was barely on the box spring, was Stephanie's body. She was motionless, and her blank eyes were frozen on the ceiling. From where I stood I could see that her throat had been slashed. Marcus grabbed his cell phone and dialed 911. He put the call on speaker.

"911, Emergency Assistance. What is the nature of the emergency?"

"We need the police! I am at the home of Stephanie Long, and we just found her murdered." He looked over at me as I wiped the tears streaming down my face.

"What is the address, sir?"

"Give me a second." I was in a daze as he spoke to me. "Misty, what's the address? Misty! What is the address?" I passed him an envelope that was sitting on the dresser, and he read it off to the operator.

"What is your name, sir, and who is there with you?"

"My name is Marcus Preston and I'm here with Misty Bishop."

"What is your relation to the victim?"

"No relation. Miss Bishop is the victim's employer."

"Okay, stay at the scene. I've dispatched assistance."

Marcus disconnected the call and came over and hugged me.

Within five minutes the police arrived and began asking us several questions: "When was the last time you saw the victim? Do you know anyone who could have done this? Did she have any enemies?"

I answered all the questions to the best of my ability and told them about the order of protection she had issued against Bernard. I informed them that her daughter was also missing and gave them her grandmother's telephone number. After feeling like we were thoroughly interviewed, they let us leave. The lead detective gave me his card and said he would be at my office in the morning to speak with the rest of the staff.

I couldn't stop crying while riding to pick up my car. She was gone! The vision of Stephanie lying on that bed was forever etched in my memory bank. It burned itself through my corneas and tucked itself in my mind. I wanted to blink the image away, but couldn't. My gut told me Bernard did this, but why? Why kill her? Was it because she didn't want to be with him, or was it because he didn't want to pay child support? It was senseless. He should have gotten himself some therapy.

"Are you going to be able to drive?"

I looked over at Marcus and nodded my head.

When we got home I went straight to the shower. My being in that room with all that blood made me feel dirty. Marcus made me some tea and had it sitting on the bed on a tray when I got out of the bathroom. I took a few sips, but it wasn't helping to settling my nerves. I went down to the bar and poured myself a double shot of Patrón, grabbed an ashtray, retrieved the joint Charmaine had given me, then went into the guest room and got fucked up.

Marcus knew I occasionally smoked weed, but I never smoked in the house. He wanted to complain, but didn't say a word.

When I awoke the next day I felt like shit, and my eyes were puffy, but I had to go to the office, and needed to get there before the police showed up. I got myself together and raced all the way there. I was relieved when I pulled up and there were no police cars in sight. I entered the office and Donald was the first person to approach me.

"Hey, Miss Misty," he cheered. He looked through the lenses of my sunglasses and saw that I had been crying. "Are you okay?"

I didn't reply. Instead, I gestured for him to follow me into my office.

"Close the door." I paused. "It's Stephanie."

"Oh brother, what happened over there last night? Did he put his hands on her again? Why doesn't he try it with someone who will fight him back for a change?"

A tear rolled down my face, and just as I looked to tell him what happened, two detectives walked in. He looked to them then back at me.

"What's going on, Misty? Did he hurt her? I'm gonna kick his ass if he did! If they had kept him in jail! How bad did he beat her up this time?"

"Dee, it's worse than that."

Before walking out into the reception area he sarcastically replied, "What could be worse, him killing her?" He approached the police with his hand extended. "Officers, how may I help you?"

The short, red-haired detective pulled out his notepad.

"Your name, sir?"

"Donald Madison. What is this all about?"

"Do you work here with Mrs. Stephanie Long?"

"Yes, and I'm also her friend. Is everything okay?"

"Miss Bishop hasn't had a chance to inform you yet?"

"Inform me of what?" He grew frustrated. He looked back at me, and my tears told him something was drastically wrong.

I led Donald and the police to my office then offered them a seat at the round conference table. I closed the door then sat at my desk.

"Mr. Madison, I'm sorry to inform you, Mrs. Long was found murdered at her home last night. We're looking for any information you can provide that may help us capture and convict the perpetrators."

It took some time for what the detective said to register, but when it did, Donald's reaction was one of outrage. He broke down then lost it on them. He wanted answers.

"What!!!!! Murdered? You want answers from me! No I want answers from you! She just had her ex-husband locked up, not even two weeks ago! She got the restraining order like the police suggested then they lock him up, and let him out two days later! If they would have kept him, she might be here now! I want answers. I want to know the name of the person who released him so they can explain to her daughter why her mother is *dead!*"

When the other staff heard the commotion they all came to the front desk. I could see them whispering amongst themselves through the open vertical blinds.

Donald yelled, "Where is her daughter at? You do even know about Samantha?"

"Yes, sir, we do. Unfortunately, at this time we're not sure of her location."

He held his head and began weeping. "If Samantha is missing, you can best believe Bernard's got her. Jesus, please don't let him have hurt that child." Donald got up and pounded his fist on the table. "I can't believe this!"

"I understand you're upset, Mr. Madison, but you will need to calm down," the second officer instructed. "Bernard is our primary suspect."

Donald eventually composed himself enough to answer their questions. One by one the detectives called everyone into my office and asked the same series of questions. When they left the staff gathered by Stephanie's desk for a prayer led by Jennifer.

I had everyone reschedule their appointments and closed the office for the day. No one was in their right state of mind to work. I stopped at a Duane Reade store and got the pictures from the New Year's Eve Party downloaded onto a disc. I also got copies made. Stephanie looked so happy. I decided to stop by her grandmother's house before going home. My phone rang, and it was Nickelle.

"Hey girlie. Whatcha doing? I need to vent."

"I'm heading over to Stephanie's grandmother's house." I sighed. "Stephanie was murdered last night."

"Oh my God, what happened to her?"

"She didn't report to work which I thought was strange. On my way home I had Marcus drive me over there to check on her, and when we got to her place we found her dead."

"You found her dead? That's crazy! I would have freaked out and ran the hell up out of that house like I saw a ghost. What did you do? Do the police know who did it?"

"No, but we all believe it was Bernard. He and Samantha have gone missing."

"Do you think he would hurt her?"

"I don't know what he's capable of. I didn't think he would kill Stephanie."

"If he lays one hand on that little girl his soul will rot in hell."

"I was helping her to make some serious moves to improve her financial situation, and get away from him."

"Have you spoken to her grandmother yet?"

"No, but I am on my way over there now."

"I know she is sickened with grief."

"I swear if I saw Bernard right now Nick, he'd be road kill!"

"Who you telling? I wouldn't even attempt to hit the brakes."

"Have you spoken to Charmaine?"

"Yeah, last night. She said Shawn won't stop calling."

"That's to be expected. She just has to stand her ground. I'll check in on her when I leave Ms. Santiago's house. You said you need to vent. What's going on with you?"

"Trey and that little dick of his might have gotten some girl pregnant!"

"What? Is that boy trying to make you a grandmother before your time?"

"That's what I said! Some girl and her mother came to my salon today talking about she's pregnant and Trey's the father. I called him right then and there! He said it was impossible, and that he always uses condoms. He said the last time he had sex with her was like six months ago, and she was sleeping with other guys before, during, and after him."

"Did she look like she could be six months?"

"She was pretty big, but who knows. I told her mother when the baby was born we could go half on a paternity test. The bitch acted as if she had a problem with that. She tried to go there with me with her ghetto ass! She said her daughter knows who she slept with and she's not putting out any money out for the test!"

"What did you say?"

"I said if her daughter knew who she slept with she wouldn't be just now coming to my door, and my son won't be claiming shit until a test is done! She went into they're planning a baby shower and need help. I told her I don't care what they're planning because I won't be contributing toward anything until I know for a fact that baby belongs to my son. If Trey is the father he'll do what needs to be done; however, we ain't doing shit until I get back some results! All she kept talking about was money with her crystal meth looking ass. I suggest she take her daughter down to the welfare center and get her an EBT card. When she started talking shit I told her to get the fuck out of my salon and to not come back until they were ready to take the test!"

"Damn, everybody got some bullshit going on! It's either feast or famine."

"Who you telling? I could kick Trey's yellow ass, but he swears it's not his. I'm going to ask Pop and Sin to have a serious man-to-man with him. He'll listen to them. He respects them."

"Hey, Nick, I just pulled up to Ms. Santiago's house. Let me get back to you later when I get settled, and when I speak to Sin I'll tell him to call Trey as well."

I took my time walking up to the door of the little white house. I lightly tapped then waited. I was actually hoping she wouldn't answer, but I could hear yelling from inside she was coming.

"Who is it?"

"It's me, Misty."

She unlocked what sounded like five deadbolts then slowly pulled the door open. "Come in." I followed her into the living room, and there was an eerie quiet.

"I am truly sorry, Ms. Santiago. I wanted to extend my deepest condolences."

"I knew something was wrong with my granddaughter when I didn't hear from her all weekend. When you called looking for her on Monday that confirmed something was terribly wrong."

"I didn't want to alarm you, but I felt the same way. She never takes off without calling. I'm so sorry this happened. We are all very upset and looking for justice."

"I went down and identified her body." There was nothing more painful than watching an old person cry. "He cut my baby's throat, Misty, and stabbed her twelve times. What would make him do something like that to her?" She broke down. "I'm so confused. Samantha is missing, and I'm worried to death. I'm afraid that animal might have kill—"

"Please, don't think like that! The police will find him, and Samantha will be back here with you before we know it. If there's anything you need, please don't hesitate to reach out to me."

"I'm going to need all the help I can get. I have a weak heart. I went down to see her body and they almost had to be rush me to the hospital. They thought I was going to have a heart attack. I can't take it."

"Whatever I can do, just let me know."

"Stephie had life insurance, but I don't know with what company, who was the beneficiary, or the amount of coverage, but I do have some money I've been putting aside from my social security checks. Maybe one day this week you and I can go over to her place and look through her papers. They said they will release her body to me sometime next week after the autopsy. Do you think you can take care of getting her to a funeral home? I'm not physically up to it."

"I'll be honored. I don't know what she personally had, but I give all of my full time employees a benefit package that includes health, dental, and a $25,000 life insurance policy. Is there any particular place you would like to have her services?"

"No, but I do want her buried with her mother."

We talked for a few more minutes before I looked to leave. Seeing the pain she was going through was tearing me up. I wrote down my cell number and told her to call me if she needed anything, and I would be in touch.

On my way home I called Charmaine. I wanted to see how she was holding up. My call went straight to voice mail, but within minutes she called back.

"You rang?" she questioned in a lethargic tone.

"Yeah, I wanted to check in on you. I also have some bad news."

"Girl, I don't need any bad news right now. I'm going through my own shit."

"I know, but it's not the type of news you can put off. Stephanie from my office was murdered last night."

Charmaine response was delayed. Like the rest of us, she was in shock. "What is this world coming to? What happened?"

"Bernard! He cut her throat. Her daughter is missing, and her grandmother is frantic. When they finally catch up with him the judge is going to throw his ass under the jail. All those people in jail missing their families and that asshole threw his away. Those inmates will see he's a punk and beat the crap out of him. He'll be someone's girlfriend before long."

"If he's anything like Shawn he might actually enjoy getting fucked up the ass!"

I giggled. "Nick told me he's been trying to contact you."

"Five times a fucking day! He can keep on calling, but he'll be talking to the voicemail. He started calling from different numbers, so I turned both my phones off. You're lucky, I just happened to be checking my messages right after you called."

"Did you talk to him?"

"Once I said what I needed to say, it's over, and there's nothing further to discuss."

"He's going to keep calling you. You can't cut yourself off from the world."

"I don't mind screening my calls. I don't want to hear his rationalization, justification, or explanation. He'll eventually get it and stop calling."

"I hope so. What are you doing now?"

"Sitting on the sofa watching television."

"Get dressed. I'm coming to get you. Let's go get something to eat, my treat!"

"I'm not really in the mood to go out, sis."

"I know, and that's why I'm coming to get you. I've been depressed before and the longer you sit in that funk the longer it will take for you to get out of it." My cell phone beeped. "I got another call. I'm on my way. I'll be there in a few, so get ready!" I clicked over to the other line before she could protest.

"Hello?"

"You have a prepaid call and will not be charged for this call. This call is from Garrett Butler, an inmate at a federal penitentiary. Hang up to decline the call or to accept this call dial five now." I dialed "5" and waited.

"Daddy!" Whenever Sin called I felt like a little girl whose father just returned home from a long business trip.

Sin chuckled. "How's my girl doing?"

"I'm okay, but things are not going good at all."

"What's happening?"

"Stephanie was murdered."

"Stephanie from your office? How and when?"

I filled him in.

"Are you okay?"

"I'm still partially in shock. It's surreal. I never saw this coming. She was just at my house, having a good time on New Year's Eve, and now she's gone. Her grandmother asked me to make the funeral arrangements. It's things like this, Sin, that make people realize just how precious life is and how tomorrow is never promised to us. I'm going to miss her dearly." Thoughts of her and laughs we shared made me sad, and knowing he was on the other end of the line was comforting. "It's crazy."

"And what's crazier is they'll let him out before me. I'm sorry for the loss of your friend. If you need anything, let me know."

"I will. If you still want to talk with Charmaine I'm on my way to pick up her."

"Okay, I'll call you back around six-thirty?"

"That's a good time. I should still be with her by then. Love you."

"Love you too, boo."

*Click.*

I walked up the stairs of the Brownstone and placed my key in the door. When I crossed the threshold, the place was upsetting. There were food cartons and plates with leftover food sitting on the counter, newspapers sprawled about the floor, and empty Sprite cans and water bottles lining the coffee table.

The mess was bothering me, so while she finished getting dressed I tidied up a bit. I grabbed a garbage bag from under the sink and started throwing things in it. I noted when she came down she wasn't looking her usual self. She wasn't wearing any make-up, and she was trying to hide her undone hair under a big hat.

We chose a local soul food restaurant. There was an available table by the window, and we were seated immediately. We mulled over the menu in silence then placed our order.

"I can't believe your assistant was murdered."

"Neither can I. Life is so short, Cha; that's why we have to live each day like it's our last." She gazed out of the window at the pedestrians walking by. "I know how you feel, Big Head. I really do, and it will get better. Do you remember when I went through my bout of depression? I didn't want to eat, get dressed, go anywhere, or do anything."

"Did it feel like you lost your best friend?"

"For me, Cha, it felt as if I lost half of my body; half of my being. I thought I was never going to get over it, but I did, and you will too."

"I'll get over it, but I don't know if I'll look at men the same after it. It's so true that a part of you dies with each relationship."

"But you also grow from every relationship as well. Sin returning didn't erase the pain I felt back then. I felt betrayed, I thought we were finished, and I had to deal with that loss. I had to go through mourning a lover that wasn't even dead."

"Well, to me Shawn is dead! What if I've contracted HIV or some other STD from his nasty ass? I trusted him!"

"That's the scary part about loving someone, is having to trust them."

"Well to shit with trust! I'm not going to trust another man!"

I laughed. "What are you going to do, become a lesbian?"

"Hell no! I'm strictly dickly, but I will revert back to my old way of thinking and concentrate of having fun and getting mine."

"Charmaine, you're kidding yourself. There's no foolproof way to safeguard your heart. We don't set out to fall in love; it just happens, and happens when you least expect it! The right man is out there waiting for you. You just have to be careful while you search for him. You never know where a person's head is until you're really involved, but an extensive background check wouldn't hurt. After Sin, I wasn't just opening myself up to anybody. A man had to convince me he was worthy."

"How do I get past the pain and disappointment? What got you past the hurt?"

"Forgiveness, myself, and you. All those times you pulled me out of the house or came in my room to hang out with me. Those were the times when I didn't think about him. I was in that room suffocating. You took my mind off of him, and the pain eventually waned."

"I don't know how you did it. How could you allow yourself to fall back in love with him? Weren't you afraid?"

"Afraid? More like petrified! I'm still afraid, and to be honest with you

I never set out to fall back in love with Sin. If anything, I was trying to do just the opposite. I was trying to end a chapter in my life. I was okay with Marcus. I was okay with my life. I was simply seeking closure. When he wrote me that first letter I didn't know what to do. It was so unexpected. I didn't know whether to rip it up, read it, or reply. I convinced myself I could handle whatever it was he had to say. I read it, and the letter was heartfelt. It took me two weeks to reply, and over the following months we continued writing. I thought we were over. Little did I know, Sin had other plans? I tried to ignore my feelings, fight them, and run away from them.

"We filled each other in on what we did during the time we weren't apart. We admitted that life was a lot better when we were together and how we missed each other tremendously. It became clear that the love we shared never died, and a huge void was filled for both of us. I felt so comfortable talking to him, seeking his advice, and he was always supportive, caring, and helpful. He was all the missing pieces to my puzzle. I felt lighter, smarter, and swifter with him. I felt complete.

"At first our letters were about our present situations and future plans. They then evolved into discussions on old times; you know with that whole era of music, fashion, and attitude." Charmaine nodded her head in agreement. "Talking about that led to us reminiscing about the great times we shared. He said he wished things had turned out differently for us and how he wished we were still together. His words were so sincere, and I felt the same way. In one letter he described with such detail the way we used to make love, and it awakened a whole bunch of dormant feelings I had for him.

"I had given him my cell number, but he never used it. One day I got a surprise call from him. The galvanizing energy was resurrected once we heard each other's voice and laughter. Out of habit he ended the call with, 'I love you, Baby Girl,' and before I could think I said, 'I love you too,

Daddy.' It was in that moment we fell back in love."

Charmaine smiled. "You two have such a great love story. You could write a book."

I winked at her then giggled. "But then he would have to kill me. Let's just leave the writing to the authors."

We finished our lunch, and she admitted that she was glad she came out. "How about we head over to Nickelle's salon and get that head of yours done?"

She looked at her reflection in the windowpane and saw the straggled pieces of hair sticking out from beneath the hat. "I look a mess! Why you let me come out of the house looking like this?"

"Because you needed to get out. I wasn't about to take a chance on commenting, and have you change your mind."

Nickelle filled us in on all her salon gossip while she did Charmaine's hair. We didn't get back to the brownstone until 5:45 PM. We kicked back on the sofa, sipped some wine, and watched *Love & Hip Hop* on the DVR.

My cell phone started ringing. I looked over at Charmaine then smiled. "That's my baby!"

After the pre-recorded message, I dialed "5" and waited.

"Hey, sexy!"

I became giddy. "Hey, Daddy!"

Charmaine sucked her teeth. "Oh, give me a break already."

I laughed then put the phone on speaker. "Sin, you're on speaker. Say hi to Cha!"

"Hey you! What's been shaking?" He would never let on that I had already informed him about her situation with Shawn.

"I don't know where to start. I met the man of my dreams then found out he likes men. I was duped, swindled, and bamboozled, brother!"

Sin laughed. "How did you manage not to see that? I thought you were a player."

"I thought so too! I may have to turn my card in behind this one. Bad-ass Charmaine caught slipping in broad daylight!"

"Not the player of the century." He laughed. "You had the wool pulled over your eyes. Got you a ewe in sheep's clothing, huh? Did he act feminine?"

"That's the thing, Sin; there were no signs. He even fucked me like a real man!"

He burst out laughing. "And what does a real man fuck like, Cha?"

"You know, like, um . . . well . . . shit, he ate the pussy!"

Sin couldn't stop laughing. "Shit, that sounds like a real man to me. Don't sweat it; it could happen to the best of us—except me, of course. Someone purposefully keeping something from you doesn't make you a fool; it makes them a liar or a sneak. In this environment I'm in you see that type of shit all day. Me personally, I'd rather jerk my dick to some sexy photos of my baby for the next fifty years than to ever resort to that. I still got plenty of vivid images in my mind of Baby Girl's legs in the air while I'm pounding that thing out! I can see those sexy lips of hers wrapped around this—"

"Okay, Sin, I don't need a play by play of what the two of you used to do!"

He laughed. "You got that. The bottom line is, you never know. I remember one time when I was out of town and my man met this he-she in a club. Off the rip I told him there was something funny about her, but he was hard up for some ass. He let the chick break him off with some head in the bathroom then brought her back to the hotel. My suite was like four doors down from his. They got to messing around in his room, and when he stuck his hand down her skirt he came up with a handful of balls!"

"Oh shit! What happened?"

"Baby Girl and I were up in our room doing our thing. I was good in the groove too! Remember, Babe?"

"Yeah, Daddy! You had me pinned up against the wall fucki—"

"Hello? Didn't I just say I don't need it blow by blow? Thanks, but back to the story."

I chuckled. "My bad, Big Head."

"Anyway, we hear all this commotion in the hall, and when I opened the door my man was trying to kill dude! He ripped that skirt off of homeboy, wrapped it around his neck, and was dragging him down the hallway. He said he was trying to throw him out the room window, but it wouldn't open all the way. The police were called and everything. I used to tell them cats to fly their shorties in like I did with Misty. It eliminated a whole lot of headaches."

The conversation with him made all the difference, and I could see her winner's spirit coming back.

"What can you do, Cha, but dust yourself off, get back on the saddle, and make sure you're riding a stallion the next time, and not a mare."

"I'm going to take a break from dating for a little while, but best believe the next man I get with will definitely be a stud; that's for sure!"

"If you ask me, I think it's better you found out sooner than later."

"Yeah, I know, but I still feel like a sucker."

"Brush that shit off. He's the one who played himself, not you. Baby Girl?"

"Yeah, boo?"

"Take me off speaker. I want to tell you something in private before I hang up."

I hit the button then placed the receiver to my ear. "Go ahead."

"I love you!"

I smiled. "I love you too, but what's so private about that? Charmaine knows you love me."

"Does she know how talking about that night gave me a clear

visualization of you riding me in that chair, and me carrying you over to the wall? Does she know that's what I'm going to be thinking about when I get my man tonight?" A naughty grin stretched across my face and Charmaine knew he'd said something fresh.

She shook her head and got up. "Ya'll nasty!" She went to the bathroom.

I chuckled. "Nah, she doesn't know, and I don't believe she wants to either."

"Good, now give me kisses so I can get off this phone."

A knock at the front door startled me. I blew him a kiss then hung up. I knew she wasn't expecting any company. I tiptoed over to the bathroom door. "Someone is at the door."

"Look through the peephole and see who it is."

I tiptoed back to the front door, but no one was there. I moved to the front window and slightly pulled back the curtain. I could see the back of a male figure, but couldn't make out the face.

Charmaine came over and stood next to me. "Who is it?"

"I don't know." I stepped to the side so she could see. She looked out and immediately recognized the person.

"It's Derrick. Can you believe that fool is still popping up over here?"

"Maybe he can help you take your mind off of Shawn for a little while."

"You might have a point." She pulled back the curtain and opened the window. "Derrick!" He turned around and she waved for him to come back.

"Charmaine, I was only kidding with you!"

"I'm not going to mess with him, but I do need to talk to him about showing up over here. It needs to stop. I enjoy his friendship, but that's all I want."

She opened the front door and let him in. I greeted him with a handshake.

"I'm getting ready to go home. You need anything before I leave?"

"Nah, I'm good." I gave her the eye and she chuckled. "I'm sure, and I'll call you tomorrow. Thanks for today, sis. I needed it!"

# CHAPTER 18

## *Funeral*

A week dragged by before Stephanie's body was finally released. I made all the arrangements for the funeral then changed my reservations to see Sin. I decided to postpone the visit a week.

I found an address book in Stephanie's desk and gave it to Jennifer. She and Donald started calling people to inform them of her impending services. All that was left to do was purchase her an outfit for the burial.

Before going to the office I stopped at Bloomingdales, where I found her a pretty dress in her favorite color, peach, and a pair of peach and gold shoes. I dropped all the clothes including pantyhose, bra, and panties at the funeral parlor. I gave the funeral director a picture of her at my party. Too often the makeup was piled on and the person looked older, darker, or lighter than they really were. I wanted her to look as natural as possible.

Her grandmother was happy to hear I'd taken care of everything. She told me she'd spoken with the detective late last night and they had located Bernard and Samantha. He was hiding out at his brother's house in Albany. We were both relieved and looking forward to her safe return.

I was extremely surprised when Jennifer announced Marcus was at the front desk. He rarely visited, and he hadn't called to say he was coming. He said he had gotten out early from a meeting and stopped by to take me out to dinner.I had skipped lunch and was hungry. We decided to eat in Manhattan at Aqua Grill.

I learned the real reason for his surprise visit was to discuss plans to move us overseas. He said he had some investment thing going on, and it was about to pay off big. He went on about the market, profits, and opportunity, but I had no interest in living abroad.

"I was thinking we should get married and move out of the country."

"Marcus, I have a life here, a career, and what about my father?"

"You need to start thinking about starting your own family. Those people at the nursing home can take care of him."

"It's an assisted living facility, and he is my family! I don't know where all of this is coming, but I'm not moving out of the country."

"I won't permit my wife to live separate from me."

"Good thing I'm not your wife then."

"Don't you love me?"

"Yes I do, but that is often not enough for longevity. I think us getting married would be a big mistake."

"I don't know what's wrong with you, but you better get on the bandwagon and quick! I told you I want kids; like five, and if you plan on having them, we got to get started. It's not like you're some spring chicken."

All I could picture while he spoke was five little people yelling, "Mommy" at the same time. "Five kids! I thought you said you wanted two? Who is going to take care of five kids?"

"You! Once we start a family your job will be to take care of our kids. You're going to close that business of yours down because you won't have to worry about working. That place is nothing but a distraction anyway. With the house and the kids you will have your hands full."

"Really? You never mentioned any of this to me before."

He smiled. "I didn't think it made a difference. With the amount of money I'm going to be making, you can stay home and be a soccer mom."

"What if I don't want to drive kids around all day and prefer to work?"

"You won't have time for work."

It sounded like he had a hidden agenda for wanting so many kids. "Marcus, just listening to you tonight tells me we have totally different views on the future, as well as other issues going on. The last thing we need to do is add five people to the equation. I have no plans of moving out of the country, staying home, playing taxi to a bunch of kids or closing the business I worked so hard to start." I expressed my desire to take a step backwards, and move out, but he continued to rattle on.

"If I want to be taken seriously at any company, it's expected I be married with lots of children. A big family shows stability."

I thought, *so that's what this was all about.* "I'm sorry to hear that, because five kids, you can forget about, and marrying you is the farthest thing from my mind."

He went on and on about marriage and kids, and what he expected of me. It was obvious we had contrasting long-term plans.

To end the conversation I said, "Yeah, Marcus, sure. I'll think about it."

I picked up my fork and began eating. I knew I wasn't going through five pregnancies. This Kitty Cat wasn't meant to push out a litter. Some women were good at managing four or more children, but not me. I would lose my mind.

My love life had been a twisted state of affairs; however, Marcus had just aligned it with one conversation. Without even thinking twice I decided over dinner it was time to end the charade. I had been putting off the inevitable and dragging my ass on moving out. I was trying to spare his feelings while he was setting me up to be the old woman who lived in a shoe. I was not going to give up my sanity or Sin in exchange for five kids and a facade of a marriage.

I would rather wait for Sin forever than settle and be discontented with Marcus. It would be more difficult to replace the friendship I have with Sin than to find another man. When Sin and I decided to seriously pursue a relationship while he was in there, we weren't prepared. We loved each other dearly, but it was my unwillingness to believe I could be without the physical aspect of a relationship and his belief that no woman could hold him down long term that held us back. However, over time he learned to trust, and I came to understand that sex was just a part of a relationship, and the older I got, the less important it became. Would the partner of a paraplegic after their accident abandon their spouse because the physical relationship is gone? Some might, but many figure out alternate methods of sexual gratification and make their marriage work.

Sin and I put in the hard work to break down each other's barriers and put all trepidations to rest. We reached deep down within to achieve an ultimate level of comfort. It might have taken years, but we accomplished what many couples sought after—unconditional love and absolute honesty. Most men wanted to know how many men their woman has slept with, but way too often they can't handle the truth. They're ready to judge or classify her as a slut if her reply is one too many for their liking.

The trick to unconditional love and absolute honesty is being able to love the person for who they are, not for what you want them to be. It's telling and accepting the truth, digesting it, discussing it, and working together to get past it. It's a great feeling to have someone you can just kick it with and be yourself around. A special someone who knows your faults and still loves the ground you walk on. Someone you feel compatible with on every level. I'm fortunate to have found that in Sin—a lover and a best friend.

If you asked Marcus what my favorite color was he would have no clue. To him that wasn't important, but to Sin it was. He knew it was fuchsia. He also knew my favorite Baskin-Robbins flavor, pizza topping, sexual position, what turned me on, and what turned me off. He even knew around what time of the month I got my menstrual. He learned these things because they mattered to him. I mattered to him. The truth was Marcus could care less. It was all about perception with him.

Marcus excused himself from the table to go to the restroom as my cell phone rang. I heard the pre-recorded message, dialed "5," and waited.

"Hey, Baby Girl! I'm sorry I didn't get to call you earlier. The phones were acting up. Can you talk now?"

"Yes and no. I'm actually out having dinner with Marcus, but he's in the restroom."

"Oh . . . Okay . . . I'll try you back another time."

"No, Daddy! When he comes back to the table, I'll excuse myself. I want to talk to you." I didn't want Sin to feel a certain kind of way.

"So what color panties do you have on?"

I smirked. "Purple, lace, thong . . . nasty boy!"

"When you get home tonight take a picture for me. I want to see them."

"You got it! You are such a big baby!" I hadn't noticed Marcus walking up from behind me as the word baby left my mouth. He pulled out his chair. I almost swallowed my tongue when I looked up and saw him, but I played it cool. I told Sin to hold on as I got up.

"I'm going to the ladies' room . . . I'll be right back." I continued talking in the bathroom. "Sorry about that. Marcus walked up on the table."

"You could have hung up."

"I know, but I wanted to finish my conversation with you."

"Misty, I know you're not a grimy chick, but—"

I snapped at him. "If you know that, then don't even finish the sentence! Whatever I'm doing is being done exclusively with you, and for us!"

"Okay. You got that. My bad, boo."

"So what kind of pose do you want me to do in your picture?"

He laughed. "You know you crazy, right?"

"Only for my Daddy!"

"Don't get yourself in trouble."

"I won't. I would've been in trouble had I hung this phone up on you." We both laughed.

"You know your man."

"Can you believe Marcus just told me I'm no spring chicken over dinner?" Sin laughed.

"It's not funny, but he's right. I am getting older and I do need to start thinking about my future, but it won't be me, him, and five kids living in some foreign country. I'll tell you about it the next time we talk, but I better get off this phone before he suspects something. Oh yeah, I had to reschedule my flight to see you due to Stephanie's funeral, but I'll be down there right afterwards."

"Okay, let me know when you're coming."

"I will. Love ya!"

*Click.*

I floated back to the table. Marcus must have noted the change in my mood, and out of nowhere got an attitude, "Who was that you were talking to?"

I nonchalantly replied, "Oh, that was Charmaine."

He wasn't content with the answer and stared me down. He was searching my face for any indication that I was lying; however, I was unruffled.

"Misty, I'm going to ask you again, who was that you were talking to!"

"I said I was talking to Charmaine! What's up with the questions?"

"Why did you get up so quickly when I sat down? It was like you didn't want me to hear what you were talking about."

"I didn't want you to hear what I was talking about! Charmaine and I were having a private conversation. I also had to use the ladies' room. I was waiting for you to come back, so yes, I got up when you approached the table. Why'd you come back so quickly?"

"There was a line. I thought I heard you call someone baby."

"You did! I called her a baby. If you would have heard the whole conversation you would have heard me call her a big baby to be exact!"

He let it go because I was becoming agitated. The whole ride home we were quiet. He kept cutting his eyes in my direction. I thought about the conversation we had over dinner. Did he really think I was going to give up my career, bear five kids for him, and move away from my friends and family? The next woman might jump at that opportunity, but not me. It was time to take matters into my own hands and get out before it was too late. On our way to pick up my car, I brought up the subject of me moving out again.

This time he became enraged. He slammed his fist down on the steering wheel then turned down the radio. "You know what, Misty? It's about time you grow the fuck up and get with the program. How long do you think you have before your clock runs out? You're not twenty-one anymore! You need to be thinking about starting a family and not moving back to the ghetto so you can run around with that whore Charmaine! You're a grown woman, my woman, and it's time you start planning for our future! I will hear none of this moving out business! What am I supposed to tell my family and the people at my job when I show up at the next function alone or with someone else? They're expecting us to be together."

"Tell them whatever the hell you want! Tell them I was too old to have five fucking kids, asshole! I moving out; now go run tell that!"

He gripped the steering wheel and accelerated down the avenue. I turned my entire body in the seat and gave him my back. I ignored him for the rest of the ride. I remained silent as he ran through two red lights.

"You're fucking ungrateful! You should be flattered and thankful for the lifestyle I'm willing to offer you! No, you'd rather run the streets with your friends like a prostitute!" He had never been so insulting.

Instead of fueling the fire I let him ramble on. As soon as we pulled up to my car I jumped out and slammed his door so hard I almost shattered the window.

When I walked in the house he tried to apologize, but I told him to save it. I knew he wasn't sorry, and knew he meant everything he said. It was just his primordial, warped way of seeing things.

✳ ✳ ✳

The detectives captured Bernard at his brother's house, and Samantha was back with her grandmother. The child was asleep during the whole incident and wasn't aware her mother had been killed. Ms. Santiago tried to explain to her that her mother was in heaven and would not be coming back, but Samantha was too young to really understand the significance of death. Ms. Santiago felt it would be helpful for her to come to the funeral and see her one last time.

The day of the funeral it was bitterly cold. I had it so the viewing was followed directly by the funeral service, and the burial was the next morning. I got to the funeral parlor early and viewed the body. They did a beautiful job with her hair and makeup. If I didn't know any better I would have thought she was asleep.

People began to arrive. Some I knew, while there were many I didn't. They made their way around the coffin and almost everyone, including the men, shed a tear. They say it's what you do in life that counts in the end. Judging by her turnout, Stephanie made a positive impression on a lot of the people. After the two-hour viewing people took the available seats within the pews while the remaining guests stood in the back. The services were heart wrenching, and Ms. Santiago had to be carried out due to chest pains. Her breakdown made Samantha cry, which caused a chain reaction. The whole place wept.

Shortly before the services were finished, I noticed a man who looked very much like Bernard slip into an empty seat at the end of the pew. I tapped Charmaine. "I think that's Bernard's brother over there."

A host of people walked past the coffin for their final farewell before the casket was closed. I walked up to the man and introduced myself. I asked if he was related to Bernard, he replied yes, and said he was his brother. I admitted to him that I was surprised he came.

"I had to come. I had no idea what my brother did. He showed up at my house that night and said he wanted to get away from the city for a few days to clear his head."

"You didn't think that was odd? You didn't think it was funny he had Samantha with him?"

"Yes, my wife and I did. He told us Stephanie went away on business and he had Samantha for the week. I swear I didn't know. My family liked her. I was one of the people who convinced her to leave my brother. He's my blood, so I love him, but I don't like him. He had issues with anyone who didn't agree with him; employers, co-workers, neighbors, me, and her. I'm ashamed of what he did. The police called and said he was a suspect in her murder. I confirmed he was at my house with Samantha, and they asked that I not tell him they were on the phone. In a matter of minutes, they had my house surrounded and him in cuffs. My neighbors witnessed the whole thing."

He passed me an envelope with his phone number written on it. "Please, give that to Ms. Santiago with my condolences. It's a check. Let her know if she needs anything she can always reach out to me. My wife and I would like to continue being a part of Samantha's life."

Marcus and I drove home in silence. I had been distant, and he had been acting suspicious, nervous, and paranoid. I asked him if there was something he wanted to talk about, but he abruptly told me no, but something was going on with him.

The burial started at 8:30 the following morning and was over within an hour and a half. Afterward Toya, Nickelle, Jasmine, Charmaine, and I stopped and had breakfast. The topic of discussion was me leaving Marcus, Charmaine's HIV test and the results. I confessed. "I remember being so arrogant when I took my very first HIV test, but after a few days of thinking about Black and who he could have slept with, I got scared."

"I thank God my gynecologist removed my IUD and Malik and I had to use condoms for the last three months; otherwise, I'd be going through the same stress as you, Charmaine. We haven't had unprotected sex since my last doctor's visit, and everything checked out fine then. Who knows what men that woman, Michelle, could be sleeping or have slept with?"

After breakfast, I drove Charmaine to the clinic and waited while she met with the counselor. She had been putting it off. I said a silent prayer. Fifteen minutes later she strolled out the door, stopped in front of the jeep, struck a pose, smiled, and then popped her collar. She hopped in, put on her seatbelt, then cheered, "I'm negative, sis, and no STD's!"

# CHAPTER 19

## *Visit with Sin*

Marcus had been acting like he had a stick up his ass. He was upset because the stock market wasn't doing well and mad that he wouldn't be getting a big bonus like he had the year before. He was disappointed that I wasn't ready to take his hand in marriage and stressed the IRS was auditing him. He was also having some problems at work he refused to discuss. We were growing more distant. The last time we'd had sex was on New Year's Eve, and that was more than a month ago.

I had spoken to Sin a few times since the funeral, but he still wasn't sounding entirely like himself. To bring his spirits up I was going to surprise him with a visit this weekend. My ticket was reserved, and my overnight bag was packed. I had already told Marcus I would be leaving this evening to look into a commercial property for Jeremy Whittaker in Arizona.

I would be with my love in less than twenty-four hours, and I couldn't wait to see him! When we spoke earlier he said he was on his way to the barber, and I hinted how I couldn't wait to run my hands over his smooth bald head. I told him I would be available and to call me later on in the evening around 8:30.

I headed to the airport and enjoyed a smooth flight. Upon landing I went straight to Enterprise and picked up the reserved rental car. I plugged the address of the hotel into the navigational system, and got there without delay. The first thing I did when I got into the room was shower then called Marcus. He was curt and our conversation lasted all of two minutes.

When Sin called at 8:35 PM I didn't mention to him I was in Arizona or that he would be seeing me in the morning. We had a good conversation, and he said he would call me sometime the next day. He said he was heading back to his cell to write me a letter. He said he had something on his chest that he wanted to discuss with me, but he didn't want to go into it over the phone.

When I woke the following morning I was excited! I was eager to see my Daddy! I took a quick shower, oiled my skin, and added a little perfumed lotion for the final touch. My hair hung in long, soft curls and my make-up was applied perfectly. I knew he would appreciate how great I looked and smelled! I slid on a La Perla bra and panties then wrapped the blue silk military style dress around my body. I opted for silk because the fabric was soft to the touch. I was dressed conservative yet sexy. I could almost pass for a flight attendant. The corrections officers didn't have a problem turning a female visitor away because she was dressed too provocatively.

Not all, but there were some C.O.'s who purposely made visiting a loved one unbearable sometimes to the point where you didn't want to return. They acted as if they were envious of the inmates. It was apparent that they despised the fact that an inmate had a better-looking woman than they did. They couldn't understand why an attractive woman would entertain a prisoner. You could see the question, "Why is she visiting him?" all over their faces. As far as they were concerned all convicts were worthless; which is far from the truth. I actually had a C.O. tell me I was too bad to be visiting some jailbird, as if that was going to get me to leave Sin and give him some play.

I drove into the visitor's parking lot and found a spot close to the building. I decided before I got out, to leave my panties in the car. I grabbed my pocketbook containing a clear pouch with twenty dollars in singles and change, my ID, and a clear lip-gloss then headed to the visitor entrance. I had seen him at this facility before and knew the process. It was the same routine every time, and if you were lucky enough to get a cool officer and people followed instructions, the process went smoothly.

I entered the building and there were two women on line ahead of me. I went to the desk and got a key for a locker. I placed my belongings in the locker less the clear bag. The first woman on line had two small children with her. One was barely walking, and the other was a newborn. The C.O. stood waiting, refusing to assist her with the kids. The second lady in line offered to hold the baby while she went through the metal detector.

After what felt like thirty minutes I finally got the chance to take off my shoes and belt and be scanned. My hand was stamped, and a group of us were escorted through a set of locked metal doors. We were led into the visiting area by another C.O. I took a seat toward the back of the room, away from the kids' play area. The visiting room was crowded. I was happy about that because I really didn't want some C.O. staring down my throat the whole visit. I sat patiently and waited for Sin to come down.

I watched the door that the inmates appeared from and finally there he was! Even in khaki's my baby was handsome. He sported a freshly cut goatee and a smooth bald head. He walked with the confidence of a king with his muscular chest. He looked around the room, but he didn't see me. I stood up as he strolled up to the front desk and handed in his ID. He scanned the room, and once we made eye contact his face lit up.

He swaggered over and stood before me then spread his strong arms. I placed my hands on his chest then stepped into his embrace. His arms felt like the wings of an angel clasped around my body. I looked up into his eyes and he kissed me ever so slowly and passionately. As he slid his tongue into my mouth I ran my hands up his back and over his head. If it wasn't for the fat, lonely female C.O. calling out his last name, we would have never stopped.

He grabbed my hand and pulled me down into the seat. "I knew you were coming, but I had no idea it was this weekend!" He smiled. "You didn't say anything yesterday."

"I know. I wanted to surprise you!"

"You did, and it's a pleasant surprise, but you should have let me know you were coming. The spot could have been on lockdown, and you would have come all this way for nothing." He leaned in and gave me a quick kiss on the forehead.

"I did call before I came. I know you like to know in advance, but—wait a second. Weren't you the one who told me to get my ass down here?"

He grinned. "Yeah, I did!"

I smiled. "Okay then, so act like you're happy to see me!"

I ran my hand down the side of his face and admired his features. He still maintained his boyish looks and athletic figure, but was a bit bulkier as if he had been lifting weights and eating lots of bread and potatoes. I looked down and even his fingernails were manicured. I ran my hand across his bald head then grinned. "It's smooth, just like I remember."

He knew I was being fresh, because I always commented on how much I loved to palm his head while he was licking my sensitive spot.

"You better watch that! As horny as I am I might just take the pussy and worry about the consequences later."

I looked him dead in the eyes. "And I would let you!"

"You look great, Baby Girl! Better than any picture you've ever sent."

"Thank you. You look pretty good yourself."

We couldn't stop smiling. Sitting there in a room surrounded by strangers didn't stop us from being in our own little world. I leaned over and gave him a quick peck kiss on the lips. He rested his arm behind my shoulders and I inconspicuously rested by body into his.

"So are you happy to see me?"

"You know I am!"

A young C.O took over the post at the front desk and Sin smirked. I looked over in the direction he had his gaze fixed on, and the young C.O. gave us a warm smile.

"He's seems cool for a corrections officer."

"Yeah, that's Walters, he's good people. He does his eight hours and gets the hell out the way."

"You can tell the fat one who was just sitting up there doesn't get any dick. She acts likes she enjoys staring down people's throats like an otolaryngologist."

"Imagine how she treats us! C.O Walters isn't like that. If you give him respect, he'll show you respect. He treats me like a man first and then an inmate. We chop it up from time to time, especially about you."

"What about me?" Before he could answer C.O Walters called him to the front desk.

I thought something was wrong until he sat back down with a slick look on his face. "What are you up to, Sin?"

He grinned. "Don't worry; I got a surprise for you! Now come here and let me taste those lips again." He pulled my face to his and tongued me down.

I licked my lips as he pulled away. "Damn, boo! You better ease up before these people end your visit and kick me out."

"Don't worry." He nodded his head in the direction of the front desk, "Walters is gonna let a brother live a little. He just told me to not go crazy, but have fun, and that's exactly what I plan on doing! They cut the budget so there's fewer eyes watching us, you feel me?"

Sin didn't waste another second before he placed my chin between his thumb and pointer finger, pulled my face to his, and gently pressed his lips to mine. It was as if everyone in the room had disappeared for those few seconds. Our tongues slowly snaked across each other's, and I was melting like butter in a hot pan. I sucked his bottom lip as he pulled away. I was glad he did, because I didn't have the self-restraint to stop.

"So how is everything going out there in the real world, Bright Eyes?"

"Touch and go is the best way to describe it. Charmaine is much better. Her results came back negative, but they say she won't be completely in the clear until she takes another two tests. I haven't really seen Jasmine that much lately. Toya retained a lawyer and is discussing divorce, and Nickelle might be a grandmother."

"A grandmother?"

"Yeah, a grandmother! Trey might have gotten some hood rat pregnant. I got distracted with Stephanie's death and forgot to tell you."

"I'm gonna get in his ass! I've stressed the importance of using condoms with him." He shook his head then heaved a sigh. "When you get home tell him to be expecting a call from me on Monday at seven o'clock sharp. So what about you? How's my Baby Girl doing?"

"Now that I'm here with you, I'm great! I told you I was moving out, and have been slowly moving my things back into the brownstone. I tried to talk to Marcus about me leaving, but he flipped out. Let's just say he wasn't receptive to me moving out. He accused me of wanting to run around with my whore friend and be a prostitute. He said I was getting old, and needed to focus on starting a family." Sin sat expressionless. I couldn't read what he was thinking. "He said I needed to get with the program; which included me marrying him, relocating to some foreign land God knows where, and closing B&B Realty. He wants me to be a soccer mom to his five kids."

"Five kids?"

"Yup, five! He basically said we needed to start on a family right away so he could look stable at work. He's walking around with a chip on his shoulder. In addition to not having sex since the first of the year, now we're not speaking, but I don't want to talk about him."

"Do you think he's going to be a problem? I can send someone over there to have a talk with him."

"I don't think that will be necessary. I'll move the rest of my things out slowly over the next few weeks, start staying at the brownstone more, and eventually just not come back."

"Are you okay with this? Are you positive this is what you want to do?"

"I'm positive. It's a little scary starting over again, but like my father told me, it's better to be alone and happy than miserable with someone. This will give me the time I need to sort out my feelings and select the right path for me. Marcus was right when he said I'm not twenty-one, and I do need to start thinking about my future. There are certain things I want and then there are the things that I need. One day I may have to decide which is more important. Lucky for us, today is not that day."

"And you're sure?"

"Yes, I'm sure!" I smiled. "Maybe I'll chill by myself until my Prince Charming comes and sweeps me up off my feet."

"I thought I was your Prince Charming?"

I smiled. "Who said I wasn't talking about you?"

He kissed me then grabbed my hand. "Let's get some stuff from the vending machine." He stood right behind me as I put the change in the slot, and I could feel his eyes burning a hole through my dress. He ran his hand down my back and rested it on my butt. His eyes could have popped out of his head when he realized I didn't have on any panties.

"So you gonna do it like that? No panties!"

I smiled then bit down on my bottom lip. "I left them in the car. Do you like?"

"Damn right I do! You must be really trying to tempt Daddy today."

By the time we sat back down we had ten dollars worth of junk food, which we probably wouldn't even eat. It was worth the ten free feels he got off my ass. We spent the next hour discussing things like his business transactions and legal affairs that he didn't want to tell me over the phone. He ran his hands through my hair, and every now and again leaned over and smelled it or gently moved a curl from my face.

An enormous African-American inmate walked up and began setting up the area to take pictures. Sin pulled a bunch of picture tickets from his shirt pocket and started counting them.

"You must have really wanted to take pictures today, huh?" He paid my last comment no mind. He continued to watch the inmate with the camera nonstop like a hawk. "You got beef with him or something?"

"Nah, Baby Girl, that's my man Tiny! I asked him for a favor."

"What's the favor? Take his time taking the pictures so you can feel me up?"

He smirked. "Something like that, but even better! Just be patient, you'll see."

They made eye contact and Sin nodded to him. Tiny moved the first vending machine closest to the C.O. desk slightly on an angle so that the left back side was flush against the wall while the other side was inched forward. He pulled the second and third machine out a few more inches. He eventually tied the ends of the canvas to the sides of the fourth and fifth machines, which he had slid all the way forward. He then nodded back to Sin, who looked over at me then smirked.

"Come on, let's go take some flicks."

He took my hand and led me over to the other side of the room where the makeshift backdrop was now hung. The pictures were taken in the corner, against the wall, on the same side of the room as the C.O. desk. From their desk they didn't have a clear view of the area because of the vending machines. The machines closest to the picture area were now situated in such a way that someone could easily slide behind the canvas unseen.

As we waited for Tiny to take our picture, Sin turned me around by my waist and pressed himself into my rear. The material of my dress was thin, and I instantly felt his erection. I literally could feel the length of his penis growing between my butt cheeks. I was so turned on! My entire being started to feel warm inside like I just took a shot of brandy on a cold winter's night. I silently thought how I should have worn my panties now that I could feel between my thighs becoming moist.

Sin gave a wink at Tiny and then nodded toward the C.O. desk. Tiny snapped two more photos of us. In between the pictures Sin was feeling me up. There were four other couples waiting on line. Tiny nodded then said, "Go ahead, you're good!" Sin grabbed my hand, discretely pulled back the side of the canvas, and we disappeared behind the vending machines.

"What are you up to?" He pressed his finger to my lips and whispered in my ear, "I'm gonna give you what we both been yearning for."

He removed his finger from my mouth and replaced it with his lips. As his tongue entered my mouth a fire shot through me. I couldn't believe we were getting ready to do this. I wasn't going to protest. I wanted him just as bad as he needed me. This was the moment we had both been praying for. He braced himself against the wall with his left palm and elbow then slid his right hand down my breast, to my waist then to my thigh. He pulled my dress up and maneuvered his fingers around until he found my hot spot. He carefully dipped his fingers in and out as my juices started flowing.

When his fingers were completely saturated he pulled them out, placed them in his mouth then sucked them clean. He knew exactly what to do to get me going, and my inner thighs were now soaked.

He smirked. "That Kitty stays wet for Daddy, don't she?"

My vaginal cavity was quivering, my legs felt weak, and I was totally ready for him. He placed his hand back in my secret garden and continued fingering me. I opened my legs a little wider so he could part my lips and play with the clit.

He had me pressed up against the wall, fingering me and kissing me ravenously. He was driving me insane. I didn't want to waste a single second because time was of the essence. I reached down and felt for his magic stick. I rubbed and massaged it through his pants. The head was poking out of his left pocket. I murmured in his ear, "It's been so long since I felt you, Daddy. I miss my dick so much."

He hadn't lied when he said he thought it grew. It was massive. I reached down and began undoing his pants as we kissed. "Be careful you don't hurt me putting that thing in me, Sin."

"Don't worry, Daddy gonna take his time."

"You better!"

My body had been craving his. This was a once in a lifetime opportunity, and we were going to take full advantage of it. I quickly loosened his pants, unzipped the zipper, and let his pants drop to his knees. I took hold of him. His dick felt so strong and thick in my hand. I couldn't completely clasp my hand around the girth. My mouth watered. I had to look at it. I pulled away from him and took a quick peek. It was just as I remembered—beautiful. The thickness, the veins, the shape, the color, it was all the same—delectable!

He undid the top three buttons on my dress, lifted my bra and hungrily took my breast into his mouth. My nipples were one of my most erogenous zones. He softly swirled his tongue back and forth as his hot breath, wet mouth and sucking sensation drove me nuts. My neatly manicured Kitty, my inner thighs, and everything in between were covered with my juices. I let out a moan, and he quickly stuck his middle finger in my mouth to stifle my sounds.

He whispered in my ear, "Ssshhh, you have to be quiet." He knew I could get loud at times, but what do you expect when something made you feel so wonderful?

I was stroking his dick with my hand and when I softly grasped his balls he let out a moan of his own. "Uuuuummmmm."

I giggled then whispered; "Now you need to be quiet." I could feel pre-ejaculation forming on the tip. "Let me taste you." I bent down and took him in my mouth. I ran my tongue around the head while lightly rubbing my fingers up and down the shaft. Before I could even really get into it he pulled me up to him.

"I can't take it. If you keep that up you're gonna make me cum, and I need to do that inside of you."

A part of me wanted to suck the life out of him, but I wanted to feel him inside of me. I licked the edges of his ears as I held him in my hand. He was so fucking hard that I could feel it throbbing. He was ready to explode. He ran his hands up my thighs and lifted my dress to my waist. He rested his palms on my ass then softly caressed both cheeks. His tongue went from dancing in my mouth to licking down my neck. I lifted my right leg and wrapped it around the back of his thigh then placed his dick between my legs and started rubbing my clitoris back and forth over his shaft.

He moaned as he placed the head to my Kitty. I slightly raised my leg, and when he entered me my eyes fluttered. It was as if someone hit me with a shot of the purest dope the streets had ever seen. My eyes rolled up into the back of my head and a calmness overcame my body.

I mumbled, "Oooohhh, Yeeeeeeesssssss, Dadddddy."

He held that position for a few seconds before trying to stroke a little deeper into me. Each stroke caused my insides to pulsate, and his dick to throb. He lifted my other leg up around his waist as I held onto him by his neck. He carefully, but steadily pumped in and out of me. My body wanted him so it unwearyingly stretched to accommodate him. If he didn't take his time he could rip me. It was as if my Kitty Cat remembered her Daddy and was giving him tight hugs and wet kisses. With each of his thrusts I felt a little more pressure, and by the time he was halfway inside of me I began to feel the strain.

He whispered in my ear, "Your too tight." He was a lot longer and much thicker than Marcus. Normally by now we would be looking to change positions, but that wasn't an option. I had to endure the pain mixed with pleasure and asked for more. I wanted him to fill my insatiable appetite.

I whispered, "Go deeper, Daddy. Deeper."

He smirked, "You ain't playing fair." He worked himself further into me as I bit down on his shoulder. I felt every inch of my insides being stretched. My entire vaginal cavity became filled to its capacity. The head felt like it was in my stomach, and pressing up against my cervix.

He held his position then stared in my eyes. "I love you, Misty."

"I love you too, Sin. Now shut up and take this pussy before we get caught!" I slightly twirled my hips twice. He tried to fight the sensation, but couldn't.

"Shit, I'm cumming," he grunted. He held my back tight and began stroking hard. I squeezed my arms around his neck as I slid up and down his shaft. His balls bounced as I took it like a real trooper. He held my ass, and pumped everything he had into me. It was an overwhelming flow of warm semen.

He stayed inside of me until his swelling went down then let my legs down one at a time.

"You have the absolute best pussy in the world!"

"Man please, after all these years any pussy would have been the best in the world." We both laughed as I straightened out my wrinkled dress. "We better get from behind this machine before we get in trouble."

"Don't worry about it. My man Tiny is watching my back. Look, my joint is still semi hard. Let me get some more. I want you to cum."

"I'm okay. I don't want to get caught."

"Let me worry about that."

He lifted my dress, picked me up, wrapped my legs around him, and slid right back in me. This time he was able to go a little longer, and we both came. I was glad we came quickly, because I was hurting.

We checked ourselves out before he took my hand and peeked from behind the curtain. Tiny gave him the nod and we slid out undetected. I walked straight to the ladies room and cleaned up the best I could with the rolls of loose toilet paper and water. We later returned to the picture area and took several more pictures.

I tried to maintain a conversation, but Sin's mind was somewhere else. He couldn't keep his hands off of me. He ran his hands through my hair, rubbed my back, caressed my face, and stroked my leg. We only had an hour left on the visit when I said, "This is the part I don't like."

"What part is that?"

"The saying goodbye part."

"Don't look it as saying goodbye; look at it as I'll see you later. Now that you're leaving Marcus you can come see me more often. What time does your flight leave tonight?"

I smiled. "It doesn't. I'm leaving tomorrow."

"That's what's up! So that means I'll get to see you again!"

"Yup, bright and early!"

He hopped up out the seat. "I'll be right back! I need to find out if Walters is working the visitor's floor tomorrow." He walked up to the C.O. desk where the two had a brief conversation then laughed. He returned to his seat and wrapped his arm around my shoulder.

"So? Is he working tomorrow?"

"Yup, bright and early!"

"So what was so funny?"

"He said I got a little sample today and now my nose is wide open, and I told him he wouldn't understand until he had some crack pussy of his own! The Sticky Icky is lethal! One more hit of that should do the trick."

"Well, if I plan on messing around with that big ass tree trunk you call a dick tomorrow I'm gonna have to soak in the tub tonight. My Kitty Cat is sore."

He put on a serious face. "Baby Girl, you do whatever it is you have to do because Daddy needs some more of that or I swear I'm gonna die."

We burst out laughing. "Don't worry, I got you, boo! Let me ask you something. How did you manage to work this out?"

"Everything fell into place for us. Walters is mad cool. He saw that I'm not like some of these knuckleheads or a troublemaker. He sees how I move and how I conduct myself. He has a lot of respect for me. We spend a lot of time talking about sports, politics, and life. I was telling him how much I miss my baby, and some of the things I want to do with you. A couple of weeks ago when the subject of my dilemma came up he said if you came while he was working he would let me rock. Tiny is a few cells down from me and he put me on to how it's done. I asked him for a favor when you first said you were coming and everything worked out on this visit. It was perfect! Did you bring another dress with you?"

"You know I did."

He grinned, "Good because I like that easy access!"

I smirked. "You always did."

"And don't forget to leave the panties in the car. That was a nice touch!"

"I got you, nasty boy! So what was your dilemma? You said he helped you out."

He rubbed his hands together. "Let's just say I might have figured out a way for both of us to be happy while I'm in here. A few more shots should do the trick. I like the way that whole thing went down!"

"Me too! I would have never thought in a million years we would get away with having sex in federal jail."

We continued talking until the C.O. announced that all visits were over. We hugged liked we weren't going to see each other the next day. I drove back to the hotel, and as soon as I got in the room I took a nap. I was going to take a shower when I woke, but decided to marinate in his scent a little longer.

I text messaged Charmaine and told her to call me. Within a few minutes she called back and I filled her in on my day. "Guess where I'm at, Big Head?"

"I don't know, tell me?"

"In Arizona, girl! I just left from seeing Sin!"

"Get the hell out of here! You didn't tell me you were going down there with your slick ass! When did you plan all of this?"

"A month ago, but I had to change my plans when Stephanie was murdered. It totally slipped my mind. When I called to make reservations they had open seats leaving this weekend. I jumped on it! I was overdue for some face-to-face time with him."

"I hear that! So how is he doing?"

"He looks really good; physically fit, skin clear, manicured. In fact he looks downright delicious! Taking where he's at out the equation I would say he's in great spirits now that he got himself some of this Kitty!"

"Wait a minute. How did the two of you pull that off?"

"Girl, opportunity came a knocking, and we got us a quickie."

"Ooooh! You're such a slut!"

"I learned from the best, so give yourself a pat on the back, ho, and yes I will be going back tomorrow for some more!"

"You go, girl! Get a nut for me while you're at it since I won't be getting any, anytime soon. Shit, how long has it been since he had some?"

"Too long, but I'm the one who's sore. As soon as I get off this phone with you I'm going to take me a long, hot bath."

"Damn, well you go ahead, because I have a date and I need to get ready."

"Who you going out with? I hope it's not Shawn!"

"Hell no! Fuck him! I'm going out with Derrick."

"Derrick? I thought you cut him off. How did he manage to get you to go out with him again?"

"Take it easy, we're only hanging out as friends. He's not stressing me for sex, and I ain't giving him none. I'm waiting until my next HIV test before I even think about sexing anyone. It's been some years since I gave old Fee-Fee here some chill time, but don't worry about me; my vibrator is getting plenty of action and giving a few of my exes a run for their money!" She laughed. "I am dating, just not screwing which means I'm going to be enjoying a bunch of free meals and watching a whole lot of new releases."

"You crazy. Be safe, and I'll call you tomorrow when I'm on my way home."

We hung up and I ordered a bottle of White Zinfandel, a turkey burger, and fries from room service. The food arrived pretty quickly and didn't taste too bad. I ran a bubble bath and five minutes after stepping into the tub my phone rang. I listened to the pre-recorded message. "Hi, lover!"

"Hey, Bright Eyes!" I could picture him smiling on the other end. "I wanted to tell you how thankful I am for your surprise visit. I really enjoyed our time together. How's my Kitty Cat doing?"

"She's tender, but never better! I'm in the tub now."

"Good. I wish I was there to put some ice on it and kiss the pain away."

I giggled. "I wish you were here too, but ice wouldn't be the only thing you'd be putting on it. Did you eat?"

He chuckled. "Yeah, but it wasn't what palate was craving."

"Maybe tomorrow there will be something better on the menu."

"I hope so. Make sure you lock the door."

"I did. I'll see you tomorrow."

"Love you!"

"I love you too, Daddy!"

I got out the tub and sat in the quiet room thinking about my day. I decided to write Sin a letter and share my thoughts. We'd had sex in some of the craziest places before, but this took the cake. No one would ever believe we fucked in a federal penitentiary. When we were younger we liked the excitement of screwing in weird places, but it was no longer about excitement. It was now out of pure desperation, and desperate times called for desperate measures.

*My Dearest Sin,*

*I'm lying here in the hotel bed thinking about you, wishing you were here with me to finish off what you started. I could see us now rolling around in this room. It would take us a straight week together to blow off the years of sexual frustration. Here I am thinking I was going to surprise you, but I got the biggest surprise of all!*

*I'm still bugging how you were able to pull it off, but that's why I love you so much! You can make the impossible—possible! Wow is all I can say about that! Kitty might be aching, but says to tell you it was well worth it, and you can best believe she'll be back for some more. (SMILE)*

*Yeah, your girl is a freak like that! It felt great spending some quality time with you. Being able to look into your eyes as we conversed face to face, feeling your arms around me, your lips upon mine, and the Sinnamon Stick was magical! I'm getting wet just thinking about it!*

*Babe, loving you comes so easy, and your presence is forever missed. I know one of these days you're going to walk out of that place, somehow, some way, and make it back to me! I have no doubt about it. I believe in you, and have faith in us!*

*Did I tell you how much I love you today? If I forgot I love you, love you, love you! You'll get this letter long after I've gone home, but know I had a wonderful time and I will be holding onto that memory forever. See you on the next visit.*

*Loving you always, your Baby Girl, Misty*

\*\*\*

Sunday morning I was awakened by the courtesy wake-up call from the front desk. I put on an olive colored wrap dress and gold stiletto sandals. I held my hair up with a large clamp, and had a few soft curls cascading down my back. I checked myself out one last time in the mirror, put on my gold Gucci shades then headed down to the lobby.

The line at the visitor's entrance was much longer today. Thankfully everyone got in without incident. I chose the same seats we sat in the day before then patiently waited for Sin to be brought down. It took ten minutes before he came strutting through the door. He handed his ID to the C.O. at the desk, looked around the room, then smiled.

He grabbed me up in his arms and gave me a big wet kiss. "What took you so long to come down? I was starting to get worried."

"I was taking a shower when they called me, but had I known you were going to look so good I would have just worn the towel down here. That color looks nice on you. It brings out the color of your eyes."

"I'm glad you like it." I ever so gently pulled his face down to mine and slid him some tongue. "What happened to Walters? I see he's not here?"

"He's working. I saw him earlier. He'll be down around ten." He smirked. "You ready to give Daddy some of that?"

"Been ready! Do you want anything out of the vending machines?"

He licked his lips then looked me up and down. "What I want they don't sell in those machines, but if I'm lucky I'll get some of your snacks behind one of them later."

I giggled. "Come on, horny boy. Walk with me. I want a yogurt and some Life Savers." We walked over to the machine, and there were a few people waiting to make a purchase or use the microwave.

He grumbled in my ear, "I wish Walters would hurry up already!"

I slightly turned and peeked over my shoulder. "Patience is a virtue."

He pinched my butt. "Forget that. I've been dreaming all night about me hitting that from the back!"

I slightly backed up into him and rubbed my ass on him. "And you'll get your chance, big boy."

I got the Life Savers and two blueberry yogurts before returning to our seat. We waited for C.O. Walters to report while Tiny set up the canopy. A few people lined up to take pictures. Walters arrived, they made eye contact, and it was a go! We made our way over to Tiny. Just as we had the day before, we took two pictures then slid behind the canopy and disappeared behind the machine for a quick lovemaking session.

As soon as we got behind the machine I pushed Sin up against the wall and aggressively began undoing his pants. He went to ask me what I was doing, but I put my fingers to his lips, "Shhh, I was been dreaming too, and I need to clear my head."

I dropped his pants and began messaging him in my hand. Once I felt the blood flowing I squatted down on the back of my gold heels and took him in my mouth.

I looked up at him as he watched my orange manicured nails slid back and forth on his shaft. I sucked and licked the tip like a lollipop. Some women don't like performing oral sex. I loved sucking his, and I stress *his*, dick! It turned me on.

When I saw his eyes slowly closing I knew I had him. I made sure not to overdo it in fear that he would cum. I ran my tongue along the front and back then gripped his balls. I swirled my tongue around the head before taking him completely into my throat. "Ummmmm, Baby Girl. That feels soooo good."

When I felt the pressure building I stood up. "Are you ready to take this from the back?"

He smiled. "Turn around!" He bent me over and threw my dress over my back. He spread my cheeks with his thumbs then rubbed himself back and forth between my legs. His manhood became lubricated with my Sticky Icky. As he situated himself to dig my back out I placed one hand on the wall and the other against the back of the vending machine.

I turned and looked up at him. "Don't get crazy back there. I don't want to be taken out of here in a wheelchair."

He gave me a slight spank on the ass. "Shut up, and take this dick." I giggled. He grabbed his rod and began playing around my opening.

"Don't tease me, Sin. You better hurry up before somebody comes." He lightly spanked my right butt cheek then admired my round ass. He ran his hand over it as he eased the tip in. We both moaned, and I giggled. "We're going to get caught."

"Baby Girl, they gonna have to beat me out of this pussy today." He slowly worked himself in and out of me with a steady rhythm. I braced myself as he picked up his pace. It was getting good to him, and his pumping caused the vending machine to slide. I removed my hand and instead held on to the back of his thighs. He bent me all the way over and dug deeper into me. The pressure was intense, but I wasn't going to tell him to stop.

"Oh, God, Daddy." He gripped my hips a little tighter and slowly pumped his load deep inside of me. All my curls had fallen out of the hair clasp, and my dress was twisted by the time he was done.

He breathed heavy. "You don't know how much I needed that!"

"Oh, I do, and I'll probably be feeling just how much for the next few days."

"As far as I had my joint up in there, fuck around, I might have knocked you up!"

We were probably both secretly hoping just one of his sperms from the last two days made it to my egg. I straightened myself out and we slid from behind the machines.

"You two were about to knock the machine over dawg," Tiny joked. "I had to use my body weight to stop it from moving, and I'm not a little dude, you know."

Sin chuckled. "And neither am I!"

I walked off in the direction of the ladies room and left them to talk. I was a little embarrassed, but shook it off. I wasn't some freak he'd just met who allowed him to fuck her on a visit. I was his lady! When I got back we took a few more pictures before returning to a set of empty chairs. We talked, laughed, and kissed for the rest of the visit.

"I love you, Misty, and although I already feel like you are, one of these days I'm going to make you my wife."

"Is that a proposal, or are you just sharing your thoughts with me?"

"Both!" He laughed.

"We need to start taking what we're doing more seriously, Sin. I have faith that one day you'll get out of here, but neither of us knows for certain when that will be. It's not cool that I have to sneak to come see you. I want to see you more than once every couple of months. It's wrong that I have to hide our pictures, our memories, and it's insane we profess to love each other so much, but . . ." I sighed in frustration. "You just don't get it. I got one man mad at me for not wanting to marry him and another who keeps making up excuses why he shouldn't."

"It's not like that, Misty. There's a lot you would be giving up, and I don't—"

"I told you before I wasn't going to bring this topic up anymore, and I would appreciate if you did the same. If you being in here is your excuse, then leave it at that. Maybe we'll talk about it when you get out. That is, if I'm still available."

"Why you acting like that? You know I want nothing more than to give you the life you deserve and the wedding you always dreamed of."

"If I didn't trust you, I would swear you were selling me a fantasy trip to nowhere. The life I want includes you, and the wedding I dreamt about all those years ago left the day you did. We're here and now, facing a lifetime in jail. That's our reality until something changes. I didn't ask for the dress, the bridesmaids, the flowers, or a big ring. I asked for the man. Wanting to get married to you while you're in here was my way of showing you my dedication. In my mind it was a way to guarantee we'd be a part of each other's life forever, and yes, maybe before I didn't think it through totally, but I know what it will take now."

I looked up at him through saddened eyes. "We both said a lot of things throughout this journey. I admit a couple of years ago I wasn't ready to forfeit certain aspects of my life, but today I'm willing to try. I've always known what I wanted, and over the last few years I've come to realize what I need. I understand the sacrifices I'm going to have to make in order to be with you, but that's not enough for you because you don't feel any woman could remain true to her vows.

"I don't agree, and feel the only way to truly know is to try, Sin. I'm willing to give it 110%. I'm willing to take the chance. The same way I was willing to take the chance and have sex with you today knowing the risk had we gotten caught. I should be ashamed, but I'm not. I'm proud to have shared that moment with you. I love you. If you want this to work, you're going to have to step out of your comfort zone and take a chance too. You can't expect me to be the only one putting it all on the line if we're both playing for keeps." He wiped the tear from my cheek. "I don't want to discuss this anymore. I put it the hands of the lord a long time ago. I just hope whoever it is who is piloting this craft has plans to take us somewhere nice and not leave me marooned on a deserted island."

Realizing I was bringing the mood down, I apologized. "I'm sorry. It was not my intent to end the visit on a sour note." I looked away from him as my eyes got watery. He hugged me, but my body tensed.

"When you get home tonight we can talk about this some more, okay?"

"Please don't try to appease me, Sin. You don't have to do that for my sake."

"Cut it out. I've been sitting here trying to do the right thing by you, and now you're giving me a hard time. I want you, Misty, more than anything, but I don't want you to resent me later. If you're willing to make that ultimate sacrifice and ready to live by the terms that come with being my wife, then I'm willing to give you everything starting with my last name. I never thought I'd say this, but I trust and believe that you can ride it out with me to the end. Your dedication and constant love has proven that, and it has not gone unnoticed. If you truly believe it can work, then I'm willing to try. That's what I wanted to talk to you about." He pulled my face to his then kissed, and kissed, and kissed me until I smiled. "I'm going to miss you."

"I'm going to miss you too."

We heard the C.O. yell that the visit was over. We hugged and kissed one final time before we were made to part ways. I sat in my rental car for like five minutes crying before I was able to pull it together. I drove straight to the airport, and while I sat at the gate I called Charmaine.

Surprisingly, she answered her phone. "Hey, sis! You on your way home?"

"Yeah," I replied sadly.

"What's the matter? Didn't you have a nice time?"

"I had a great time."

"So why are you pouting?"

"How do you know I'm pouting?"

"Because I can hear it in your voice. Every time you leave him you're sad."

"It breaks my heart when I have to leave him, Cha."

"I know, but you got to be grateful. You got to spend some quality time with him, and managed to get some dick yesterday."

I laughed. "No girl, I managed to get some great dick yesterday and today!"

"I know he tore that shit up too!"

"Like a gorilla in the mist! The subject of marriage came up again."

"Oh boy, so that's what got you upset. Don't sweat it. Once you move back in here I'm gonna tell him when he calls the house you're out on a date with a real nice man. I bet that will put some fire under his ass!" She laughed.

"You're so stupid! He's actually the one who brought it up and he seems more open to the discussion." My other line beeped and I looked down at the caller ID. The screen read caller unknown. "That's him on the other line. Let me call you right back."

"It's okay, just call me when you get home, and tell him I said hi!"

I listened to the pre-recorded message then accepted. "Hello."

"You got to the airport okay?"

"Yeah, I returned the car and I am sitting at the gate. I want to thank you."

"Thank me for what?"

"For being you. You make me so happy Sin."

"That was sweet. I thought you were mad at me."

"Maybe a little frustrated with the situation, but not mad at you. It's my choice to be in love with you. The same way it will be my choice to walk away if it ever comes to that. Are you happy now that I got my black ass down here to see you?"

"Yes, and don't think I didn't catch that slick shit you just said. You know your man would never sit back idly and watch you walk away. I'll never let that happen. I got big plans for you, Mrs. Butler! And, yes I'm happy! I feel great! Better than I ever thought I would be in here."

"I'm glad I was able to help you out. They're calling us to board the plane. I put something in the mail for you. You'll get it sometime next week."

"Get home safe and I'll talk to you tomorrow. I love you!"

"And Miss Bishop loves you too."

"You trying to be funny?"

"Not at all? What's the joke? Isn't my last name Bishop, Mr. Butler? I'll talk to you later, Sin. Smooches!"

*Click.*

I hung up before he could say anything. I wanted him to think about that.

I was flying high, and it wasn't because I was aboard a plane. If it wasn't for the fact that I was returning to a home where Marcus awaited me, it would have been a perfect day.

I located my car at the short-term parking lot at Newark Airport then made my way home. When I arrived the house was dark. The volume on the TV was off as Marcus sat quietly watching the news. He barely acknowledged me; which was cool with me, because I didn't feel like talking to his dumb ass.

I went upstairs and unpacked. I placed the dresses to the side with the intention of dropping them off at the cleaners. I sat down on the bed, and after a few seconds changed my mind. I got up, grabbed the small bundle of clothes then headed to the laundry room. I walked over to the washing machine, poured in some Woolite, set the gentle cycle, and threw everything in. I didn't feel like explaining anything to Marcus if he decided to play hamper hunter and delve through my dirty laundry.

### ***SIN***

After calling Misty I went out to the yard and sat on the bleachers. There was a basketball game going on, but I really wasn't watching it. My mind was on her. My man Jahad walked up and sat beside me then bumped my shoulder with his.

"What it look like, Sin? You look like you're in deep thought. You just left the visit and you already missing wifey," he joked.

I laughed. "Something like that. I'm going to marry her."

"We've had numerous conversations on this topic, and I know your stance on penitentiary marriages. So when you say marry her are you speaking hypothetically or actuality?"

"Jah, Misty systematically destroyed every element of my argument and on this last visit. She made it clear that even the sex issue isn't an issue. At this point any reluctance on my part is gonna look more like me not wanting to do it, opposed to me not wanting to restrict her life."

"Do you really think she's ready? Right now she means what she's saying, but who knows what can happen when reality sets in."

"You know I've contemplated all those thoughts, Jah. Honey's a grown-ass woman. Trust she's weighed out her options and come to the conclusion that being my wife would fulfill and enhance her life more than being with someone else. She's totally down for a brother. She's out there on her grind, making connections and creating new revenue for us. I'm proud that so much of what I showed her was retained and is being used."

"So you're saying, you believe this is the right decision?"

"Yes, we make a mean team! She believes, more than I do, that there is a great chance of me overturning my conviction and getting out of here."

"She knows you have proven that you're a man not to be doubted so having faith in you means a great probability that she'll see you stroll the streets of the city again, and once that happens. . ." Jahad gave me a devious grin.

I smirked. "That's right, Jah! Watch out, world!"

"Are you sure you wanna to get married now? Misty is a beautiful woman, but we both know there's a lot of pussy out there, and with you back on the streets it's gonna rain from the sky. You gonna have women coming at you from all angles. You sure you ready to pass that up?"

"Where they at right now, Jah? I got joints trying to get at a nigga, but they ain't putting in no work or fight to get me up out of here. Misty laid it down so good she didn't leave any room for the competition. The way I see it, they don't deserve the tip of my dick. Baby Girl done locked this player down!"

"Hot damn! The girl's a genius," Jahad said then cut up laughing.

"She's as proven as I am so why not believe she knows exactly what she's doing? My girl got this shit all planned out. If she believes in me why not show the same faith in her? Why not believe in her judgment?"

Jahad stood up then patted my shoulder. "Well then there's only one thing left to find out."

"And what's that?" I asked waiting for the punch line.

"What size is the ring?"

*Baby Girl,*

*I was sitting here and found myself surrounded by so many examples and declarations of your love for me. Today I walked through an incredible demonstration of infinite love as I picked through your old letters and admired your pictures. What a package you present—supportive, encouraging, dependable, intelligent, tenacious, giving, caring, and honest. I need not even mention your sexiness. I couldn't block that out even if I tried. You are truly a blessing to me, and I cherish what we share.*

*Taking everything in, I smile as I look back over the years and recall the feisty cutie that intrigued me on 155th Street so many years ago. A real man recognizes the jewel he has in his lady, and I am as real as they come! You have grown into a tremendous woman of excellence, and the woman you are has never been more evident than on your last visit.*

*You explained in no uncertain terms the length you'd be willing to go to see us together. I've never been shy about expressing my reservations concerning making our union official. I felt it would be such a confining and restrictive commitment on your part. The standards have always seemed too high for any woman to uphold in my eyes, but after the days spent together I find myself reevaluating that position.*

*I said a lot of things about relationships, marriage, and incarceration over the years. Many of my opinions on the topics were dead-on, for I have seen many fall victim to the strain of this path, but I can't deny your effect on me. Your love is the fuel that powers me, and the depth of my emotions has no floor, just as the height soars and has no ceiling. I stand strong alone, but with your energy I feel invincible!*

*Your soul mirrors my own. Your sexuality strokes the fire in my loins, and my hands crave the feel of your skin. You are everything I could wish for, and I can't wait until I can act out every single fantasy that has graced my vivid imagination. I have deep faith in the plans that have been laid to restore my freedom, but regardless of what the future holds, as long as you're in the equation, my life will be a success.*

*I believe it is time for us to take things to the next level. What do you think? For me marriage is now seriously on the table. No more being stubborn and bull headed. I'm man enough to admit . . . you proved me wrong! We can discuss this more the next time you are within my reach. That should motivate you to get your ass back up here (Smile). Damn, I miss you. What I wouldn't give to be looking down into those beautiful eyes right now as I say all this to you.*

*P.S. Your Sin-namon stick is lovesick. He wanted me to ask you to ship him a bottle of your special Sticky Icky ointment. He says he has a stuffy nose, and that's the only thing that will clear it up. (LOL)*

# "YOU PROVED ME WRONG"

*Had they asked me was I capable of ever settling down with just one woman, I would have said HELL NO! Why would I when I have so many at my disposal? Then one hot day on 155th it was like an angel had sent me a gift. Before me sat a young girl with the prettiest eyes, and she stole my heart to my surprise. She was everything I wanted and needed in a mate. You still being here shows me it was fate. You proved me wrong!*

*Had they asked me after being sentenced to 60 years do I think a woman is capable of riding it out with me until the wheels fall off, I would have said HELL NO! They don't make them like that! Then one day this beautiful creature walks into the jail. It felt like that same angel from my past special delivered my mail. You took your place by my side. You said, "Daddy, I'm here to stay, and I'm down to ride. I want to co-pilot. Let me be your tour guide." You proved me wrong!*

*Had they asked me after my first year if I believed a woman was capable of truly loving me under these conditions while still honoring me and selflessly giving of herself? I would have said HELL NO! That kind of love doesn't exist. But here you still stand, hand in my hand, loving me stronger with each passing day, never asking for anything, never looking for pay. You proved me wrong!*

*Had they asked me last year would I ever get married while in here, I would have said HELL NO! No woman would be able to honor her vows! But if any woman can do it, I believe it's you. Your tenacity, determination, and unwavering love tells me I'm about to be proven wrong yet again. Misty, I'm ready and want to try.*

*Forever yours, lovingly*
*Garrett (Sin) Butler*

# CHAPTER 20

## The Ultimate Gift

I folded up the letter I received from Sin this morning. It had been two months since I'd seen him.

Even with the weather warming up I was still being given the cold shoulder. Marcus was downright frigid. Things between us had gone from all right to impossible. We had been avoiding each other like the plague. Most nights I stayed at the brownstone, and the nights I stayed at the house I slept in the guest bedroom. The mere mention of ending it and me leaving caused a number of arguments. He became belligerent. Instead of conflict I continued to discreetly move things out. My plan was to be completely gone by the time he returned from his next business trip.

I had been feeling overexerted lately and didn't have the energy to fight him. Between avoiding him, arguing, moving my whole summer wardrobe, and running my business, I felt depleted like I was running on empty. I admit I was in part to blame for the downward spiral in my relationship. I allowed my loving Sin to create a greater distance between Marcus and me. However, the distance was already there. I believe if it wasn't Sin eventually it would have been someone else who wooed me away. Does it even matter who's to blame when it's over? What matters is moving on and trying to end things amicably.

Friday night came and Toya invited me over for dinner. Her kids were with their grandmother for the weekend, and she thought it would be nice to host a girls' night. I jumped at the opportunity to get out of the house and eat some of her great cooking. Charmaine, Nickelle, and Jasmine had all confirmed, but at the last minute Jasmine conveniently couldn't make it. She claimed to have a date, but she probably still felt funny hanging with me or Charmaine after what happened at the spa. Nickelle was telling us how Jasmine's boyfriend borrowed $2,000 from her and was now not calling her back.

When I arrived, Toya was in the kitchen stirring pots. She was an excellent cook. I tried to get her to start a catering company, but she was leery. I stripped off my coat, hat, and boots then took a seat on the sofa. We talked for a few minutes before she disappeared back into the kitchen. Nickelle and Charmaine were drinking apple martinis and playing tennis on the Wii game system. They tried to get me to join them, but I wasn't interested. I opted to watch them from the leather sectional.

I must have dozed off, because I was awakened by Toya tapping me on the leg. "Misty, wake up! Come on over to the table. The food is ready."

She made blackened catfish, red rice, and steamed fresh vegetables. Charmaine wasted no time and dug right in. Nickelle was working on seconds by the time I finished my vegetables. Seafood was normally my favorite, but tonight for some strange reason I wasn't feeling it.

"You barely touched your food, Misty. What's the matter with you? Are you sick?" Toya asked.

"No, I'm just feeling a little out of it. I haven't had much of an appetite in the last two weeks. I've been doing a lot of running around, and it must be catching up with me."

"Try doing some sleeping the next time you're in bed," Nickelle joked.

"Girl, please, the only thing going on in my bed is sleep. Marcus and I haven't done the nasty in I don't know how long. Our sex life is nonexistent."

"Maybe you're coming down with something," Charmaine said.

"I don't feel sick or have a fever. I actually feel like I'm suffering from exhaustion. If you would have let me, I could have slept on that sofa all night long."

"I remember feeling like when I was pregnant with Ky'elle."

Charmaine looked over at me then smiled.

"What?"

She picked up her fork, grinning as if she knew something the rest of us didn't. "Oh, nothing."

Toya bought some movies from Target and suggested we watch one. I helped pack the dirty dishes into the dishwasher while Charmaine refilled everyone's glass. The movie wasn't playing for ten minutes before I felt myself nodding off. When I woke the credits were rolling. I stretched as all three them peered over at me smiling.

"Well hello, sleeping beauty," Toya joked.

"We were talking about you while you were catching up on your beauty rest, and I think I know why you're so tired."

"So tell me, Doctor Charmaine, what's your diagnosis?"

"You're pregnant!"

I burst out laughing. "Why would you think that? I just told you Marcus and I don't have sex, and last time we did he used a condom."

"Years ago when you were pregnant by Sin all you did was sleep. When was your last menstrual?"

I had to search my mind. I remembered having one two weeks before seeing Sin, but I couldn't recall the date of my last cycle. I had been doing so much I'd lost track. I hadn't even noticed I missed it. A nervous feeling went through my body as if I was being questioned by my parents. "I don't remember, but I don't think I am pregnant."

"Misty, I've known you almost all of my life, and I have never seen you sleep this much or pass up Toya's cooking, especially fish. You're the only person I know who can go to bed at five o'clock in the morning, get right back up at eight-thirty, run around for ten hours, and not be tired."

Nickelle giggled. "Yup, she's pregnant!"

"No, I am not! I haven't been intimate with Marcus since New Year's Eve!"

Charmaine smiled. "I don't mean to blow your spot up, but who said anything about Marcus being the father? You did have sex with Sin."

I froze. My head started twirling. Could it be? Could I have gotten pregnant on the visit?

Nickelle cheered, "Wouldn't that be special? Misty and Sin finally having a baby!"

I couldn't think straight, and my heart was beating in my throat. The faces of Marcus and Sin flashed in my head. A part of me was elated to possibly be carrying the child of the man I was so very in love with. The other part of me was suffering from anxiety. I never thought I would be faced with a reality that included being pregnant by a man doing an unfathomable amount of time, nor did I ever anticipate having to explain to Marcus how I snuck to see Sin, got lucky on the visit, and came home knocked up. This was too much. This was some made-for-television crap. Opposed to getting myself all worked up over nothing, I ended the conversation. "I doubt very seriously I'm pregnant. I'll call and make an appointment with my gynecologist tomorrow."

Charmaine protested, "Oh, hell to the nah! I can't wait that long! If your doctor is anything like mine you could be waiting a month for an appointment. That's entirely too long! If I'm going to be an auntie I need to know now! I'll be right back."

"Where are you going?"

"To the Rite Aid to get you a pregnancy test!" Before I could object she and Nickelle grabbed up their coats and were heading out the door. Toya was beaming.

"And what are you so happy about over there?"

"I'm happy because once you get past the initial shock; you'll realize what a blessing God has bestowed upon you and Sin. If you are pregnant, whatever you need I'm here for you, Misty. I see how you were with Trey as well as my kids, and I think you'll be a wonderful mother. You're not getting any younger, and deep down inside this is what you ultimately wanted. You can do this. You know we all got your back."

I sat and contemplated. I did want to have a baby, and for the longest I wanted it with Sin. I put the thought in the back of my mind after the miscarriage of our first child, and then the thought was completely eradicated by his long sentence with no conjugal visits. Was I ready to be a single mom? Was he going to be happy about this? How would Marcus react once he found out? What would people think? All these things buzzed around in my head.

I finally exhaled and answered with my heart. I was ready! Everything I had done up to this point was preparing me to be a mother. I could take care of this baby by myself—physically, financially, and emotionally. I believed Sin would be overjoyed. This was something we both wanted. My friends and family would be supportive, and at this stage in my journey who cared what Marcus or anyone else thought? It was my life!

"You're right, Toya. I can do this!"

My stomach flipped as we waited for Charmaine and Nickelle to return. I knew what I was going to do, but was still nervous. I was trying to remain levelheaded. I didn't want to get my hopes up and have it be a false alarm. Now that I had gotten past the point of acceptance, I would be disappointed if I wasn't.

Charmaine and Nickelle returned thirty minutes later with three different home pregnancy kits. I went into the bathroom and set up each test on the counter. I read the directions, peed, and processed all three sticks then placed them on top of the boxes. I returned to the living room and waited for them to process.

Nickelle was growing inpatient. "It's got to be time! Go check and see if the results are ready."

She couldn't take the anticipation while I stalled. "Okay, okay," I said as I got up in a huff. I walked toward the bathroom with mixed emotions. Every good and bad thought floated through my mind as I took that long walk. I was prepared for the worst and hoping for the best. I closed the door and said a silent prayer before looking down at each stick.

They each stick gave the same results: POSITIVE! POSITIVE! POSITIVE! I looked in the mirror then placed both hands on my flat stomach. It hit me. *I'm carrying Sin's baby!* I yanked open the bathroom door and screamed, "I'm pregnant!"

They all ran into the bathroom and started hugging me. "Oh my God, you're having a baby, sis! I'm so happy for you! I'm going to be an auntie!"

"I hope it's a boy! It's so cool having a son," Nickelle cheered.

"No way! Girls are better," Charmaine challenged until the voice of reason set in.

"It doesn't matter what the sex it is as long as the baby is healthy. Now what are you going to do about Marcus, Misty?" Toya questioned.

We walked back into the living room.

"What can I do, Toya? It's over. I'm not that type of female who would let him believe this baby is his, and I'm not sticking around until I start showing. I do care about him, but I'm not in love with him. I've been slowly moving out, but now I need to get out like yesterday. I made my bed, and now I plan to lie in it with my baby." I smiled. "I can't believe this! I'm pregnant!" I became overwhelmed and began crying. "I hope Sin isn't upset."

"Upset? Girl, please, you're delusional," Nickelle joked. "What's there to be upset about? He might just try to break out of there when you tell him. I'm glad me and him had that little talk."

"What talk?"

"It was a while ago. I told him he better stop dragging his ass and figure out a way for you two to be together before somebody beats him to punch! I told him to knock your ass up, but who would have thought?"

I laughed. "He did! He actually listened to you for once."

"Misty, seriously, if the two of you share a fraction of the love you have for each other with that baby, everything will be fine. I basically raised mine by myself although Malik was there. He didn't change a diaper nor fix a bottle. Whatever you need, I'm here for you."

"Thanks, Toya. I guess that's it. We're having a baby!"

Charmaine rose from her seat. "And I'm going to be an auntie!" She came over, and hugged me tight, then yelled, "Group hug!" Toya and Nickelle joined in. We sat and discussed my pregnancy a little more before calling it a night. I was thrilled, and couldn't wait to tell Sin!

* * *

The weekend flew by, and on Sunday morning Marcus unexpectedly packed a bag and said he had to leave for business. I was happy to see him go, but thought it was strange given that he'd ignored two calls from his secretary and hadn't been in to the office in two weeks. Something was definitely up with him. He was walking around with wrinkled shirts and razor stubble. We were at least cordial before, but with the passing days he was becoming nastier and nastier. I told him I was moving out, but he said now was not a good time. He said he had a lot going on and would discuss it when he got back on Tuesday. I had other plans. I intended to use his time away to vacate the premises.

Monday started off on a good note. I had a restful sleep, I was in a great spirits, and I had a clarity that I hadn't had in a long time. I showered, ate some oatmeal, and then got dressed. I went into my home office before heading out for the day. I needed to retrieve the letter I had written to

Sin. I walked to my desk and noted the drawer was closed, but unlocked. I thought it was odd because I always made sure to lock it. I didn't think much of it since the envelope was still sealed. I snatched it up, threw it in my bag then headed out the door. The traffic was light, the sun was bright, and I was smiling for good reason.

Around 3 o'clock my cell rang. It was Sin!

"What's good, Baby Girl?"

"Everything, Daddy! I'm feeling so blessed today! I was hoping to hear from you all weekend. How's my lover doing?"

"I could be better. I'm feeling a little boxed in, but you sound like you're in a great mood. Sounds like you got something good going on?"

"Oh, I do! I'm on top of the world right now! I can't remember a time when I was this overjoyed!"

"Well, rub some of that good stuff off on me. What's going on, a new contract?"

"No, it's one hundred times better than that! Over the weekend I learned something of great magnitude. I got confirmation, and I almost still can't believe it myself! I would say it's the closest thing to a miracle I'll ever see!" I was so hyped that I got him excited.

"So tell me! What is it?"

"Now it wouldn't be any fun if I just told you, but what I can do is give you a clue. Hopefully by the time you call me back later you will have figured it out."

"Come on, Baby Girl. I'm not in the mood for riddles."

I whined, "Come on. Entertain me." He was reluctant so I pretended to beg, "Pretty please. I promise it'll be worth it when you figure out the answer."

He sighed. "All right, go ahead."

"Okay, now do you remember when we went to Hawaii?"

"How could I forget that? We had a bomb-ass time!"

"Perfect! On the first night when we got back to our room and were in bed you asked me what I wanted more than anything in this world. I told you there were two things. We had an in-depth conversation, and you made me a promise. I'll give you a clue. I wanted two things, but I managed to get one of them two months ago when you had me *cum* to see you. Think about it, and call me back tonight."

"That's not fair. You know my memory isn't as good as yours."

"Come on, *DADDY*, at minimum you're going to have to try if this is going to be any fun. There weren't that many promises you didn't keep or things I wanted and didn't get. Especially something I wanted more than anything in this world. I knew you were going to do this, though." I laughed. "So I came prepared. I have one last clue for you. It's a poem."

"I like your poems!"

"Listen up. Okay, here it goes! Who knows whose nose, long fingers, or ten toes? It has yet a name for me to proclaim, but it's growing bright, like a flashing headlight. Like a Cracker Jack's surprise, hidden deep down inside, a reflection of your eyes, I'll love till I die." I giggled then repeated it for him one more time. "You're smart Sin! I know you'll figure it out!" I gave him a kiss through the phone then hung up before he could ask me for another clue.

Nickelle and Toya called the office to check up on me. Charmaine also called to confirm she was spending the night. She was going to help me pack the rest of my things as well as go with me to the gynecologist in the morning. I knocked out everything I needed to do then went home and started packing. I ate then decided to take a quick nap. I crashed on the sofa and waited for Sin to call. Shortly after seven my ringing cell phone woke me. It was him! "How you doing," I made sure to stretch out the word "*DADDY*?"

"How am I doing? I'm doing marvelous thanks to you little," he stretched out the word, "*MOMMY!* I'm feeling like the luckiest man in world!"

I giggled. "And why is that?"

"I got the answer!"

"I knew if you put your mind to it you'd figure it out. Was it fun?"

"I can't lie, it was. I did have to put some thought to it. I went back to my cell, laid down, and then took myself back to that trip, back to that conversation. I kept asking myself, 'What the hell was it we talked about in Hawaii?'" He chuckled. "You know I had to dig deep into the crevices of my mind. I can remember all kinds of numbers, but stuff like that is your forte. I tried different angles. I was like 'two months ago,' but all that did was generate visuals of back shots, and I was stuck there for a minute. That shit felt like it was pulled straight from the pit of my stomach!"

I giggled. "Yeah, and then took up residency in mine." We both laughed.

"I drifted back to Hawaii, and that first night. That was cool allowing my mind to recapture that moment. I recalled us going to dinner, walking on the beach, going back to the room, and making love. There's a common factor, but in-depth conversation? I had to close my eyes, relax, and let my mind travel back to that place and time. For a minute it felt like I was actually there lying up in that bungalow with you. I saw the dark room filled with the faint glow of the moon that was glistening off the water, and reflecting off the walls. I saw us cuddled up in that king size bed, enfolded in the softest white Egyptian cotton sheets. Yeah, we had a nice time."

"I remember laying there with you in my arms as I gazed out into the starry sky. I recalled that conversation and you saying you wanted a real family more than anything in this world. You wanted to marry a man who respected, valued, and loved you. A man you would honor and trust with your life. A man you would be proud to give a son. I remember joking that you already had the man, and all we had to do was work on the marriage and the son. My promise was once I slowed down we would make that a reality. You see, Daddy was listening. Now aren't I a man of my word?"

"Don't get all cocky. Only half of the promise was kept, and that was by chance," I teased.

"But I will make good on the other half, and that won't be by accident, Mrs. Butler!"

"Umm hum, it sounds good, Mr. Butler. So we're okay? I was a little worried for a quick second."

"I'm ecstatic! We're better than okay—we're terrific! I picked up your picture once I figured it out and haven't stopped kissing it since! I don't know about you, but I feel like I was just given a new lease on life! And for the record, it wasn't by accident. It was all in my plan!" He got serious. "You know you're going to have to move up out of his spot immediately."

"I know, and I already have Charmaine coming over tonight to help me pack. Marcus is away and won't be back until tomorrow night. Cha is going with me to my first doctor's appointment tomorrow. I'll eventually look for a place, but in the interim I'm going to stay at the brownstone. I think it's best. Plus Auntie Charmaine won't let me out of her sight anyway. She's probably more excited than the both of us!"

"So how far along are we? I mean are you?"

I laughed. "I would think about eight weeks. I'll know for sure when I see the doctor, but I already know it was that back shot that did it!"

"That was indeed a direct path for my heat seeking missile! Before your next visit I want you to get in contact with Big Ant. He's taking care of something for me, and I want to make sure it's ready the next time you come down. I can't wait until you start showing. I want to rub on your belly. I hope it's a boy and looks just like his father!"

"And what if it's a girl?"

"Then she'll be as beautiful as her mother, but more spoiled!"

I blushed. "Can you believe it? Misty and kid."

"Nah, fix that. It's the Butlers', Baby Girl! I was waiting for the next time you come down so we could talk about that."

"I know. I got your letter. Hold on one second. Cha is out front." I saw her car pulling up across the street. "Let me open the door and let her in." There was a brief pause. "Sorry, Daddy, where were we? Oh, yes, I read it, but I didn't reply. I figured we would talk when we were face to face. I'll look for a flight for next weekend."

"Sound's good! Let me talk to Cha real quick."

"Okay, hold on." I waited for her to put her bag down then passed her the phone. "Sin wants to talk to you."

She covered the receiver with her hand. "Did you tell him yet?"

"Yeah, I gave him two clues and he got it!" I reminded her to be careful what she said on the phone. His calls were monitored.

She nodded then hit the speaker button. "So what's good, bro?"

"Everything! Baby Girl tells me you're going with her to the doctor tomorrow."

"Yeah, I'm going to be her doctor's appointment slash Lamaze partner!"

"Thanks for stepping up, Cha. I really appreciate it! Let me get your cell number so I can add it to my list just in case I need to talk to you." She read off the cell and house number to him, and just that quick he memorized them. "I got some information I need to give you in case she needs anything, but I'll get that to you later. Do you have a camera?"

"Yeah, I always have it with me."

"Cool! Make sure you take lots of pictures!"

"I got you! I'm gonna to take plenty of pictures of her stomach as it grows. I can't wait until her belly gets fat! You should see her right now. Thank god she got pretty teeth because the girl is smiling from ear to ear. She's actually glowing! You know what? I got my camera with me right now! You go ahead finish talking to her while I snap a picture of her telling you the good news!"

She passed me back the phone and went searching through her

pocketbook. She came back and started snapped pictures of us talking. She then excused herself and went upstairs with her overnight bag to take a shower.

"Baby Girl, I tip my hat to you! You are indeed an incredible woman! I salute you for always believing in me and never giving up on us, even when I did. Your positivity radiates and shines on all that you love."

I could hear the overwhelming emotions as his voice cracked. He cleared his throat. "You allowed me back in your life when some wouldn't have given us a second chance under the circumstance. You held onto what you believed to be true, and you remained determined, focused, and unwavering. You've given so much of yourself, and shown me love and loyalty beyond measure, and now this! This is the ultimate gift we could share. This is unquestionably a sign that my plan is coming to fruition!"

"Okay, enough. What is this plan you keep talking about?"

He laughed. "I'll tell you about it when you come to see me."

"Uh-huh, you always up to something.

"Just know I got our best interest in mind, and I love you so very much!"

I joked, "The last time you had my best interest in mind, I got left." I laughed. "I'm just kidding. I love you too! You've made me a very happy woman, and you're all the man I need! All I want now is for you to bring that big dick over here, and let me wrap these juicy lips around it."

"Which lips?"

I smiled. "Both! They equally miss that sweet dick of yours!"

I heard a creak in the wood floor behind me, and when I turned around Marcus was standing there. He snatched my cell phone from my ear and pushed me onto the sofa. Hard creases formed across his brow. His lips were chapped and he had the look of a madman in his eye. He started yelling as he pointed the phone at me, "Who the hell are you in my house talking about their dick? Is this that jailbird boyfriend of yours?"

"What did you just say?" I was shocked.

"You heard me, whore!" He raised the receiver to his mouth. "Is this Garrett?" The call had reached it maximum length, and had already disconnected. He threw the phone on the floor. "Misty, you better do some explaining and fast!" He began pacing back and forth in front of the fireplace.

"Marcus I'm sorry, but it's over. I told you I'm leaving you. I will have the rest of my things out of here by tonight."

"You think you're going to humiliate me and leave me for some fucking felon?"

I looked at him with contempt.

"That's right, Misty; I know all about you and Mr. Garrett 'Convict' Butler! I read all of his letters and watched your fucking porno before I left. I found a video of you and him fucking upstairs in my DVD player! My fucking DVD player, Misty! I couldn't understand why. Why would you be looking at that after all this time? I thought I got rid of him the last time!"

When Sin was in Otisville I would visit him every other weekend. Marcus found a visitor's slip and made me promise to never go see him again. Oddly enough, weeks later Sin was transferred to the facility in Arizona. Marcus was under the impression we had stopped corresponding, but we hadn't. His curiosity must have led him to my office.

"So you broke into my desk?"

He paced back and forth becoming angrier and angrier. "The desk, in the office, in my house! Yes! I found all the letters and cards you've kept hidden in there! I put them in order by date then sat down and read them all; the poems, the greeting cards, and the freaking love letters. I read every raunchy note detailing what he wanted to do to you. You two are pathetic! Do you want to know what I did? I sat down and wrote him a letter of my own!"

"You did what?" I got up from the sofa. "I don't know why you did that, because it won't change a thing"

He pushed me back down.

"I'm sorry, Marcus, but it's time we go our separate ways. I'm leaving you."

"You're just like all the rest of the ungrateful bitches I've come across! You think you're just going to up and leave me? I'll tell you like I told him: I will never see you two together. It will be over my dead body!"

"Marcus, it's over! You can't keep someone who doesn't want to be held."

"Well if I can't hold you, then he won't either!"

All I could think to do as I watched him grab up the iron poker from the side of the fireplace was to protect myself. I pulled my feet up to my chest, tucked my head between my knees, and then covered my head. He held the iron within both of his hands and swung it like a bat with full force at my head. I blocked the first swing with my arm and heard my bone snap. The second swing was a crashing blow that caught me on the side of my head and sent me flying to the floor. My mind temporarily went blank. As I regained consciousness I realized he was dragging me into the kitchen by a handful of my hair. I tried to get loose, but I was too weak. Blood dripped into my eye as I tried to kick my feet and wail my arms to no avail. I managed to call out for help. I screamed for Charmaine, but my voice was low. It gradually regained some strength.

"Help... Help me! Charmaine help!"

"Shut up," he yelled as he slammed the back of my head into the side of the kitchen cabinet. "No one is going to help you! I have serious problems going on at work, and you're wasting time writing him!"

He punched me hard in the face, and when I tried to fight him back, he lost his mind. I fought for my life as he tried to grab a knife off the counter. He repeatedly punched and kicked me as I tried to crawl away. As I began to fall unconscious, he got hold of the knife and thrust it into my back.

When Charmaine reached the kitchen she watched helplessly as he turned me over and plunged it into my chest. She screamed from the doorway of the kitchen, "What have you done?"

He was startled when he saw her and as she charged at him he dropped the knife and took off out the kitchen door.

She snatched the phone up off the kitchen counter, and dialed 911. She sat beside me on the cold kitchen floor and waited for help to arrive.

"Cha, tell Sin I love him."

"You tell him yourself! You're going to be okay, Misty."

"I don't know. I'm starting to feel real cold." I looked into her eyes. "Cha, I'm scared."

As my eyes started to close, she shook me. "Whatever you do, don't go to sleep. You have to stay awake! The ambulance is on the way!" She shook me again, and I fully opened them. A tear ran down the side of my face. She looked down and there was a massive amount of blood pouring out of my chest. She grabbed the kitchen towel and applied pressure to my chest and back. I was shivering.

"Do you want a blanket?"

I nodded. She ran to the sofa and grabbed the throw and placed it over me then went back to applying pressure. The ambulance finally arrived as I was fading in and out.

"Cha, I want you to do something for me. If I don't make it…"

"Don't talk like that! You're going to be fine! You have to! We're having a baby."

She looked over at the EMT. "DO SOMETHING! HELP HER!

The EMT stuck needles in my arm, bandaged me up, and placing me on the gurney. I was wheeled out and secured in the back of the ambulance. They raced down the highway with sirens blaring.

I took the oxygen mask off of my face then whispered, "Tell Sin it's not his fault, and not one single day did I ever regret. Tell him me and the baby will be waiting for him in heaven."

I began to cough up blood, and I saw the panic in her eyes, which frightened me. The EMT put the mask back over my face.

"Tim, press on it! She has internal bleeding."

"Just hold on, sis! We're almost there! You and the baby will be fine." She grabbed the EMT's arm, "PLEASE SIR, HELP MY SISTER!"

I could feel myself losing the battle as she took my hand.

"Just hold on a little longer. You have to keep your eyes open, Misty."

I fought to remain focused, but everything was becoming blurry. She squeezed my hand as my eyes closed.

"Goddamn it, Misty. YOU HAVE TO FIGHT!"

Tears ran down my face, and I knew I was fighting a losing battle. I could hear my heartbeat slowing. It was losing strength, and lifelessness was settling in like rigor mortis.

"Step aside, miss, we're losing her!"

I felt my hand slipping from hers. "Cha, (*COUGH*) . . . *I love yo* . . ."

Charmaine began screaming frantically as I gurgled up blood. "SOMEBODY DO SOMETHING! YOU CAN'T LET HER DIE! SHE'S PREGNANT! PLEASE! HELP HER! MISTY, NO! PLEASE, PLEASE, PLEASE DON'T GO! FIGHT, DAMN IT!"

"Her pressure is dropping, Tim. She needs blood."

"COME ON! HURRY, HURRY, HURRY! God, please I beg of you, let us get her there in time. I may not always act like it, but I believe in your power." I felt Charmaine squeeze my hand. "MISTY, HOLD ON!"

It felt like I was having an out of body experience. Everything around me was moving in slow motion as they work on me. My ears became deaf, and the only sound I could hear was a muffled, low-pitched ringing. My body felt like it was descending backwards in a large body of water; sinking deeper into the unknown, deeper into the darkness.

"We're losing her, Tim! I'm going to administer a shot of Atropine. Step aside, miss!"

My hand dropped from Charmaine's, and the machine started going haywire. "NO, NO, NO!! JESUS NO! YOU CAN'T TAKE HER. YOU CAN'T LEAVE ME LIKE THIS!"

*Boop* . . .

# AUTHOR BIO

Jeanine Mayers is passionate about uplifting young women and teens. Having defied the odds and boasting a successful career in the private sector, she uses her platform as an author and motivational speaker to empower audiences to personal development and growth.

In her debut novel, *Infinite Love—The Pursuit*, Jeanine approaches relationships, social matters and women's sexual issues from a unique perspective. As a life-long resident of New York's South Bronx, Jeanine has first-hand experience with the big-city living she writes about in her books. She masterfully melds the opposing worlds of Corporate America and street-smart savvy with compelling storylines and true-to-life characters. The passion, fear and determination intertwined throughout her novels permeate every woman's fundamental hunger for love.

CPSIA information can be obtained
at www.ICGtesting.com
Printed in the USA
LVOW12s1800211016

509750LV00002B/455/P